phlg

D1287781

SAMUEL'S RETURN

Center Point
Large Print

Also by Susan Lantz Simpson and available from Center Point Large Print:

The Mending
The Promise
The Reconciliation
Rosanna's Gift
Lizzie's Heart

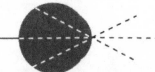

**This Large Print Book carries the
Seal of Approval of N.A.V.H.**

SAMUEL'S RETURN

Susan Lantz Simpson

CENTER POINT LARGE PRINT
THORNDIKE, MAINE

This Center Point Large Print edition
is published in the year 2022 by arrangement with
Kensington Publishing Corp.

The text of this Large Print edition is unabridged.
In other aspects, this book may vary
from the original edition.
Printed in the United States of America
on permanent paper sourced using
environmentally responsible foresting methods.
Set in 16-point Times New Roman type.

ISBN: 978-1-63808-421-1

The Library of Congress has cataloged this record
under Library of Congress Control Number: 2022936836

This book is dedicated to my wonderful readers. Thank you so much for your encouragement and support!

Acknowledgments

Thank you to my family and friends for your continuous love and support.

Thank you to my daughters, Rachel and Holly, for believing in me and dreaming along with me. (Rachel, you patiently listened to my ideas and ramblings, and Holly, I couldn't have done any of the tech work without your skills!)

Thank you to my mother who encouraged me from the time I was able to write. I know you are rejoicing in heaven.

Thank you to Dana Russell for all your support and for arranging signings every time I have a book released.

Thank you to Mennonite friends Greta and Ida for all your information.

Thank you to my wonderful agent, Julie Gwinn, for believing in me from the beginning and for all your tireless work.

Thank you to John Scognamiglio, editor-in-chief, and the entire staff at Kensington Publishing for all your efforts in turning my dream into reality.

Thank you most of all to God, giver of dreams and abilities and bestower of all blessings.

Prologue

Samuel Mast dragged in a huge gulp of fresh air, filling his lungs to near bursting. Ever so slowly he released the air through pursed lips. How *gut* it was to be back in Southern Maryland. He had missed the place even more than he realized. Wide-open spaces. Fields dotted with two-story farmhouses. Barns with tall silos beside them. Horses and cows grazing lazily in the fenced-in pastures. It would be ever so *wunderbaar* to dig his fingers in the rich, dark soil again. *Jah*, he was home to stay.

He tipped back his head to watch the cottony clouds skitter across the bluer-than-blue sky and had to clap a hand to his head to hold on to his straw hat. A person would think Samuel had never seen farmland before. Of course there were houses and barns and farms in the other places where he had lived, but this place was special. Had it really been ten years since he boarded the big van that carried him and his family to the first faraway town his *daed* insisted they move to? Seemed like a lifetime!

In a way, it had been a lifetime. He'd been a mere *bu* of seventeen, just beginning his *rumspringa*. So many changes had occurred in his life over the years. But this place looked remarkably unchanged. Would *she* be the same, too?

Chapter One

She didn't know how a house could seem so quiet with three young *kinner* inside it, but with Becky out enjoying an evening with her soon-to-be in-laws, silence crept through Lena Troyer's house and wrapped around her soul. If this was a foretaste of how things would be when Becky married Atlee Stauffer and moved out for *gut*, Lena wasn't sure she'd be able to endure the void.

Becky had moved into Lena's house before Matthew was born to help Lena care for Mary, Eliza, and the house. Lena's status had changed from *fraa* to widow when she was barely pregnant with Matthew, so she'd needed all the help she could get. But Becky hadn't just moved into Lena's house. She had moved into Lena's heart as well. She had become family. While Lena was happy Becky had found someone to share her life with and to help raise her unborn *boppli*, she would surely miss the girl something fierce when she was gone.

Simply put, Lena was lonely. She loved her *kinner* with every fiber of her being, but they couldn't satisfy that need for companionship. Joseph had been a *gut* husband, and Lena had loved him dearly. She would always love him, but the fingers of loneliness had been rippling up

11

and down her spine and plucking her heartstrings. Seeing the love blossom between Becky and Atlee had made Lena wistful and, *jah*, envious. Was the Lord Gott trying to tell her it was time to move on with her life?

Lena blew out a sigh that sent her *kapp* strings fluttering. She grabbed an errant strand of dark brown hair and poked it back beneath the *kapp*. Right now, though, it was time to get everyone ready for bed. She had already nursed the *boppli* and tucked him into the cradle next to her own bed. Three-year-old Mary and one-and-a-half-year-old Eliza still looked at books on the rag rug near the woodstove. They must be tired, they sat so quietly. The only sound came from the slight rustle as they turned the pages. Eliza appeared ready to topple over any second.

"*Kumm*, girls, let's get to bed."

"Can't we wait for Becky to get home? We need to tell her *gut nacht*." Mary used her most cajoling voice.

"She might be late. You'll see her in the morning. Please put your books in the basket."

Lena could see Mary's disappointment, but the girls were going to have to get used to not seeing Becky on a daily basis. Mary pulled Eliza to her feet. Both little girls shuffled over to the basket and dropped in their books.

"*Gut* girls." Lena smiled at her precious *dochders* who looked so like her. There didn't seem to be any of Joseph in them at all. Maybe Matthew would look like his *daed*. Already she could see a few of Joseph's expressions on the infant's face. It was too soon to tell much about his looks yet. Sometimes she feared Joseph's image was fading from her memory altogether.

Ach, Joseph, you left me too soon. Our kinner will never know you except through stories I tell them. The ache in her heart had finally dulled after nearly a year. Becky's presence had helped a lot. The girl had been a true blessing. Lena believed she and her *kinner* had helped Becky through a rough patch, too.

The poor, dear girl had arrived home in Southern Maryland alone, scared, and in the family way. She had run out of her baptismal service and headed straight for New York to experience life in the big city. Unfortunately, she had gotten taken advantage of. The marriage she believed was legal and binding turned out to be a sham. The man she thought was her husband didn't really care about her and died of a drug overdose. Becky fled the city and returned to Maryland an entirely different person than she was when she left. The flirtatious and sometimes inconsiderate girl had grown into a caring, compassionate, loving young woman. She would make a *wunderbaar fraa* for Atlee and an excellent *mudder* for her little one.

Lena sighed again, gripped the wooden arms

of the rocking chair, and pushed herself to her feet. She should climb into bed herself as soon as she had the girls settled. She needed to get rid of her gloomy thoughts and try to sneak in a few hours of sleep before her hungry son awoke. She'd leave on a propane-powered light so Becky wouldn't have to enter a completely dark house.

This might be the last time Becky crept into Lena's house at night, and Lena was tempted to stay up to talk to her. Becky let slip that she and Atlee would be published on Sunday and married the following Thursday. That meant there was a lot of work to get done in a short amount of time. It also meant the end of their nightly chats after the *kinner* had gone to bed. Lena wished Becky and Atlee every happiness. Truly she did. But oh how she was going to miss that girl!

Lena had barely reached the stairs when she heard the jiggle of the front door. She paused with one hand on the banister. "Becky?" She kept her voice soft so she wouldn't awaken the *boppli*, though he probably wouldn't have heard her even if she yelled.

"*Ach*, Lena! You're still up. I thought you might have gone to bed because the light was dim."

"I was on my way." She headed back toward the living room.

"I don't want to keep you up. I know you must be tired."

Not half as tired as I'm going to be after you

14

leave. "I want to hear all about your plans. I can tell from the sparkle in your eyes and your dreamy expression that you and Atlee and the Stauffers were planning a wedding."

"I know we aren't published yet, but our circumstances are a bit different. Because we're getting married so soon, we've had to step up the preparations."

"It's so exciting! *Kumm* sit and tell me all about it."

"Are you sure? You need your rest."

"I'm sure." Lena hooked an arm through Becky's and propelled her to a chair in the living room. "We won't have many more evenings to have chats. I want to take advantage of every one of them. I can sleep another time."

Before she sat, Becky threw her arms around Lena. "I'm going to miss you."

"And I will miss you, but you are *wilkom* here any time. You do know that, don't you?"

"I know."

"Soon you'll be busy with your husband and *boppli.*"

"But never too busy to visit you. And you'll bring the *kinner* to see me, too. Right?"

"Definitely. Now, tell me your plans."

An hour later, both women yawned and rubbed their eyes, but neither seemed motivated to budge from their chairs.

"I suppose we should go to bed. I've kept you up long enough." Becky was the first to stir from her comfortable position. She held out a hand to Lena.

"I should be helping you up. You're the one in a delicate condition."

"I'm tougher than I look."

Lena laughed. "That you are. I am so happy for you, dear Becky."

"*Danki.* And I am indebted to you for taking me into your home and under your wing."

The women shuffled to the stairs and trudged up in single file. At the door to her room, Becky paused. "*Ach,* Lena, I nearly forgot to tell you."

"What's that?"

"Atlee's *mamm* said Samuel Mast has returned to St. Mary's County. He's buying the old Stoltzfus place. It will be *gut* to have that house occupied again. I always thought it was much too pretty a place to sit empty."

Lena's hand flew to her chest, where her heart skipped a beat before thumping in double time. She stifled a gasp. "Samuel?" The single word escaped her lips in a whisper.

"*Jah.* He was a few years older than me, but you knew him, ain't so?"

Lena nodded. The hand on her chest toyed with the *kapp* string dangling over her shoulder. "I knew Samuel Mast."

● ● ●

She prepared for bed by rote. Only after she crawled beneath the covers did she realize she had hung her purple dress on a peg and pulled on her nightgown. She reached up to pat her head. *Jah.* She'd removed the *kapp* and plaited her hair into one long braid. She lay on her back and stared at dark shapes in the room illuminated only by a thin moon beam from the window on the opposite wall. Becky's innocent question echoed through the chambers of her brain. "You knew him, ain't so?"

Lena knew Samuel Mast all right. She'd spent a *gut* two years trying to forget Samuel Mast. What was he doing back here? And he was buying property? That meant he planned to stay. She rubbed one hand across her furrowed forehead and patted her suddenly queasy belly with the other. Her breath came in short pants and her heart tried to fly out of her chest.

Calm down. You're an adult now. You aren't the fifteen-year-old girl with a king-sized crush on the older bu. *You are a grown woman, a* mudder *with three* kinner. *Get hold of yourself.* Lena forced a few slow, deep breaths to go along with her pep talk.

Gradually her taut muscles relaxed and her heart rate approached a normal speed. She needed to think rationally. She needed to go to sleep and not think at all, but that was about as likely to happen as cows were to fly. Maybe she wouldn't run into Samuel anywhere. She'd see him at church, of course, because the old Stoltzfus place was in her same district, but they would sit on opposite sides of the room. They wouldn't have to mingle at all.

Lena rolled onto her side. She'd think of something else. Something happy, like Becky's wedding. That would be such a joyous occasion. Ten years ago Lena dreamed of marrying Samuel Mast. Ugh! Lena threw off the covers and bolted upright. *Get out of my head, Samuel, just like you got out of my life!*

A faint rustle and smacking sound from the cradle on the other side of her bed alerted Lena to Matthew's awakening. If she could get to him before he began to fuss or cry, he'd probably drift right back to sleep after nursing. Maybe then she'd be relaxed—or fatigued—enough to close her own eyes and give her weary body a few minutes of rest.

Lena stumbled into the kitchen a few hours later with heavy footsteps and bleary eyes.

The teakettle already sang on the back burner of the wood cook stove. She had a gas stove, too, but the kettle always sat on the wood one. A perky Becky sat at the table as close as possible to the propane-powered lamp because the sun had not yet cast much light in the window. Her thread

18

box sat beside the blue fabric she concentrated on.

"Your wedding dress?"

Becky glanced toward the doorway. "*Jah*. Not many brides have to worry about their dresses being too tight in the midsection, I don't imagine. I've made it as loose as possible, but I can tighten it later."

"It looks like you're about finished with it."

"I am. I'm hemming it now." Becky looked up again and squinted. "You look terrible."

"*Danki*. Nice of you to notice."

Becky giggled. "I didn't mean anything bad. You're as lovely as ever, but you look exhausted."

"Uh-huh. Don't try to smooth things over now." Lena shuffled to the cupboard to pull out a mug. "A little tea should help."

"A little sleep might be a bigger help."

"I'm afraid it's too late for that now. Matthew will be hungry again soon."

"Why don't you go back to bed after you nurse him? I can take care of the girls."

"*Nee*. You have plenty to do. Besides, I have to get used to being on my own again."

"I feel bad for deserting you."

Lena laughed. "You aren't deserting me, silly girl. You're beginning a brand-new life of your own. A new adventure. A new chapter in the Rebecca Zook story."

Becky raised her eyebrows. "You should be a

writer, Lena. Those are pretty poetic words."

"It's a wonder I can get a sensible thought to *kumm* out, as tired as I am." Lena hoped the whistling teakettle made enough noise to cover that little slip of the tongue. She didn't want Becky to feel guilty for leading her own life.

"*Ach*, Lena! I still hate leaving you to take care of the house and the *kinner* and everything else all by yourself. It's so much for one person to do, especially one small woman."

"Women have been taking care of all those things since time began. I might be scrawny, but I'm pretty strong. Don't you worry about me."

"I will, though. I want to help you."

"You have helped me more than you know. You supported me through some rough spots and toiled harder than any workhorse. It's time for you to make your own home with Atlee." Lena dunked a tea bag in her mug of steaming water. "Would you like some tea?" When she turned around she saw tears shimmering in Becky's eyes. "I hope I see tears of happiness in those green eyes and not tears of sadness."

Lena carried her mug to the table and dropped onto a chair beside Becky. She reached over to lay a hand on her *freind*'s arm. "Don't you remember we agreed to be roommates, so to speak, until one of us married? And I told you that would most likely be you. I saw how much Atlee cared for you even then. I knew it would only be a matter of time before you both admitted your feelings and did something about it. I truly am very, very happy for you."

"*Danki*, Lena." Becky sniffed. "I'm going to miss you."

"I will still be right here. And wild horses won't keep me from your house when that *boppli* arrives. I'm going to be his or her honorary doting *aenti*."

"I'm counting on that." Becky jabbed her needle into the little tomato-shaped pincushion. "There. It's done." She gathered all the straight pins and dropped them into a plastic box. "Lena?"

"Hmm?" Lena blew on her tea before taking a sip.

"Did thoughts of Samuel Mast keep you awake last night?"

Lena coughed as the tea slid down the wrong way. Her eyes watered and her nose ran. She patted her chest where the scalding liquid seemed to have stalled. "Whatever made you ask that?"

"I saw your reaction last night when I mentioned his return. You looked like you'd seen a ghost, as the *Englisch* say."

"I-I was surprised to hear he'd moved back here, that's all."

"Shocked is more like it, I'm thinking."

"Maybe."

"Any particular reason why?"

"He's been gone a long time. I assumed it was

a permanent thing. Who would ever have guessed he would return to Maryland from wherever he's been all these years?" Lena paused but couldn't resist asking, "I-is he alone, or did he bring family with him?"

"He's alone, I believe."

"Oh."

"He was special to you at one time, ain't so?"

Chapter Two

Lena hoped the heat she felt creeping up her neck and onto her face didn't make her cheeks glow as bright as the moon on a starless night. She hurried to raise the mug to her lips and take a sip to stall for time. Any other day, one of the girls would interrupt such an important conversation. Where were they now? Lena raised her eyes only enough to see Becky still staring at her expectantly. "Special?" she croaked. "We were *kinner* when he moved away."

"You weren't so young. You were out of school, ain't so?"

"Fifteen," Lena whispered. She coughed to clear her throat that suddenly became so clogged she could scarcely get air to flow, never mind her voice. She jumped when Becky laid a hand on her arm.

"You cared about him. I can tell."

"It was a silly teenage thing. I hadn't even begun my *rumspringa* yet."

"That doesn't mean you couldn't have feelings for someone. Do you still care?"

"*Ach*, Becky. I've lived a whole lifetime since those days. I'm a widow with three *kinner* now. And I loved Joseph."

"I know you did. But a lot of people love more

than one person. They don't always marry their first love."

"At fifteen and seventeen we certainly weren't planning any wedding." Lena forced a nervous laugh. "Did you love any of the fellows you stepped out with before Atlee?"

This time Becky's face flushed crimson. "Not at all. That was all foolish flirting."

"The *bu* in New York?"

Becky's hand scrunched her blue wedding dress until Lena's hand covered it and stopped the motion. "I only thought I loved him because I was alone and scared. I was too naïve. I believed his pretty words. Now that I have Atlee and really understand what love is, I know the feeling for Vinny wasn't love at all."

"Are you absolutely sure it's love with Atlee?"

"Completely."

"I thought so, but I wanted you to be sure without any doubts."

"I don't have a single doubt." Becky slapped the table. "How did you do that, Lena Troyer? We were talking about you and Samuel Mast. How did we end up talking about me?"

Lena smiled and shrugged. "It's more interesting to talk about you. How are the wedding plans *kumming* along?"

"Fine. I'll need to do lots of baking."

"I'll help. Will your folks be arriving soon?"

"*Nee*. Mamm wrote and said Grossmammi

24

took a turn for the worse. They won't leave her."

"I'm sorry, Becky. I know you miss them. I had so hoped they would make it here for your wedding."

"Me, too, but my *bruders' fraas* will help. Atlee's *mamm* and *schweschder* will help, too."

"And I will help. We'll get everything done up just right, so don't worry."

"I'm not worried. The important thing is that Atlee and I are ready. The other stuff is just fluff—nice, of course, but not necessary."

That dreamy expression that crossed Becky's face made Lena feel wistful, almost envious. She chased those emotions away. She would not be melancholy. This was a happy time. She wouldn't do anything to spoil Becky's day. "You have a *gut* attitude. Let's plan what food we need to prepare and make sure we have all the ingredients."

"Okay, but you have time to finish your tea and eat breakfast."

Fussy little sounds reached them before either woman could rise to concoct breakfast. "Maybe I don't!" Lena pushed back from the table.

"I'll get breakfast thrown together while you tend to the *boppli*."

"Sounds like a plan."

"Lena?"

"Hmm?"

"What happened between you and Samuel?"

"That's another story."

"I'm a *gut* listener."

Lena offered a wobbly smile. "I know you are, dear one. I'll keep that in mind. Now I'd better go tend to that fussy fellow."

"I'll help the girls, too, while you nurse Matthew."

Lena opened her mouth to protest. She had to get back into the routine of doing everything herself. Becky spoke before she could utter the first syllable. They'd become so close that Becky could correctly guess her thoughts.

"I know you can do everything for yourself, and soon you won't have me here every day. So let me do all I can while I'm here. Let me have a few more days to help the girls. I love them, too, you know."

A lump rose like a boulder in Lena's throat. Tears blurred her vision. All she could do was nod and scurry from the room before sobs overtook her. She surely would miss Becky. She had grown to rely on her, not just as a helper, but also as a close *freind*.

Lena changed and dressed Matthew, answering his little coos with babbles of her own. He was so much more alert and active now, and could even wait a few moments for his feeding. Lena heard the girls giggling with Becky in their room down the hall. She smiled as she settled herself with Matthew in the oak rocking chair she'd used for each of her *bopplin*. Nursing always helped her relax and did today as well, until unbidden snippets of a long-ago conversation played out in her mind.

"I'll be back for you, Lena. You'll be grown up, and I will have some work skills under my belt. We'll be ready to plan a future then."

"*Nee*, you'll probably find another girl wherever it is that you're going."

"I won't even be looking. There isn't a girl anywhere out there who could compare to you." He reached out to tuck a dark strand of hair under her *kapp* and then stopped a tear in its tracks with his thumb as it traveled down her cheek. "Please don't cry, Lena. You're the only girl for me. I promise."

"I don't know what to do without you, Samuel. I'll be ready to start my *rumspringa* soon. I had hoped . . ." Embarrassed by the words that almost leaped from her tongue, she clamped her lips together.

"I had hopes, too. Our hopes don't have to die. I have to go with my family right now. I'm only seventeen, so I have to do what my *daed* says. But that will change soon."

"It will seem like forever to me."

"Me, too. I have your address, though, and I'll write to you."

"Will you? Promise?"

"Of course. Everything will work out all right. You'll see."

But Samuel Mast kept none of his promises. He didn't return for Lena. He didn't even write a single letter. Promises evidently meant nothing to him.

Matthew stopped nursing and looked into Lena's face. "I'm sorry, sweetie. I'll slow down my rocking. I about threw us out of the chair, ain't so?" She rocked at a more moderate pace so Matthew would resume nursing. Lena stroked the soft cheek. Samuel had been right in one respect. Things had worked out—just not as she'd originally planned.

Lena had mourned for Samuel the same as if death had claimed him, but after a long, long while, her heart gradually mended. And Joseph Troyer was there when the wound had scabbed over. He had been a loving, gentle husband and a *gut* provider. He gave her three beautiful little ones who she loved with all her heart. And she had loved Joseph, too, maybe not with the same passion she had loved Samuel, but in a somehow softer, more subtle manner. That other love was only some silly emotion teenagers experienced, wasn't it? She'd missed Joseph terribly since he had been gone. Only recently had she begun to crawl from beneath her grief. Becky had been instrumental in helping her return to life.

Mary and Eliza rushed into the room to give their *mudder* a hug. Their clatter didn't faze

Matthew one bit. He had grown used to their noise. He continued to nurse as if he and Lena were the only people in the room.

"We're going to help Becky make pancakes!" Mary jumped up and down while clapping her hands. Eliza attempted to mimic her older *schweschder* and would have fallen flat on her face if Becky, who had followed the girls into the room, hadn't reached out a hand to steady her.

"Are you sure you want these two to make pancakes?" She tried to look serious, but the edges of her lips curved upward.

Becky smiled and nodded. "We'll have fun, and I know the girls will be a big help."

"Without a doubt."

"We'll make some pancakes for you, too, Mamm."

"Great! I'm as hungry as a bear." With the hand that wasn't supporting Matthew, Lena reached out to tickle each girl. They were still giggling when they trooped downstairs with Becky. Mary and Eliza were going to miss Becky as much as she would. Lena vowed to spend extra time doing something fun with them. Surely she could carve a little time out of her busy routine for that. In a minute she would tiptoe downstairs to peek into the kitchen. She was certain she would be met by a cloud of flour as soon as she poked her head in the door.

● ● ●

Samuel rubbed his eyes as he stumbled into the cold kitchen. It might be spring outside, but winter still reigned inside the drafty, two-story house that had sat empty for too long. Some pancakes or eggs would sure be great about now, but without wood or propane, hot food would be out of the question, as would refrigerated food. He needed to weatherproof the house, buy propane, buy groceries—once he got the propane to power the refrigerator—and eventually cut and split wood. He'd better make a list of all the chores so he didn't forget anything. He had a feeling he would be adding more and more items to that list.

A rumble from his stomach reminded Samuel he'd have to eat whatever he had on hand to hold him over until he could purchase an assortment of food. A half-stale, convenience-store powdered doughnut or an equally unappetizing semisquished granola bar? The rumble grew louder and more ferocious. Maybe both. He'd compose that combination to-do-and-grocery list while he choked down his meager breakfast. There must be a scrap of paper and a pencil nub around here somewhere.

Samuel fought his way through a maze of cobwebs to a small desk in the corner of the kitchen. That would be the logical location of writing paraphernalia. He grabbed his lower back when he bent to yank open a drawer. First order of business was to pay a visit to Bishop Menno Lapp, who'd said he had a spare bed. Sleeping on the cold, hard, wood floor another night and worrying about being run over by mice or whatever other critters might have taken up residence in the abandoned house were not at all conducive to restful slumber.

For all the disarray of the rest of the house, the desk was surprisingly tidy. The fact that its contents were rather scant helped with that, for sure. A spiral notepad and an assortment of pencils ranging in size from full length to barely graspable, tooth-marked to smooth, rolled around in the middle drawer. In the bottom drawer— once he wrenched it open—Samuel found empty hanging file folders still in excellent condition. These would *kumm* in handy once his business got up and running. *If* it got up and running.

When he'd contacted Bishop Menno before making the move back to Southern Maryland, the bishop assured him the skills of a blacksmith and toolmaker would be in demand. Samuel's experience working as a builder for a construction company would be useful as well. It had been the bishop, in fact, who had connected him with the person handling the sale of the Stoltzfus property, now to be known as the Mast property. Hard to believe he was owner of this twenty-acre farm with its barns and silo. Owner of this sturdy, two-story farmhouse. His gaze swept the room, prompting him to amend that last thought to "owner of this mess"!

Samuel sighed. He reached way down inside himself to pluck up a positive attitude. He *would* get this farm producing again. He *would* get this house cleaned up. A second glance almost made him lose his grip on that rosy outlook. He dragged in a deep breath. It was nothing a little elbow grease couldn't correct, ain't so? Well, maybe a lot of elbow grease.

He debated his plan of action. Samuel would like to get the house in livable condition before he brought in any supplies or furniture. But he didn't know if there could possibly be any cleaning supplies here that would still be usable. He might very well have to go to the store to purchase a mop, a bucket, a broom, cleansers, and other assorted items before he could even begin to restore the house to a semilivable condition. He should add a can of air freshener to his list. A big can. Samuel hadn't quite adjusted to the musty odor permeating the air, and he'd been trapped in here with it all night.

Before he could put any plans into action, the crunch of buggy wheels on the gravel-and-dirt driveway drew his attention to the filmy window. *Ach*! He needed window cleaner, too. Not only one buggy rolled toward the house but a whole procession of gray buggies followed suit. Samuel certainly wasn't prepared to receive guests. He crossed the kitchen to close the desk drawers that still yawned open before he dashed outside to determine the meaning of the buggy brigade.

"*Gut mariye*, Samuel!"

The voice rang out before the body it went with emerged from one of the buggies. Samuel shaded his eyes from the glare of the early morning sun. He squinted at the first buggy and was rewarded with an identification of the voice. "*Gut mariye*, Bishop Menno."

The bishop jumped from the lead buggy with the spryness of a much younger man. "How was your first night in your new home?"

Cold. Sleepless. Fraught with animal skitterings that kept his imagination working overtime. Hungry. Make that starving. Samuel said none of these things, though they were all true. He opted for the simple answer. "Fine."

Bishop Menno chuckled. "Fine, as in you didn't get run over by field mice, or fine if you like sleeping on a hard floor, or fine if you can stand the growling of your stomach echoing through empty rooms?"

Samuel laughed. "It sounds like you've spent a night or two here."

"I can only imagine." The bishop waved for the buggies to pull forward before he approached Samuel. "I've brought help."

Samuel cleared his throat to protest, but the

sound died before it could exit his mouth.

"Don't be stubborn, son. Don't refuse our help. You'll never get this place running if you don't accept help. We all work together, ain't so?"

Samuel shrugged. "I suppose so."

Martha Lapp, the bishop's wife, approached the two men. "*Wilkom* back, Samuel. It's *gut* to have you home, and it's *gut* to have this place occupied again. Don't you worry. We'll have this place in ship shape before you know it." She waved toward the buggies where women hopped out laden with brooms, buckets, and all sorts of things Samuel didn't recognize.

"What . . . ?" Shocked by the number of people who had converged on the place, Samuel couldn't seem to convert his thoughts into words.

"We're having a frolic!" Martha laughed. "A rather impromptu one because we didn't have a lot of advance notice you were moving in here. At any rate, the women will get your house all spick-and-span while you and the men see what needs to be done in the outbuildings."

"I haven't been to the store to buy cleaning supplies."

"We've got everything we need, so we'll get started. That way we should be done in time for you to move in furniture."

"I don't have any furniture, actually."

"We've got that covered, too." Bishop Menno broke into the conversation. "Remember I told you we had a bed you can have, mattress and all? Well, Martha rounded up a few other items, too. It seems nearly everyone had some kind of furniture they weren't using."

Martha's eyes crinkled at the corners. Her entire face participated in her smile. "We've got you a table and chairs for the kitchen and a few chairs for the living room. It will be right homey. Then, when you get a chance, you can add whatever you like."

"*Danki*. I don't know what else to say."

"There isn't a need for words. We're glad to help. We'll go ahead and get started with the cleaning. We even brought food for the noon meal. Everything is under control." Martha strode toward the buggies where the other women waited.

Samuel quickly surveyed the crowd of women. Even from this distance, he could tell a small, thin, dark-haired beauty was not among them. Surely she hadn't changed so much that he didn't recognize her. Lena had haunted his dreams so many nights in the past ten years that he would recognize her mere silhouette, and it was not dancing among the shadows of the women milling around outside his house.

"I feel so bad I wasn't in church to hear your big announcement." Lena felt like stomping her foot and poking out her lower lip in a pout like

Mary used to do when she was two years old.

"I know, but it isn't like it came as a surprise to anyone that we were published and will marry so soon. How is Eliza?"

"Better, I believe. At least she's kept down some soup and crackers. She and Mary are still napping."

"*Gut*. I want everyone well on Thursday."

Lena couldn't help but notice the apprehension that crossed Becky's face. "What is it? Is something wrong?"

"*Nee*. At least I hope not."

"Uh-oh. What does that mean?" Lena laid her sleeping *boppli* in the cradle and gave her undivided attention to the young woman in front of her.

"I, uh, we, invited everyone to the wedding."

"Okay. That shouldn't be a problem. We've got enough food planned to feed half the state." At Becky's silence, Lena prodded further. "Why the worried expression? I figured everyone would want to see you and Atlee take your vows, so the number of people won't be a problem."

"Samuel Mast was at church today. He was invited along with everyone else."

Lena's heart lurched and her breath caught. She forced a calmness she did not feel. "That's all right, Becky. I have to face him. We live in the same community, so we'll run into each other all the time."

Becky threw her arms around Lena and hugged her tight "I was so afraid you'd be angry or upset."

Lena patted Becky's back. "Stop fretting, silly girl. Everything is fine. The past is past." But was it?

Chapter Three

Thursday, Becky's wedding day, dawned bright, sunny, and unusually warm for mid-April. Most Amish weddings occurred after crops were harvested and canning and preserving had been finished, but it wasn't totally unheard of to have a wedding at a different time of year. Lena thought this was the perfect time for Becky and Atlee to get married.

Spring meant newness, rebirth, rejuvenation. Becky and Atlee were certainly new people. Becky had blossomed from a flighty, flirtatious girl into a kind, loving, responsible young woman. Atlee had shed his prankster, joking ways and become a hardworking young man ready to take on the responsibilities of the head of a family. Together they would create a new life and a home for Becky's *boppli* and any other *kinner* they might have.

Lena could hardly contain her happiness for her *freind* who had grown closer than a *schweschder*. She tamped down the trace of envy that tried to penetrate that ray of sunshine. Maybe it was a *gut* thing to experience a teensy bit of longing. Perhaps that indicated that Lena was finally emerging from the gloom of grief she'd been wallowing in since Joseph's death. When she thought about it, she'd actually been climbing out of that pit of despair ever since Becky came to live with her. Another reason to be grateful for Becky.

Lena sat Mary and Eliza on the couch and admonished them to keep still after making sure they were completely ready for the wedding. She needed to nurse Matthew one last time and then slip into her Sunday dress after the threat of a wet burp had passed.

"Do I look all right? I know I'm not supposed to worry about my appearance, but I want to make sure everything is right, I . . ." Becky paused to gulp in a breath.

"Whoa, girl. Slow down or you will be too exhausted to attend your own wedding. I've heard of nervous brides, but you take the cake." Lena clucked her tongue in mock chastisement. She couldn't hold the serious expression, though, and burst out laughing.

"What's so funny?"

"You!" Lena wiped her eyes. "You look absolutely beautiful."

"I look fat."

"Never in a million years."

"I know everyone is aware of my condition, but I don't want to look heavy for my wedding."

"I can assure you that you look far from heavy. You probably won't look heavy at nine months. You're like me. You'll look like a twig with a knot in the middle."

Becky wrinkled her nose. "I'm not sure that's a compliment, Lena."

"Well, I meant it in a *gut* way. Actually, you probably aren't quite as skinny as I am." Lena held out a thin arm as proof.

"I don't think you gained anything but the exact weight of the *boppli*, and it all disappeared the moment he was born."

"Why don't you sit down and read to the girls before they get antsy? As soon as I nurse Mathew and change, we'll load up our food and head out."

Becky nodded.

"And Becky?"

"*Jah?*"

"Breathe."

Becky inhaled deeply. "Right."

Lena didn't dare let Becky take the reins after they all piled into the buggy. The poor girl would probably drive them right off the road and into a deep ditch. Because Becky's parents had moved from the area and Lena didn't have space to host the wedding, Becky's oldest *bruder*, Emanuel, and his *fraa*, Sally, had agreed to have the wedding at their place. From the corner of her eye, Lena could see Becky alternately wringing her hands and picking her nails. "It's a *gut* thing Emanuel's house isn't far or you'll have every finger bleeding."

Becky promptly tucked her hands beneath her thighs. "Sorry."

"You weren't annoying me. I'd just hate to see you get blood all over that new dress." Lena reached a hand over to pat Becky's knee. "You don't have doubts, do you?"

"Doubts?"

"You aren't sorry you agreed to marry Atlee?"

"Never! I don't have any doubts about him at all."

"What, then?"

"Lena, what if I can't be a *gut fraa* to Atlee? What if I mess this up? I've made a fair share of messes in my life and then some."

"You love Atlee, ain't so?"

"With all my heart."

"And he loves you?"

"*Jah.*"

"Then you won't mess things up. This will be a new experience for both of you, and you will learn together. Everyone feels a little nervous to embark on a new chapter in life."

"Were you nervous before your wedding?"

"Absolutely. But Joseph was, too, so we were in the same boat. We learned to mesh our lives and to create a home together. You and Atlee will, too."

"I hope so. That's what I want."

"I don't have any doubts about you two, Becky dear. I can see the love you share. I can see the way Atlee wants to take care of you and protect you. His excitement about the *boppli* is so sweet."

"Most couples don't start right out as parents."

"You'll have a few months for just the two of you to adjust and to set the course for your lives. And you'll make changes to suit you as you go along. Besides, a lot of couples become parents within the first year of marriage, like I did, so you're only a couple of months earlier than us."

"I guess so."

They rode in silence for a few moments. Even Mary and Eliza kept mum in the back of the buggy. At least neither was sick today.

Becky pulled her hands from under her legs and picked at her nails again.

"What is it?"

"*Ach*! Sorry." Becky gripped her hands and left them in her lap. "I'm nervous to have everyone looking at me, remembering my past."

"We are all your *freinden*. We care about you. The past is just that. Past. Gone. You were a girl. I daresay most adults in the crowd did at least one thing when they were young that still makes them cringe. None of us is perfect. We learn from the past and move on. You did. Everyone will see a *wunderbaar* young woman taking her vows with an equally *wunderbaar* young man."

Becky squeezed Lena's arm. "*Danki*. I can always count on you to help me."

"You can, indeed, and I will always be here for

you. You are the little *schweschder* I never had, and I am grateful for all you've done for me."

Becky swiped at her eyes. "You're going to make me cry."

"Only happy tears are allowed today!" Lena had to blink the moisture from her own eyes. *Remember that!*

Mary leaned against one of Lena's arms and Eliza against the other after nodding off in the middle of the three-hour service. Matthew dozed in her arms. Lena feared she wouldn't be able to move when the time came to do so. The actual wedding, or exchange of vows, occurred at the end of a service that was much like an ordinary church service. The ministers did focus on passages of scripture that dealt with marriage and loyalty, though. Poor nervous brides and grooms had to sweat through the whole service before their special part.

Lena gently nudged Mary and Eliza awake right before the exchange of vows. She knew they wouldn't understand, but she wanted them to at least see Becky and Atlee pledge themselves to each other. It would probably be better for everyone, though, if Matthew remained asleep. If he awoke and wanted to nurse, she would have to take him out and then miss the wedding herself.

She knew without lifting her gaze whose eyes bored into her. She hadn't any need to search the

43

person out. That same icy-hot sensation traveled up and down her body exactly as it had when she was a girl. Back then, she would look up, meet those eyes across the room, and venture a small smile. She would not give into the temptation to look up today. She wasn't that girl anymore and hadn't been for quite some time. She was a woman on her own with three small *kinner*.

Lena focused on Becky's pale face as she joined Atlee in front of the ministers. Lena prayed for courage for her *freind* and that the girl could speak her vows confidently. She prayed the couple would have a happy marriage and would always be *gut* to each other. She held her breath when it was Becky's turn to answer the questions asked by the ministers.

Becky spoke loudly, clearly, and confidently. There wasn't even a trace of trepidation. Lena exhaled. Atlee had not faltered, either. The love between the two was palpable. Had she and Joseph looked at each other like that at their wedding? She didn't have any pictures and she certainly couldn't ask anyone. That would be a strange question indeed. Lena raised the arm that hadn't grown numb from holding Matthew and swiped at the tears before they could trickle down her cheeks.

"Mamm?" Mary's whisper held a note of concern.

"Happy tears." They were, weren't they?

Lena wouldn't even glance in his direction, but still he was powerless to move his gaze away from her. He'd heard she had a sick little one on Sunday, so he hadn't been able to have an initial meeting with her then. Years ago, if he stared at her, she felt it and looked at him. Did she feel anything at all today?

Samuel tried to concentrate on the sermons. He'd attended enough Amish weddings in his life that he'd probably heard every variety of wedding sermon imaginable. It wouldn't be difficult to tune back in when his mind stopped wandering through its collection of memories.

Had Lena thought about him at all over the years? Apparently she didn't have too much trouble getting over him because she'd married and produced three *kinner*. If only Daed hadn't dragged the entire family around the countryside like nomads wandering in the desert.

Their first stop in Pennsylvania wasn't bad. It was at least close enough that Samuel might be able to slip away for an occasional visit to Maryland. But *nee*, Daed hadn't been satisfied there for long. Next, he whisked them away to Indiana, and Samuel's hopes of visiting wavered. Still, he planned to work hard, save his money, and buy a bus ticket or hire a driver to make his trip to Maryland. He never wanted Lena to believe he'd abandoned her. He had always planned to return to her somehow. He'd written several letters but had never received any reply. If Lena had written, the mail had never reached him. *Hard to hit a moving target.* Samuel tried not to let bitterness creep back in.

They'd barely settled into a routine in Indiana when Daed took another notion to move. Samuel could tell his *mudder* had grown weary of packing and unpacking only to pack again. He'd heard her mumbling more than once that Daed should have gotten the restlessness out of his system before bringing a *fraa* and *kinner* into the picture. Yet she obediently packed and trudged along behind Daed. What choice did she have?

The next stop on Daed's secret agenda had been Pinecraft, Florida. He'd left the buggy and horses with a neighbor in Indiana for what he called "safekeeping," and they took only the bare necessities south with them. He probably knew the new location wouldn't be permanent either. Florida had totally taken Samuel by surprise. It might have been all right for a vacation but not for a home.

Samuel couldn't adjust to the blazing heat, the oppressive humidity, the bugs big enough to ride on, or the lack of buggies, horses, cows, and any other vestiges of farm life. He'd felt like he had dropped from another planet and landed smack in the middle of some alien world. Apparently the contrast must have been too great even for Daed because he soon had them headed back to Indiana to collect their belongings.

The last stop had been Wisconsin, about as different from Florida as possible. And cold! Were winters ever frigid! The ice and snow didn't seem to faze his parents, though. His parents acted happier than they had in any other place they'd lived. Samuel suspected Mamm had been so relieved Daed had found a place he wanted to stay that she wouldn't have cared if they lived at the North Pole.

Samuel's heart had stayed in Southern Maryland all through the gypsy years. Even if Lena had moved on with her life—and how could he blame her if she had?—Maryland was in his blood. It was the one place he belonged. The community, located in a rural county far from any cities, was small enough that everyone knew everyone else. There was space enough between farms, but members weren't isolated from one another. Most folks farmed and had small businesses at their homes. That always appealed to Samuel.

When he contacted Bishop Menno, the man had seemed delighted that Samuel wanted to return. He even helped arrange the transfer of property so Samuel would have a place of his own. He had finally developed skills he could use to earn a living. After his *daed*'s death and Mamm's remarriage, he finally felt free to forge his own path.

He thought he had been prepared to see Lena again, but he hadn't expected the pain he experienced when she refused to look at him. Would she ever give him a chance to explain his circumstances? Could he ever do anything to earn her forgiveness?

Samuel tuned back into the service in time to hear the happy couple pledge their love to each other. He had a sinking suspicion he would remain single all his days and lament the loss of what could have been. The bride and groom smiled blissfully at each other while loneliness squeezed Samuel's heart.

Chapter Four

Lena spent the whole reception dinner keeping her eye on her girls or helping make sure everything progressed smoothly. She felt like the *mudder* of the bride even though she was only about four or five years older than Becky. At least Matthew napped in a cradle in the corner of the kitchen so she didn't have to worry about him. It was a *gut* thing the little fellow was used to sleeping with chaos reigning all around him. With him down for the count, Lena's hands were freed up to help out. As soon as she got the girls fed, she would persuade them to take a nap with some of the other *kinner*.

She deliberately avoided looking anywhere near where the young, unmarried men gathered. That didn't mean she didn't feel the pull, though, like a nail drawn to a magnet. She simply refused to yield to it. She would stay busy, preferably in the kitchen, to make sure she abided by that resolution.

"Have you eaten anything?" Saloma Stauffer, Atlee's *mamm*, sidled up to Lena and pulled her hands from the soapy water where she washed yet another sink full of dishes.

"I don't believe so."

"Well, if you don't remember, that most likely

means a morsel of food never crossed your lips. *Kumm* and eat. Someone else will scrub a while."

"I'm fine, really."

"You won't be so fine when you pass out and fall on the floor, or worse yet, you drop your head into that dishwater and drown."

Lena laughed. "I don't think there's any danger of that happening."

Saloma tossed her a dish towel. "Dry your hands and grab a plate."

"I'll just eat something here in the kitchen in case Matthew wakes up."

"He's sound asleep. Join the festivities."

"I, uh, I'd . . ."

"I'm sorry, Lena. I didn't mean to be insensitive. It must be hard attending a wedding after your loss."

And with my first love out there watching my every move. "*Jah*," she whispered, "but I'm so happy for Becky and Atlee. They make a *wunderbaar* couple." Lena hoped to steer the conversation away from herself.

"I think so, too. Though to be honest, I had my doubts at first."

"I know. Everyone had to look beyond Becky's past. She has really grown into such a caring, responsible young woman."

"She has indeed. And we're looking forward to meeting that *boppli*, too."

50

Lena laughed. "To spoiling that *boppli*, you mean."

"Most likely." Saloma chuckled. "I can keep an eye on Matthew for a few minutes. I promise I'll fetch you when he wakes. Go have some fun."

"I'm too old to have fun."

Saloma laughed so hard she had to wipe her eyes. "You're so ancient at what, twenty-five?"

"I feel as old as dirt. I have three *kinner*."

"You became a *mudder* young, and you're still young. You need to take a few minutes for yourself now, while the little ones are napping." When Lena hesitated, Saloma tugged at her arm. "Off with you, now. I've got six *kinner*. I think I can handle your *boppli* if he wakes up. If you don't eat something, you're going to dry up and blow away."

"*Danki*, Saloma." Lena couldn't very well admit her trepidation to the older woman. Surely Samuel had gone home by now and her fretting was for naught. She slipped outside and headed to the big barn where the meal had been set up. For an instant, she considered hurrying off behind the barn and pretending she had gone inside for food. Fear of getting caught made her stay on course.

Lena mumbled under her breath and slowed her steps. She had deliberately stayed occupied in the kitchen to avoid mingling with the crowd of wedding guests. She figured her absence wouldn't be noticed, but Saloma never missed a thing. She not only realized Lena hadn't put in an appearance, but took it upon herself to remedy that situation. Lena hoped that most people had finished eating and visiting and were ready to head home by now. The young unmarrieds would stay around for more activities, but they wouldn't pay any attention to her.

She slipped into the barn where people continued to sit at tables or mill about. If she moved slowly so as not to draw any attention, she would snag a plate, plop a few finger foods on it, and beat a hasty retreat to the kitchen or the front porch or the woods. Anywhere but right in plain view of every watchful eye in the place. Lena withdrew a plate from the stack and promptly dropped it when a deep voice spoke right behind her.

"There you are!"

She didn't need to turn around. She'd heard that voice in her dreams for years. She didn't need to see the brown hair with flecks of gold that always reminded Lena of the acorns that speckled the ground beneath the old oak tree in her parents' front yard. She didn't want to see the fern-colored eyes. She retrieved the plate with trembling hands.

"I'm sorry. I didn't mean to startle you."

"It's okay," Lena mumbled without turning around.

"How have you been?"

"Fine." As fine as a woman could be who'd lost two men she had loved and now was raising three youngsters alone.

"Could you turn around so I don't have to talk to your back?"

Could you disappear like you're so gut *at doing and leave me alone?* She dropped the plate back onto the table. "I need to check on my *boppli.*" She jumped when strong fingers encircled her arm.

"Don't go, Lena. Please get something to eat."

Lena peeked at the hand that so easily wrapped around her entire arm. *He probably thinks I'm so skinny I should eat the table and all. He probably thinks he can stand me in the cornfield to scare the crows away. He probably . . .* Why should she care what he thought? "I-I'm not hungry."

Samuel kept one hand on Lena's arm as if afraid she would bolt, which she would do given the opportunity. With the other hand he laid a couple of slices of banana bread on the plate and added raw vegetables and pickles. *Great! Now he's going to feed me!*

"Here. At least have a little something." He thrust the plate practically in Lena's face. Pickle juice flowed around and under the bread. "Ugh! This is pretty unappetizing, isn't it?"

In spite of herself, Lena giggled like a nervous schoolgirl. "*Jah.*"

53

He set the plate back down. "I've always loved to hear you laugh."

She sobered instantly when the thought, *Then why did you never return or write?* shot through her brain. She pulled her arm from his grasp.

"Can we talk, Lena? Please?"

"I need to . . ."

"Check on your *boppli*. I know. Your little ones are all adorable. I'd like to get to know them. The girls are as pretty as their *mudder*."

Lena sucked in a gulp of air. Her neck and face burned. It was too late for sweet-talking at this point in time. If he didn't need her in his life ten years ago, she didn't need Samuel Mast in her life now.

"Here. I'll grab you some unpickled banana bread. You can eat it while we talk." Samuel selected a fresh piece of bread and laid it on a clean plate. He reached for Lena's arm, but she backed away. He turned a questioning expression on her. "What is it?"

"I am perfectly capable of choosing my own food, Samuel Mast. And what makes you think I want to go off and have any kind of conversation with you?" Lena's ire rose, as did her voice. She fought to control both.

"We need to talk."

Lena dragged in a deep breath and held it while she counted to fifty by fives. She lowered her voice to barely above a whisper. It would not be a *gut* thing for anyone to overhear any discussion they might have and spread the details along the grapevine. "I do not *need* to talk to you, nor do I *want* to talk to you. You didn't feel it was necessary to communicate with me for the past ten years, so don't waltz back into town and think we can pick up where we left off. We were young back then. Life moved on. I'm a *mudder* with three *kinner* now. End of story."

She had said more than she intended. Lena snapped her mouth closed and brushed past Samuel. She had to get away. She wanted to rant and rave. She wanted to accuse and blame. She wanted to sob and moan. She would do none of those things, at least not here on public display.

"Lena, wait!"

His voice was low. Was that a plaintive note she detected? Sadness? Dejection? Whatever it was, it tugged at her soul and pierced her heart. She stopped in her tracks but didn't turn around.

"I'm sorry."

Still Lena kept her back to him. She couldn't look into Samuel's eyes. More important, she couldn't let him look into hers. The eyes were said to be the window to the soul. Samuel had always been too *gut* at reading her thoughts simply by gazing into her eyes. Did he still have that ability? She couldn't take the chance that he did.

"Did you hear me?"

She nodded. The lump that clogged her throat prevented any words from exiting.

"I never wanted to hurt you all those years ago. I never even wanted to move to all those places my *daed* dragged us to."

"They have mail service everywhere." Somehow, those few words squeezed past that boulder before she could swallow them back down.

"I know. I tried to write."

"I never received so much as one single note."

"That's because the letters didn't make it to the mail."

"I see. I wasn't important enough." Lena started forward again.

"*Nee*. You were the most important person in the world to me."

"Not mailing letters, not visiting—those sure are odd ways to show you care."

"Let me explain."

"Lena!" A voice called loud and clear. "I'm sorry to interrupt you, dear."

"*Ach*! It's Saloma. Matthew must be awake." She hurried to reach the barn door. "You don't need to explain anything," she flung over her shoulder to the man staring at her.

Lena pulled in two deep breaths to calm her nerves. If she remained agitated, the *boppli* would pick up on her mood and be fussy. "Here I am, Saloma. Is Matthew upset?"

"*Nee*, but he's rooting around and I'm afraid

I can't supply his needs." Saloma chuckled and patted the infant in her arms. "Did you get something to eat, dear?"

"I'm fine. I can take him." She didn't dare tell Saloma she hadn't so much as inhaled a crumb or the woman would likely force-feed her. She reached out to take Matthew into her arms and to snuggle him close. She inhaled the sweet scent of the sun-dried swaddling blanket.

Lena turned to follow Saloma's gaze. Samuel stood just outside the barn. The late-day sun highlighted the gold strands in his hair. He smiled and gave a little wave. "I'll talk to you later, Lena," he called.

She whirled around and bent to kiss Matthew's head. The nerve of that man! "You didn't interrupt a thing, Saloma. Is my little fellow getting hungry? *Kumm* and your *mamm* will feed you."

"I changed him before I brought him out."

"*Danki.* You didn't have to do that."

"It's great to take care of a little one. It keeps me in practice."

Lena cocked an eyebrow at the older woman.

"Not for any *bopplin* of my own, I assure you. Aiden is my last one. I love him dearly, but if he'd been my first, he might have been an only child. I'm hoping my *kinner* provide me with lots of little ones to love."

Lena smiled and tried to relax. "I'm sure you

will be a magnificent *grossmammi*. I pray you will have a whole bunch of *bopplin* to lavish attention on."

"I hope so. In the meantime, I get to spoil every tot I have contact with."

"I suppose Mary and Eliza are still napping?"

"They were when I brought Matthew outside."

"*Gut.* Then I'll have a few minutes with my little man." Lena felt the eyes that bored into her back as she marched toward the house, but she refused to give in to the temptation to turn around. She slowed her pace a bit when she noticed Saloma's struggle to keep up.

"Did Samuel Mast say or do something to upset you, dear?" Saloma's words were punctuated by gasps.

Lena stopped short and nearly caused the older woman to collide with her. "Of course not. Why do you ask?" She wasn't really telling an untruth, she reasoned; she'd been upset before Samuel even opened his mouth. And she shouldn't have been angry about his appearance. He had every right to return to Maryland. He was a grown man and could certainly reside anywhere he pleased. She didn't have to like his choice, but it wasn't any of her business. Just like her life should be none of his business.

"You seem peeved, and you're walking like you can't get away from the man fast enough."

"I'm sorry I'm moving so fast, Saloma. I'm

usually chasing after two active little girls." Lena forced a little laugh.

"Hmm. I'm not so sure. If my memory serves me correctly, you and Samuel were kind of sweet on each other back in the day. I know we older folks aren't supposed to notice those things, but we do."

"That was a silly teenage crush. We've both grown up and gone on with our lives."

"I'm not so sure Samuel has moved forward with his."

"Of course he has. I don't know why he chose to settle here after being away for so long, but he's free to live wherever he likes, I suppose."

"I could make a pretty accurate guess as to why Samuel returned to Maryland, if the way he stared after you is any indication."

Lena's face heated. Her cheeks had probably turned cherry red. "*Ach!* You're talking nonsense, Saloma."

"Am I?"

"For sure." But was she?

Well, he'd certainly gone about that all wrong. Samuel rubbed a hand across his smooth chin. Even to his own ears he had sounded cocky and demanding, not penitent and concerned, as he had hoped to sound. How had his words and his attitude gotten so turned around? He wanted so much to talk to Lena, to explain his actions, to beg forgiveness for leaving her in the lurch, to somehow make amends. It seemed like he'd only angered her and further alienated her. How could simple, *gut* plans have gone so awry? Would he ever get the opportunity to tell Lena he had written her dozens of letters, most of which his *daed* had found and destroyed? He'd definitely had words with Daed over the interference, but in the end had been powerless and totally unsuccessful in reasoning with the man.

It was time to slip away from the wedding festivities. He might be a young, single man, but his heart had been claimed long ago. Samuel didn't belong with these young folks who would be pairing up, laughing, and celebrating the marriage of their *freinden*. He had nothing to celebrate. Not yet, anyway. But one day he would, Gott willing. He watched Lena enter the house before hitching his horse to his recently acquired, secondhand gray buggy.

Chapter Five

How did she ever manage before Becky came to live with her? Lena scorched the oatmeal, burned the eggs, and charred the toast. She had been cooking for years. Why was she so flustered and discombobulated today? Becky had gotten married only yesterday, so this was her first day without help and companionship. She would adjust to doing everything herself once again, wouldn't she? She would keep telling herself that. Surely missing Becky must be her reason for her distracted state this morning. The fact that she'd lain awake most of the night rehashing the encounter with Samuel over and over again had nothing to do with her clumsiness.

Ach! Two hungry little girls would put in an appearance in a matter of minutes. She needed to salvage something from this mess that was supposed to be their breakfast. Lena lifted the lid from the pan on the back burner of the stove. She could probably scrape out just enough oatmeal for three relatively small bowlfuls. Thankfully, Eliza didn't eat big portions yet. Mary, though, could put away some food. As little as she was, Lena didn't know where the girl stowed all the food she consumed. She must be going through a growth spurt, or else she had a hollow leg.

The eggs were a hopeless mess. There really wasn't any way to fix burned eggs. Lena snatched a butter knife from the drawer and scraped the black coating from the overtoasted bread. There. If she slathered on some homemade strawberry jam made from last year's berry crop, all would be well. Oatmeal and toast would have to suffice this morning. She wouldn't attempt a new batch of eggs. As distracted as she was, she might burn down the whole house! If Mary or Eliza was still hungry, Lena would drag out the box of corn flakes from the cupboard.

How long would it be until things returned to normal? Lena pushed down that faint whisper of "never" that echoed through her brain. As if it wasn't hard enough to accept that Becky wouldn't live with the Troyers any longer, now Samuel Mast's appearance had to complicate life even more.

Why did he have to return after all these years? And why did her heart skip every other beat when she saw him or even thought of him? *Silly woman. You are too old to act like a schoolgirl.* Infuriation, that's all it was. He infuriated her with his assumption that she would jump at his beck and call, that she would eagerly take up where they had left off.

Lena absentmindedly reached for the pan to dish out the oatmeal. She ended up grabbing the hot side of the metal pan instead of the handle.

"Ouch!" She dropped the pan back onto the stove. It was a *gut* thing the oatmeal was too pasty to slosh out all over the place. She definitely did not need another mess to contend with. She blew on her smarting fingers. "It's all your fault, Samuel Mast!"

"Who are you talking to, Mamm?" Mary stood in the kitchen doorway rubbing sleep from her eyes. Eliza clasped Mary's hand. Her other thumb was jammed in her mouth. Both were tousle-headed, but they were dressed. Sort of.

Lena had been so preoccupied, she hadn't heard the girls approach. Usually their clatter and chatter warned her as to their whereabouts. "I'm talking to myself, I suppose."

Mary giggled. "You're funny, Mamm." Eliza giggled in imitation of her big *schweschder*.

"I guess I am at that." Lena smiled at her precious girls. She blew on her fingers once more.

"We got dressed all by ourselves."

"So I see." Somehow she would have to rearrange their dresses without hurting their feelings. They tried so hard to be helpful.

"I had to help Eliza, you know." Mary puffed herself up as big as possible.

"*Danki.* I certainly appreciate your help. Why don't we go upstairs and comb your hair before we eat breakfast?"

"I'm hungry."

"Hungry," Eliza echoed.

"I'm sure you are, but you don't want to eat your hair when it gets in the way, do you?"

Mary giggled again and wrinkled her nose. "That wouldn't taste *gut*."

"Exactly. So let's go brush and braid your hair."

"Okay." Mary sighed, as if this whole hair-fixing thing was a huge inconvenience. Eliza copied that sigh with her thumb still filling her mouth.

"Let's hurry so you poor, starving girls can eat your breakfast."

Lena managed to ever-so-subtly alter the dresses a bit after she braided the girls' hair. They made it back to the kitchen in a jiffy. Lena let the girls help by placing napkins and spoons on the big, old oak table. She sprinkled chocolate chips on top of the oatmeal bowls in a smiley face pattern not only to offer a little treat but also to camouflage any scorched taste the oatmeal might harbor.

If the breakfast was less than ideal, the girls didn't notice. Mary dug into her oatmeal, delighted with the chocolate smile. Lena spooned a bite into Eliza's mouth. Ordinarily she would let Eliza feed herself, but she did not want to have to change Eliza's clothes or scrub the floor.

"When will we see Becky again?" Mary asked around the bite of toast in her mouth. Strawberry jam oozed out to give her a red mustache.

"Please don't talk with food in your mouth." Lena reached to wipe Mary's mouth with a paper napkin.

"Will Atlee still *kumm* to play with us?"

Lena could tell Mary missed having a *daed* around. She probably had a few vague memories of Joseph playing with them. Eliza stared at her as if waiting for an answer, too. "Well, you know, girls, Atlee and Becky got married yesterday. They need some time to set up their own home, but I'm sure they will visit as soon as they can."

"I wish they lived here."

Lena found herself wishing the exact same thing, but her house wasn't designed for two families to live in comfortably. Becky and Atlee would live with Atlee's recently married *bruder*, Sam, and Sam's *fraa*, Emma. The situation probably wasn't ideal for two couples just starting out, but at least the house was large enough to accommodate two families. Sam and Emma would have the downstairs, while Atlee and Becky would occupy the upstairs. They would make do with that until Atlee and Becky's own house was ready for occupancy. Lena hoped that would happen before Becky's *boppli* arrived.

She'd busied the girls with chores after breakfast. They acted as if they enjoyed swirling dust cloths around. Of course Eliza mainly waved her cloth in the air, but she pranced about as if she was performing the most important task in the world. Lena had to turn away to hide her smile. They were such dear little ones.

After feeding the girls their noon meal and nursing Matthew, Lena managed to get all three down for naps. Blessed peace reigned for a while. She longed to curl up with her knitting or to nap herself, but that luxury would have to wait . . . and wait. Lena hadn't had the opportunity to while away the afternoon since she was a little girl. Once she had grown old enough to be of significant help around the house, her days of lollygagging about came to an abrupt end. But she had felt as elated as Mary and Eliza that she had become useful to her family.

Enough reminiscing. Lena flew about the kitchen mixing up a meat loaf and pressing it into a loaf pan, peeling potatoes to boil and mash later, and gathering up other items she would need to round out their supper. If she could get supper preparations out of the way, she would help the girls bake cookies when they awoke. They were all sorely missing Becky. Even though Lena had other chores to finish, they all needed a fun diversion today. Stacking wood for chilly evenings and getting in laundry from the line could wait a little longer.

Samuel continued to kick himself for the way he'd handled his encounter with Lena at the wedding reception. How could he ever get her to listen to his explanation for why he hadn't returned to Maryland sooner? Maybe she sensed his excuse was flimsy and would never listen. All he had managed to do yesterday was make her angry, or at least perturbed. *Nee*, angry was more like it. How could he get her to at least be civil? Even though Samuel had hoped for so much more, couldn't they at least be *freinden*?

He snatched off his straw hat and fanned himself with it. He pulled a handkerchief from a pocket and mopped his face. The day was actually pleasant, with a gentle breeze, but mending this old fence surrounding the pasture had proven to be an arduous, sweat-producing task. He scarcely even noticed the cooling breeze.

Samuel straightened to get the kink out of his lower back and surveyed the small field. If he ever got the fence repaired and the shed cleaned out and transformed into a stable of sorts, it would be perfect for the animals he wanted to purchase one day.

Sheep. He envisioned a field of wooly, white, black-faced sheep. His *mudder* was an avid knitter and always lamented that high-quality yarn was in such short supply locally. She often mail-ordered the materials she needed. So there must be a big market for *gut* yarn. Samuel had always liked sheep. Some people called them dumb animals, but he had found them to be gentle and smarter than they were given credit for. He had helped neighbors in various places with their sheep, so he had a little experience to draw on. Although most farmers in the Southern Maryland community raised cows or chickens, a few had sheep, so he could pick those farmers' brains, too.

Lena's parents had raised a few sheep at one time, but the animals were more like pets. He'd heard her parents died in an accident not long after Samuel's family had moved away. Was that when Lena turned to Joseph Troyer? If he remembered correctly, Joseph had been several years older. Maybe Lena believed Joseph would take care of her after her parents passed. She used to enjoy knitting and often showed him items she had stitched. Would she be interested in raising sheep with him?

"Go on with you, man!" The horse munching grass in the shade paused to look at him, making Samuel feel foolish for speaking aloud. He sighed. Lena couldn't stand the sight of him at present, and she would most likely avoid him at all costs every time they happened to be in the same place. Somehow he had to earn her trust. He slapped the hat on his head and turned back to the broken-down fence. He would think of something.

Chapter Six

"I saw you, you little sneak." Lena smiled and tapped Mary's hand. The girl stared with big, questioning eyes. Lena struggled not to laugh at Mary's feigned innocence. "Don't pretend you don't know what I'm talking about. I saw you pop those chocolate chips in your mouth." Mary gulped and opened her mouth wide to show it was empty. "You're going to choke swallowing them whole."

"Me?" Eliza obviously wanted in on the act.

Lena handed her younger *dochder* a chocolate chip and watched to make sure she chewed it. "Now, let's put the rest in the batter unless you want plain cookies."

Mary and Eliza both wagged their heads. Mary grunted as she attempted to stir the heavy, sticky dough, but she refused to give up.

"Would you like me to check to see if it's ready to scoop out?" Lena knew Mary's hand must be aching, but she admired the little girl's determination.

"Okay." Mary held out the spoon.

"You've done a splendid job, girls." Lena whisked the spoon around the bowl a couple of times to scrape any unmixed batter from the sides. "I believe we're ready." She passed each girl a small scoop and helped them gather enough dough to form cookies. Both had flour-dotted cheeks, chins, and noses. Lena wouldn't be surprised if her own face sported some of the same powder.

A thump outside the back door gave them all a start. Eliza's scoopful of dough slid right off the side of the pan. Her quick little fingers snagged the hunk and almost deposited it in her mouth before Lena could grab her hand. "We don't want to eat it uncooked. Raw eggs can make you sick." Lena shook the sticky glob out of Eliza's hand and tossed it aside. She grabbed a rag to wipe the remaining goo away.

Thump! Thump! What could be making that noise? It reminded Lena of wood thrown onto the rack. Surely Atlee hadn't *kumm* to stack wood on the day after his wedding. She would step out and send him on his way. She had planned to do that chore herself as soon as the cookies had all been transferred to wire cooling racks.

"Girls, I want you both to sit right here while I check outside. Mary, show Eliza this book. Look at all these yummy pictures." Lena handed Mary a cookie cookbook someone had given her long ago. She moved the big ceramic bowl still half-full of cookie dough and the cookie sheets out of reach. It wouldn't do to tempt her little bakers to make their own cookies or to eat raw dough.

Lena gave a final glance over her shoulder to

make sure the girls sat quietly before poking her head out the back door to locate the cause of the thumping sound. New pieces of wood had been stacked on top of her dwindling pile near the door. How did it get there? She stepped all the way outside in time to see a man push a wheelbarrow loaded with wood toward the house. She squinted into the afternoon sunlight. He appeared too tall to be Atlee. Although Atlee was at least six feet tall, this man had him beat by several inches. Who in the world . . . ?

Lena gasped. Her heart stuttered and she nearly stumbled. When the man stopped to remove his hat and mop his brow, she knew exactly who had been stacking wood. Who else had that sun-kissed brown hair? She stomped in his direction. "What do you think you're doing?" She drew herself up as tall as her five-foot three-inch frame would allow and planted her fists on her hips.

"I know exactly what I'm doing. Nice to see you, too, Lena."

Oooh! He was infuriating, that's what he was. "I planned to do that as soon as my cookies were done."

"Well, now you don't have to."

"I'm perfectly capable of doing my own work."

"I'm sure you are. Can't a fellow be neighborly?"

"We are not neighbors."

"We're all neighbors, ain't so? Isn't that what the Bible teaches us?"

"I, uh . . ." Lena sputtered and stopped. Her forehead tightened into deep furrows.

"Cookies, did you say?"

"You wouldn't be interested."

"Since when wouldn't I be interested in cookies? I don't eat a lot of sweets, but I do like cookies. Don't you remember when I ate nearly a whole dozen chocolate chip cookies? They are my favorite, you know. What kind are you making?"

Heat crawled up the back of Lena's neck and wrapped around her face. She stared at the ground and mumbled, "Chocolate chip." She peeked upward in time to catch Samuel's smile. She didn't understand why it irked her, but it did. Surely he didn't think she made chocolate chip cookies because he liked them. She didn't even know he planned to show up at her house today. And she wouldn't have made him cookies if she did know!

He continued observing her with that hopeful, expectant look. What was she supposed to say? Was she supposed to eagerly invite him inside for a snack? *Nee.* That wasn't going to happen. Yet the Christian thing to do would be to offer him a treat and a drink because he'd been stacking *her* wood. A little imp inside her reminded her that she didn't ask him to perform the chore for her.

Could she turn on her heel and march back to her girls and her kitchen? Could she be that rude?

She could not. Her *mudder* had taught her to be polite and hospitable. It was the right thing to do, even if she did not want to. But that didn't mean she had to invite Samuel into her home. She could bring him some cookies outside if he was still here when they came out of the oven.

"Mamm, we looked at the book. Can we finish the cookies now?" Mary's head popped out the back door. Eliza squeezed through the gap Mary created.

"*Ach*, Mary! You let Eliza out!"

Samuel dropped the handles of the wheelbarrow and let the load slam to the ground. He crossed the distance between them in several long strides. "I'll nab her."

Before Lena could protest or unglue herself from the spot where she stood, Samuel scooped up Eliza in his muscular arms and tickled her before depositing the giggling little girl into Lena's waiting arms.

"Me, too?" Mary didn't want to be left out of any merriment.

Samuel bent to tickle Mary. "You must be Mary, and the wiggle worm must be Eliza."

Mary giggled. "She's my *schweschder*, not a worm."

"Ah, I beg your pardon."

"Who are you?"

"My name is Samuel. I am—was—a *freind* of your *mudder*'s." He chucked Mary under the chin.

Was. You got that right. Lena bit her tongue to keep those words from spewing out.

"You're funny." Mary giggled again.

Lena wanted to hustle her girls inside and bolt the door. Samuel needn't try to win over her *kinner*. Only a sense of obligation kept her from doing exactly that.

"We're baking cookies," Mary announced.

"So I heard."

"We need to get back to our work, girls, ain't so?" Lena reached for Mary's hand and tried to turn toward the door.

"Can't Samuel *kumm* in for cookies?" Mary pulled on Lena's hand, insistent on an answer.

My little girl is showing better manners than I am. "They aren't even baked yet, silly goose, but we'll bring Samuel some later if he's still here." Lena hoped he got the implied message and was long gone by the time the cookies were done.

"I might just have to wait around for some." Samuel winked at Lena.

Lena quickly averted her gaze. There came that sudden flash of heat again. The man was much more persistent than she remembered. She chose not to respond to him. "Let's go, girls."

"He's nice, Mamm."

Lena hoped she had shepherded Mary out of

Samuel's hearing range. She didn't dare turn to see if he caught the comment.

"Ain't so, Mamm?" Mary tugged on Lena's skirt. Apparently she wasn't going to let Lena get out of answering.

"Hmmm. I suppose." Lena needed to divert the little girl's attention. She certainly didn't want her *dochder* to get attached to Samuel Mast in any way. That could only lead to disappointment and heartache. She would not let anyone hurt her little ones. It never ceased to amaze Lena how akin to a mother lion she became the instant after she gave birth to her first *boppli*. She loved Mary, Eliza, and Matthew fiercely and would do anything to keep them safe. "Let's wash our hands and get those cookies in the oven."

"We washed our hands." Mary looked at her hands, turning them this way and that, as if looking for a speck of dirt.

"*Jah*. We did wash them earlier, but we've been doing other things. A *gut* cook washes again before returning to her baking."

Mary ran for the sink. "I'm a *gut* cook, ain't so?"

"Me, too." Eliza ran behind her *schweschder*.

Lena chuckled. "You are both *gut* cooks."

Thirty minutes later, the tantalizing aroma of chocolate wafted through the kitchen, making their stomachs rumble and their mouths water. Lena placed a hand over the top of Mary's to help her transfer cookies to the cooling rack. Eliza sat in her high chair with a small cup of water, waiting patiently to sample a cookie.

Mary pointed to the cookies that had been cooling. "Are those ready to eat?"

"I believe you can sample one as soon as I pull this last pan out of the oven. Why don't you spread out napkins for you and Eliza?" Lena handed Mary the paper napkins.

Mary grabbed the napkins and hopped up and down. Excitement glowed in her eyes. "It's time, Eliza! We get to s-s-sample cookies." Eliza caught Mary's fervor and banged on the high-chair tray. Mary spread out napkins for each of them before turning to Lena with a scrunched-up face. "What's a s-sample?"

Lena laughed. "It means you will try a cookie. You get to eat one." She held up one index finger.

"*Gut.*" Mary plunked down at her place at the big oak table. She barely sat before popping back up. "What about Samuel?"

"What about him?"

"Can we take him some cookies?"

"We'll see." Lena hurried to lay a cookie on Mary's napkin, hoping to distract her. She broke a cookie into bite-sized chunks for Eliza. On her way back to the counter to transfer the last batch of cookies to the cooling rack, her gaze drifted to the window. *Gut.* Samuel was not in sight. Maybe he had given up on the notion of eating cookies and set out for home. She snagged a still-warm cookie from the rack and closed her eyes in bliss as she chewed the chocolate treat.

"Any cookies for a starving man?"

Lena's eyes flew open at the deep voice sounding at her back door. She swallowed her now tasteless bite of cookie and promptly gagged. She hastily swiped at the moisture from her eyes with the back of one hand. Did the man have some uncanny sense that his name had been mentioned? Why hadn't he gone home? Why had he even returned to Maryland instead of staying wherever his family lived? Was she going to be plagued by surprise visits or coincidental run-ins the rest of her life?

She coughed to clear her throat of the lump lodged there. Lena couldn't be certain if it was only a bite of cookie or if the crumbs had adhered to the wad of dread clogging her windpipe. She snatched up a handful of cookies and wrapped them in a napkin. Perhaps she could appease him with this meager offering and send him on his way.

Lena hurried to the door with the cookies. She didn't want to appear ungrateful or rude, but she didn't want Samuel to stay either. "I know you must have a thousand things to do. I appreciate your moving the wood for me." She held out the napkin-wrapped treat. That didn't sound too rude, did it?

"I also mucked out your stalls and tended the horses for you." Samuel pushed back his hat.

"You shouldn't have done that. The bishop's son and several others take turns helping me with that. Sometimes I do it myself." Lena bristled at his shocked expression. "I am perfectly capable of doing hard work myself. I might look small and weak, but I assure you, I am strong. I've had to be."

Samuel threw up his arms as if in self-defense. "I don't doubt your strength for a single minute, Lena. Or your determination. I remember well how you can do whatever you set your mind to doing."

Lena exhaled the breath she had been subconsciously holding.

Samuel softened his tone. "I didn't mind the chore. I was already here, so I saved someone else a trip. Don't deprive people of the blessing of helping."

"*Danki*." Lena wavered in her decision to send Samuel on his way. How could she not offer him a drink and a chance to sit for a minute after all his hard work for her? True, she hadn't asked for his help and would have refused it if she'd had the chance, but it was all over and done now. Samuel had considered helping to be a blessing. She'd have to think about that later.

"Lena?"

"Huh?" Had he asked her something and her straying thoughts made her miss it?

"Can I wash my hands?"

"Sure." Lena moved back a step to indicate Samuel could enter. With his hat pushed back, she could clearly see those eyes that always reminded her of the bright green ferns that grew close to the creek on her parents' property. She used to tease Samuel about his fern eyes. Did he remember? She mentally shook herself to dislodge the memories of long-ago hikes and picnics. "The bathroom is through here." Lena pointed out the way.

"Hi! Our cookies are *gut*!" Mary called out around the bite she still chewed.

"Please don't talk with food in your mouth." Lena threw a stern look in her *dochder*'s direction.

Mary hung her head until Samuel spoke. "If you helped bake them, I'm sure they are scrumptious." Instantly she brightened and licked the chocolate from her lips.

A little dart pierced Lena's heart. Her girls missed having a *daed* around. Atlee had tried to lavish attention on them when he visited Becky. She couldn't expect him to continue visits now that he and Becky were married. She would simply have to do a better job of being *mamm* and *daed* to her precious little ones.

Or remarry.

Lena sighed. She needed to banish that little imp that continued to whisper into her ear. She scurried back to the kitchen and laid the napkin full of cookies on the table. She split another cookie to give half to each girl. "This is all for now. I want you to eat your supper."

"From the look of those faces, those cookies must be yummy." Samuel patted Mary's head as he passed by her chair.

"You can sit beside me." Mary gave him a shy smile.

Samuel winked and slid onto the empty chair beside the little girl.

Lena's heart ached more. She needed to hurry and get Samuel out of her house and keep him out before Mary began forming any attachment.

Eliza banged on her tray. Obviously she didn't want to be left out. Great! Now both of her girls vied for the attention of a man Lena had worked hard to remove from her heart and mind. She would not let him sneak back into her life or into her *dochders'* lives.

Chapter Seven

"Hey, little one! I see you." Samuel reached out to scoot the high chair closer so he could talk to Eliza, too.

Lena seethed. How dare he jump into their lives! She had been having a fun day with her girls and Samuel Mast had to *kumm* along and spoil it. She watched him drag the napkin full of cookies across the table. He moved in slow motion and made a big show of undoing the napkin and pulling out a cookie to entertain his enthralled audience of two.

He can only spoil the day if you allow him to do so. That's right! She was in charge of her thoughts and moods. She would not allow him to mar their happiness. She'd try not to anyway.

"Mmm!" Samuel chewed the bite of cookie and rolled his eyes. "This might be the best chocolate chip cookie I've ever eaten, and I've eaten quite a few in my life. They are my favorite, you know. Whoever baked these did a superior job." He took another bite and heaved an exaggerated sigh.

Mary giggled. "We baked them, silly. Mamm, Eliza, and me." Eliza giggled whenever Mary did.

"You sure are *gut* bakers."

Lena had had enough. She needed to get

Samuel to leave. It was hard enough for the girls to adjust to Becky being gone. They didn't need to start liking Samuel only to have him pull a disappearing act, as he was known to do. *Be fair, Lena. He had to leave with his family. He was young. What other choice did he have?* "He could have *kumm* back."

"What? Did you say something, Lena?"

Ach! Had she spoken aloud? How embarrassing! How was she going to cover that slipup? "I said I'll be back. With a drink. What would you like? I don't have any *kaffi* made, but I can brew tea right quick. Or there's milk." Now she was babbling. Samuel would think she'd lost her mind for sure. Hmpf! Why should she care what he thought?

"Water will be fine, Lena. Don't go to any trouble."

"Tea or milk wouldn't be any trouble." She at least had to make an effort to be polite.

"I like water just fine."

"Okay." She turned her back on the cozy little scene at her table. Too cozy. She didn't want Samuel cozying up to her girls. It took every ounce of her willpower not to stomp across the floor to retrieve a glass from the cupboard. She tried to ignore the rumbling deep voice and the childish giggles behind her. *Just get the water, Lena, and then get him out of here!* Her resolution to hang on to the happy day had all but disappeared. *Breathe, smile, breathe.*

She plunked the glass of water on the table and scurried around to the high chair with a wet cloth in her hand.

"Can't you sit down with us for a few minutes, Lena? Have a cookie. Relax."

This is not a happy, little family scene that you brazenly inserted yourself into, Samuel Mast. These are my kinner. *You don't have any claim on them, on us. You shouldn't even be here.* Harnessing these thoughts and bridling her tongue had given her a pounding headache. "I have work to do. I'm sure you must have a lot to straighten out at the Stoltzfus place."

"It's the Mast place now." Samuel smiled. "I do like the sound of that."

"*Jah*, well, I'm sure you have plenty to do there." Eliza squirmed as Lena wiped chocolate from her mouth and fingers. "Besides, I want the girls to eat their supper in a little while. I don't need you to keep sneaking them bites of cookies."

"Uh-oh. We got caught, girls."

"*Mudders* have eyes everywhere. Didn't your *mamm* ever say that to you?"

"Probably."

Lena lifted Eliza from the chair and set her on her feet. "Wipe off your hands, Mary. You and Eliza can help me get the laundry off the line."

Samuel finished the last of the cookie he'd

been nibbling and tucked the others back into the napkin. He gulped a half glass of water without stopping and set the glass on the table. "I know a dismissal when I hear one."

Guilt stirred inside Lena's soul. "I don't mean to be rude, but we've all got work to do." Yet those words did sound rude. Once she spoke them, though, she couldn't stuff them back inside her mouth. "I do appreciate your hard work, but please don't feel you have to take us on as your charity project. We're doing fine."

"That isn't what I was doing at all. I was . . ."

"What? You were what?"

"I only wanted to help."

"*Danki*, but I'm managing fine." Most of the time.

"What about your fields this spring and summer?"

"Several of the younger men needed more farming space. They rent my fields. It works out for all of us. They get to farm. My fields get used. And I get a little income from the rent." Younger men? When did she start considering herself an older woman? When she became a parent or when she became a widow? She was only twenty-five, not exactly ancient.

"That sounds like a fine arrangement." Samuel picked up his hat.

"Play?" Eliza must have remembered how Atlee always played with them before he left.

"Can you play with us?" Mary expounded on Eliza's request.

Samuel opened his mouth to speak, but Lena rushed to answer before he could get out a sound. "Samuel did not *kumm* to play, girls. He has a lot to do at his house. Who is going to get the laundry basket for me?"

"I got the hint, Lena. I know you want me to leave. It's okay. I sense that I make you nervous."

Try flustered, annoyed, angry, perturbed, upset. Any of those words might be a better choice. "Not really."

"That's all right. I hope you will get used to seeing me around because I plan to stay in St. Mary's County now. We will run into each other all the time. And I can help you whenever you need someone to help. All you have to do is say the word." With that, Samuel gave each girl a pat on the head and slipped from the house.

Lena closed her mouth. She had only just realized that it hung open. "I won't be needing you, Samuel, so don't hold your breath waiting for me to call on you for help," she whispered.

Cracking her shell was definitely not going to be easy. Samuel shook his head as he clucked to the horse to get the buggy moving. He realized that time had marched on, and that he couldn't pick up the relationship where they'd left off. They'd barely been more than *kinner* when he left, but his feelings for her had been real. And they had never died. Seeing Lena brought those half-buried emotions out of hiding.

Of course he had tried to deny those feelings, and he had managed to push them down a little deeper when he'd heard through the grapevine she had gotten married. He had been crushed at the news, but he understood her desire to move on. As far as she knew, he'd fallen off the earth and was gone forever. He had made a genuine attempt to forget her smile and her dark, velvety eyes, but her image could pop into his mind without any warning whatsoever.

Since his *mudder* had finally been able to correspond with old *freinden* from Maryland after his *daed*'s death, Samuel had heard about the birth of each of Lena's *kinner* and the death of her husband. He wouldn't deny that her status as a widow played a part in his move, but he had always planned to return to Maryland as soon as the opportunity presented itself.

Samuel raised a hand to his smooth chin. Even if Lena never wanted to trust him with her heart again, couldn't they at least be *freinden*? Couldn't she accept his help as she'd done with other men in the community? He chuckled. Those little girls sure were cute, and smart. They must have gotten that from Lena. He remembered what a fine scholar she had been. She always had perfect spelling papers and scored highest on arithmetic tests.

He shook the reins to prod the horse to move a wee bit faster. Time to pull his mind back from its wanderings. As Lena said, he did have a lot of work to do to get his place in shape. He needed to focus on that right now. Maybe some idea of how he could at least win Lena's trust, if not her heart, would present itself as he mended more of the fence or shored up the barn.

Lena hummed softly as she rocked and nursed Matthew. The girls had been tucked into bed for a *gut* hour, so it was *mamm*-and-*boppli* time. Usually this last feeding of the evening was so relaxing. She could rock and let go her cares from the day. That was not to be this night.

"Either you've gained a ton of weight, little one, or my arms have grown weaker." Lena shifted Matthew in her arms to relieve her aching muscles. He paused in his nursing to gaze into her face. She bent to kiss the top of his fuzzy head. "You have your *daed*'s hair, but I believe your eyes are going to be brown like mine and your *schweschders*'." The infant resumed eating and closed his eyes, obviously content to be close to his *mudder*'s heart.

Lena deliberately slowed her breathing to encourage her body to release its tension. She raised a hand to manually smooth the furrows she felt puckering her forehead. She massaged each temple, making little circles with two fingers. If only she could obliterate troubling thoughts the same way. Somehow she had to *kumm* to terms with Samuel's presence in the community. He bought property, so he wouldn't likely leave any time soon, that was for sure and for certain. The sooner she accepted that fact, the better for her emotional well-being.

With all three little ones down for naps early Saturday afternoon a week later, Lena bustled around the kitchen, preparing food for supper and for Sunday. She rejoiced that she hadn't seen or heard from Samuel since the day she and the girls made cookies. Had he finally gotten the message she had tried to send? They absolutely could not be that besotted young couple they had once been. Too many changes had occurred. She had responsibilities now. She had three *kinner* who depended on her to care for them and to make the right decisions. She couldn't let them down or subject them to anyone who might break their tender little hearts as hers had been broken.

Trepidation gradually crept in as the day wore on. Tomorrow was a church day. That meant she would at least have to see Samuel, if not talk to him. Could she merely exchange pleasantries if necessary? Or would she be able to avoid him altogether? *Ach*! There wasn't any use worrying about that now. She would finish her preparations and take the *kinner* outside when they awoke. She'd enjoy what remained of this beautiful spring day.

Buggy wheels crunched on the dirt-and-gravel driveway. The sound floated in the open window and brought a smile to Lena's face. Maybe Becky had decided to pay a visit. The girl had only been gone a couple of weeks, but it certainly seemed much longer. They could catch up after church tomorrow, of course, but there would be other people around, preventing a private conversation. Lena dried her hands on a yellow dish towel and hurried to the back door. She stopped short when she hopped off the last concrete step. "What are you doing here?"

"*Gut* afternoon to you, too." Samuel's lips twitched, as if he tried to hold back a smile. "Are you always so congenial to visitors?"

I'm only abrupt with the ones I'm not thrilled to see. Calm down, Lena. Don't let him get to you. "Too late," she muttered.

"What's that?"

"Nothing."

"Usually when someone says 'hello,' the other person answers with some similar *nice* comment."

"Is that so? Well, never let it be said that I am unkind." Lena forced a pleasant tone that sounded sarcastic even to her own ears. "Hello,

Samuel. What brings you by? Was that better?"

"Only slightly, but I'll take it."

Lena unclenched her hands and relaxed her hunched shoulders. She could do nothing to slow her runaway heart.

"I've brought you something."

"Samuel . . ."

"Hold on!" Samuel threw up his hands as if warding off an attack. "Let me show you." He reached into the back of the buggy and pulled out a flat of begonias. The little green plants already sported delicate pink-and-white blooms. "See?"

"They're beautiful, but . . ."

"I bought a bunch from Bylers' nursery to try to spruce up my place a bit, but I'm afraid I went overboard. I ran out of spots to plant them, so I thought I'd bring the rest to you."

"My place needs sprucing up, huh?" Lena glanced around her yard. A few daffodils and hyacinths still bloomed, but she hadn't had time to do much yard work. She certainly hadn't purchased any flowers. Keeping food on the table had been the priority. The property could use a little brightening.

"I didn't mean it that way at all. I remembered you always liked begonias."

"I still do. They will bloom all summer."

"I remember the little potted begonia you gave my *mamm* the summer before we moved. It had pink-and-white-ruffled blooms almost like roses.

Do you know my *mudder* dug it up and replanted it every place we moved?"

"She did?" He remembered that plant? How many fellows would take note of the blossoms and notice their *mudders* hauled the plant with them all over creation?

"She did indeed. I'd be happy to plant these for you, if you show me where you want them."

The gesture was touching, but she still did not want to let him into their lives. "You don't have to do that. I can get the girls to help me. They'll like digging in the dirt."

"Why don't we all plant them?"

We? There wasn't any "we." Why would he think that there was? "The girls are still napping."

"Maybe they'll be awake by the time we get organized and fill the watering can."

There was that "we" again. "I don't think . . ."

"Mamm?"

Lena looked over her shoulder to where Mary stood in the doorway, rubbing her eyes. "Is Eliza awake, too?"

Mary nodded at the very same time a yawning Eliza pushed past her. Lena rushed to snatch Eliza before she tumbled down the steps. "You still look sleepy to me." She kissed the little girl's cheek.

"Pretty." Eliza pointed to the flat of begonias on the ground beside Samuel's buggy.

"Hello, sleepyheads." Samuel's wide smile

91

took in both little girls. "Would you like to help your *mudder* and me plant the pretty flowers?"

Lena glared. How did he have the audacity to ignore her previous comments and involve her *dochders* in his scheme? Only moments earlier she'd told him she and the girls would plant the flowers. Now, without her permission, he had dragged her little ones in on his plan. "We can do it later so we don't hold you up."

Mary had already skipped down the steps and raced over to the flowers. "Can we do it now, Mamm? Please?"

Eliza bounced in Lena's arms so hard she had to stand the tot on the ground. How could she refuse now without crushing their little hearts? They had been through so much. Mary's request was such a simple thing, and both girls were so eager. She could smack Samuel for putting her in this awkward position. She would be a real ogre if she denied their request. She sighed. "Okay."

Mary giggled and clapped. Eliza aped her *schweschder*. It didn't take much to make them happy. Lena supposed she could endure a few more minutes in Samuel's presence. "Is Matthew still sleeping?"

Mary nodded and, as usual, Eliza mimicked.

Samuel clapped his hands. "All right. Where do we want to put these plants? I have an assortment of colors."

The flowers truly were beautiful. Lena loved

flowers, and as Samuel knew, she was particularly fond of begonias. Their hardiness and variety made them special. Or maybe their ability to spread out into large clumps and bloom all season endeared them to her. Despite her misgivings and her aggravation with Samuel, she experienced more than a teensy bit of excitement at planting the flowers. Splashes of color here and there around the house would do so much to lift her spirits.

Lena stooped down to her *dochders'* level. She pointed out different locations in flower beds around the yard. "Should we put some here and here?" Both girls nodded. "Go stand by the spots so Samuel and I can bring the plants and tools there." Lena's breath hitched and her heart skipped a beat when her words, "Samuel and I," sunk in. She hadn't said their names together in years. Why did goose bumps march up and down her arms?

Eliza contented herself by playing in the dirt, but Mary proved to be helpful. She patted soil around the newly transferred plants and exclaimed over each blossom. Samuel helped Lena pull weeds as they moved up and down the flower beds, leaving them tidy and neat. They laughed at the girls' antics and teased them about their dirt-smeared faces. Lena didn't know when it happened, but at some point her guard relaxed and she found she actually enjoyed herself.

That shouldn't be, should it? She was a widow with three small *kinner*. Shouldn't she be more serious? Certainly she shouldn't be giggling like she didn't have a care in the world or working alongside a man she did not trust.

She jerked any trace of a lingering smile from her face.

"You have a beautiful smile, Lena. Don't stow it away."

She didn't realize Samuel had been studying her. Her cheeks burned. "I have to check on Matthew." She spun around and headed for the house. "*Kumm*, girls, let's get cleaned up." She didn't stop or even slow down but simply flung over her shoulder, "*Danki* for the begonias."

Chapter Eight

"You're allowed to have fun, Lena!"

She didn't turn around or even indicate she heard him. She simply pulled the two little girls close to her, like a hen tucking its chicks under its wings, and kept moving. Did saying she had a beautiful smile send her into a tailspin? Samuel didn't know what possessed him to give voice to that thought. *I should have kept my mouth closed.*

They had been having fun. At least he had been. The girls giggled and played, obviously enjoying themselves. Even Lena talked and laughed. The furrows etching her brow disappeared and little crinkly lines fanned out around her doe eyes when she laughed. But a door slammed shut, locking any joy behind it as soon as he mentioned her smile. Why?

Did Lena hate him that much? *Nee,* she wouldn't hate him. Lena could never hate anyone. That much he knew. Neither would it be like her to hold a grudge. At least the Lena he once—and still—cared for wouldn't hold one. It must be a matter of trust. Surely she understood that he hadn't willingly left Maryland ten years ago. He had been subject to his *daed*'s will and whims back then. His leaving must have caused her great pain.

"*Jah*, so much pain that she ran straight into Joseph Troyer's arms." Samuel glanced around quickly and heaved a sigh of relief that only a rabbit and two squirrels heard his muttering. He should not have said such a thing, even under his breath. He should not even think such a thing. Lena had every right to marry another man. They had not had any formal commitment. None of the letters he'd written had reached her, so she probably assumed he'd forgotten all about her and what they had meant to each other. How could his *daed* have been so deceptive, so cruel? He had apparently wanted to cut all ties with his past and forced his family to do the same.

Samuel had never forgotten Lena. He had carried her in his heart and mind all these years. He only wished he could tell her, or that she would at least give him the chance to tell her. He stopped to retrieve a forgotten trowel nearly hidden in the lush, green grass. He carried it to the shed to store with Lena's other gardening tools. He surveyed their handiwork on the way back to his buggy. The flowers sure looked pretty. In his heart he knew Lena liked them. He smiled when he remembered how much she looked like her girls when she first saw the plants. She'd been tickled pink. He wouldn't have been surprised if she had hopped up and down and clapped her hands in glee. Her eyes grew as round as dinner plates and glowed with excitement. He chuckled at the thought.

That's it! He snapped his fingers. He could erect greenhouses on his property. He could grow begonias, geraniums, petunias, pansies, and all sorts of plants to sell to Amish and *Englisch* customers. That would be a *gut* way to supplement his blacksmith and tool business. Someday, he hoped, his *fraa* could take over the greenhouse, if she wanted to.

Of course lots of Amish grew plants to sell, but there always seemed to be a need. Everyone loved flowers. And flowers would be a lot better than sheep. At least he wouldn't have to feed and shear them. Well, maybe he'd still purchase a few sheep. He had always been partial to the black-faced ones.

With a new spring in his step, Samuel practically jogged to the buggy. He threw one final glance at the house before climbing inside. He smiled and waved at the two little faces pressed to a front window. Adorable little girls. Like their *mudder*.

Lena dragged her weary body out of bed. Hadn't she closed her eyes only moments ago? She blinked twice to clear her bleary eyes enough to focus on the battery-operated clock on the nightstand. She rubbed her eyes and blinked again. Was the clock right or had the batteries given out? She picked it up and drew it closer to her face. Yikes! The second hand moved in its steady rhythm. The clock had the correct time. She would have to hustle to get herself and her three *kinner* dressed, fed, and off to church on time. Plus, she'd have to hitch the horse to the buggy. Why did she feel like covering her face with her hands and weeping into them?

Because you got spoiled, that's why. Becky had taken such a huge load off her shoulders when she moved in after her return to Maryland. Now Lena had to resume handling all the responsibilities herself. *You did it before. You can do it again.* She jumped out of bed, squared her shoulders, and sniffed back the urge to cry. She had too much to do to wallow in self-pity. She quickly made her bed before pulling her blue Sunday dress from the wall peg. Because it was Sunday, she wouldn't be cooking a big breakfast. Instead, they would have bowls of cold cereal and slices of banana bread.

It had been a struggle, but Lena managed to stay awake and alert during the three-hour church service. Becky sat with her and helped when Eliza and Matthew got fidgety at the same time. She didn't allow her gaze to stray to the men's side, even though the temptation was great. She didn't need to look over there to confirm that it was Samuel's gaze burning a hole clear through to her soul. How would she ever discourage his attention? Did she want to? *Of course I do. Stop being ridiculous!*

"Mamm, there's Samuel. He waved." Mary tugged on her skirt to get her attention as they walked from the barn to the house.

Lena's face burned. "Okay," she whispered at Mary's persistent tugging. She shrugged her shoulders at Becky's raised eyebrows.

"He brought us flowers." Mary shifted her attention to Becky.

"Did he?"

Lena figured she had better offer some sort of explanation. "He had bought some begonias to plant in his yard and had extras."

"I see. That was nice of him."

Lena nudged her *freind*. "Wipe that smirk off your face, Becky Zook, I mean, Becky Stauffer. It was purely a neighborly gesture. That's all."

"You don't have to defend yourself. I'm sure Samuel was only being neighborly, as you say." After a moment, she spoke in a more subdued voice. "You know, Lena, it really would be quite all right for you to be interested in someone."

Lena gasped and nearly tripped over Eliza as they headed to the kitchen. She hoped she would be able to grab a quick plate of food for the girls and hurry home. She could eat later, and she certainly didn't feel much like socializing today.

Becky reached for Lena's arm to steady her. "It has been more than a year."

"I know."

Becky patted her *freind*'s thin arm. "I hope you find someone else when you're ready. I want you to be happy."

Lena smiled. "Spoken like a newlywed. I am happy with my *kinner*."

"You know what I mean."

She did. Lena missed having someone to share smiles with over the girls' antics, someone to sip a cup of *kaffi* with early in the morning, someone to hold her when she was frightened or weary. But those days were over. And she was okay with that. Most of the time. Some of the time?

Samuel had worked so hard the whole week that he'd fallen into bed too exhausted to conjure up a coherent thought. A dozen men from the community, young and old, had helped him shore up the old barns so he had a safe, dry place for his horses and buggy and a separate space to set up his equipment that had been packed and stored in the driest corner of the barn. He needed to get his business operational as soon as possible. His savings would soon dwindle to nothing if he didn't start earning money pretty quickly. Several men already had work for Samuel to do. That was a *gut* thing.

He had even squeezed in a little time to begin

assembling the greenhouse he'd purchased from a fellow in another district. It was probably too late in the season to raise flowers or vegetable plants. Most people had already prepared their gardens and flower beds. The greenhouse would be ready for next year, though. He might be able to start some fall plants. That should work out well. He would start some greens or broccoli, or potatoes. He should also be able to raise chrysanthemums for the fall. Folks loved their deep red, rust, and yellow hues.

Today, Samuel absolutely had to tackle a chore he had been postponing. With clean clothes dwindling as fast as his savings, he had to make peace with that old wringer washing machine. Surely it couldn't be that hard to figure out, could it? Probably every eight-year-old Amish girl knew how to operate one. If he could use machinery to make tools and horseshoes, a washing machine shouldn't be too daunting.

Then again, maybe it could! Samuel had the gas. The hoses were connected. Everything appeared functional, but the contrary contraption still had him stymied. He could shoe a horse without getting kicked or stomped on, and he could hammer a barn roof without pounding a nail into his hand or tumbling off and breaking his neck, so why couldn't he tame this beast?

How ridiculous! How pitiful! Lena washed and hung out numerous loads of laundry every week with little ones under her feet and Samuel couldn't even make the washer work. Funny how Lena crept into his every thought despite the fact that she deliberately tried to avoid him, as she had last Sunday. That hurt. But not nearly as much as his finger, which was now caught in the wringer. He yanked it free and popped it into his mouth. He studied the machine from every angle. What was he missing? There must be some small but significant detail he had missed that would render this hateful gadget operational.

"Samuel? Are you here?"

The voice sounded like Miriam King's. Miriam and Melvin were older neighbors who had been so encouraging and welcoming. They'd helped him settle in, and he had helped Melvin with farm chores.

"I'm here." Approaching footsteps halted abruptly, as if she wasn't sure which direction to take.

"Where?"

"I'm fighting with this washing machine. I think it's winning the battle." Samuel heard a chuckle, followed by resumed footsteps.

"*Was ist letz?*"

"I don't know what's wrong with the contraption."

"Perhaps it's the operator."

"That could very well be true. I'll let you in on a little secret." Samuel lowered his voice, as if about to impart some important, confidential information or to confess some great sin. "I've never used one of these things before."

"What?" Miriam threw back her head and cackled. Her white prayer *kapp* bobbed atop her salt-and-pepper hair.

"Shh!"

"*Ach*, Samuel." She wiped her eyes. "You are such a comical sight. If only you could see yourself."

"I'm glad you're amused. At least I've entertained you today."

"That you have."

"Can you tell me how to get this monster to work?"

"Of course I can. I've been doing laundry for a hundred years. Well, not quite that long, but it seems like it."

"Then you are the very person to instruct me."

"I don't suppose you would have learned how to use a washing machine because you're a *bu*."

"*Nee*. My *mudder* never taught me. She ran the household with my younger *schweschders*' help, after they got older, that is. I worked outside. I do know my way around the kitchen, though." Samuel winked at the old woman. "I can fry an egg with the best of them, and I can make a pretty decent cup of *kaffi*."

"Eggs and *kaffi* wouldn't be a very balanced diet, but at least you won't starve."

"I can cook other things. I can fry bacon. I can bake a potato and boil vegetables. And I'm a whiz at opening and heating canned soup. But for the life of me, I can't figure out how to make this machine do anything but attack my finger."

Miriam cackled again. She reached for his hand and held it close to her face. "You might want to put ice on this finger. However did you manage to do this?"

"The beast grabbed me and mauled my finger." He pulled back his hand to examine his bruised and swollen finger.

"I can't say I have ever been attacked by my washing machine. Why don't you let me do your laundry for you? We can't have you getting injured every time you need a clean shirt."

"I appreciate the offer, but I wouldn't dare impose on you. Can you give me some pointers, or at least tell me how to appease this creature?"

"Samuel Mast, after all you do to help Melvin and me when you've got so much of your own work to do, your laundry is the least I can do to repay you."

"I don't want to be repaid. I like helping you and Melvin. And you've helped me tremendously, too. I couldn't have gotten this place in livable condition without you."

" 'Twas the whole community that did that."

"Everyone helped, and I'm grateful, but you two have helped the most. Melvin's advice alone has been worth more than gold. And the casseroles you sneak into my kitchen from time to time have been lifesavers."

"Well, until you get yourself a *fraa* to take care of you, it's the least I can do."

Samuel's cheeks burned. They must be as red as overripe tomatoes. He had been thinking about a *fraa* while tangling with the washing machine. Correction: He'd been thinking about Lena and her *kinner* living with him. "I don't see that happening any time soon," he mumbled, "so you'd better show me how to make peace with this thing." He gave the washer a kick.

"We never know what the Lord Gott has in store for us, Samuel. A special woman for you could *kumm* along any day, but in the meantime, I will give you a quick laundry lesson."

Lena had managed to get a whole line of freshly washed diapers and infant clothes hung out to flap in the gentle breeze. A line of little girls' dresses danced behind them. *Kinner* sure went through a lot of clothes! She absolutely had to get some mending done while Matthew slept and the girls played with their dolls. Before she knew it, the garden would be producing and she'd have green beans to can, cucumbers and beets to pickle, and jams and jellies to make.

She sank onto the rocking chair and reached for her nearly overflowing mending basket. Lena plucked out one of Mary's dresses and began letting out the hem. Either the girl was going through a growth spurt or she was going to be a tall woman. Lena was on the short side at five feet three inches with shoes on, and she couldn't think of a single tall person in her family. Joseph had been taller by about six inches, not especially tall for a man. Not nearly as tall as Samuel.

"Ow!" Lena jerked and glanced down at the finger she'd poked with the needle. A bubble of blood swelled and trickled away from the puncture site. She grabbed a tissue from the box on the lamp table and wound it around her finger before she stained the dress. She certainly didn't need one more piece of clothing to scrub today.

Lena jabbed the needle into the fabric so she could examine her finger closer. It was all Samuel's fault. If he hadn't popped into her mind, she would have been paying attention to her stitching. She unwrapped her finger to see if the bleeding had stopped. She dabbed at the wound again and sighed. *Forgive me, Lord Gott, for blaming Samuel for my own clumsiness. And for my mean-spiritedness on Sunday.*

She hadn't exactly been mean. She'd simply ignored the man. Maybe that was the same as being mean. Anyway, she figured she should confess while she was in a penitent mood. Next time she saw him, she'd probably be angry or aggravated or confused and would need to ask for forgiveness again. That seemed to be the way things went with them. She checked her finger again and deemed it okay to resume her stitching. She vowed to concentrate on sewing or supper or the weather or anything else besides Samuel Mast.

"Mamm?"

"Hmm?"

"Will Samuel be back?"

It was a *gut* thing she hadn't been about to plunge the needle into cloth or she surely would have speared a finger again. Where had Mary's question *kumm* from? Just when she had resolved to lock the man out of her thoughts, her *dochder* shoved him through the keyhole.

"Mamm?"

"Why do you ask?"

"It was fun planting flowers with him."

"*We* can plant more flowers, and vegetables, too."

"With Samuel?"

Why did Mary's eyes sparkle? How had the man wormed his way into her little girl's heart? How did she tell her Samuel wouldn't be back if she could help it? "He is busy with his own place and work. We girls can take care of planting, ain't so?"

"I guess so."

Was that a note of dejection? Lena didn't want her little girl to be sad. She had already experienced more loss than any little one should have to face. "Hey!" Lena snapped her fingers. "Maybe we can invite Becky to plant flowers with us. That would be fun, *jah*?"

Mary brightened. "*Jah*. Let's ask Becky."

The diversion had been successful. Besides, it truly would be great to spend time with Becky. All too soon the younger woman's *boppli* would arrive, claiming his or her *mamm*'s attention. Now Lena needed to get a message to Becky, or maybe they would take a ride to visit the newlyweds.

Lena snipped the thread on the second dress she had rehemmed for Mary and rubbed her burning eyes. Maybe when Matthew started sleeping through the night she would stop feeling like a team of horses had trampled her. She could purchase some vitamins the next time she visited the grocery store in case she was deficient in iron or some other mineral. *You are deficient in sleep because your brain can't shut down during the few minutes your head does rest on the pillow!* Lena stared out the window to give her eyes a break from the close-up work. How did a person shut down her thoughts?

"Mamm, I'm hungry."

"Hungry," Eliza echoed.

"Oh my! I suppose it is time to eat." Lena scooted her mending basket out of the way and pushed to her feet. She could heat up leftover macaroni and cheese and vegetables pretty quickly. And there were still apple muffins, too. She'd put the food on the stove and then nurse Matthew, who surely must be awake by now.

Lena got the girls situated at the table and a bib tied around Eliza's neck. The sound of buggy wheels on the gravel drive reached them through the open window. She set Mary's plate in front of her and broke a muffin in small pieces for Eliza to nibble on while she saw to the visitor. As she reached for a paper towel to wipe her hands, the back door opened and a voice called out.

"Is anyone home?"

"Becky!" A green bean flew from Mary's mouth at her exclamation. Eliza giggled. Then Mary giggled until a coughing fit overtook her.

Lena rushed around the table to pat Mary's back. "Here. Take a sip of water." She handed the little girl her cup. "*Wilkom* back to the loony bin, Becky!"

Becky laughed. "I've missed you all."

"You have not. You've been too busy."

"I've been busy, but not so busy I didn't miss my family. I consider you my family, you know."

"That we are. You don't have to be related by blood to be family." Lena moved Mary's cup of water back from the edge of the table before she had more to clean up than an escaped green bean.

"Are you all right, Mary? I didn't mean to

make you choke." Becky studied the little girl, who nodded and beamed at her.

"Her silliness made her choke, not you." Lena pulled out a chair. "Have a seat. I'll fix you a plate."

"You don't have to do that. I had a big breakfast."

"You're also eating for two. You'll need your strength."

"Where is your plate?"

"I haven't gotten to that yet. I was getting the girls settled first." Eliza chose that moment to reach for her plate, sitting barely out of her grasp. She wiggled so much the entire high chair wobbled. "Hold on, little one." Lena scooted over to hand Eliza her food. Now that she could supervise, she would let the little girl feed herself. She tucked a spoon in the little hand and encouraged Eliza to use it instead of her fingers. "You can watch her while I fix your plate and then I'll take over, or you can feel free to fix your own plate."

"How about if I watch this little rascal while you eat?"

"You're the one expecting a *boppli*."

"You're nursing one, and you look like you've lost more weight that you definitely did not need to lose."

Lena glanced down and only then noticed how much looser her dress hung on her lean frame than it had only a few weeks ago. "I guess I haven't felt like eating a whole lot lately." At Becky's frown, she hastened to add, "But I have been drinking milk and juice."

"We'll have to talk about your lack of appetite later. Now, I will make sure this little girl doesn't paint her hair with gooey cheese while you put food on your own plate."

"Okay, Mamm."

Mary giggled. "Becky isn't your *mamm*."

"I know, dear one. I'm teasing." Lena smiled at her older *dochder*.

Becky's foot tapped on the linoleum floor. "I am not teasing. You go pile food on that plate, and I don't mean a gnat's portion, either."

"Bossy, aren't you?" She headed for the stove. "How about if I fix your plate while I'm here?"

"Fine."

Becky chatted with the girls while eating the mound of food on her plate. Lena caught her *freind*'s periodic glances at the noodles and vegetables still clumped on her own plate. For some reason, she could only pick at her meal. Up until a few weeks ago she'd had an insatiable appetite but couldn't gain weight. She chalked that up to nursing because the same thing happened after Mary and Eliza were born. Now she could barely choke down enough food to give her a little energy to get through the day.

When the girls began fidgeting, Lena knew they

111

were finished eating. "Let me put them down for naps and then we can visit."

"I'll put them down while you finish eating." Becky wagged a warning finger in Lena's direction. "Eat. I mean it."

Lena raked macaroni and cheese onto her fork while Becky wiped little hands and faces. She raised the fork to her mouth when Becky turned back to look at her. Even if she wanted to, which she didn't, she could not force the fork between her lips. The macaroni held all the appeal of worms. "Ugh!" She laid the fork back on the plate. Maybe the green beans would be a better choice.

Then again, maybe not. Lena couldn't eat a single one. She would have to get rid of the plate before Becky returned, though, or she'd surely receive another tongue-lashing. She jumped up from the table and quickly scraped the uneaten meal into the scrap bag before setting her plate in the sink. She returned to the table to clean the high-chair tray and the table.

"I'm an adult. I shouldn't have to sneak around to hide uneaten food in my own house." She continued to mutter as she ran water into the sink.

"What's that?"

Chapter Nine

Lena jumped. She hadn't heard Becky's approach. She squirted way more liquid dish soap into the sink than she had intended. Little bubbles floated toward the ceiling. Now she'd have to double rinse the dishes. "You scared ten years off my life, Becky Stauffer."

"I'm sorry. Who were you talking to? Is someone hiding under your sink?" Becky bent down, pretending to look under the sink and in the bottom cabinets for some mystery person.

"Very funny. I was talking to myself. I tend to do that from time to time."

"Do you answer yourself, too?"

"On occasion."

"Hmm. We might have to see about that."

Lena flung a dish towel at the younger woman. "You're quite the comedian today. Marriage must agree with you."

Becky's cheeks flushed a delicate pink color that made her pale hair seem lighter and her green eyes brighter. "I suppose it does."

"Seriously, Becky, I'm so glad you're happy. You are practically glowing and the joy almost bubbles out of you." Lena couldn't remember ever feeling that way herself. She had been happy on her wedding day and during her marriage, but it was a quiet happiness, if there could be such a thing. More like contentment. Not a bubbling-over, ready-to-burst, jump-up-and-shout exuberance. Becky's joy was nearly palpable. Lena wanted to scoop up armfuls of it and bottle it for herself.

"Did you hear me, Lena?"

Oops! Her mind had galloped away from the kitchen and her hands swirled the dish cloth around and around on the same plate. "I'm sorry. What did you say?"

Becky snatched the plate from Lena's hands and rinsed it. "That one is quite clean. I said I want you to be happy, too."

"I've told you before, I'm happy with my *kinner*. I am blessed to have them."

"I know you are. They are precious, and I know they bring you great joy. I'm sure I'll feel the same way about my own little one." She patted her growing abdomen. "In fact, I already feel that way. But I want you to have someone to share your life with, to talk to, to share laughs and hugs with."

Had Becky been privy to her earlier thoughts? "I've been down that road, Becky, so what you are saying isn't totally foreign to me."

"Were you and Joseph happy?" Becky laid a hand on Lena's arm. "Forgive me. I don't mean to be nosy. You told me some about Joseph when

I lived here with you. He sounded like a very *gut* man."

"He was, and we were happy." Lena's voice dropped lower, as if she spoke only to herself. "Maybe it wasn't the shout-to-the-world, glow-in-the-dark, leap-from-the-rooftop happiness that some people have." She felt Becky's hand tighten on her arm, but sudden tears kept her from seeing clearly. What must it feel like to experience such elation? She would never know.

"It isn't too late to have that."

Lena sniffed and blinked back the tears. "I had my chance already. I might be the teeniest bit envious of you, but I am so glad you are happy, dear girl. You've been through so much. You deserve to be this ecstatic. And I truly am thrilled for you and Atlee. It's obvious how much he cares for you."

"It is not too late for you," Becky repeated a bit more forcefully. "You are young. Many people who have lost a spouse remarry and are even happier than they were before."

"Maybe older people. I'm part of a package deal. Whoever loves me would have to love my *kinner* or it would never work."

"I was a package deal, too."

"I'm sorry, Becky. I didn't mean to be insensitive."

"You weren't at all. I did not take offense. I had qualms about Atlee really accepting my *boppli*, but I know he truly is thrilled that he will be a *daed* soon. He acts exactly as I expect every soon-to-be parent behaves, and it is so sweet." Her cheeks grew brighter.

Lena laughed. She shook soap suds from her hands and embraced her *freind*. "You are so cute! You and Atlee do make the perfect couple, and you will be great parents."

Becky returned the hug and then pulled back to look at Lena's face. "I didn't think it possible, but I believe you are even thinner than before. Will you please tell me what's troubling you so much that you aren't eating or sleeping?"

"Who said I wasn't sleeping?"

"The big, dark circles under your eyes shout out that story."

"Oh."

"Sometimes it helps to share your burdens, you know."

Lena sniffed. Why did she so often find herself on the verge of tears lately? "It's only my own silliness. I need to deal with the issue and let it go."

"Does it have anything to do with Samuel Mast?"

Lena turned her attention back to the dishes. She plunged her hands beneath the suds and felt around for hidden silverware. "Samuel's showing up out of the blue has made things difficult. 'Awkward' might be a better word."

"How so?"

"He dredges up memories better left alone."

"And feelings, too?"

Lena shrugged. "It was a long time ago. Like I said, it's my own silliness that I need to get over."

"Feelings aren't silly."

"I didn't say anything about feelings. I said memories. You're the one who attached feelings to the problem."

"You can't have one without the other, can you?"

Lena shrugged again.

"Then tell me about your memories." Becky pulled Lena's hands from the water and handed her the green-checked towel. Then she tugged her toward the table and pulled out one of the sturdy oak chairs. "Sit."

Lena sat but didn't feel like talking, even to her dearest *freind*. The two had shared many secrets and dreams while Becky lived in the Troyer home. They'd shared hopes, fears, and burdens. Becky had even taken on the role of midwife's assistant at Matthew's birth. They had become as close as any two *schweschders* could ever be, but Lena resisted diving into the past. Becky pulled up a chair, plunked down, and clasped her hands in her lap, as if waiting for some magnificent story to be told. "There really isn't much to tell."

"Tell me anyway."

"We were young. Barely beginning our

rumspringa. Samuel began talking to me after church. Even though I was only fifteen, he would visit or take me for drives. We only had eyes for each other."

"Did you have that earthmoving feeling with him?"

Lena couldn't stop the smile that tugged at her lips. "I did. But we were young. Practically *kinner*."

"Young people can have strong feelings that can last a lifetime."

"That's true, but ours obviously didn't."

"What happened?"

"He left."

"By himself?"

"His family moved. He had to go with them."

"So he didn't *choose* to leave you."

"*Nee*." Lena gulped down the sob that clawed its way up her throat. "I was devastated. I thought he was the one for me. I thought he felt the same way." She swiped at an escaped tear. "I guess not."

"You said he was young, and his family moved. What choice did he have?"

"None at that time. He could have written, though. When I realized I wasn't likely to ever receive a letter or visit from Samuel, Joseph was right there waiting. He was kind, dependable, honest, and trustworthy. He was older and ready to settle down. When my parents died after their buggy was hit by that dump truck, Joseph was there for me. I felt safe and cared for with him. It seemed perfectly natural for us to marry, and we were content together. We had a *gut* life."

"I'm sure you did." Becky reached for one of Lena's hands. "But now Samuel is back. Maybe it was meant to be."

"What was meant to be?" Lena's spine stiffened and her muscles tensed.

"You and Samuel." Becky's reply was a mere whisper.

"Whatever I had with Samuel is in the past. The past stays in the past."

"Until it *kumms* roaring into the present."

"Well, I'll have to make sure it turns right around and heads back where it belongs."

"Lena Troyer, you were so wise and so perceptive when I returned to Maryland. You helped me recover from my terrible experience in New York. You helped me forgive myself and move on. You encouraged me to trust Atlee and to believe he really cared. When I tried to push him away, you convinced me I was throwing away my happiness." Becky only paused a moment to gulp in a breath. "Well, you were right. If I hadn't given Atlee a chance, I wouldn't have a *wunderbaar* husband and *daed* for my *boppli*. I wouldn't know the bliss we now share. And here you won't give Samuel the chance to even be a *freind*."

"My situation is a little different. Atlee never stole your heart and ran off with it. He never crushed your dreams."

"Like you said, you were practically *kinner*. He had to obey his *daed*, didn't he?"

Lena shrugged, and then gave a reluctant nod.

"Samuel has tried to talk to you on several occasions, ain't so?"

"*Jah*."

"And he brought those beautiful begonias blooming outside your door."

"He did."

"It seems like he's trying to make amends. Did he have an explanation for his silence all these years?"

"He said something about his *daed*. I, uh, cut him off, though, and wouldn't let him cast the blame on someone else or make up excuses. It's too late."

"What if what he wanted to tell you was the truth?"

The truth. Did Samuel intend to tell her the truth or some pretty little story he'd concocted to worm his way back into her life, her heart? She couldn't let her heart be smashed to smithereens by Samuel Mast again. That was that.

But Becky's words plagued Lena the rest of the day. She replayed them while she folded diapers and infant clothes fresh off the clothesline. She heard them as she nursed Matthew and read to the girls. She pondered them as she prepared supper and cleaned the kitchen after eating. Now she heard their echo as she readied herself for bed and another night of tossing and turning.

Maybe she should have held her tongue and not told Becky anything about her past with Samuel. She certainly hadn't intended to share that information. Becky had a way of drawing it out of her. When had the girl grown so intuitive? Could Becky possibly be the teeniest bit right? Should Lena at least give Samuel a chance to explain and unload any guilt he'd been carrying around? Hmpf! He must not have experienced too much remorse if he could wait ten years to confront her. Seeds of doubt kept threatening to germinate in her mind, confusing her whenever she thought she was beginning to make sense of things.

Freinden. Becky had mentioned that. Could she and Samuel be *freinden*? She certainly didn't need him to be any more than that. She had her little ones to consider. Their needs and their happiness had to *kumm* first. Becky didn't understand that yet. She would soon, though. Lena sighed. The best solution for everyone would be for her to steer clear of Samuel Mast. Wouldn't it?

Chapter Ten

Miriam King's words rang truer than she probably realized. Samuel needed a *fraa*. He wanted a *fraa*. But not any woman would do. He only wanted one woman. The one he had always wanted. The one he hadn't been able to shake out of his head these past ten years.

Sure, he had tried to forget her. He'd attended the young folks' singings wherever they lived and chatted with a few girls. He even drove a couple of them home, but romance never bloomed. It didn't help matters that if he fell for a girl in Florida, he'd have to stay in Florida, and he did not want to do that. The heat and humidity practically reduced him to a puddle of human flesh, and he didn't cotton to the idea of hunting down those gigantic bugs that slipped into the house. The frigid temperatures in Wisconsin didn't suit him, either. He didn't fancy the notion of caring for animals when it was so cold he had to chisel the ice from the water with his frozen fingers.

Maryland was just right. Of course they saw their fair share of hot, humid, muggy days as well as cold, windy, snowy days, but there was a lot of in-between weather that made the extreme days bearable. Plus, Lena lived here. Even though his *daed* refused to allow communication with their former community for some unfathomable reason, his *mudder* sneaked peeks at *The Budget* when she visited some of her *freinden*. She practically memorized the news written in the Southern Maryland section and repeated it to him when they were alone. She'd told him of Lena's marriage and of her widowhood a few years later, along with all the other births, deaths, and marriages she remembered from her readings.

That news of Lena's marriage almost did him in. He'd been heartbroken. He'd felt betrayed— until he discovered all his letters had been confiscated by his *daed*. How could Daed have been so cruel? When Samuel demanded a reason, his only answer had been, "It's best to cut ties with the past." Samuel had begged for more of an explanation but had gotten none. Had he done something to someone in the Maryland community, or had someone hurt him in some way? Samuel had racked his brain but couldn't think of a single explanation before realizing his *daed* didn't want them to communicate with people in any of the places they'd lived.

Once he found out about those letters, he'd understood why Lena had married. She obviously believed Samuel had forgotten all about her. After her marriage, he did try to forget her. He tried to make himself care about several girls, but nothing worked. Not a single one measured up to Lena. He had to return to Maryland, and not merely because the weather was more to his liking. He had to see Lena again to determine if there was any hope for reconciliation. If she out-and-out rejected him, he would then have to find a way to erase her from his mind and heart and move on with his life.

Moving on without her would be near impossible, especially living in close proximity, but he'd trust the Lord Gott to help him. His fervent prayer, though, was that the Lord would soften Lena's heart toward him.

Samuel's first glimpse of the girl he'd loved told him she was the same beautiful girl inside a strong woman. Life had obviously been very difficult for her. She was even tinier than he remembered, but there didn't seem to be anything small about her faith, her strength, and her determination. Somehow, he admired and loved her more than ever, even though she thwarted his every attempt to offer friendship. *Please, Lord Gott, help her be willing to give us another chance. Show me how to get through to her.*

Not a single plan came to mind, but Samuel vowed to stay vigilant and to help Lena in whatever subtle ways he could. Maybe he could slip over unnoticed and take care of her yard work. That must be difficult for her to tend to with three small *kinner* to keep an eye on at the same time. Such cute little girls. They would probably grow up to be beauties like their *mudder*. And Matthew looked like a healthy little fellow. It would be a long time before he would be able to help Lena with anything, though.

Satisfied with his idea, Samuel whistled as he checked his tools. He had several men bringing horses over today to be reshod and he wanted to be ready for them.

Somehow, in the busyness of her day, Lena had found time to bake a chocolate cake, frost it, and hide it from Mary's sight. Her firstborn turned four years old today, and she wanted to surprise her later with a cake and a small gift. She had to guard her tongue to keep from revealing the biggest surprise or else the little girl would bounce around all day and pester her about the time. Becky had promised that she and Atlee would *kumm* to dinner and bring ice cream to serve with the cake. Lena smiled in anticipation of Mary's reaction.

How in the world had her *boppli* gotten to be four already? Whoever said *kinner* didn't stay *bopplin* long had been absolutely right. Time had flown by. Before she knew it, or was ready, Mary would be old enough for school. *I'd better not dwell on that or I'll start bawling.*

With the morning chores, the noon meal, and naptime behind them, Lena found herself growing excited for the evening. It would be fun to visit with Becky and Atlee. Most likely the girls would have Atlee playing with them without needing to be very persuasive. Lena hummed as she rolled out dough for biscuits. A roast surrounded by carrots and potatoes already simmered in the oven.

"Can I help?" Mary tugged at her *mudder*'s skirt.

"*May* I help?"

"What?"

"We should say, 'May I' instead of 'Can I.' "

"Oh."

"I suppose the birthday girl can help." Lena tore off a length of wax paper and laid it on the table. She sprinkled flour across the paper and pinched off a hunk of dough for Mary to roll around.

"Help?" Eliza tried to climb onto the chair next to Mary.

"Hold on, little one." Lena scooped her up and deposited her in the high chair. She covered the tray with wax paper and gave Eliza her own lump of dough. "It's a *gut* thing I made a double batch." She quickly cut out her biscuits and arranged them in the pan before helping the girls form at least one glob resembling something edible.

"Why are there so many?" Mary pointed to the pan holding more biscuits than usual.

"In case we want leftovers." That was the best excuse Lena could render on the spur-of-the-moment, but it seemed to satisfy Mary's curiosity. She scrubbed the table and high chair and wiped gooey little fingers while the biscuits baked.

A commotion at the back door grabbed her attention as she slid golden brown biscuits out of the oven. "Could you check to see who's there, Mary?" The little girl would be so pleased to see Becky and Atlee. To be honest, Lena was every bit as excited as Mary and Eliza would be. *I must really be starved for adult conversation.* She loved being with her *kinner* all day. She adored them, but it sure was nice to have adult companionship once in a while.

"This must be the birthday girl?"

Lena sucked in a breath and held it. The deep voice certainly did not belong to Becky, and it didn't sound at all like Atlee, either. It sounded exactly like . . .

"Hello, Lena."

"*Ach*! What . . . ? How . . . ?" In her flustered state, she couldn't form a coherent thought, much less get untangled words out of her mouth.

"Would you believe I happened to be in the area, so I decided to stop in?"

"*Nee.*"

"Would you believe . . ."

"Try the truth, Samuel."

"I heard someone was having a birthday, so I stopped by to offer my best wishes." He twisted his straw hat in his hands. He smiled at Mary before offering Lena a lopsided grin.

"And how would you know today was Mary's birthday?"

"A little birdie told me."

Mary burst out in a fit of giggles. "Birds can't talk."

Lena couldn't prevent the pucker on her forehead from turning into a scowl. Samuel should not have intruded on her family's little birthday celebration. How did he even know about the birthday? Why did he feel compelled to acknowledge it? How could she tactfully tell him to leave?

"Is someone here having a birthday?" Another voice floated in to them from the back door.

"Becky!" Mary's eyes grew as round as saucers and her entire face glowed.

"Happy birthday!" Becky rushed into the room with Atlee on her heels. She stopped short, nearly causing him to plow into her back. "Oh my! I didn't know you had company, Lena."

"You're fine." Lena reached out to pat her *freind*'s arm. "Samuel stopped by to wish Mary a happy birthday, but he hasn't yet told me how he knew about it." She tapped one foot like an impatient schoolteacher waiting for her scholar to recite a lesson.

"I'm afraid that's my fault." Atlee peeked over

his *fraa*'s shoulder, a sheepish expression on his face.

"Really? How so?" Lena looked from one man to the other. "I mean, Mary's birthday is not any big secret, but we don't want any little head to swell from all the attention."

Atlee swiped his straw hat from his head and fanned himself. He crooked a thumb in the other man's direction. "Samuel came into the dairy and we got to talking. I guess I mentioned we'd be celebrating this momentous occasion."

Samuel nodded. "That's for sure, but it was my idea to stop by. I do have a little gift, if that's okay."

Mary hopped from one foot to the other. "Can . . . may Samuel stay? You said we had extra biscuits."

Lena forced a tight smile. *Nothing like my own* dochder *putting me on the spot.* How could she refuse? She couldn't. That's all there was to it. She would have to make the best of this awkward situation or else risk appearing the stingiest woman in the world. Not to mention, she'd cause her little girl great disappointment. "Sure."

"What can I do to help you?" Becky's eyes roved the kitchen.

"Not a thing. Everything is just about ready. You could check on Matthew, if you want."

"Of course. I need all the practice I can get."

As Becky shuffled off, Atlee lifted Mary high

in his arms and twirled around. "Are you having a *gut* birthday?"

"*Jah*."

"Me, too." Eliza, not wanting to be ignored, held out her arms.

Before Lena could react, Samuel lifted the tot and copied Atlee's move, though he twirled a little slower. Lena bit her tongue and turned away. She spooned drippings from the roasting pan into a small saucepan to prepare gravy. Her tongue would probably be too sore to even attempt to eat.

Becky, with Matthew in her arms, sidled up close enough to whisper, "Are you all right?"

"Is there another choice?" She stirred the gravy a bit more briskly than necessary and pasted a smile on her face before turning to face the men and girls. "We're almost ready."

Mary had been so excited she had trouble settling down to eat her supper. Eliza, who took cues from her big *schweschder*, played with her food until a stern look and firm voice from her *mamm* caused her to change her ways. The adults talked quietly, though Lena had very little to say. Samuel's presence had put a damper on her spirits. His position directly across the table from her made it even harder than usual to choke down a morsel of food. Thankfully, the men devoured their meal quickly, and Becky, with the pressure of her advancing pregnancy, could only consume small amounts at a time.

Lena insisted that Becky relax while she cleared the table, but she couldn't keep the younger woman from helping with the dishes. Atlee and Samuel took the girls in the living room to play. Matthew had outgrown the infancy stage, so Atlee was brave enough to take charge of him as well. She wished Samuel would leave. She didn't need him getting chummier with her *kinner*.

"Why don't you sit and keep me company while I wash the dishes? It won't take me long." Lena pulled a chair close to the sink.

Instead of sitting, Becky snatched the dish towel from its hook. "Why don't I dry so the chore goes faster?"

"It isn't necessary."

"You don't have to treat me like I'm fragile. You've been through this three times yourself."

"Exactly. So I know how tired and miserable a woman feels toward the end."

"I'm okay."

"You look tired and, well, a little wrung out."

Becky laughed. "Aren't you full of compliments?"

Lena playfully punched her *freind*'s arm. "You always look lovely, but carrying a *boppli* around inside your body gets tiresome. Are you sleeping well?"

"I'm trying."

"Hmm. I'm thinking that means you aren't sleeping much at all. Maybe the newest little Stauffer will be here soon."

"Not yet! Not until next month!"

"They tend to arrive on their own schedules. You're ready, aren't you?"

"Is anyone ever ready?"

Lena laughed. "As ready as we can be, I suppose."

"I've washed all the little clothes and blankets. You saw the beautiful cradle Atlee had his *bruder* make, so his or her bed is ready."

"Are you still planning to give birth at home, or did you decide to go to the midwife's birthing center?"

"Home, for sure. I'm so glad that enough of our house has been completed so we could move in. I'm sure Sam and Emma are glad, too. Laurie said she didn't see any reason why I couldn't have a home birth. Everything has been going fine."

"Great. I'm sure everything will continue to go fine." Lena turned her attention to the silverware she fished from the bottom of the sudsy sink. She jumped when Becky grabbed her upper arm. "What is it?" Had the girl experienced a sudden pain? Lena's heart pounded.

"You'll be there, won't you? You'll help Laurie with the birth?"

"I definitely want to see your little one arrive in

this world." Lena patted Becky's hand and gently loosened the death grip on her arm. "I'm not sure what I'll do with three little ones, though."

"When?"

Startled, Lena gasped and spun around to look toward the doorway. Honestly, did the man have some sort of superhearing ability that enabled him to be privy to the kitchen conversation? "*Ach*! Eliza! You'll fall." Lena rushed forward with hands outstretched to snatch Eliza from Samuel's shoulders.

"She's fine, Lena."

"She's just a *boppli*. She'll topple off." *What do you know about* kinner? Samuel spoke before she could voice that thought.

"Relax. I'm *gut* with little ones."

"Really?" She knew her tone conveyed her doubts, but that couldn't be helped. She couldn't exactly reel the words back in once they hung out there in space.

"Trust me. My *mudder* had three more *kinner* after we left Maryland. I might have been the oldest son, but I did my share of entertaining the little ones. I love *kinner*." He gave a little bounce, causing Eliza to sway as she erupted into giggles.

Lena drew in a sharp breath and stretched out her arms again. "Maybe I'd better take her."

"She's all right. Honest. I wouldn't do anything to hurt her."

But you didn't have any qualms about hurting a bigger girl. A competing voice in her head countered, *He had to go with his family.* Would she always have this tug-of-war going on inside her brain? "It makes me nervous to see her up there." But if memory served her correctly, Joseph used to let Mary perch on his shoulders. Mary had squealed with delight exactly the same way Eliza was doing.

"When do you need someone to watch the *kinner*?"

"Becky and I were talking about . . . oh, never mind."

"We were talking about when my *boppli* arrives. I want Lena to be with me."

Samuel's cheeks reddened, but he seemed to take the topic in stride. "I'll watch them."

"I don't think . . ." Lena began.

"If the midwife picks you and the *kinner* up on her way to Becky's house, you can drop them off with me and be about your business."

"*Danki*, Samuel, but I'm not sure that would be appropriate. I can probably get Atlee's *schweschder* or one of the other ladies there to mind them."

"Everyone will be busy if it's like the way things were at my house when my younger siblings were born. I don't think it would be inappropriate. Unusual, maybe, but not improper. Anyway, keep it in mind as an option."

"Danki." Becky's voice held some measure of relief.

"Why don't we have cake now? Then I can get the girls ready for bed." And Samuel can go home.

He deposited Eliza in the high chair and tied a bib around her neck as deftly as if he performed the task every day. He kept the little girl entertained while she waited.

Lena set the chocolate cake in the middle of the table. Mary giggled and Atlee chuckled in the next room. Apparently both were having fun. "We need our guest of honor."

"Atlee!" Becky called. "Dessert! That will get him in here. He has a huge sweet tooth."

Scarcely had the words left her mouth when Atlee bounded into the room with Mary on his heels. "Ah, look, Mary. Chocolate cake. If you don't like chocolate or if you're too full, I can take your piece for you."

"I like chocolate. I'm not full."

"Gut try, Atlee." Becky shook her finger at her husband. "I happen to know that Mary loves chocolate, so there isn't a chance she will forfeit her piece of cake. I'm sure there will be enough for you to have seconds, though."

They sang to Mary and enjoyed slices of cake with vanilla ice cream until Eliza resorted to finger painting the high chair tray with chocolate frosting. Lena jumped up to wipe the little girl's hands and face with a wet cloth while Becky helped Mary remove the chocolate mustache from her mouth.

"Did you want a second slice?" Lena picked up the knife to cut another piece.

Atlee patted his stomach. "I think I'm full, believe it or not."

"Samuel?" Lena glanced his way but avoided looking into the green eyes she used to enjoy gazing into. *That was a lifetime ago, Lena!*

"*Nee*. I'm not usually a big sweets eater, but that sure was tasty."

Lena placed the cake back in its covered pan. "It must be time for presents, then." She had to laugh at Mary's wide-eyed expression.

"For me?" The four-year-old seemed almost afraid to ask the question.

"Of course for you. It's your birthday." Lena hurried to hug her big girl. "You have to have a few presents on your birthday." Lena placed several wrapped boxes on the table.

"Oooh!" Mary touched the flowery paper on the biggest gift and fingered the small box, obviously trying to decide which to open first. Excitement conquered patience. She tore into the big package. "A new dress!"

"I've let out the hems of your dresses so many times, I figured I'd better sew a completely new one."

Mary shook out the folds of the blue dress and

held it out. "It's so pretty. I believe it will fit fine."

The adults chuckled at the little girl's pronouncement. The dress had been constructed exactly like all her other dresses, but the color was fresh and the fabric crisp.

Lena held out her hand. "I'll lay it aside for you so it doesn't get dirty."

"*Danki.*" Mary passed the dress to her *mamm* for safekeeping. She unwrapped a coloring book and crayons and a beginning reading book.

Becky presented her with a package wrapped in animal print paper. Mary tried to identify all the animals before tugging the paper loose. She carefully picked off the tape and folded the paper. "Can I save the paper, Mamm?" She smiled at Lena's nod of consent. She opened the box and lifted out a tub of small, white-spotted, black blocks.

"They're dominoes," Becky explained. "I'll show you how to play the game, or else your *mamm* can teach you."

"Or you can line them all up just right and knock them down. That's even more fun. I'll show you how to do that." Atlee laughed. "That was my favorite way to play dominoes."

"Show me!"

"I will. It might have to be on my next visit, though, because it's getting late. I see a little girl with sleepy eyes who might fall asleep in her high chair any minute."

Samuel cleared his throat. "I have a little gift for you, too, Mary."

Lena bristled. "You didn't have to do that." She knew she sounded snippy but couldn't help it.

"I wanted to. It isn't anything grand, but I thought you might like it." Samuel held out a lump wrapped in crumpled tissue paper.

Mary took the oddly shaped package and unwound the crinkly paper. She gasped. "It's a horse! Look, Mamm, it's a horse!" She raised the sleek, dark, wooden horse high. "It's *wunderbaar*. *Danki*, Samuel."

"That is very nice." Becky ran her hand over the smooth wood. "Did you make it?"

"I did. I'm not much of a woodworker, but I used to enjoy playing around with carving during those long, cold Wisconsin winter nights. I made toys for my *bruders* and *schweschders*."

Eliza banged on the tray, obviously wide awake now. "See? See horse?"

Samuel reached into his pocket. "You know what, Eliza? I have a little horse just your size right here." He scooted over to set a smaller version of Mary's horse in front of the younger girl.

"Pretty."

"Like you." Samuel smiled and tweaked her nose.

"Samuel, I . . ." Lena wasn't at all sure what to say.

He held up a hand like a stop sign. "I wanted to do it, Lena. Please don't deny me the pleasure of giving gifts."

Lena swallowed any words she might utter and nodded. "That was very nice of you. *Danki.*" The least she could do was be polite and show gratitude.

"*Ach!*"

"Becky, what is it?" Lena whirled around to stare at her *freind.*

Chapter Eleven

Becky gripped the high back of the sturdy oak chair. Her face had turned chalky. Lena rushed to her side and threw an arm around her. "Did you get a hard kick?"

Becky shook her head.

"A-a p-pain?" Atlee wore a pained expression himself.

"*Jah*," Becky gasped.

"*Kumm* in the living room and sit on a comfortable chair." Lena kept a firm grip on her *freind*'s arm and led her from the kitchen. "Can you see to the girls?" She flung the words over her shoulder but couldn't be sure either man standing with mouths agape would be capable of taking charge.

"Of course."

That voice belonged to Samuel. Lena knew that for sure and for certain. Poor Atlee probably still stood as if he'd been planted in cement. She hoped Samuel could enlist his help and get his mind occupied with something besides his nearly palpable fear. She eased Becky onto the sofa. "Better?"

"I think so. What do you suppose that was? It's too early for the *boppli*?"

"*Bopplin* arrive according to their own

140

schedules, not ours. You know, I had false labor a couple of times with Mary. Laurie told me to drink water and lie on my side to see if the pain stopped. It did until it was truly time for the birth. Would you like to lie down?"

"Not yet, but I'll try the water."

Lena raised her voice. "Atlee, would you please bring your *fraa* a glass of water?" She heard a bump that sounded like someone had run into a chair. She hoped Atlee could manage to bring the water without dumping it everywhere. Joseph had been nervous at Mary's birth, but she didn't recall his being paralyzed with fear.

Five seconds later, Atlee stumbled into the room, sloshing only a little water over the sides of the glass. He held it out for Becky and then knelt on the floor beside her. "Are you all right, *lieb*?" He stroked her arm. Becky managed a smile and nodded.

Lena perched on the edge of the opposite chair and studied the tender scene. It was so sweet how the young couple tried to reassure each other when they were probably both frightened. Their deep love couldn't be hidden even if they tried to do so. "Drink some water." Lena hated to interrupt the moment, but as of yet, Becky hadn't taken a single sip of fluid. They needed to determine if this was false labor, true labor, or something entirely different. It would take some time to summon the midwife if she was needed.

Becky finally took a gulp of water as Atlee continued to stroke her arm and watch her face. A pain shot through Lena's body and lodged in her heart. It had to be an ache of longing, of loneliness, rather than a physical ache. Had Joseph ever gazed at her so tenderly? Surely he must have and she simply didn't remember. How could a person forget so much in a year?

As she continued to watch, Atlee lovingly, gently brushed a loose tendril of his young *fraa*'s honey-gold hair from her cheek. He tried to poke it beneath her *kapp* but settled for tucking it behind her ear. Lena smiled despite the pain in her core.

Childish giggles followed by a deep chuckle echoed from the kitchen. At least the girls seemed at ease with Samuel, for some unexplainable reason. They weren't fussing or crying, so that was a plus. Maybe he had told the truth about his experience caring for his siblings. Maybe she could trust him some small amount. She didn't have much choice but to do so at this point. Becky needed her, and she needed someone to mind her *kinner*.

"Are you feeling better?" Atlee's voice came out whisper soft.

"I-I think so." Becky took a few more swallows of water before setting the glass on the small lamp table next to the sofa. She reached for her husband's hand.

"Do you want to go home now?" Atlee raised Becky's hand to his lips, completely oblivious to the fact that Lena sat opposite them. Or perhaps he didn't care if he had onlookers. Maybe his *fraa* was more important to him than anything else at the moment.

Lena's eyes watered. Oh to be so cherished! "You're *wilkom* to stay here tonight if you don't want to make the trip home."

"I-I think I can make it. I hope I didn't frighten the girls."

Lena smiled. "From the sound of things in the kitchen, I'd say they've forgotten all about your hasty departure from the room."

Becky nodded. "He seems like a *gut* man."

"Things aren't always what they seem." Lena couldn't stop the frown that tugged at her forehead.

"But sometimes they are, and we need to realize that." Becky yanked on Atlee's hand so he would help her stand.

"Possibly," Lena whispered. Could it be the young woman was wise beyond her years? After all, Becky had survived some terrible times when she ran off to New York. She'd done much soul-searching before finally accepting the Lord's grace and forgiveness. Perhaps her experiences had given her some special sort of insight. Only time would tell if Samuel Mast was what he seemed.

Becky's groan as she stood brought Lena's attention back to the problem at hand. Was this *boppli* eager to be born this evening or merely tricking his or her parents? "Are you having another pain?"

"*Jah*." The word emerged wrapped in a gasp. Becky's free hand flew to her stomach. Atlee flinched, causing Lena to assume Becky's other hand squeezed the life out of his.

Lena tried to guess how much time had passed since the previous pain. Most likely it had been a *gut* ten to fifteen minutes. "Do you want to sit back down?"

"*Nee*." Becky panted to catch her breath. "I think I want to go home."

Atlee's face exhibited pure panic. Lena almost laughed, but figured the one-time joker of the community would not find any humor in his present situation. Poor fellow. He was probably terrified to go home alone with a laboring woman.

Lena sidled up to Becky and placed a hand on her *freind*'s belly. Becky wasn't very big for being so near her due date, but Lena had never gained much weight with her pregnancies, either. This little one felt low, as if he'd inched his way down to escape from the womb. She could feel the tightening beneath her palm when Becky sucked in a shaky breath. It sure felt like a contraction to her. Having birthed three *kinner*, she'd had her fair share of those.

"Should I go call Laurie?" Atlee wrapped an arm around his *fraa* and pulled her close. Becky leaned her head against his chest and waited out the contraction.

"First *bopplin* take a long time, ain't so?" Becky's face showed hope mixed with fear.

"Every birth is different." Taut muscles relaxed under Lena's hands as the contraction ended. She wasn't an expert on the technicalities of the birth process, but that contraction sure felt strong to her, not at all like early labor. Having the *Englisch* midwife check her progress might be a *gut* idea. "Do you have your birth kit at home or is Laurie supposed to bring it?"

"It's at home."

"Then maybe we should get you home, just in case."

"You'll *kumm*, too, won't you?" Becky clamped a hand around Lena's wrist. "If this is true labor, will my *boppli* be all right? It's too early. Laurie said next month." Her sentences grew choppier, as if she struggled to catch her breath.

Lena patted the hand that threatened to cut off all circulation in her arm. "Many infants arrive early, and they're fine. Mary was two weeks early. Let's get word to Laurie and get you settled at home. Now, take some deep breaths for me." She sensed Becky's mounting fear and wanted to keep her from hyperventilating and growing dizzy. Lena knew Becky wanted her to accompany the young couple home. She wanted to be there to help, too, but she had her own *kinner* to consider. Being a single parent could be so hard at times.

"You'll *kumm*, won't you, Lena?"

If Becky's grip grew any tighter, Lena feared her bones would shatter. "I'll have to bring the *kinner* with me. Maybe we can get Malinda to watch them." Atlee's *schweschder* had helped care for Mary and Eliza during Matthew's birth, so hopefully they could enlist her assistance again.

Becky nodded and loosened her grip only slightly. Lena used the opportunity to slide her arm free. "Atlee, why don't you hitch up the buggy while I gather up my *kinners'* things?" She eased Becky backward. "You sit back down, dear, until we're ready."

Atlee, on Becky's other side, helped his *fraa* perch on the edge of the sofa. He kissed her cheek. "We'll stop at the phone shack to call Laurie. Do you have her number?"

"I have it, Atlee. Don't worry. I've still got the number stored in my memory from Matthew's birth." Lena scribbled the number on a scrap of paper. "Here. You two go now." She wanted to add "hurry," but didn't want to alarm the parents-to-be any further.

Samuel poked his head into the room. "I heard

146

your plans. I can drive over to watch the *kinner*. I can stay as long as you need me."

Lena hesitated and then nodded. She had no other option. If things went according to her makeshift plans, Samuel would be relieved of his duties as soon as possible and could be on his way.

"You're going to leave me?"

Lena could tell Becky tried hard to be brave, but her wobbly voice said otherwise. "Only long enough to snatch up Matthew, the diaper bag, and a few things for the girls. I'll be back in a flash. You aren't having another pain, are you?"

"It's starting to feel tight again." Becky rubbed her belly in a circular motion.

"I'll wait a moment." Lena reached one hand down to gauge the contraction. She waved her other hand at Atlee to get him moving out the door. They needed to get Becky home where she wanted to be before travel became impossible. Atlee flew from the room, almost tripping over his own feet. "Careful!" Lena called. They certainly didn't need to add an injury to the confusion they were already dealing with.

When she believed Becky would be fine for a few minutes, Lena dashed upstairs to gather up things her little ones might need. She hoped they would all sleep, but Matthew would probably want to nurse soon. Maybe she could sneak him out of the crib without waking him to buy them a little extra time.

Atlee rushed in the door at the same moment Lena hopped off the last step. She stopped in the kitchen long enough to thrust a sleeping Matthew into Samuel's arms. She might have chuckled at his surprised expression if she hadn't been so concerned about Becky. Did his experience with *kinner* include infants as well?

Poor Becky cut off her soft moan as soon as Lena collided with Atlee in the living room doorway. "It's okay to make noise," Lena assured her.

"I don't want to frighten the girls."

"They aren't paying a bit of attention to us." Lena hoped that statement was true.

"*Kumm, lieb.*" Atlee gently pulled Becky to her feet. "I can carry you if you want."

"I can walk."

Atlee tightened his arm around her and walked her toward the door. Becky leaned heavily on her husband as she shuffled along. She glanced back long enough to say, "I'm so sorry I spoiled Mary's birthday."

Lena hurried over to the couple and patted her *freind*'s arm. "You didn't do any such thing. You get settled in the buggy and I'll be right there with the *kinner*."

"I can bring the girls with me, Lena, if you take Matthew. I'm not sure I can watch him and drive

148

the buggy." Samuel slipped into the room, lightly bouncing the infant in his arms. Lena marveled that he did not hold him awkwardly as most single, young men would do. *Nee*, Samuel held Matthew with perfect ease, as if he'd been toting *bopplin* around all his life.

When Lena realized he was waiting for her answer, she stumbled over her words. "I, uh, I'm not sure."

"They'll be fine. We'll drive right behind you. I promise I won't drag race the buggy and crash into a tree or anything."

He smiled that charming smile that lit his whole face, the smile that had always made Lena smile, the smile that had always melted her heart. Once upon a time, that is. Now she had to make an instant decision. Time was wasting. How long would it take to get the girls situated in the back of Atlee's buggy? If they dawdled, precious minutes would lapse. "Okay. I have a bag here for them."

"I'll get it. Don't fret and frown, Lena. They will be fine. We'll be along shortly."

Lena tugged Matthew from Samuel's arms. "Girls, Samuel will bring you to Becky's house. Be *gut*." She snatched up the diaper bag and sped out to the buggy that Atlee practically lifted Becky into. She had barely gotten herself and Matthew situated when Atlee clucked to the horse and spurred the animal into probably the fastest trot he'd done in his life. She prayed Becky didn't feel every little bump and pothole they took at their fast pace.

The buggy stopped with a jerk beside the phone shanty near the end of a neighbor's driveway. Before Atlee could climb out, Lena tapped him on the shoulder. "I'll make the call." She figured Atlee wouldn't quite know what to say to the midwife. His relief that he wouldn't have to do the talking was almost comical. Lena thrust Matthew into Atlee's arms and hopped down. She wanted to tell Laurie to hurry because this seemed to be the real thing, and she was certain Atlee did not want to deliver the *boppli*. It wasn't exactly high on her list of things she dreamed of doing, either.

Becky puffed through another contraction as Lena crawled back into the buggy. She patted the girl's shoulder. "It's okay, Becky. We'll have you home and settled in a jiffy." Thankfully, Atlee took that hint, and away they flew.

"Laurie?" Becky gasped.

"She's on her way."

"*Danki*, Lord Gott," Becky and Atlee whispered simultaneously.

When Matthew began squirming and fussing, Lena threw a blanket over them and let him nurse. By the time they reached the Stauffers' house, he would be content with a full belly and she would be ready to help. "Atlee, let's get

150

Mary puffed up. "I am big. I'm four now."

"That's right. And Eliza is getting big, too." He tickled her under the chin, hoping to turn the scrunched-up face into a smiling one. "If your *mamm* has an apple, we'll take it along for Stockings' treat. He wouldn't like birthday cake."

"I like birthday cake." Mary glanced at the cake pan that held her chocolate cake.

"Me, too." Was that a smile he saw tugging at Eliza's mouth?

"I know you do, but horses aren't so fond of cake. They do like apples, though."

"We have apples." Mary ran to the fruit bowl on the kitchen counter. It sat just close enough to the edge that she could pluck out a bright, red apple.

"*Gut.* We'll bring that one with us." Samuel took the apple from her and tucked it into a pocket. "Your *mamm* put some things she thought you might want in that bag by the door. Why don't you bring your dominoes, too?"

"Do you know how to play?"

"I certainly do. I'll teach you."

"Horse?" Eliza ran to the table to try to snatch her little horse from the high-chair tray.

Samuel saw the wheels spinning in the child's mind and knew she would attempt to scale the chair any second. He leaped forward. "I'll get it for you. You can take your horse." He tucked it into Eliza's little hand and folded her fingers over it. "Are we ready?" He didn't want to take much time and give Lena something else to worry about. She already mistrusted him. He didn't want to add more fuel to that fire.

He didn't wait for any reply. Samuel tucked a girl sideways under each arm and groaned as he pretended to stagger to the door. The little howls of delight warmed his heart and relieved his concerns. If he could make them laugh, they would be fine. He tilted Mary down so she could grab the bag. "Are you strong enough to carry that?"

"I'm strong."

"All right. Let's go." He waddled to the door and set down the girls. He herded them outside and pulled the door closed behind them. "Last one to the buggy is a monkey's *onkle*!" The girls giggled and ran, with Samuel bringing up the rear. "It looks like a tie to me. You are both fast runners."

"Apple?" Eliza remembered the horse's treat.

"Let's give it to him after he's taken us to Becky and Atlee's house. He'll enjoy it more then." Samuel lifted first Mary and then Eliza into the buggy. "Stockings, go!" The horse took off and the buggy jerked forward.

"Stockings, go!" the girls cried together amid more giggles.

Samuel sighed in relief. He did it. Actually, the girls did it. They rebounded beautifully. They really were adorable *kinner*. How could they not be? They were Lena's. He sang a silly song and laughed along with them.

Lena settled Matthew in a little nest of blankets in a far corner of the bedroom because there wasn't anyone around to watch him just yet. She wondered if the girls were okay. It wasn't that she didn't trust Samuel to be kind to them. She truly would never believe he could be mean, at least not to *kinner*. She simply was unaccustomed to leaving her girls with anyone, particularly a near stranger. Mary and Eliza certainly seemed at ease with Samuel, though, nearly as comfortable as they were with Atlee. A soft moan drew her attention elsewhere.

"Becky, are you all right?" Lena straightened up from tucking Matthew into his makeshift bed. "Do you need help changing?"

"I-I think I can manage." She paused a moment to gasp. "Do you think this truly is labor? I wouldn't want to drag Laurie here for nothing."

"I'm sure midwives are used to false labor, strange twinges, hysterical new parents—the whole deal."

"*Ach*! I haven't been hysterical, have I?"

Lena laughed at Becky's horrified expression. "Not in the least. You've been very calm. I'm proud of you, though I'm probably not supposed to say that." She reached to help Becky's fumbling fingers remove the pins from her dress. "And to answer your first question, I honestly think Laurie will be needed here."

Becky squeezed her *freind*'s hand. "I'm so excited! I'm so scared!"

Lena laughed again. "Both are perfectly normal." She hugged the younger woman.

"I hope the *boppli* isn't too small, that he's ready to be born. I've read everything Laurie gave me at least three times, and it seems the lungs don't mature until near the end."

"We will trust the Lord Gott that all is well with him or her. But you are completely normal to worry about your *boppli*. We all did that—at every birth. Now, where is your birth kit? I want to get the waterproof pads on your bed. You do know that Laurie will need to examine you, right?"

"*Jah*. I remember from Matthew's birth." She shook out her dress and headed for the hooks on the wall.

"Don't worry about hanging it up. I'll do it in a minute. You change before another pain hits."

"I don't want Laurie to see a messy house."

"Your house is far from messy."

"I wonder when Atlee will be back." Becky's voice came out muffled while the nightgown covered her face.

"I'm sure he will be here soon." *I wonder when Samuel will be here with my girls*. Lena kept her own fears to herself.

"I don't have to get into bed, do I? I feel better walking around."

"You'll have to lie down for Laurie to check you, but then she usually lets women do just about anything they want. Midwives are generally pretty flexible. You can give birth up or down or upside down."

Becky offered a nervous giggle. "I think I'll skip the upside down part."

"*Gut* idea. With Mary and Eliza, I paced, I knitted, I rocked in the rocking chair, and I refolded tiny clothes ten times. Matthew came quite a bit faster."

"I remember." Becky drew a hand to her mouth and bit down on a knuckle.

"I see the wheels turning. What do you want to ask? You know you can ask me anything. If I don't know the answer, I'll try to find out—or I'll make something up."

Becky burst out laughing. "You're *gut* for me."

"I certainly am glad to hear I'm *gut* for something." The two women chuckled together.

A noise downstairs interrupted them. Lena waited for the sound of footsteps, but none came. "I know I heard something."

"I thought Atlee had gotten home."

"There it is again. It's at the front door. It must be Laurie. None of our *freinden* would bother to knock."

Becky nodded but then gripped the top of

the dresser and sucked in a ragged breath.

"Breathe, Becky. Let me get the door. I doubt she'll hear me if I yell from here. Are you okay for a minute?"

Becky nodded again, but her face registered a mixture of fear and panic.

"Hang on. I'll be right back." Lena flew down the stairs and yanked open the front door. "*Gut.* You're here, Laurie. Oops!" Lena almost ran headfirst into Samuel. The girls had stopped to pick clover from the yard. She patted her pounding chest. "You got here fast. I thought it was the midwife because you knocked."

"I don't know Becky well, so I didn't want to barge in. I got here as soon as I could so you wouldn't worry about the girls on top of everything else."

"*Danki.*" She didn't mention that she had indeed been concerned about her girls' welfare. "Atlee hasn't gotten back yet and, as you know, we're still waiting for the midwife. I need to get back to Becky." What would she do with two little girls while she helped a laboring woman? Matthew was a bit easier to deal with, but two active, older *kinner* was a different matter.

"Don't worry about Mary and Eliza. I'll play with them for a while. We'll go outside and then play with Mary's dominoes."

"Are you sure?"

"Absolutely. You go."

"Malinda should be here soon to relieve you."

"I'm not worried."

Lena worried, though. She imagined herself a wishbone, tugged on one side by her *kinner* and the other by Becky. *The girls are fine. The girls are fine.* She silently chanted the words with every inhalation and exhalation. Becky was the one who needed her right now. Lena raced back up the stairs to find Becky hunched over beside the dresser. One hand rhythmically rubbed her belly. The other was fastened onto the furniture with a white-knuckled grip.

"You're doing fine. Just remember to breathe."

"Laurie?"

"That was Samuel and the girls. He'll stay with them until Malinda gets here."

"*Gut* man, Lena." Becky panted.

Lena shrugged. She wasn't so easily persuaded. "Give him a chance."

"We'll worry about him later."

"You convinced me to give Atlee a chance."

"*Jah*, but . . ."

"Becky?" a voice called from below.

"*Kumm* on up, Laurie," Lena answered. She heard Becky's sigh of relief. She almost echoed that. Lena probably could handle the birth herself as long as there weren't any problems, but she rejoiced that she wouldn't have to do so.

"I hear we have a baby coming, right, Becky?" Laurie set down her bag. "Let me wash up and we'll see how you're progressing. Can you crawl onto the bed while I wash?"

"I'll help her." Lena took one arm and nudged Becky toward the bed.

"It's too early, ain't so, Laurie? Will my *boppli* be all right?"

"Due dates are only estimates. You've had a completely normal pregnancy. I believe the baby is fine. I'll be right back."

By the time Laurie had examined Becky and foretold an imminent delivery, Atlee had returned with Malinda and Saloma. As she'd done when Lena gave birth to Matthew, Malinda quickly volunteered to watch the little ones. Darkness tinged the sky, so she scooped up Matthew and called the girls inside. Atlee sat with Becky and talked her through contractions until he appeared to be in as much pain as Becky.

"You don't have to stay," Becky gasped.

"I don't want to leave you."

Saloma clamped a hand on his shoulder. "Take a break, Son. We have women's work to do here."

A masculine voice called to Atlee. "*Kumm* pace down here for a while. You can wear a hole in this rug, too."

Lena swallowed a giggle. Amazing! Samuel still hung around.

Atlee bent to kiss Becky's forehead and brushed a loose strand of golden hair from her cheek. Lena heard his whispered, "I love you," before he shuffled from the room. She saw his look of despair and anguish and knew he wanted to stay by his *fraa*'s side. She smiled at him, mouthed, "Everything will be all right," and then prayed her words rang true. Although birth was a natural, normal process, occasionally something went wrong. Becky was young and strong, though. Her *boppli* would be fine.

Atlee nodded before stalking away.

Samuel called again, "*Kumm* on, Atlee. I'll even pace outside with you. We can trample down the grass so you won't have to mow it."

Atlee stomped down the stairs. "How would you feel if it was your *fraa*?"

The words had been mumbled, but Lena heard them. Had Samuel?

Chapter Thirteen

He would probably be in worse shape than Atlee. Samuel feared he would have to be dragged from his *fraa*'s side. He would want to draw the pain from her body and take it upon himself. He would want to cradle her in his arms, wipe her brow, and give her every ounce of strength he possessed. Especially a tiny, delicate woman like Lena.

Samuel couldn't imagine any other woman he would want to share such an experience with. Whenever he thought of a *fraa* and *kinner*, Lena was the woman in his little, imaginary family. Their *dochders* would be tiny replicas of Lena, with dark brown hair and chocolate-drop eyes. Their sons would have his green eyes and grow to be big, strong *buwe*.

Ach! Who was he kidding? Lena could barely tolerate his presence. She only invited him to stay for supper to be polite, and she only trusted him with her *kinner* because she had been desperate. Would he ever be able to win her back? Even though they had been young, they'd had something special. Could they recapture any of those feelings? He still felt the same after all those years.

You can't give up, man. You have to keep

trying. There isn't another woman alive who can substitute for Lena. His heart would only admit her. Samuel sighed. At least her girls liked him. Maybe that would be a point in his favor. He pulled himself from his mental ramblings when Atlee reached the bottom step. A more pitiful fellow he'd never seen.

"Hey, do you want to get some air?" Samuel clamped a hand on the younger man's shoulder.

"I didn't want to leave her."

"I know you didn't. She'll be fine, and soon your *boppli* will be here." If the shoe was on the other foot, Samuel wouldn't take any comfort from those pretty words. He would feel as dejected and as worried as Atlee looked.

"I should be there. She's my *fraa*."

"I understand."

"Do you?"

"I wouldn't want to leave someone I loved, either." Samuel couldn't prevent his gaze from straying to the stairway, even though he knew Atlee watched him.

"I believe maybe you do. Let's walk." Atlee nudged the taller man with an elbow. "Not too far, though."

Warmth spread through Lena's heart at Atlee's words and actions. She had never doubted his sincerity, but this evening he'd proved his acceptance of Becky's *boppli* as his own. He behaved as every other *daed* she'd ever witnessed at other births she had attended. Granted, he and Becky were still newlyweds, but the depth of love for the woman and infant were totally obvious. Lena would have to remember to tell Becky all these things later so she could treasure them in her heart.

Had Joseph behaved in a similar fashion at Mary's and Eliza's births? Somehow, in the throes of labor, a woman's attention was not generally focused on whoever else was in the room. Of course Lena remembered Joseph had been there holding her hand until the women shooed him out, but she couldn't recall specific words or gestures. How could a person forget so much in a year? Sometimes she couldn't recall his face clearly or hear the tone of his voice in her mind. Memories seemed to be seeping away. Did that have to happen to allow a person to move forward?

Lena had been a single parent since the second month of her pregnancy with Matthew, trying to do everything on her own. Until Becky appeared, that is. The girl proved to be a blessing in many ways before, during, and after Matthew's entry into the world. It was Becky who walked through labor with her the last time. Becky mopped her brow, held her hand, and supported her as she pushed with all her might. Now she wanted to do the same for her *freind*.

"You're doing great, Becky. It won't be much longer. Right, Laurie?" Lena prayed Laurie would confirm her words.

"She's right. The baby is ready to emerge in only a few more contractions. You're doing a splendid job." Laurie laid a hand on Becky's hard belly. "Are you ready to push?"

"*Jah.*"

Becky's voice was little more than a croak. Lena promised to give her a sip of water after this next effort. She wiggled herself behind Becky to hold her shoulders as the girl bore down.

"It's a good thing you're so thin, Lena. You can fit in the small places." Laurie chuckled as she got ready to catch the baby.

"I guess being skinny can have some advantages. At least I'm a strong skinny, not a weak one."

Becky started to giggle, but the sound was swallowed by a moan.

"*Gut* girl, Becky. You can do this." Lena knew the poor girl must be exhausted, but she also knew how much physical and emotional strength she had. "You'll be cradling your *boppli* before you know it."

"I hope so." Becky gasped and collapsed against Lena at the end of the contraction.

Lena reached for the cup on the bedside table and offered the laboring woman a quick sip of water.

Laurie patted Becky's leg. "Maybe the next push."

"Atlee?"

"We had to kick him out, remember? I'm sure he's fit to be tied."

Becky only had time to nod before another contraction swelled and all her attention reverted to the task of delivering her infant.

Lena found herself grunting along with Becky. If she could have taken on the contraction for the younger woman, she surely would have. She offered another silent prayer for the well-being of the new *mudder* and her infant.

"It's a girl, Becky!" Lena cried as she suctioned the newborn's mouth and nose with the little bulb syringe.

"I knew it!" Lena squeezed Becky's arm. "I knew you would have a golden-haired little girl." She stole a glance at Saloma, who had tears streaming down her face as she watched the midwife dry her first grandchild.

"Here, Grandma." Laurie passed the infant to Saloma. "You hold the baby while her mama and I finish up here."

Becky strained to sit up so she could see her *boppli*. Lena knew the younger woman's arms ached to hold the precious bundle she had been waiting for. "You'll get to cuddle her in a few minutes. I know you can hardly wait."

"She's absolutely perfect. She's got all her fingers and toes," Laurie confirmed.

Saloma shuffled close to the bed so Becky could see her *dochder*. The poor girl burst into tears. "My *boppli*." She sniffed and tried to swipe at the flood coursing down her cheeks.

Lena pulled a tissue from the box on the table and dabbed at the new *mudder*'s tears. "I did the very same thing when I first laid eyes on Mary. Birth is truly a miracle, and each new life is a blessing."

"That's for sure," Saloma whispered. "She looks like you, Becky dear. Fair skin, honey-gold hair, even greenish eyes."

"We're all done here." Laurie straightened and began cleaning up. "Why don't you get comfortable so you can nurse that little girl?"

Lena helped Becky wiggle into a more upright position and plumped up a couple of pillows before poking them behind the girl's back. As if on cue, the newborn let out a lusty wail.

Saloma laughed. "Her lungs work fine." She bent to kiss the tiny head before settling the infant in Becky's outstretched arms.

"Get Atlee now?" Becky croaked. She tried clearing her throat, but still her voice came out gravelly. She cradled her little one close.

"Here. Take a sip." Lena held out the cup of water. "You must be parched. And hungry, too. We'll get you something to eat in a few minutes."

Thundering footsteps and a commotion at the doorway drew every woman's attention. A disheveled young man skidded to a stop, apparently unsure if he should enter. "Becky?"

"Come inside, dad, and meet your daughter." Laurie laughed. "And you look like you need to sit down."

"*Dochder*? We have a *dochder*?" Atlee dashed across the room. He stroked the infant's cheek with one index finger before bending to kiss Becky's lips. "Are you all right?"

"Fine now that you're here and I know the *boppli* is healthy."

Lena watched the happy scene with a jumble of emotions. She was ecstatic for her *freinden* and the love that enveloped them like a cloud. Oh, how *wunderbaar* it would be to be close to someone again, to share the milestones of their *kinners'* development, to share dreams and goals. She gave herself a mental shake. She'd had her turn. Now it was Becky's turn, and she would rejoice for her. "Does this little angel have a name?"

Becky looked into her husband's adoring face and smiled. "Do you want to tell them?"

Atlee patted his *fraa*'s arm. "You can."

With the hand that didn't clutch the infant, Becky reached out to grasp the hand of the man hunched over the bed. "Because of all the love and mercy shown to me by the Lord

168

Gott and by all of you, her name is Grace."

Saloma brushed at a fresh crop of tears. Lena swiped at the moisture gathering in her own eyes and was sure she heard a sniff from the doorway, where Samuel peeked in.

"That's lovely." Laurie found her voice first. "A beautiful name for a beautiful baby. Congratulations."

"*Danki* for everything," Becky whispered.

"You are very welcome. You did all the hard work, Becky. I simply assisted. Now, let's get this babe nursing before she goes into a deep sleep. Perhaps we can find some nourishment for her happy but weary parents, too."

Saloma cleared her throat several times. "Lena and I will prepare a healthy snack and bring it upstairs. Please stay for a bite to eat, Laurie."

"I believe I'll accept your kind offer. Let me make sure the baby latches and nurses well, and then I'll be downstairs."

Lena followed Saloma to the door where Samuel still lingered with an expression that could only be longing on his face. At least that was Lena's interpretation. Could he be wishing for a family of his own? Did men feel that same tug at their hearts that women did? What should she say to him? Anything or nothing?

Saloma spoke before Lena's brain could give her tongue a message. "Go have a quick peek. After all, you worked hard keeping Atlee sane tonight." She nudged the big man and chuckled. "Hurry before the baby nurses."

Samuel's face flushed pink, then beet-red. By the time he got his feet to move, the color had crept up to both ears. Saloma chuckled, and Lena put a fist to her mouth to stifle a giggle. Most likely Samuel would hightail it out of the room on their heels.

"Let's make some sandwiches." Saloma linked her arm with Lena's and led the way toward the stairs. When another bedroom door cracked open far enough for Malinda to poke her head into the hallway, her *mudder* relayed the news of Grace's birth.

"The *kinner*?" Lena hadn't heard so much as a peep. She hoped her little ones hadn't given Malinda any problems.

"They're all sleeping like little cherubs."

"Great." That was one less worry. Heavy footsteps behind her told Lena her guess had been accurate. Samuel had paid his respects and scurried from the room, leaving the new family and the midwife behind. Maybe he would go home now. Lena couldn't believe he had tarried so long, except he probably had provided support and diversion for Atlee.

Saloma looked over her shoulder at the man towering over them. "*Kumm* grab a sandwich, Samuel. You must be hungry, too. I sure appreciate your keeping Atlee company. The boy would have gone crazy or driven us crazy otherwise."

"I suppose I could use a sandwich if you have enough."

"Pshaw! There's always enough food. In fact, I stocked Becky's refrigerator with some sliced meats and salads only yesterday in anticipation of the birth. Something told me to get things ready."

Lena stumbled as she neared the bottom of the stairway and almost missed the last step altogether. If a big hand behind her hadn't grasped her arm, she would have sprawled out flat on her face on the wood floor.

"Are you all right?" The deep voice came from so close behind her that the little hairs on the nape of her neck quivered. A chill snaked up her spine. Her arm burned beneath the grasping hand. *Traitor,* she silently admonished her body.

Chapter Fourteen

I was all right until five seconds ago. A simple touch or voice should not wreak such havoc on a person's emotions. Not after ten years. "I'm fine. Just clumsy."

"You are not clumsy, Lena. You're probably dead on your feet."

"It's not that late. Besides, Becky and Laurie did the work up there." She nodded at the ceiling.

"Sometimes emotional strain is harder on a person than physical pain."

As if you have to tell me about emotional duress. She'd fallen into the pit of psychological turmoil more than once in her life and had only climbed out by hanging on to her faith in the Lord Gott. She didn't want to delve into that, though. Not tonight. Not with Samuel. "That I know." She kept her answer simple in the hope of dissuading further conversation.

"I suppose you do."

Suddenly realizing Samuel still had a hand wrapped around her upper arm, Lena pulled away. Space. She needed to put distance between them. "I need to help Saloma."

Samuel's hand dropped against his leg with a smack. "I can help, too."

Lena tossed a questioning glance over her shoulder.

"What? I can work in a kitchen. I do it all the time. A man alone still has to eat. I might not be capable of concocting an elaborate meal, but I can make a decent sandwich." He patted his belly. "I haven't wasted away yet."

"Your stomach is flat." *Ach!* She shouldn't have let on that she noticed anything about his appearance.

"Maybe so, but it's not sunken in to meet my backbone."

Lena laughed in spite of her resolution to remain aloof. Samuel always had been easy to talk to and fun to be with. Apparently some things about him hadn't changed. She, on the other hand, felt a hundred years older. Hopefully, she was a thousand times wiser. She hurried to the kitchen before they could converse any further.

"What have you got?" Lena forced brightness into her voice that she didn't feel. Confusion, hurt, disappointment, and fatigue all vied for attention. She wanted to recapture that earlier joy at the miracle of birth. She surveyed the assortment of deli meats and condiments Saloma had spread out across the kitchen counter. "It looks like you have enough food to feed the entire community for a week! You have every kind of meat known to man."

"I figured because this was a first birth it might

take a while, and people would need lots of sustenance. Becky surprised us, though."

"She did indeed. She did great."

"For sure." Saloma spread mayonnaise on several slices of bread. "I know Atlee will eat a couple of sandwiches. I'll fix one for Becky. Why don't you put something together for Laurie and Samuel?"

"I can fix my own. You two have enough to do."

Saloma whirled around. "Samuel Mast, you have a seat in the other room. You can tell Lena which kind of sandwich you want before you leave."

"You ladies worked harder than I did."

"You kept Atlee calm. That had to have been a major undertaking." Saloma chuckled as she added cheese slices to the sandwiches she was preparing.

"Atlee did fine. He'll make a great *daed*."

Lena peeked up from the turkey sandwich she'd begun making for Laurie in time to catch the wistful expression on Samuel's face. Did he want *kinner*? Probably his own, for sure, but not someone else's. *Ach!* Why in the world did such a thought race across her mind?

Saloma picked up the thread of the previous conversation. "Tell Lena what you want on your sandwich."

Ham, two slices of cheese, tomatoes, pickles,

174

and a smidgeon of mayonnaise. Funny how Lena remembered that tidbit. But Samuel's tastes could have changed completely over the years.

"I really can make it myself, but if you won't let me, I'll take ham, cheese—two slices, please—tomatoes, and some of those pickles. And only a tiny bit of mayonnaise."

Lena burst out laughing.

"What's so funny?" Samuel frowned, but the edges of his lips curled up as if they wanted to smile.

"Nothing." Lena gathered the fixings and got busy.

"I believe I'll drag my sleeping *kinner* out so the new little family can have their house to themselves. I'm sure they will have plenty of visitors soon enough." Lena stifled a yawn.

Saloma clamped a hand on Lena's shoulder. "*Danki* for all your help. I know Becky was glad you were here."

"I wouldn't have wanted to miss little Grace's birth for the world. I peeked into the room a few minutes ago to see if they needed anything and they were all asleep." Lena's smile turned into a yawn.

"Exactly where you need to be. I can help you hitch up, or maybe we can persuade Samuel to do that. Where is he?"

At that precise moment, the back door banged

shut and heavy footsteps tromped into the kitchen. "Did I hear my name?"

"I was telling Lena maybe we could get you to hitch her horse."

"I . . ."

Lena smacked her forehead. "I must be sleep-deprived or crazy. I didn't bring my buggy here. I rode with Atlee and Becky."

Samuel cleared his throat. "I was going to ask if you were ready to leave. I just hitched up my buggy and can drop you and the *kinner* off."

Lena reviewed her options. She could spend the night here, which she hated to do because she felt it was important for the new family to have time to themselves, or she could wait around until someone else visited and beg a ride. Or she could accept Samuel's offer. Why did it have to be him?

"That sounds like a plan to me, Samuel." Saloma made the decision for them.

"I'll help you carry out the *kinner*. It's rainy and nasty now."

"Wait!" Lena wasn't used to someone else making decisions for her, but she really didn't have a choice at this point. "Let me pack up everything and take that out first." She resigned herself to spending even more time in Samuel's presence.

"*Gut* idea. Let me know when you're ready for me to carry things out."

• • •

The temperature had nose-dived and the heavy rain made it feel downright cold. Lena clutched Matthew close to her and sat ramrod stiff on the edge of the buggy seat. Where had the cold wind come from? She hadn't been prepared for such a drastic temperature change. After all, it was summer. They shouldn't need buggy blankets to keep them warm. Mary and Eliza leaned against each other on the back seat huddled under the quilt Samuel found stashed beneath the seat.

"I really don't bite, Lena. You can move a little closer so our shared body heat can warm us a little. A storm must be brewing, or there's some big weather system change."

"I-I'm f-fine." Her chattering teeth told him the exact opposite. She hoped they'd reach her house before any storm hit. The girls were afraid of storms, and she wasn't overly fond of them herself.

"And that's why you're shivering worse than the last shriveled-up leaf on an oak tree in a windstorm."

Lena laughed in spite of herself. "You still have a way with words." She tugged the *boppli* closer. "Actually, Matthew helps keep me warm."

"Well, could you scoot over a little for my sake? I'm freezing!"

Lena's muscles released a bit of their tension as she chuckled again. If he was kind enough to stay throughout the entire labor, birth, and after, the least she could do was honor his simple request. She slid an inch closer.

"That's certainly a big help."

"All right." Lena moved a bit closer. She gasped when her arm brushed against his. That same electric current she'd always experienced at his touch shot through her body. Did he feel it, too? She wiggled to put a little distance between them. Even though it was too dark to discern the expression on his face, she could tell Samuel turned to look down at her. She pretended she didn't know.

A lightning bolt zigzagged across the black sky illuminating the entire world. A thunder clap rocked the buggy an instant later. Lena gasped, the horse reared, and the two sleeping little girls, instantly awake, cried out.

"It's okay, girls." Lena tried to offer comfort, but her own heart pounded so hard it ached. "Strange weather for the end of July."

"Very strange." Samuel called out to the horse in a soothing voice and urged him on.

A sudden blast of wind nearly lifted the buggy from the road. Samuel spurred the horse to run faster.

"I don't like this," Lena whispered so Mary and Eliza wouldn't detect her fear.

"We're almost home."

Lena clutched Matthew so tightly she wondered

that he didn't holler. The girls whimpered in the back of the buggy. Her sigh of relief when the buggy turned onto her gravel driveway was cut short when debris and dirt swirled around them, frightening the horse even more. "Samuel?"

"It's okay." He reached out to pat her leg, and for once she didn't flinch or scoot away.

The wind howled furiously. More debris swirled by, and another jagged streak of lightning split the sky. *Hurry! Hurry! Hurry!* She braced herself for the next boom of thunder. Surely her heart would burst through her skin.

Samuel stopped the buggy as close to the back door as he could. The horse pranced and whinnied, anxious to get out of the storm. "Take the *kinner* inside. I'll put my horse in the barn and check on your animals."

Lightning slashed the sky again. "Hurry, Samuel. Get back to the house quickly."

He patted her arm. "I'll be fast. Let me lift the girls down. Do you need help getting them inside?"

"They're terrified. They'll run, I'm sure."

"Okay. Let's go."

A wall of rain blasted them immediately, as if the lightning had ripped open the sky to unleash the torrent. "Run, girls. Mary, take Eliza's hand." Lena tried to shelter Matthew, but they were all instantly drenched before they'd jogged two steps. Thunder rattled the windows and the girls shrieked. They stood as if cemented to the spot. Lena would have to lay Matthew inside and return for the girls. Before she could act, Samuel scooped a girl under each arm and ran for the back steps.

Lena unlocked the door and nudged it open with an elbow. Samuel deposited the two wet, shivering *kinner* right inside the door and sprinted for the buggy. "Hurry!" she whispered her plea before slamming the door against the wind. A ping against the glass warned her that the wind flung hail at the house. This was not any ordinary storm. "Let's get dried off." Lena wanted to get the girls away from the windows in case the glass shattered. Maybe they should run to the cellar. Where was Samuel? Lena tried to calm herself. He had probably dropped them off only moments ago. It only seemed like hours.

Suddenly the whole room lit up as bright as when the noonday sun streamed through the curtainless windows. The faint odor of sulfur tainted the air. The crash that followed shook the house. Mary and Eliza screamed. Lena wasn't sure, but she thought she screamed along with them.

Chapter Fifteen

"Samuel." The word was no more than a whisper. Had a tree crashed down right outside the house? Had it landed on the barn or, worse, on a man running from the barn? Lena had to find out. What if Samuel was hurt? She had to help him. But what of her three frightened little ones? *What should I do, Lord Gott?*

She didn't have time to debate with herself, to weigh the pros and cons as she usually did. She needed to act. Now. *Move feet!* "*Kumm* quickly, girls." Lena led them to the big storage closet under the steps. She pressed the switch on the giant flashlight so the beam would dispel the shadows. She breathed a prayer of gratitude that the batteries were strong.

"We're going to play store." Lena pulled an old quilt from a box and threw it on the floor. She laid Matthew in a little nest she made in the quilt's folds. "Go back to sleep, my sweet one."

"How?" Mary and Eliza spoke as one. Their hands were still so tightly clasped, Lena feared they'd grown together.

"Well, you can take the items out of the boxes and arrange them however you want in your pretend store."

"We can open the boxes?"

Gut, Mary was getting excited. That would be a big plus. "These three boxes here." Lena pointed to the ones she meant. "You need to stay right here with Matthew. Storekeepers can't leave their shops unattended."

"What about you?"

"I'll be right back to see your amazing store. I have to see if Samuel needs my help. I want all three of you to stay in here. Do you understand?"

"*Jah*, Mamm." Mary's quivering lips belied her pseudobravery. Eliza merely nodded and kept a tight hold on her *schweschder*'s hand.

"That's my big girls. I love you." With a final glance at her *kinner*, Lena snatched up a smaller flashlight from the shelf and raced through the kitchen to the back door. Her heart galloped faster than she'd ever prodded her horse to go. *Please let him be all right. And please don't let me have wasted too much time.* She'd had to ensure her little ones' safety, but that ate up precious minutes. Lena heard Mary directing Eliza in a grown-up voice and smiled. They would be all right. *Please keep them safe, Lord.*

She yanked a shawl from the hook by the back door but didn't know why. She was already soaked to the bone, and the shawl wouldn't offer any real protection from the deluge right outside the door. Hail still pinged off the roof. She jerked open the door and fought the wind to push it closed behind her.

"Samuel!" The wind took her voice and threw it back at her. She gasped at the sight of the big tree that, only by the grace of Gott, had fallen away from the house. She shrieked at the lightning that streaked all too close and the deafening boom of thunder. Where was Samuel? He should have finished checking on the animals by now.

Lena cried out when something sailed through the air and struck her cheek. The surprise and the pain caused her to stumble on the slippery ground. She threw out her hands to break her fall but still landed hard on her knees and elbows. The flashlight flew from her hands and rolled away. It must have broken because its comforting little beam of light disappeared. Lena's cheek throbbed, and her knees and elbows protested their rough treatment.

She raised a hand to her cheek, then jerked it away. If it had merely been wet like the rest of her body, she would have taken little notice. But her hand felt sticky, too. With the next bolt of lightning that tore the sky, Lena saw the red stain. Blood. She couldn't worry about that now. With a grunt, she pushed to an upright position. What had struck her? She forced her aching knees to bend. She had to find Samuel. Something could have injured him, too.

Lena pressed the edge of the shawl to her cheek. The wind nearly blew her off her feet. Already wobbly from her fall, she struggled to remain standing. "Samuel!" She wouldn't have believed it possible, but the storm seemed to be worsening. If only she had her flashlight to see how to avoid any other debris that might be littering the yard.

"Oomph!" There shouldn't have been any huge obstacle between the house and the barn. That was her last thought before she tumbled to the ground again. Momentarily startled, Lena lay where she landed. The rain and wind had practically numbed her by now. At least numbness would obscure the pain. She tried to push up again, but a wave of dizziness washed over her. She lowered her head for a second as another mighty blast of wind roared around her. Creaking and snapping trees alarmed her. Would a tree limb crash down on her at any moment? She had to get her bearings and get on her feet.

"Lena!"

A faint light bobbed toward her, but the angry wind carried her voice away when she called out. Again she tried to stand, but the wind pressed her down. Before she could try to scramble to her feet once more, a light was thrust into her hands and strong arms lifted her from the ground. The roaring wind now sounded like the freight train that used to haul coal along the old train tracks during Lena's childhood. "Samuel?"

"*Jah*. Hold on."

How the man ran at top speed while carrying

her was beyond Lena's comprehension, but he ran as if she didn't weigh any more than a feather. She clung to his neck, trying to avoid choking him. Her *kinner*. She had to get to her *bopplin*. They must be terrified. A loud crack followed by a crash broke through the rumble of thunder. That falling tree must be awfully close.

Samuel set her on her feet as soon as they got inside the back door. Lena sped toward the closet as fast as her limp would allow. She ignored her throbbing elbows and knees and stinging cheek. She heard Samuel's heavy footsteps right behind her. All three little ones were crying when Lena pulled open the closet door. "It's all right. Mamm is here." She opened her arms to the girls as Samuel squeezed past her to retrieve Matthew.

"I'm so scared, Mamm," Mary whimpered and buried her face in Lena's shoulder.

"Scared," Eliza echoed. Huge tears leaked from her enormous brown eyes.

Lena hugged them tight. "I know, but you have been my big, brave girls." She glanced up to find Samuel rocking and crooning to Matthew. *Danki, Lord, that they are all fine and the house is still standing.* The wind suddenly stopped growling, leaving an eerie silence in its wake. They must have barely escaped the full wrath of a tornado. She prayed it didn't touch down anywhere, leaving a path of destruction behind. "Is it gone?" she mouthed to Samuel.

"I think so." He touched his own cheek and nodded at Lena.

At the same instant, Mary pulled back to look at her *mudder*. "Mamm! You're hurt!"

She was also soaked and freezing, but she was alive. "I'm all right. The wind blew something that hit my face."

Samuel scooted closer. "We need to clean that wound. I think it's safe to leave the closet now."

Lena shuffled backward toward the door with Eliza still clinging to her skirt. "It's okay, little one." She tried unsuccessfully to loosen Eliza's grip. "We need to get dry, right?"

"They will be fine for a few minutes while I clean your cheek." Samuel shifted Matthew to one arm and reached for Lena's arm with his other hand.

She stepped back out of his reach. "I'm perfectly capable of cleaning my own wound." She certainly did not need to be so close to him that their faces nearly touched. It was bad enough the man had carried her like a *boppli*. She could halfway justify that because the situation had been extreme.

"I know you're capable of doing anything you set your mind to. Sometimes it's hard to do your own doctoring, though. *Kumm* on."

Before she could retreat farther away, he grasped her arm. He thrust Matthew into the crook of her other arm and tugged her toward the bathroom. "Really, Samuel, I'm not a *kinner*. I can take care of myself." The girls giggled. At least they had recovered from their terror.

"I am well aware of both of those points."

Still, he did not let her go. True, she would have dashed far out of reach if he so much as loosened his grip, but there seemed little chance she would have the opportunity to do so. Lena's heart thudded against her ribs, and a strange tingle burned the length of her arm. She should not be this close to the man. She should not allow him to touch her or to even breathe the same air she struggled to breathe.

Why had dragging in oxygen become so difficult? She had to resort to gasps. Why were her thoughts such a jumbled mess? She must have hit her head one of the times she fell. "This is ridiculous, Samuel. I need to tend to my *kinner*." She yanked hard enough to cause Matthew to wobble, but still Samuel held fast.

"They are fine. They need to know that their *mamm* is, too. With dried blood all over your face, they're probably scared you're badly hurt."

Lena finally stopped resisting and allowed Samuel to tow her into the bathroom.

"Do you have a first aid kit or some hydrogen peroxide so I can clean the wound? I don't want to use alcohol."

"*Nee*! Not alcohol. That would burn like crazy. There should be peroxide under the sink."

"If I let go, will you promise not to run off?"

Lena considered her options. She glanced down at her free hand. Dried blood kept her from easily flexing her fingers.

"What happened to your hand?"

"I probably scraped it when I fell." She shifted Matthew so she could check her other hand. It, too, was caked with dried blood.

"We'll clean those as well."

"Honestly, I can wash my own hands."

"Do you have injuries anywhere else?"

Lena absolutely would not confess to the stinging pain along her knees and shins, and she certainly would not investigate those wounds now. "I'm fine," she mumbled instead.

"Right." Samuel rinsed a washcloth and gently swiped at her cheek.

Lena winced. If plain water stung enough to bring tears to her eyes, what would anything stronger do? She clamped her bottom lip between her teeth. Maybe she should have laid Matthew down so she wouldn't squeeze him in half or drop him.

"I'm sorry. I'm trying to be gentle."

In all fairness, Samuel had used the utmost care. Her wound must be raw to cause such pain. "It's okay." Somehow Lena squeezed out the words between her clenched teeth. She braced herself for the hydrogen peroxide while Samuel uncapped the bottle. With very gentle strokes, he swabbed the saturated cloth across her cheek. "Y-you must have done this before."

"I've doctored up my younger siblings more times than I can count when my *mudder* was in the middle of canning or something." He laid the cloth on the sink and studied Lena's cheek. She tried not to squirm under his scrutiny. "It doesn't look deep enough to need stitches, and the active bleeding has stopped. Face and head wounds tend to bleed a lot even if they aren't deep."

"And you know this because . . ."

"I've been in a hurry shaving a time or two and obtained a few nice nicks to show for it."

"Oh." Why did her cheeks burn anew? Shaving wasn't all that personal.

Samuel squirted a little antibacterial ointment on his finger and dabbed it on the wound. "There. Do you want me to cover it with a bandage?"

"I don't think that will be necessary."

"Let me see your hands."

"Trust me, Samuel, I can wash my own hands."

He reached for Matthew. "Let me hold him while you wash."

Samuel must have cared for his younger siblings an awful lot to be so at ease with her three little ones. Lena handed Matthew over and stuck her hands under the faucet. Again, stinging pain made her catch her breath. Once the dried blood had been washed away, though, her hand wounds didn't look too bad. She'd tend to her knees later. She blotted her hands dry and hung the towel on the rack. "Now I've got to get these *kinner* into dry nightclothes and tucked into bed for whatever is left of the night."

"You need some rest, too."

"And so do you." Mainly, she had to get Samuel out of her house before dawn tinted the sky lest someone think he'd spent the night here. That would never do.

"I'll help you with the *kinner*."

"That isn't necessary. I'm used to doing everything."

"You keep telling me that, and I don't doubt your abilities for a second, but if I help you, you can get everyone to bed faster."

Why did he have to make so much sense? Lena couldn't remember when she had felt so exhausted. Rest was in order for all of them. "Okay. You put dry clothes on Matthew and I'll see to the girls."

"Sounds like a plan. *Kumm* on, little man."

"I sure hope Becky and her *boppli* are okay. They were upstairs. If a tree fell on the house or anything . . ."

"I'm sure they're fine."

Lena stopped and looked over her shoulder. "How can you be so sure?"

"I didn't hear any sirens, so I assume there weren't any lightning strikes or injuries anywhere close by."

"I pray you are right." Lena continued toward the kitchen, where she found her two little girls curled up together on the floor with the damp quilt from Samuel's buggy wrapped haphazardly around their tiny bodies. She pulled Eliza free from the tangled quilt and lifted her limp body from the floor. She juggled the girl's weight until she could free a hand to shake Mary awake. "Let's go to bed." Groggily, her older *dochder* struggled to her feet.

Before they could move, a thump sounded at the back door. Lena's heart hiccupped. What in the world was that? She shot a worried glance at Samuel, still standing in the kitchen doorway with Matthew.

"Lena? Lena Troyer, are you all right?"

Chapter Sixteen

It must be three in the morning. Why on earth was Bishop Menno at her door? And Samuel was standing in her kitchen, holding her *boppli* like he belonged here. Could things be worse?

"Lena?" The pounding came again.

She fought to catch her breath. She had to answer the bishop, if only she could get her voice to slide past the boulder in her throat. This did not look *gut* at all. *Feet, move!* Lena waddled to the door with Eliza clutched in her arms and Mary clinging to her wet skirt.

After what seemed like the longest trek of her life, she reached the door. She had done nothing wrong. There was absolutely nothing bad going on here. Would the bishop believe her? Lena had never given him any reason to mistrust her in the past. She wiped her free hand on the dress, an action that was useless; her dress was wetter than her sweating palm.

"B-bishop Menno?"

The man stood in her doorway, his countenance illuminated by the lantern in his hand. Rain spots glistened like crystals on the lenses of his wire-rimmed glasses. He was a tall, wiry man but appeared smaller hunkering under a yellow, waterproof slicker. Amazingly, the rain had dwindled to barely a drizzle. More drops fell from the bishop's salt-and-pepper beard than from the sky.

"I came to check on you. You have some trees down. We will cut them up for you tomorrow. I guess that would be later today, though, because it's after midnight." He held up an intact ceramic flowerpot. How did the thing manage to survive the raging storm unscathed? "I nearly tripped over this, so I brought it to the house with me."

Lena's free hand flew to her injured cheek. So that's what had threatened to knock her head off.

"You've been hurt."

"It must have been that very pot that struck me when I was outside." She almost said, "When I went looking for Samuel," but caught those words before they could slip out. She should ask the bishop to *kumm* inside for tea or water or something. But then he'd know Samuel was here. She didn't have anything to hide, but looks could be deceiving, especially to the bishop.

"You were outside in the storm?"

"Becky Stauffer had her *boppli* tonight. I had been with her. It was storming when we got home. Would you like something to drink?" Lena's tongue flapped like it was loose at both ends. She had been with Becky. That just didn't happen to be the reason she was outside when the flowerpot sailed through the air like a missile. And she did have to be a polite hostess even

193

though it was the middle of the night, didn't she?

Why didn't Samuel leave earlier, as she wanted him to? Why did she let him bring her home at all? In the space of mere seconds, a zillion questions whizzed through Lena's brain. If she had refused Samuel's offer of a ride, she would have had to wait for the midwife to finish her work and drive them home in her tiny car. If Samuel hadn't been here when she fell, she could have been more seriously injured when the tornado roared through. On the other hand, if Samuel hadn't been here, she wouldn't have gone back outside in the first place.

Everything was too tangled up and frustrating. Lena called back her wandering mind and realized she'd been holding her breath waiting for the bishop to reply to her question. *Please don't let him want to step inside.*

"*Danki*, but I'd better let you and the little ones get to bed. I need to get a bit more sleep myself." He stifled a yawn, as if to prove his point. "I only wanted to make sure you were all right."

"I appreciate that."

"Everything went okay with Becky?"

"*Jah*. She had a fine little girl named Grace."

"*Gut*. I'll tell Martha about the *boppli*. I'm sure she'll want to take food over to them." He waved toward the yard behind him. "We'll be by tomorrow to take care of the debris." With that, he turned and let the darkness claim him. Mist

194

swirled around the thin lantern beam until it completely swallowed the light.

Lena watched for a moment and then stepped back to close the door. She couldn't resist the huge sigh of relief and whispered a prayer of gratitude that the formidable bishop had not entered the house. She turned to find Samuel's gaze fastened on her.

"I'm sorry to have put you in an awkward position, Lena."

"It couldn't be helped." Not at this point, anyway. What was done was done.

"I think he would have understood my presence here, wouldn't he? He wouldn't have jumped to the wrong conclusion, ain't so?"

Lena shrugged. "It's hard to say. I'm just glad he didn't want a drink of water or anything. I can get the *kinner* to bed, Samuel. You must be exhausted, too."

"You might as well let me help so I don't run into the bishop on my way home."

Would this night ever end? She wanted nothing more than to crawl into bed and sleep for a week. She swallowed a wry chuckle. By the time she laid her head on the pillow, Matthew would want to nurse again. Sleep was a rare and precious commodity for *mudders*. Lena rubbed a hand across her forehead and deliberately worked to smooth the furrows. "All right. Let's go." She didn't think the bishop would return. Besides, the man should be home snoring in his bed by the time Samuel headed out.

Lena led the way upstairs. She clicked on a battery-operated lamp on the chest of drawers and quickly pulled out a dry diaper and night clothes for Matthew. "I can change the diaper." If she did that, she might as well dress him and tuck him into the crib. Samuel could leave.

"I can change a diaper."

Lena whipped her head around and raised her eyebrows.

"What? You don't believe a man can change a diaper?"

"Not an unmarried one, and maybe not many married ones, either."

"I'm a *gut* diaper changer. Maybe not a great one, but I can get the job done."

"Your *mudder* had you do all that for the younger ones?"

"Sure. She needed help sometimes. I was the only person available. I didn't mind."

"Such a *gut* son." Lena didn't realize she had spoken the thought aloud until Samuel answered her.

"I tried to be." He laid Matthew on the changing table and began peeling off damp clothes.

Apparently Samuel told the truth. He obviously had things under control here. "Let's go, girls."

"Are we going to brush our teeth?" Mary's voice was heavy with sleep.

Malinda had probably given the girls all sorts of treats, but Lena was too tired to worry about cavities now. "We'll brush them extra-*gut* tomorrow." Mary nodded against her leg. Poor thing was probably too tired to utter another word. Eliza had already become deadweight in her tingling arms.

In the girls' room, she laid Eliza on the bed and shook her arm to restore circulation. She pulled out a nightgown and stripped off the damp clothes. "Can you put on your nightgown, Mary?"

The exhausted little girl mumbled that she could and set about removing her own clothes. Lena struggled to get Eliza's floppy arms through sleeves but finally had her ready for bed. She'd worry about the tangled hair later. She slid Eliza closer to the wall so Mary could climb into bed beside her. Poor lamb stumbled and would have fallen if Lena hadn't grabbed her and tucked her in beside her *schweschder*. She kissed each little cheek and adjusted the covers. "Sleep well, my angels." Now if Lena could get Matthew tucked in without waking him, she might catch a few winks of sleep herself.

"*Ach*, he's in bed already!" When Lena crept back into Matthew's room, she found him settled in the crib.

"You really didn't think I could do this, did you?" Samuel grinned. "Surprise!"

"I admit I had my doubts. I humbly beg your pardon."

Samuel laughed. "I'm glad you haven't lost your sense of humor."

"My mind, maybe, but not my sense of humor."

"You always could make me laugh."

Even in the dim lamplight, Lena noted the wistful expression that crossed Samuel's handsome face. He had always made her smile in the past, too. They had been *gut* for each other. Back then. Now was a whole different story.

"I should leave so you can get out of your wet clothes and get some sleep."

She would change clothes, for sure, but she had a sneaking suspicion that either her whirling thoughts or her *boppli* would prevent much sleep from occurring. "I think the clothes have melded with my skin."

Samuel chuckled again. "Bishop Menno should be home by now, don't you think?"

"I can't imagine why he wouldn't be."

"I'll head out, then. I will probably help with the downed trees later."

"Please don't trouble yourself. You might have a mess to clean up at your own place." Besides, if one of them slipped and innocently referred to "last night," they would raise a lot of eyebrows, and she would have a great deal of explaining to do.

"We'll see." Samuel patted her arm as he

brushed past her, sending a prickle from her shoulder to her fingertips. *"Gut nacht,* Lena."

"Gut nacht. And *danki."*

As she had suspected, sleep refused to claim her regardless of how tightly she squeezed her eyes shut or which position she assumed or how many times she plumped her pillow. Matthew still slept, so he couldn't be blamed for her restlessness. Samuel Mast was the problem. He had messed up her life once and now he was threatening to do it again.

Lena rolled over and groaned. *I'm too tired for this. Why won't my brain shut down and give me some peace?* She had made so many adjustments in her life. She'd coped with being a widow and a single parent. She'd dealt with Becky's departure when she married Atlee and moved out of the Troyer house. Now she had to adjust to Samuel's return. How much more could a person stand?

She bolted upright. "Why, Lord Gott? Why do I have to deal with more hardship?" She flopped down with a gut-wrenching sigh. It wasn't her place to question the Lord. The pot didn't ask the potter why he made it. Neither should she question her maker. "Help me, Lord. Oh, help me."

Chapter Seventeen

Samuel made a quick check of the barn and animals to make sure the storm hadn't caused any problems before hitching up his horse. "I hope you had a *gut* rest so one of us can stay awake on the way home." He gave Stockings a final pat before climbing into the gray buggy and starting for the Stoltzfus place—*nee*, his place.

He couldn't pinpoint a time when he had been more tired than he was right now. His bed called to him, but he would only have a few hours at best to spend there. Stockings' plodding picked up speed the closer they got to home. The poor animal probably wondered why he'd been disturbed so much in one evening. He wouldn't get much of a rest, either, but at least he'd been fortunate enough to eat and snooze while his owner had been otherwise occupied.

Samuel heaved a huge sigh of relief when the buggy's wheels crunched on his own gravel driveway. At last. He'd see to the horse as quick as a flash, dash up the steps, and flop onto his bed. His clothes were merely damp now as opposed to wringing wet. The dampness didn't bother him much at this point. He'd gone from chilled and soaked to cool and damp to numb and resigned. The only part of his body that seemed to be alive at the moment was the one thing he wished would shut down. His brain. It played images of Lena over and over. How could she look so beautiful when they'd been so bedraggled and frightened?

Fright didn't begin to describe the emotion that shot through him when he saw her lying on the ground. He thought she'd been struck by lightning or thumped on the head by a falling tree limb. He'd died a little bit himself when he assumed the worst. Only when he saw her struggle to get to her feet had his heart kicked back into some semblance of a normal rhythm.

If anything happened to Lena, he didn't know what he'd do. Even if she never wanted a relationship with him or didn't want to so much as breathe the same air he did, he would fall apart if she was badly injured or worse. Samuel shook himself. Simply letting his mind travel down that path sent chills up his spine. He would rather think of Lena's lovely smile, her dark hair and eyes, her sweet *kinner* or . . . What or who was at his house? At three in the morning?

Samuel sucked in a sharp breath that whistled as it escaped between his clenched teeth. Any idea of sleep vanished quicker than the dew on a mid-July morning. This could only be Bishop Menno, and Samuel doubted the man was making a social call. He almost chuckled at the thought. He'd better get a grip on the sarcasm before he opened his mouth to speak to him.

Before jumping from the buggy, Samuel grappled with possible ways to begin a conversation. "What are you doing here?" seemed rather rude. "I didn't do anything wrong," screamed guilt. Hmm. Perhaps he'd better let the older man begin and simply follow his lead. This couldn't be *gut*. As had been his way from his scholar days, he'd get the hard things, the most unpleasant tasks, out of the way first. He took a deep breath, forced his hunched shoulders to relax, and hopped to the ground.

Even though Samuel hoped he'd been wrong, it was indeed the bishop who crawled from the other buggy. In the dim light from the battery-operated buggy lamp, Samuel couldn't tell if the man's face registered anger, shock, fatigue, or all three. He would make himself wait to hear whatever accusations, recriminations, or warnings were issued before offering any defense.

"Samuel."

Just his name? The bishop must be debating which words to choose, too. "Bishop Menno. I thought you'd be home asleep by now." Oops! So much for waiting for the bishop to speak his mind first. Did those few words sound sarcastic to the man's ears? Samuel hoped not. It certainly was not his intention to be sarcastic or disrespectful.

Bishop Menno cleared his throat. "I'm not sure

why you were hiding, but I know you were at Lena Troyer's place."

How? Could the man see through walls or read minds? Samuel nearly choked on his own saliva. He fought not to cough as he searched for words. "I, uh, wasn't hiding." Well, he sort of was, if staying out of sight constituted hiding. "I was seeing to Matthew."

"I don't know what your intentions are, but please don't cause Lena pain or embarrassment. She has been through enough."

"I would never do anything to hurt Lena or her *kinner*. I know Lena has had hard times. I'm only trying to help." Samuel didn't need bright light to see the man's bushy eyebrows rise heavenward. "You saw how the girls clung to her. They were frightened by the storm. Lena couldn't very well see to the *boppli* and tend to the girls at the same time."

"You'd be surprised at what women can do. For generations, since the beginning of time even, women have been caring for *kinner*, and usually for more than three at a time. What were you doing there in the middle of the night?"

"Lena told you Becky had her *boppli*."

"And how does that concern you?"

"I had stopped at Lena's yesterday to wish Mary a happy birthday. Atlee and Becky were there, too." Samuel was aware that his words spilled out all over themselves, but he was powerless to stop them. He paused only to gulp in a quick breath of air. "Becky's pains started. She wanted Lena with her, so I went along to watch the *kinner* until Malinda arrived."

"You watched the *kinner*?"

"Sure. Why not?" Yikes! He didn't sound like he was questioning the man's authority, did he? He didn't want to get on the bishop's bad side. He wanted acceptance back into the community, not rejection or even ostracism.

"Not many young, unmarried men would volunteer to care for a *boppli*."

"Lena didn't have a whole lot of choice at that point. Besides, I cared for my younger siblings a lot." Samuel wasn't sure how much of his family life he should reveal, but he wanted this stern man standing in front of him to have a little better understanding of how life had been for him.

"Really?"

"*Jah*. My *mudder* had more *kinner* after we left Maryland. I didn't have any *schweschders* old enough to help, so I often gave Mamm a hand with the younger ones. We moved several times. It was very hard on Mamm to keep starting over. I think it took a toll on her emotional and physical health."

"I see. It's a *gut* thing you could help her, then." The bishop stroked his long salt-and-pepper beard and cleared his throat. "Lena is an entirely different matter, though."

Samuel's patience began to ebb as much as his energy. Couldn't this conversation have waited until they'd both gotten at least a couple of hours of sleep? He was operating on sheer willpower at the moment, and his brain wasn't processing quite as clearly as it should. He certainly didn't want to say or do anything to cast an unfavorable light on Lena or himself. "I realize that, Bishop Menno. As I said before, I would never do anything to hurt Lena or compromise her *gut* standing in the community."

"Not willingly, perhaps, but being alone with her in her house in the middle of the night is not acceptable."

"That would not have happened if Lena had not needed a ride home from the Stauffers' house, and if it had not been storming."

"You should have dropped Lena off at the door and continued on your way."

Samuel barely resisted the urge to roll his eyes, even though the older man probably wouldn't have seen it in the dim light. He couldn't, however, suppress an exasperated sigh. "Ordinarily I would have done that, but the *kinner* were frightened of the storm, and the rain poured down in sheets. Could you have put out a woman and her three little ones and driven off?" Now he'd probably just cooked his own goose, but his loosened tongue ran away with itself. "If I had left Lena's at that moment, I would have run smack into the tornado or whatever caused that horrible wind and roaring noise."

Bishop Menno stroked his beard so hard that Samuel expected the man to holler with pain any second. Surely he didn't doubt Samuel's words. If the man had been driving at that time, he must have experienced one wild ride. If he'd been sitting outside Lena's house, it was a wonder he hadn't been propelled clear across the county.

He stopped yanking at his beard and rubbed that same hand across his forehead. He sighed loud and long, as if resigning himself to the situation. "I understand, Samuel. I would not have left Lena alone to get three frightened *kinner* safely inside, either. And it would have been foolish to put your own life in jeopardy by driving headlong into that storm. It was quite windy."

"Quite windy"? That had to be the under-statement of the year. It was like saying the grass is a little green. Samuel needed to satisfy his own curiosity. "How did you drive in that tempest?"

"The storm wasn't so bad out my way, and it had already passed through here by the time I arrived. You know how tornadoes can be. They hop, skip, and jump from place to place. One house can be devastated and the next one untouched. I got here in time to observe the aftermath."

The older man stopped speaking. Samuel wasn't sure if he should wish the bishop a *gut nacht*, although it was now morning, or if he should invite him inside, or simply wait for more condemnation to be heaped on his head. Did Bishop Menno believe a single word he'd said? Samuel was spared formulating any sort of comment because the bishop must only have paused to gather more steam. Would this night, or day, or whatever it was ever end?

"Why did you stay at Atlee and Becky's place after Saloma and Malinda arrived? I thought you said Malinda came to tend to the *kinner*."

"She did. I stayed for Atlee. He was about to wear a hole through the floor with all his pacing. I tried to occupy his mind a little and lend whatever support I could. The poor fellow was a wreck." Could that be a smile lurking at the corners of the bishop's mouth? Was that the reason for the twitching facial muscles Samuel could observe even in the dim light?

"I can picture Atlee doing exactly as you said."

To Samuel's surprise, Bishop Menno chuckled, and not merely a polite little laugh. The sound erupted into a full belly laugh. Samuel wasn't sure what struck the usually somber man so funny, but he much preferred laughter to chastisement.

The bishop swiped a hand across his eyes. "I shouldn't laugh at Atlee's expense, but it is a bit humorous to picture our practical joker in years gone by pacing like every other expectant *daed*."

Samuel smiled at the memory of Atlee's

nervousness, but he wasn't at all sure he'd do any better if it was his *fraa* about to give birth. "He definitely wore the shine off the wood floor and bit off most of his fingernails."

"I suppose you did some *gut* there if you were able to keep Atlee from climbing the walls."

"I did my best."

"Just do your best not to cause Lena any problems."

"I don't have any intention of causing her problems."

"Sometimes our *gut* intentions go awry. I won't stand by and watch you lead her astray."

"Why would you think I'd do such a thing? Do I seem like an evil person? I assure you, I am not."

"I never said you were evil. A young widow can get terribly confused and make the wrong decisions. Tread lightly is all I ask."

"I don't think I have any choice. Lena scarcely wants to be anywhere within sight of me." This time a sigh did escape. Samuel was weary, frustrated, and confused. He didn't want to spar with the church leader. He wanted to go to bed.

"I believe you are a *gut* man, Samuel, and I believe Lena needs a *gut* man in her life. I'm not saying that man is you, necessarily. But don't try to force things to happen. You have been gone a long time. Things change. People change. Take one day at a time and see how things go.

You might find Lena is not right for you. Or you might eventually resume what you started years ago."

Abruptly, Bishop Menno turned and, without so much as a farewell, strode to his waiting buggy. Samuel was more perplexed than ever. So the bishop knew he and Lena had feelings for each other ten years ago. Apparently the man missed little that went on with his flock. Here he and Lena thought they'd been so secretive when they were young. Silly. How many secrets could one really have in such a small, close-knit community?

Even more disturbing was the thought that everyone assumed he wanted to pursue Lena again. Was he truly that obvious? Would Lena *kumm* around? Would her heart soften toward him? Could she give him the chance to show he cared? He so wanted to be that *gut* man Lena needed in her life.

Chapter Eighteen

If she hadn't been nursing a *boppli*, Lena would have added a few extra scoops of *kaffi* to the pot. The one cup she allowed herself in the mornings ever since she suspected she was expecting Matthew was simply not going to provide the jolt she needed to get her through the morning, let alone the day. She'd have to dig down deep inside and pull up some willpower from wherever it lurked.

For some strange reason, it always seemed that when the girls went to bed late, they got up early. Lena was going to have two cranky little ones on her hands in a couple of hours. Naptime would definitely have to be early today. At least she was able to get breakfast over and the kitchen cleaned before anyone arrived to work on the downed trees.

Lena threw out the pot of *kaffi* she'd made earlier and started over with a fresh pot in case any of the men wanted a cup. For sure and for certain they wouldn't want that nasty stuff she'd tried to swallow. When the sound of squabbling reached her from the living room, Lena figured she'd better get Mary and Eliza involved in the baking. The girls were seldom at odds with each other unless they were sick or exhausted. With a sigh and a silent plea for strength, Lena dried her hands on a checked dish towel and followed the sound of escalating voices.

She pasted a smile on her face and infused a cheerfulness she didn't feel into her manner. She clapped her hands to get the girls' attention. "Hey, girls, would you like to help me make some brownies to take to Atlee and Becky and some cookies for the men who *kumm* to work here today?"

"*Jah!*" Mary forgot all about the issue she'd had with Eliza and jumped to her feet. Her little *schweschder* followed her lead.

"Okay. What should we make?"

"Why are the men working here?"

Lena shuffled over to the window and peered outside. She crooked a finger, signaling for Mary and Eliza to join her. She lifted a girl in each arm and nodded out at the two fallen trees. "They have to saw those trees and get them out of here."

"Oh."

Mary didn't appear too interested in the trees at the moment, but Lena suspected that would change once the men began sawing. "Who's ready to bake cookies?" She lowered both girls to the floor.

"Me!" Mary cried with the enthusiasm only a four-year-old could muster. "Can we make supercookies?" Her eyes sparkled.

Catching Mary's fever, Eliza hopped up and down, repeating, "Super."

"I'll have to see if we have all the ingredients. We usually use candy and chocolate chips and little marshmallows. Let's see if we have all those things. Atlee would love those cookies for sure."

"Can we see the new *boppli*?"

"Maybe. Let's get busy with our baking."

Lena kept little hands busy stirring and rolling balls of dough. She wasn't even aware that the men had arrived to work until she heard the buzz of chain saws. Immediately Eliza ran to her *mudder* and buried her little face in Lena's skirt. "*Nee. Nee.*" Her whimpering nearly broke Lena's heart.

She stooped to pull her younger *dochder* into a hug. It seemed only natural the *kinner* would be frightened of loud noises for a while after last night's storm. "It's okay, sweetheart. It's only the men sawing those trees I showed you. Remember?" Eliza nodded against Lena's leg. "Well, that's a *gut* noise. The men are going to cut up those trees so we'll have lots of firewood this winter and can stay nice and warm. We'll watch after we finish here."

When the timer rang, Lena pried Eliza's hands loose so she could move. "Let's check this batch. Do you think they will be done?"

Eliza nodded again, but inched along right beside her *mamm* all the way to the oven.

Lena grabbed two quilted potholders to slide the trays filled with fat, golden-brown super-cookies from the oven. She gave an exaggerated sniff. "Mmm! These smell delicious. When they've cooled off a bit, we'll take some out to the men." Thank goodness they had made the brownies first, so they could clean up when the last two trays of cookies were done. She stretched to gaze out of the kitchen window. Which men had showed up to help?

He paused to catch his breath. He raised an arm to his forehead to swipe the edge of his blue shirtsleeve across his dripping brow. A quick glance at the house told him absolutely nothing. Samuel couldn't tell if anyone inside stirred or not. Most likely Lena had been up for hours taking care of the *kinner* and the household chores. He hoped she'd gotten more sleep than he had. If she'd slept for five minutes, she would have him beat.

Samuel didn't even make the attempt to go to bed after Bishop Menno finally ended his inquisition and drove down the driveway. By the time Samuel had unhitched Stockings and gotten the exhausted horse settled, he would have had one measly hour to sleep. His mind probably wouldn't have shut down in that brief time.

Instead, he made a pot of coffee so strong it could have jumped from the pot to the mug all by itself. After two cups of that foul brew and nothing to eat, Samuel expected to be jittery all morning. He only hoped he didn't cut off an arm or leg or, worse yet, injure someone else. The caffeine had him wide awake for now, but he couldn't guarantee that he wouldn't crash when its effect wore off.

Samuel turned back to the monstrous limb he'd begun sawing. He thanked the Lord Gott this mammoth tree hadn't fallen on Lena's house or on one of them. He shuddered at that thought despite the sweat running down his back like a raging river. How could he let Lena know the bishop was aware they were together last night?

That didn't sound right even in his own mind. They weren't actually together. He never wanted anyone to get the wrong idea or spread a false story. Their entire evening and early morning were perfectly innocent. Anyone with half a brain should be able to understand that. But sometimes people misconstrued the facts and added their own flourish as they passed tidbits along. Samuel truly didn't believe most people intended to be gossips, but human nature had a way of making people want to repeat a *gut* story. The embellishment came with the retelling.

He remembered a game they'd played as *kinner* where someone whispered a message that, in turn, was whispered to the next person and so on down the line. By the time the last person repeated the message aloud, the whole thing had changed. They used to howl with laughter at the mix-up. If the bishop inadvertently alluded to Samuel's nocturnal presence at Lena's house, a whole nasty can of worms could be opened. He couldn't let Lena suffer any embarrassment or ridicule because of him.

Samuel stole a glance at Bishop Menno, who helped saw the other fallen tree. The wiry man worked as hard as any of the men half his age. He didn't even look sleep-deprived. Why should he, though? He probably went straight to bed when he got home and slept like a log until he smelled *kaffi* perking. After unloading his concerns onto Samuel's shoulders, he could return home with a clear conscience. Though Samuel had no reason to feel guilty, he felt burdened all the same. He grunted as he lifted the saw to get back to work.

Ach! The bishop was merely doing his job. He didn't accuse me of any wrongdoing, but I'm sure he'll be watching my every move. That was all right. Samuel hadn't done anything to be ashamed of, nor did he intend to do so. If caring about someone and wanting to help them was a crime, then he was guilty of that alone. Didn't the Bible say to help others?

The soft, melodic voice he'd heard in his dreams over the past ten years penetrated his brain and interrupted his mind's ramblings. When had Lena *kumm* outside? She must have slipped

215

out as silently as a mouse with laryngitis. He'd never even heard a door bang closed. Maybe he could catch her attention before she approached Bishop Menno.

So Samuel did show up. Lena couldn't be sure when she glanced out the window. Bishop Menno came, too. He'd said he would, though, and she'd never known the man to go back on his word. She hazarded a quick glance at Samuel and started when she found him staring at her. She knew that expression on his face. He used to look at her the same way when he tried to send her some kind of silent message. What was he trying to tell her today?

Ach! She couldn't stare like some moonstruck teen. If Samuel needed to tell her something, he'd simply have to *kumm* right out and say it. Lena turned her back on the tall, muscular young man who was even more handsome than she remembered. She would pass out cookies to the men working on the other tree first. She spied large thermoses of water on a nearby cart but would bring tea outside to them after she doled out her treats.

The bishop paused and shot her a pointed look. Was she supposed to understand its meaning? What was it with men and their cryptic glances today? She was way too tired to try to decipher hidden meanings. She attempted a smile as she approached the man. "*Gut mariye*, Bishop Menno. *Danki* for helping out and for rounding up all these fine helpers."

"*Jah*. I told you we'd be by to get things squared away here." He yanked off his straw hat and swiped a hand across his face.

"Would you like some cookies? Freshly baked. The girls and I just took them from the oven a few minutes ago." Maybe she could hurry and slip away while the bishop stuffed a cookie in his mouth. If only he would go ahead and select one! It was all Lena could do not to pick the plumpest cookie from the pile and jam it in the man's mouth herself. She wanted to scurry back inside the house. Her nerves had been stretched to the limit.

Finally the bishop selected two medium-sized cookies. Now she could move on. He broke off a chunk of one of the cookies but spoke before he popped it into his mouth. "Lena, about last night . . ."

"Hey, Lena! Are those cookies? I could sure use one or two or three." The other men laughed at the comment.

Lena juggled the tray in one hand and put the other to her forehead to shade her eyes. "Atlee Stauffer! Is that you? Why aren't you home with your *fraa* and new *boppli*?" Lena marched in Atlee's direction, completely forgetting about Bishop Menno's words hanging in the air.

"You helped us so much. Now it's my turn to help you. Besides, my *mudder* is there. Malinda is there. Emma is there. I think every woman in the community has converged on the house. I couldn't even get near my *fraa* and *boppli*."

Lena laughed. Atlee may have grown up and taken on a man's responsibilities, but a fun-loving *bu* still lived inside and sometimes tried to escape. "How are they doing?"

"Fine, as far as I can tell."

"Did you get any sleep?"

"Becky and I dozed for a little while after she fed Grace. Can you believe it, Lena? I'm a *daed*!"

Lena squeezed the young man's arm. "You are indeed, and you'll be a fine one."

"I sure hope so." Atlee lowered his voice. "It scares me a little, to tell you the truth. I mean, Becky and I read all the booklets the midwife gave us, we love little Grace with all our hearts, but it's such a big responsibility."

"You're right about that. But we're all here to help. You and Becky will work together to give your *dochder* the best life possible. Be thankful you have each other." How nice it would be to have someone to share the burdens and joys of parenthood!

"I am thankful. Every night I thank the Lord that Becky and I have each other and now Grace, too."

Lena smiled and held out the tray. "Then the

Lord Gott will help you to be *gut* parents. Would you like a cookie?"

"Would a drowning man like a rope?"

Lena chuckled and shook her head. There would be a lot of love and laughter in the Stauffer household for sure and for certain.

"My favorite. Your supercookies." Atlee stuck one in his mouth and swiped two more from the tray.

"Hey, Atlee, leave some for the rest of us!" Without looking, Lena knew that voice belonged to Roman, one of Atlee's younger *bruders*.

"I'll save you one."

Lena smiled at the bantering and continued her rounds. She might have to whip up another batch of cookies. She called back to Atlee, "I'll try to check on Becky and Grace later, if you don't think she already has too many people fussing over her."

"Becky would always want to see you."

The men sawing and chopping the second tree stopped and watched Lena's approach. She smiled. They looked like a bunch of scholars waiting to be told it was time for recess. "Don't worry, fellows. Atlee didn't take all of them."

"That's a wonder!" someone called out.

A few of the men guzzled water and several poured a cup on themselves to cool off. "I'll bring you all some tea in a few minutes." From the corner of her eye, Lena noticed Samuel trying to catch her attention. She'd get to him in turn. She didn't want to be observed carrying on a lengthy conversation with him. She didn't need people putting two and two together and ending up with the wrong answer. She and Samuel were not a couple, nor would they ever be.

At last Lena held out the tray to Samuel. Why did the tray suddenly wobble in her hand? She'd kept it steady up until now, when it was even heavier. She needed to use her other hand to keep from dumping cookies all over the ground.

"Finally it's my turn. I'm starving." Samuel selected two cookies. He made a big show of sniffing one. "One of the sweetest smells ever." He dropped his voice to a whisper. "He knows."

"Pardon me?"

"He knows. Bishop Menno knows I was at your house."

A jolt like a lightning bolt shot through Lena's body. That must have been what the bishop had been about to say when Atlee called out for cookies. *Bless you, Atlee, for buying me a little more time to think this through.* How did Samuel know? Had the bishop already spoken to him? Did the man accuse them of wrongdoing? Surely Bishop Menno would understand the situation. Well, she would make sure he had the right information.

Samuel made a big to-do over the cookies. Lena figured he did so to cover up the whispers he interspersed with his comments. "I explained."

Lena nodded and turned away. Eyes bored into her back. They could only belong to Bishop Menno. She didn't want to give him more reasons to reprimand them if indeed he believed the worst. Lena would get the tea outside to the parched men and then look for an opportunity to set the bishop straight. She couldn't let this matter fester any longer. Even as a scholar, she did not procrastinate. She'd always learned the hardest spelling words first and worked the hardest math problems before the easy ones. If something was tough, Lena wanted to get it over with, same as Samuel, if she remembered correctly.

She hurried into the kitchen, checked on the girls, who played with a tea set on the living room floor, and made sure Matthew was sleeping soundly in the cradle that he would soon outgrow. Her last *boppli* was growing much too fast. He already rolled over and tried to get to his knees. Soon he would be crawling and then walking. Lena would need to pack away the cradle before long. She couldn't bear to part with it, though. Perhaps she would stow it in the attic for Mary and Eliza to use with their own little ones one day.

Lena snatched up a bag of paper cups and her two biggest pitchers filled with iced tea. Now to juggle it all and get outside without sloshing tea everywhere. She gasped when the door opened right as she prepared to push against it. She struggled to regain her balance. "*Ach*! Bishop Menno! I was on my way out with the tea."

"So I see. I believe it can wait a minute or two."

"Okay. I had planned to talk to you after I handed out the tea."

The man's bushy eyebrows quirked, but he did not speak.

He's waiting for me to hang myself. Well, that won't happen. I didn't do anything shameful. "I thought you were about to say something to me when Atlee interrupted begging for cookies."

The bishop allowed a teensy smile. "Atlee is still a character, ain't so?"

"That he is, but he has grown up a lot."

The man nodded. "I didn't *kumm* in to discuss Atlee. I wanted to ask about last night."

"That certainly was some storm, wasn't it?" Why did she have a sudden attack of nerves? Where did her conviction go? "Was it as bad at your house?"

"*Nee*. It seemed to jump right over us."

"That's *gut*. I guess you know Samuel helped out at Atlee and Becky's place last night, and that he brought me and my *kinner* home."

Bishop Menno nodded and waited for Lena to continue.

"It was a blessing, actually, that he was here to help me get them safely inside before the hail and howling wind began. They were pretty scared."

Lena paused to drag in a deep breath before taking the plunge. "I can assure you the visit was purely a necessity. I didn't have my own buggy and needed a way home. It was not a social call at all."

"Samuel said as much."

Samuel was right. The bishop knew all. Was that a trace of skepticism in his voice? If so, Lena needed to dispel any false notions the man might have. "I know I am a single woman now, and I intend to stay that way. I have my three *kinner*, and they keep me plenty busy. I am not looking for a man." Her cheeks burned. What an awkward conversation!

"You don't need to stay single, you know."

"Maybe not, but that's my plan."

"Sometimes the Lord Gott has other plans for us."

Lena's mouth dropped open. Did he expect her to marry again? Surely he didn't think that just because Samuel returned to Maryland she would automatically hop on the marriage wagon. "I-I never considered remarrying."

"Sometimes it's not *gut* to be alone. You have the little ones to consider. And you're still a young woman."

"But . . . but . . ."

"I'm not saying you need to rush into anything, and I'm not trying to push you to consider Samuel. He only just returned. But I can see that he cares. He can't hide that even if he tries. I'm only asking you to use caution. Don't get into compromising situations that would cast you in an unfavorable light and cause tongues to wag."

"I assure you that won't happen. Samuel would not have been in my house in the middle of the night if a tornado had not been blowing over."

"I understand." He paused to tug on his beard. "I only want what is best for you, Lena. Use *gut* sense, like you always have, but don't close yourself off to love and companionship."

The bishop turned and pulled open the door, holding it wide for Lena to pass through with her loaded tray. Sudden tears burned her eyes and clouded her vision. Frantically, she blinked them away before approaching the men with the cold drinks. That conversation certainly hadn't been what she expected. Great! Now she had yet another perplexing situation to ponder.

Chapter Nineteen

Samuel's heart plummeted to his toes when he caught sight of Bishop Menno heading toward the house. He wished he'd had a chance to tell Lena about his own inquisition. Even more, he wished the bishop would let the whole matter slide. Samuel tried to concentrate on cutting the wood to avoid amputating any body parts, but his mind had its own agenda.

What was the bishop saying to Lena? Would Samuel be able to talk to her when the other fellows left, or would Bishop Menno hang around, keeping his hawk eye on Samuel? He jumped at the slap on his back.

"Whew! These have been stubborn trees." Atlee fanned himself with his straw hat.

"*Jah.*"

"I didn't mean to startle you."

"That's okay." Or it would be okay once his heart beat normally again.

"Why are you so jumpy?"

"I'm not."

"You could have fooled me. You nearly leaped to the sky with my simple little touch."

"I wouldn't exactly call that blow to my back a 'simple touch.'"

Atlee guffawed. "Aw. It wasn't that hard."

"Let me pound on you and then you can tell me if it was a little touch."

"Okay. Okay. I suppose I don't know my own strength."

"*Jah*, but smell isn't everything."

Atlee pretended to sniff himself. "You're so funny, but I don't smell that bad."

"We all smell that bad."

"All right. Maybe we do at that. I wanted to say *danki* for keeping me from going crazy last night."

"I tried."

"It helped. I was so worried. I know childbirth is a normal thing, but things can go wrong. I was so afraid something would happen to Becky or the *boppli*."

"You don't need to apologize. I'm sure every new *daed* feels the same way."

"I guess. I kind of remember Daed pacing when Aiden was born, and he was the sixth one."

"I suppose if you care about someone, you always want them to be fine."

"How about you?"

"Huh?" Samuel wiggled as a rivulet of sweat tickled his back.

Atlee nodded toward the house. "You're worried about what the bishop might say to Lena."

The words came out as a statement, not a question. Atlee certainly didn't miss much.

Still, Samuel tried to dodge the comment. He shrugged. "Why should I be?"

Atlee rolled his eyes. "I was there last night. I know you took Lena home. Our work today tells me how bad the storm was here. I would be very surprised if you did not stay to help Lena. But if the bishop got wind of that, he might decide to have a little chat with both of you."

"What are you, a mind reader?"

"Just smart."

Samuel sighed. "The bishop showed up here to check on Lena. The tornado had passed over with a deafening roar. The *kinner* were terrified. I was holding Matthew in the background when Lena answered the door with the girls hanging on to her skirt. Bishop Menno didn't see me, but somehow he knew I was here."

"You *thought* he didn't see you. The man has more eyes than a spider."

"Apparently."

"I'm sure he understands why you were here. Becky and I can vouch for you and Lena."

"*Danki*, but I don't believe that will be necessary. I'm pretty sure he understands the situation. And I'm sure he feels it's his duty to issue a little warning, though."

"Warning?"

"To behave myself. Not to hurt Lena." Under his breath, Samuel added, "Like I would ever do that."

"Lena's been through a lot, and things haven't been easy for her."

"I understand that, but . . ."

"It actually was a blessing Becky showed up and stayed with her. I think it helped Lena trust again, in addition to helping with her *kinner* and household tasks."

"She had trust issues because of me," Samuel mumbled.

"That was a long time ago. You've been gone ten years, ain't so?"

"*Jah*."

"Well, I would think she would have gotten over your leaving in all that time. But her parents and husband all passed on, so she might have trouble believing someone else would stay around."

"And if I left once—even though it was out of my control—I could leave again. So it would be better to keep me at a distance, too. Is that what you're saying?"

"Something like that."

"When did you get so wise?"

Atlee shrugged. "Every now and then even someone like me can figure out a few things."

"Don't sell yourself short. I think you've always been a keen observer and assessor of character."

"I can tell you still care. Just go slow. Give Lena time."

"Right. We'd better finish this job." Before returning to work, Samuel glanced toward the house. Bishop Menno was just stepping outside. Their eyes locked for a moment. The older man nodded and mouthed words that Samuel interpreted as, "Give her time." Samuel nodded in return. That seemed to be a common theme. He'd have to cultivate patience and work ever so hard to stifle the urge to gather Lena into his arms and never let her go again.

Lena grappled with that strange conversation. Did Bishop Menno really expect her to marry? Soon? Life would be easier for the men in the community if they didn't have to pitch in to do work around her house in addition to all their own chores and work. But was easing everyone else's burdens a reason to marry? What about her *kinner*? Would they accept another man for a *daed*? More important, would a man accept them as his own?

She successfully avoided looking at Samuel. She slipped around the men, leaving cups of tea within reach, and beat a quick retreat. When she reached the privacy of her own kitchen, Lena raised the cool pitcher to her burning cheeks. Had all the men seen the bishop enter the house? Would they assume she had committed some transgression?

Well, she hadn't. Lena forced herself to breathe

normally. She would have stayed hidden inside the house if she hadn't promised the men more tea. Now if she could feed the girls a quick meal and get them and Matthew down for an early nap, maybe they could visit Becky later. She'd really like to get her *freind*'s opinion about all the crazy, mixed-up thoughts swirling in her head. She didn't want to burden the new *mudder*, though, so she'd have to play it by ear.

The girls were still so tired from their lack of sleep the previous evening that they cooperated beautifully at naptime. She might even have to wake them up so they didn't snooze for so long that they couldn't sleep when night fell. Lena dropped onto the rocking chair with a groan to nurse Matthew. She'd have to force her eyes to stay open so they didn't both tumble from the chair.

Lena hummed softly until the disturbing thoughts snuffed out the song. She was expected to remarry. She knew that. It was their way. But she wouldn't be forced to marry. Other folks had spoken to her about marrying again, but she had pooh-poohed the idea. The bishop, though, had never mentioned any expectations he might have.

It certainly wasn't as if there was an over-abundance of eligible men for her to choose from in their community. Old Nathaniel Yoder was just that—old. Ten days older than dirt. Not that there was anything wrong with being old. They would all be old one day, the Lord Gott willing. But at twenty-five, she was much too young to be paired with a man who must be at least seventy.

Isaiah Kurtz was a widower with six *buwe*. Six. *Buwe*. Lena truly didn't think she could handle that. And they were not docile, peaceful, little cherubs. They usually ran about shrieking or poking at one another or otherwise creating mayhem. Though they certainly were not angels themselves, she could not subject her sweet little girls and infant to that. *Ach*! She couldn't subject herself to that! Isaiah had been searching for a *fraa* and even stuttered out an invitation to her to go for a ride several months ago. She had politely refused, and he hadn't asked again.

Lena might be lonely at times, but she could be happy being a single *mudder*. Couldn't she? Her little ones kept her busy. And there was always housework, gardening, canning, and sewing to occupy her days. Any loneliness crept in at night, when Lena missed having another adult to converse with. Becky had filled much of that void when she'd stayed with them, but now Lena was back to talking to herself in the evenings.

And then there was the matter of relieving the men of their burden of caring for her place when they were already so busy. Although they never complained, it must be hard for them to take on extra duties. So remarriage had its pros and cons.

Lena didn't want to have a marriage without love, though. She had loved Joseph. Maybe she hadn't been head over heels in love, but she'd loved him in a different way. She loved the sweet, gentle, kind man he was. A person didn't need to see fireworks or hear bells ring for a marriage to be content. Sure, dramatics might create excitement, but surely other people had more ho-hum marriages and were perfectly happy.

She thought about couples she knew fairly well. Did they have an exciting or boring relationship? She smiled when Atlee's and Becky's faces floated across her mind. Of course they were newlyweds, but she couldn't imagine they would experience very many dull moments in their marriage. Phoebe and Benjamin and Malinda and Timothy all seemed to have more exciting relationships than she'd had with Joseph, but who knew for sure?

And who needed exciting? She didn't have time or energy for excitement. She was completely happy with her life. Well, mostly happy. *I wonder what it's like to be so crazy in love that you see shooting stars and feel like turning cartwheels.*

Lena vaguely remembered something akin to such feelings, but that was a long time ago. She'd stood on the fringes of adulthood back then, so quite possibly mature women didn't experience such mountaintop emotions.

"Lena?"

The deep voice calling from the back door startled her and nearly caused her to drop Matthew. "*Jah?*"

Atlee poked his head into the living room. "I'm heading home to check on Becky and Grace, and then I have a delivery to make. Some of the other men are leaving, too, but a few will keep plugging away at splitting. Would you like me to hitch up your buggy so you can visit? Or would you want to ride with me?"

Lena chuckled softly. "We tried that last night and it had a whole host of repercussions."

"I suppose it did." Atlee laughed along with her. "I can hitch up your horse."

"I appreciate your offer, but I can do it later. I'm not sure how long the girls will nap, and I don't want the poor horse to get overheated waiting for us."

"Okay. I'll see you later, then."

"For sure. *Danki* for your help."

Atlee nodded and retreated the way he'd entered. Lena wanted to call after him and ask who remained to work, but she didn't dare do that lest Atlee read something she didn't intend into her question. She'd find out soon enough when they left to visit Becky. But her plan was to slip away as quickly and as unobtrusively as possible.

Lena managed to thank the men for their hard work without looking any of them in the eye when they were finally ready to leave. She hurried to the buggy and, despite her jittery fingers, easily hitched the horse. Now she wanted to focus on Becky and Grace, not on the fern-green eyes that she knew bored into her back.

Chapter Twenty

"I must have timed that just right. All your other company has gone home." Lena smiled as she crossed the room to where Becky sat in the rocking chair with her *boppli* in her arms.

"*Jah*, I've actually been alone most of the day. Saloma, Malinda, and a few other women came early this morning. They brought some food and *boppli* items."

"*Gut*. I promise we won't stay long."

"It's fine to stay as long as you like."

"I know how tired you must be, but you certainly don't look like a woman who just gave birth." Lena paused to fix Eliza and Mary with a stern look. "Girls, please play quietly with your puzzles and toys. Becky will let you peek at Grace in a little bit." The girls immediately sat in a far corner of the room and took out their toys.

"Sit. Talk to me." Becky nodded to the armchair near her rocker.

"I'm sure everyone brought you casseroles or soup or something."

"For sure. I've got more noodles around here than a noodle factory. I'll gladly send some home with you."

"Well, I did not bring noodles. In fact, I didn't

bring anything healthy or nutritious at all. I brought chocolate."

"Great! I can't bear to look at another noodle or chicken and rice casserole. I've put pan after pan in the refrigerator. Please take some home with you."

"We'll see."

"What I want to see is the chocolate you brought. I've tried to eat healthy all these months. I need some junk food about now. I need chocolate!"

Lena laughed at her *freind*. She remembered feeling the same way after each of her *kinner* was born. "I brought dark chocolate brownies and a few of my supercookies."

"I'll start with a brownie."

"It's the hormones and the nursing that make you so hungry. Are you drinking plenty of fluids?"

"I'm trying."

"How about a cup of milk with the brownie?"

"Sure. I guess milk is healthy, so it can balance out the sweets. I might have to drink two cups because I want at least one cookie after the brownie."

Lena laughed harder. "You are starving! Didn't you eat any breakfast or some of those yummy casseroles?"

"Saloma cooked eggs and bacon for us. I had a few bites of eggs, but to be honest, the smell of bacon sort of turned my stomach inside out. She cooked the eggs in the bacon grease, so I had trouble getting those down, too. Do hormones cause the nausea?"

"Probably. You had a lot of morning sickness, so maybe your body is trying to adjust."

"I don't know why they call it 'morning sickness.' Mine lasted all day."

"If you don't think chocolate will upset your stomach, I'll cut you a brownie."

"A big one? I'm sure I'll be able to tolerate it."

"Why not? You'll burn off the calories with nursing."

"Is that why you're so skinny?"

"I've been scrawny all my life, but I'm sure the nursing and all the physical work this time of year adds to that problem."

"Well, cut yourself a brownie and then talk to me."

Lena made sure the girls played nicely and laid Matthew in Grace's cradle for a moment. She hurried to the kitchen to prepare Becky's snack. She returned to the living room balancing two napkin-wrapped brownies and a plastic cup filled with cold milk. She eased down the cup to the little side table and passed Becky her brownie.

"Are you able to eat while holding the *boppli*?"

"Sure. I understand I'll have to learn to do all sorts of things while holding her."

"True."

Becky took a big bite and rolled her eyes. "Mmm. A little taste of heaven. Now, tell me what happened."

"Let me get Matthew out of Grace's cradle."

"He's fine. Leave him there."

"Some *mudders* don't like sharing their cradles with another infant."

Becky made a clicking sound with her tongue. "Not me, for sure and for certain. Matthew is family. I helped bring him into the world. Well, I helped a little bit." She bit off another gooey chunk of brownie.

"You helped a lot." Lena eased herself onto the chair on the other side of the little table. It always amazed her how fatigue hit her as soon as she sat down, as if it was waiting for the opportunity to pounce on her. As long as she stayed moving, she could keep going.

"I was worried about you all last night. The storm hit not long after you left."

"It was pretty bad, but we got the *kinner* inside before that tornado passed over."

"We? Did Samuel stay?"

"He didn't have much choice. It certainly wasn't my preference. He helped me carry in the *kinner* before racing to check on the animals and put his own horse in the barn for protection. I settled Mary, Eliza, and Matthew in that big closet under the stairs and went out to look for

Samuel when he didn't return. I feared a tree limb had thumped him on the head."

"It looks like it got you instead."

Lena raised a hand to her sore cheek. "The wind picked up every loose object and sent them flying. I think it was a flowerpot that autographed my cheek."

"Ooh! That must have hurt."

"For sure. Samuel found me and helped me get inside. The little ones were so scared."

"I would have been, too. We didn't get such a bad storm here."

"You probably wouldn't even have noticed. You and Atlee were totally absorbed with little Grace."

"Probably. When Atlee came in a while ago, he mentioned the bishop went inside to see you. Is everything okay?"

Great! Did all the men pick up on that? The grapevine would be humming. She'd be the topic of many conversations, exactly what she did not want or need. "Let me do some cleaning for you." Lena leaped to her feet.

"You sit right back down. I know your evasive tactics, Lena Troyer."

"What evasive tactics? I can sweep or mop or do any laundry you need washed."

"I don't need anything done. Malinda swept earlier, the laundry is on the clothesline, and Saloma tidied up when she wasn't thrusting

239

a plate of noodles in my face. She must have thought I hadn't eaten in a week."

"I'm sure she just wanted you to regain your strength."

"I feel fine."

"But you're still running on adrenaline from the whole birth experience. Have you had any rest?"

"For your information, I've been napping when Grace does."

"*Gut.* So what can I do for you?"

"You can tell me what's going on behind those big, brown eyes that look awfully tired today."

"It was late, or actually early morning, by the time I could get to bed. Daylight appeared not long after I closed my eyes."

"You didn't have to return here today. Grace and I are fine."

"I needed to see that for myself. Has Laurie been by?"

"She has, and she said Grace and I are 'splendid.' Her word, not mine. Now stop changing the subject."

Lena heaved an exaggerated sigh and leaned her head against the back of her chair. "Does the man have some uncanny sixth sense?"

"Who? Bishop Menno?"

"*Jah.* How does he know everything that goes on day or night? It's strange."

Becky laughed. "I used to think so, too, and I was a little afraid of him."

"Only a little?"

"Okay. A lot. Martha is so bubbly and outgoing, but her husband seems so stern and serious."

"Do you suppose he's always been that way, or do you think the seriousness of his position changed him?"

"I'm sure the job has changed him. He takes his responsibilities seriously." Becky pinched off another bite of brownie and poked it into her mouth.

"Poor Martha. I hope the man isn't so poker-faced when they're alone." Lena shivered.

Becky laughed and coughed at the same time. "*Ach*! I need a drink."

"Sorry." Lena leaned over to hand her *freind* the cup of milk. "Are you all right?"

"I think so." She glanced down at the infant in her arms. "That didn't faze her one bit."

"Newborns generally sleep pretty soundly."

"*Gut* to know. By the way, I have seen Bishop Menno smile."

"Go on!"

"Really. His lips curved up a tiny bit at the corners, so I took that as a smile. The man was kind to me when I returned to Maryland. He believed my wild story and allowed me to join the church. I think he will be fair. Can you tell me what happened?"

Lena started with leaving Becky's house, arriving home as the storm hit, and the bishop's surprise visit. She ended with the man's admonition today to behave herself and his urging to consider remarriage. "I'm completely *befuddled*."

"By Samuel?"

"*Nee*, silly. By the bishop."

Becky inched forward in her chair, taking care not to jostle Grace, and reached out to pat Lena's knee. "He might have a point."

"What do you mean?"

"Have you ever thought of remarrying? I know we talked about getting married a long time ago, before Atlee and I got together, but have you thought of it recently?"

"Why would now be any different? Once in a blue moon the notion creeps into my mind, but I chase it right back out."

"I thought you might be a little lonelier now that I don't live with you anymore. I'm not saying I was the best company ever, but you know what I mean."

"You were the best company, and I do miss you, but that doesn't make me want to run right out and get married."

As if on some mysterious cue, the back door opened and heavy footsteps clomped toward the living room. Lena turned toward the doorway right as Atlee entered.

"Atlee, you're home already!"

"*Jah*. I handled the delivery and then said I wanted to get home to check on my girls."

How sweet. Lena caught the loving gaze the couple exchanged. What a blessing they had found each other.

Atlee crossed the room in three long strides. He bent to kiss Becky's cheek and to pat the bundle in her arms.

Lena's eyes misted at the tender scene. Joseph would never have kissed her cheek or even held her hand if another living soul had been present. Atlee, apparently, didn't have any qualms about showing his love for his *fraa* and *boppli*. The sight almost made Lena want to run out and get married. Almost. Not every man was as open or affectionate or even as considerate as Atlee. How would she find such a man? She wouldn't. That was not her goal. But what did she want?

"Lena?"

"Huh?" She looked from Becky to Atlee. What had she missed while her mind took a hike?

"Atlee asked if you brought more of your scrumptious cookies."

"Ah, but what do I see here, dear *fraa*? Could it be the remains of a brownie or a cake?"

"Brownie. Dark chocolate." Becky licked her lips. "It was delicious."

"And you didn't save me a morsel?"

Lena burst out laughing at Atlee's hangdog expression. "Fear not. There is a whole pan full of brownies in the kitchen. I don't know which of you has the bigger sweet tooth." She shook her head at them. "Poor little Grace is headed for a life filled with cavities or obesity."

"My little girl will only eat healthy foods." Atlee looked down his nose as if he was superior to Lena.

"Like her *daed*? You might have to make a tweak in your diet, my *freind*."

"I'm going to tweak it right into the kitchen this very moment."

Lena chuckled, pulled the embroidered pillow from behind her, and hurled it at the retreating man. "He's crazy, Becky."

"I know."

"But you wouldn't have him any other way."

"I love him exactly as he is."

Lena struggled to ignore that familiar little pang of longing that shot through her again. "You are blessed."

"Indeed."

"I'm going to run out to get your clothes off the line while Matthew is content."

"You don't have to do that."

"I want to. Somehow I can't picture Atlee folding sheets without wrapping himself up like a mummy." Becky's laughter followed Lena out of the room.

When she returned, Lena lifted Matthew from the cradle and laid him on a blanket on the floor. She scattered a few toys around so he could practice lifting, reaching, and rolling. Then she took Grace in her arms and rocked to and fro. "Why don't you go do whatever you need to do while I hold her?"

"She'll be ready to nurse again soon."

"That's all right. She isn't eating her fists yet or anything. Go take a bathroom break or grab a cookie."

"I do need a quick break."

"Take your time."

Becky nodded and whisked from the room as Lena swayed and hummed to Grace. Her mind ambled without an agenda. How sweet this newborn was! Matthew was rapidly leaving this stage behind as he learned to do more and more things. Soon he'd be toddling behind his *schweschders*. Lena experienced a pang of regret that he would be her last *boppli* and her only *bu*. Wouldn't he?

If she gave Isaiah Kurtz a chance, she'd have six more *buwe*. Rambunctious, loud *buwe*. She shuddered, startling Grace.

"What was that face about?" Becky giggled.

"What face?" Lena knew she had shivered, but she didn't realize she had made any comical expression.

"That scrunched-up forehead, wrinkled nose, and I-smell-a-dead-fish look?" Becky tried to demonstrate but burst into a fit of giggles.

Lena couldn't help but join in the laughter. "I was just thinking!"

"Of what? Cleaning toilets?"

"My, but living with Atlee must have turned you into a clown."

"Well, you certainly didn't seem to be having any pleasant thoughts. What or who were you thinking about?"

Grace finally worked a tiny fist to her mouth and sucked on it. Her paper-thin eyelids fluttered. Her eyes would pop open any second. She'd probably test those lungs, too. "Are you ready, Mamm? This little one is giving her hunger cues."

Becky gingerly lowered herself to the rocking chair and held out her arms for her *boppli*. Lena dropped to the floor to play with Matthew and coax him to crawl while Grace nursed.

"Your thoughts?" Becky prompted.

"I was thinking that Matthew was my last *boppli* and my only son."

"Not necessarily."

"Unless I give into Isaiah Kurtz's invitation to go for a ride and see where that leads."

Becky laughed again. "Because you made that awful face, I can tell how much that idea appeals to you."

"Six rowdy *buwe*. Would you want to take that on?"

Becky shook her head. "I can't say that is a job I would want to tackle. I'm completely happy with my little girl."

"Exactly. I'm happy with my three."

"You'd be happy with other *kinner* of your own."

"With Isaiah?" Lena knew her voice emerged in a nerve-grating screech but couldn't control it.

Becky laughed so hard that little Grace's eyes popped open to stare at her. "I assume that isn't an appealing idea, either."

"I'm *gut* with being a single parent."

"There is another option."

Chapter Twenty-One

Lena began gathering up the toys surrounding Matthew. She was pretty sure she knew where this conversation was headed and did not want to travel down that road. "You won't let me do anything around the house, so I should get these rascals of mine out of here so you and Atlee can enjoy some of those noodle casseroles for supper."

"There you go again—running away from something and hoping that will make it vanish into thin air."

"I'm not running away."

"*Jah*, you are. Lena Troyer, you are the strongest woman I know. You've borne a lot on those tiny shoulders of yours and carried your burdens well. I haven't known you to be afraid of much, except maybe big, hairy spiders. But you certainly are afraid to face your feelings."

"I don't have any particular feelings to face or fear."

"I think if you examine your heart and if you are honest with yourself, you will find that is not true."

"Are you saying I am a liar?" Lena wagged a finger at her *freind*.

"*Nee*, but you are in denial."

Lena stuffed toys inside her bag and gathered her *boppli* close. "I'm not doing any such thing."

"I'm not trying to make you angry, Lena. Help me understand why you won't even give Samuel Mast the time of day, much less a chance to earn your trust and affection."

"I've traveled down that dead-end road before and I'm not interested in doing it again."

"You were practically *kinner* then. Would you hold a grudge for something he couldn't help?"

"I'm not holding a grudge." Lena tickled Matthew, eliciting a string of giggles that brought a smile to his *mamm*'s lips.

"Okay. Blaming, then. You blame Samuel for the actions of his parents?"

"Of course not. He didn't have a choice about leaving with his family. I understand that."

"Then what's the problem?"

"He didn't care enough to contact me all these years, so why should he be allowed to traipse back into my life as if nothing ever happened?"

"Have you given him an opportunity to explain?"

"It's not important. I've moved on. My life is fine the way it is."

"We all could use *freinden*."

"I have *freinden*."

"Of course you do. And you know Atlee and I are always here for you. But it seems like Samuel is bending over backward to show he cares. Can't you allow him to at least be a *freind*?"

Lena shrugged. "I don't know. Maybe a casual acquaintance."

"An acquaintance is someone you nod and smile at and then go on your merry way."

"Exactly. That's all I need from Samuel." Lena picked up the blanket Matthew had been lying on.

"Can't you reconsider?"

"Why are you championing his cause? You probably don't even remember the *bu* of ten years ago."

"True, but I see a kind man who obviously has some sort of feelings for you. Strong feelings, I'd say."

Lena shrugged again.

"Don't close yourself off to a possible relationship, my *freind*. That's all I'm saying."

Becky's words echoed Bishop Menno's words from earlier in the day. Were those two in cahoots? They sure seemed eager to link her with Samuel Mast. Well, she had lots more to consider than just herself and Samuel. She had three little ones who needed the best she could give them.

"You deserve happiness, Lena, and your *kinner* deserve a *daed*. I don't mean you should rush into anything you aren't ready for or don't want to do. You were so helpful to me and I want to return the favor. I want you to be as happy as I am with

Atlee. It's certainly your choice. Just consider all the options."

Lena's throat ached from holding back sobs. Her eyes threatened to unleash a flood of tears. All she could do was nod.

"Hey, you aren't leaving already, are you?" Atlee's deep voice boomed across the room, penetrating the cloud of solemnity hanging over the room.

"We had a very late night, as you might recall. I need to get these little ones home, fed, and tucked into bed."

"Speaking of fed, you are going to take some of these casseroles off our hands, aren't you? I mean, we'd love to share our bounteous gifts with you." Atlee bent at the waist in an exaggerated, sweeping bow.

Becky and Lena both broke into giggling fits.

"Please. I'm begging you to take some of this food home with you. Then you won't have to cook and you can all go to bed early." Atlee's pleading look was as comical as his speech.

"But this food was meant for you and Becky so she won't have to cook for a few days."

"There are enough noodle casseroles in there for a whole slew of people for weeks. Trust me!"

"Atlee, you're a big eater. You'll need that food."

"I've never eaten that much casserole in my life. Please, please grab a few bowls to take with you. I'm begging."

Lena looked over her shoulder at Becky and winked. She was enjoying Atlee's antics and was glad he hadn't outgrown his fun-loving spirit. "Atlee, those ladies who took the time to prepare that food meant it for your family. They would be crushed to know you gave it away."

"I won't tell if you won't. I promise."

"Should I make him beg some more, Becky?"

Becky finished nursing Grace and rearranged the blanket. "This is rather fun, but I suppose we should put him out of his misery."

"*Danki*, dear *fraa*. Now will you please convince this stubborn woman to take home some food?"

"Who are you calling stubborn?"

"You. Now *kumm* pick out whatever you'd like."

Lena still hesitated. She hated to take food meant for Becky's family.

"Please, Lena, before the man drives us all crazy. Take a look at the offerings and take something home with you."

"Take a lot of somethings," Atlee mumbled.

Lena laughed. How *wunderbaar* it must be to have a convivial, playful marriage. Her relationship with Joseph had been much more subdued and not very playful at all. It had been amicable and caring, but not particularly romantic or fun. A person could live without romance and fun, but they sure would be nice.

She trailed behind Atlee. "All right, let me see what you've got."

Atlee opened the refrigerator and pointed to the dishes jammed inside. "Hey, would you mind dropping off a dish of food for Samuel? I told him I'd send him something. He was such a big help to me."

Lena's jaw dropped. The only sound she could squeak out was, "What?"

"You'll pass right by his place. It would save me a trip out. I'd like to stay with Becky and Grace."

Atlee knew how to get to her. It was important for the little family to bond. Lena knew that. She also knew she didn't want to go anywhere near Samuel Mast's house.

"Please?"

"Oh, all right. But for the record, I'm not happy about this. I'm only doing it because I love you all."

Samuel had worked in his shop the few hours since returning home from Lena's place, mainly organizing his supplies and straightening up because he didn't have any shoeings scheduled. He and a few other fellows had finished splitting and stacking wood for Lena and then dragged the useless branches to the woods to rot and return to nature. He tried to tell himself he should not feel slighted that Lena had not spoken to him when she left. She had issued a blanket *"danki"* to everyone and hustled the girls to the buggy.

He shouldn't have been surprised, though. She'd probably experienced humiliation or shame or maybe even anger that the bishop had approached her in full view of any of the men who glanced up from their tasks. He shouldn't feel at fault—he needed to bring her and the little ones home last night and he needed to ensure their safety—but guilt crept in all the same. Lena would never warm up to him if he got her into a pickle with the bishop. Would she warm up to him anyway?

Patience, Samuel, patience. How often had he repeated that mantra and still he had not mastered the virtue? He would try very hard to be patient. Success was doubtful, though. He was the kind of fellow who wanted to step in, fix things up, and move on to the next project. He was pretty sure he shouldn't compare a relationship to some sort of project. He really did know the difference. He knew feelings had to grow and that relationships took time to develop. He would have to be attentive and helpful without being overbearing. He would have to be kind and loving—not hard to do with Lena. Most of all, he would have to give her time.

An approaching buggy called Samuel back to the present. Would a customer really be arriving this late in the day? He was so weary, but he needed to build up his business. He'd probably have to schedule the person for tomorrow unless he wanted to wait around while Samuel prepared his tools and got everything ready.

He shaded his eyes with one grubby hand and studied the buggy that had drawn close enough for him to count the occupants. One adult. It looked like a woman. Two smaller shapes. *Kinner?* Could it be Lena? His heart lurched and every drop of moisture evaporated from his throat. What would she be doing here? This must be pretty important because she probably figured the bishop would be keeping an eagle eye on her. He hoped nothing was wrong.

Samuel set out at a brisk walk that turned into a jog. Every thump of his heart was a prayer. *Please, Gott, let all be well.* When he heard Lena call, "Whoa," he raced the last few steps to the buggy. "Lena." He panted and tried to drag in enough oxygen to continue. "Is something wrong?" He tried to look past Lena to make sure the little ones were all right.

Mary and Eliza smiled, waved, and offered a shy, little "hi."

"Where's Matthew. Is he okay?"

"He's in his safety seat behind me. He's fine. I'm so sorry I frightened you. Truly, there is nothing wrong."

Samuel's relief was so great that he practically collapsed against the buggy. He'd always cared about Lena, but how had he grown to care about the *kinner* in such a short time? Granted, they were part of Lena, which made them special to start with. But each one had unique personalities and qualities. He'd begun to figure that out and appreciate their differences in all his time with them—was it just last night? It seemed eons ago.

He licked his dry lips and swallowed the dust in his throat. His pummeling heart had slowed to a respectable rate. He reached for a tone of voice somewhere between playful and serious. "Then to what do I owe the pleasure of a visit by three lovely ladies and a dapper fellow?" The girls giggled. They might not have understood his words, but they picked up on his teasing manner.

"Atlee said he promised to send you a casserole or two. He's up to his eyeballs in noodles." Lena gave a nervous-sounding laugh.

Samuel saw her picking at her fingernails, even though she'd tried to hide her hands in the folds of her dress. She didn't need to be nervous around him. He'd never do anything to hurt her, at least not deliberately. She probably believed differently, however. A tiny wave of disappointment washed over him that she had visited at Atlee's bidding and not because she wanted to see him, but any excuse to see Lena was a *gut* one.

He chuckled, hoping to put Lena at ease. "He

did say he wanted to unload some of the food filling his kitchen."

"I brought you two different things. One is a tuna noodle casserole. Now don't wrinkle up your nose. I'm sure it's delicious."

"I'm sure. What's the other one?"

"A spaghetti casserole."

"I'll start with that one."

Lena laughed a genuine laugh this time. "Anyway, you'll need to return the dishes to Becky and Atlee so they can get them back to the rightful owners." She leaned closer to him and lowered her voice as if there were spies around to catch her words. "And keep this hush-hush. Becky doesn't want to hurt anyone's feelings by giving away their food."

Samuel had the sudden, almost irresistible urge to pull her even closer, but he didn't dare even touch her. He pretended to zip his lips and mumbled, "I won't breathe it to a soul." The girls giggled again. "In fact, I'll put the food in my own bowls so I can return these tomorrow."

"Do you have bowls?" Lena immediately clapped a hand over her mouth.

Samuel chuckled at Lena's obvious embarrassment. "I do indeed. I didn't set up housekeeping totally without supplies. I don't have a lot of extra things, but I'm okay on the basics."

"Of course you are. Forgive me, Samuel. I didn't mean to imply you lapped your food out of cardboard containers and swigged milk from the carton. Sometimes my tongue takes off completely on its own without waiting for directions from my brain."

Samuel threw back his head and laughed. "I admit mine does the same thing. I do have to confess that I have drunk straight from the milk carton a time or two, but I've learned some manners. I always use a cup now."

Lena laughed. Her gaze roved over the yard, and Samuel wondered what she thought. He'd been working very hard to get the place into shape. He knew it was ridiculous, but he wanted her to like his changes. He craved her approval of his handiwork. That might be prideful or wrong, but he needed some encouragement, some little sign that she liked the result of his efforts.

When a huge smile spread across Lena's small face, Samuel nearly melted. That smile still reached down to caress his soul as it used to do, as it always would even if they never got back together.

"*Ach*, Samuel! The flowers are beautiful. Begonias. Big, bushy, white and crimson begonias. They're splendid. You did buy every color, didn't you?"

"I couldn't decide which to get. When we planted the flowers at your house, I told you I remembered how much you liked begonias."

"You did. And you said you bought a lot of

them, but I wasn't expecting this many. Your yard looks very pretty."

"I was hoping you would like what I've done so far. I even remembered which colors you said you liked together."

"My! You remembered all that?"

"And so much more." *Like how soft your little hand was between my two big, rough ones. How your eyes dance and crinkle when you're happy. How your laughter has a quality unmatched by any musical instrument I've ever heard anywhere. How you used to look at me with eyes full of promise and love.* Jah, *I remember many things.*

Lena dipped her head, but not before he caught sight of the pink stain that crept up her neck and across her cheeks. Could she be remembering similar things?

She cleared her throat. "Well, it looks like you've put in a lot of hard work. From what I can see, the house and yard look *wunderbaar.*"

All for you, dear Lena. You are in my mind with each task I undertake. "*Danki.* I'm still working on things."

"It all takes time, especially when you are also working or babysitting rambunctious *kinner,* or calming an expectant *daed* at the same time." She laughed. "I'm impressed with all your work."

Samuel wished he could invite her in to show her the inside of the house and to get her opinions

259

and advice. After all, he hoped she would live there with him one day. "*Danki*, Lena. That means a lot to me."

"Well, I'd better get going before the, uh, these girls start whining for supper."

He knew she had started to say, "before the bishop drove by," or anyone else who might report to the church leader. He understood. "Sure. I appreciate your dropping off the food."

"Not a problem."

He was sure it had been a big problem. He was equally sure it had been Atlee's or Becky's idea for Lena to bring the casseroles, especially because he didn't really need the food. He doubted she would have actually volunteered for the job. He took the dishes she passed to him and promised to return them to Becky. He stood still and watched as she expertly turned the buggy to head down the driveway. He waved and watched until the buggy rolled out of sight. Another lonely evening stretched out before him.

Chapter Twenty-Two

Lena collapsed onto the rocking chair she'd pulled close to the open living room window, hoping to catch whatever hint of breeze whispered into the room. Drained. That's what she was. Totally and completely drained of energy, motivation, and even desire to move. If she'd had sense, she would have held off this crash until she reached her bed.

After arriving home and tending to the horse, she whirled through the kitchen to put supper on the table. She silently thanked Atlee and Becky for insisting she bring food home with her. If the *kinner* had had to wait for her to cook something, they would have had a serious meltdown that wouldn't have been at all pretty.

Lena had cleaned up the kitchen, bathed the *kinner*, read a Bible story followed by prayers, and tucked three little bodies into bed. If she hadn't had to return to the lower level of the house to check the doors and windows, she would surely have crawled into her own bed, clothes and all. But she'd become slightly paranoid about making sure downstairs windows were closed and locked at night ever since becoming a widow.

She set the chair in motion and leaned her head against the thick back cushion. She was too tired even to sigh. That shouldn't be right, should it? Maybe she needed to buy a bottle of vitamins. Extra-strength ones.

Lena closed her eyes. The house had finally grown silent. Even the creakings and groanings of the old building had ceased. Now she could concentrate on the world awakening outside the one window she'd left open. Crickets sang, bullfrogs croaked, and somewhere in the distance an owl hooted. Nature's symphony. If she'd been sitting out on the step, Lena might have glimpsed a shooting star, but she was too weary to walk that far. The chair gave a soft squeak as if in answer to the critters outside. Ever so gradually, the tension in her shoulders and back eased.

She deliberately put tomorrow's chores out of her mind. She would need to deal with those soon enough. If she could make her body obey, she'd drag herself out of this chair, but it refused to cooperate. She settled more deeply into the cushion and turned her head slightly so the wisps of breeze skimmed across her face, tickling the little hairs along her neck like a miniature caress.

Images of bushy begonias floated by right beneath her eyelids. She squeezed her eyes tighter to make them disappear. They didn't. Her brain apparently had its own agenda as well. She was amazed that Samuel remembered so much from the past, things she'd pushed from her own memory.

Lena supposed that was the sort of relationship they had back then. Although they'd been young, they'd shared the most minute details of their lives and were happy to do so. Of course there had been excitement and fun, stolen hugs and whisper-soft kisses on the cheek, but there had been seriousness as well. She remembered Samuel's talk of wanting his own business, along with farming and raising animals. Sheep. He'd mentioned sheep because he knew how much she enjoyed knitting. She smiled at the memory of Samuel taking her hand and squeezing it as his excitement mounted. He was smart and capable. He could do whatever he set his mind to. She hadn't any doubt about that.

This would never do. Thoughts of Samuel Mast should never linger in her mind. She needed to sweep them from the corners of her memory. The past was past. Samuel was past. Joseph was past. Mary, Eliza, and Matthew were present. Who knew what the future held?

The next church Sunday, Lena did her best to maintain a low profile. She skittered out of the Swareys' big, swept-clean barn as soon as the last prayer concluded and speed-walked to the house with Matthew bobbing in her arms. She quickly busied herself in the kitchen and let the younger, unmarried girls handle the serving.

All of this was because she'd picked up on Samuel's vibes during the church service and caught him staring at her several times. Lena couldn't have Bishop Menno or anyone else thinking there was something brewing between the two of them because that was absolutely not the case.

After they finished eating, Lena let Mary and Eliza play under the watchful eyes of some older girls. Matthew napped with other little ones, so Lena could help restore the kitchen to order. Becky sidled up to her and whispered, "I got the dishes you put in the buggy."

"I didn't put any dishes in there. Remember, I brought them to your house the last time I visited."

"*Ach*! That's right." Becky tapped her head. "I don't know what's wrong with my brain these days."

"It's new *mudder* brain. You're sleep-deprived and your whole day revolves around a needy *boppli*. We've all been there." Lena patted her *freind*'s arm.

"It does go away, ain't so? Things do get back to normal?"

Lena smiled at Becky's worried expression. "It will be a new normal because your whole life has changed, but your brain will function correctly again."

Becky heaved an enormous sigh. "That's a

relief. I guess Samuel must have put those dishes in the buggy."

"That's likely, I'd say. Hey, where is that sweet little Grace?" Lena didn't have any desire to discuss Samuel Mast.

"Poor thing has been oohed and ahhed over so much that she's completely tuckered out. She's sleeping."

"Then you should be resting as well."

"I need to visit a bit. Maybe talking to other women will help clear the cobwebs out of my head."

Lena dried the last bowl and hung the dish towel on a hook to dry. "You're doing fine, Becky. Being a new *mudder* is hard work."

"And I only have one. How do you manage with three?"

"I get into a routine, and the *kinner* know the routine, too. You helped me establish that when you lived with me. Mary and Eliza are getting big enough to help out a little, too."

"They are terrific little girls."

"I think so, but I may be just a tad biased." Lena playfully elbowed the younger woman and laughed.

"Look out there." Becky nodded toward the open window.

Lena's gaze followed Becky's until it rested on a group of young *kinner* playing with none other than Samuel Mast. It appeared that he was attempting to teach them some game.

"Isn't it great how he takes such an interest in the little ones?"

Lena's heart skipped a beat and then banged. It looked like Samuel would be the topic of conversation despite her best effort to avoid it. She couldn't keep the hint of a smile from her lips. He did look sweet out there with the *kinner*. She started to turn away but whirled back with a gasp. For an instant she felt faint. There stood her Mary, clasping Eliza's hand, watching Samuel's every move. Mary was so intent that she didn't even swat at the big horsefly buzzing right past her. Sadness stabbed Lena's heart. She couldn't deny the obvious, and the sudden realization nearly made her sob aloud. Her little ones needed a *daed*.

She couldn't hear his precise words, but Samuel must have called to the girls. She saw him wave a hand, beckoning to them. He didn't need to call twice. Mary set off at a trot, towing her younger *schweschder* behind her. Lena heard childish giggles. Even though the other *kinner* surrounding Samuel were a bit older, he didn't hesitate to include the little girls. Bless him! They needed that attention. Apparently they craved it more than she knew.

Maybe Lena should step outside and stay close by in case some of the older ones became a little too aggressive. *Nee*, Samuel would watch over them. He wouldn't let anyone pick on Mary and Eliza, or ridicule them if they didn't catch on to the game quickly enough. Lena wasn't sure how she knew this, but she was as sure of that fact as she was that the sun would rise in the east in the morning.

"The girls will have fun. Samuel will watch over them, don't you think?"

Becky spoke Lena's thoughts aloud. Lena nodded. "I expect so."

"Would you like to get a cookie or two and go watch them?"

"You and your sweet tooth!"

"I was thinking about you. You didn't eat very much unless you sampled food while you were hiding here in the kitchen."

"I wasn't hiding, not exactly."

"Exactly what would you call it, then?"

"Helping. Getting food ready for all the hungry folks waiting for it."

"I see."

Lena swatted her *freind*'s arm. "Get your cookies if you want them. We'll peek in at the *bopplin* and then step out for air, if you want. See, I can be sociable."

"Wonders never cease."

While waiting for Becky, Lena remained near the window but out of direct view of anyone outside. The warmth of the kitchen had made her drowsy. She could almost drift off to sleep on her feet.

"How nice to play with the young ones."

The sugary voice drifting in from outside instantly pulled Lena from her drowsy stupor. She crept a little closer to the window and tilted her head only enough to put a face with that voice.

"I don't know if you remember me, Samuel. I'm Sarah Swarey. I'm sorry I haven't had the chance to speak with you or to welcome you home before now."

Sarah. Emma Swarey Stauffer's cousin. If Lena remembered correctly, Sarah was older than her and maybe even older than Samuel. The girl had never married. Lena wondered why. Sarah wasn't displeasing to look at, with her light brown hair and eyes and a smattering of freckles across her nose. Rather ordinary, but there was nothing wrong with ordinary. Lena stood rooted to the spot and practically held her breath so she wouldn't miss any of the exchange between Sarah and Samuel.

"*Danki*, Sarah. I do remember you." Samuel turned away and directed his attention to a little *bu*. "Here. Like this." He demonstrated how to flick his wrist to throw a Frisbee. Lena didn't see how the Frisbees came to be there, but green, yellow, blue, and red plastic discs dotted the yard. Samuel must have bought out the discount store's entire supply and brought them here for the little ones to play with. How thoughtful.

"How thoughtful of you to bring toys for the *kinner*."

Somehow when Sarah voiced Lena's thought, the words sounded phony. *Stop it, Lena. You aren't being at all nice.*

"Well, this group is too young for the volleyball game and too old to play with the toddlers. I've been watching them for several weeks and thought this might be a *gut* activity for them."

"Splendid idea!"

Splendid idea! Lena singsonged the words in her head and instantly chastised herself. *What is wrong with me?*

"What are you looking at?" Becky held out an oatmeal raisin cookie.

"N-nothing. Just, uh, the *kinner*." Absently, Lena took the cookie from Becky's hand and bit off a chunk.

Becky scooted closer so she could peer out. "What is she doing there?"

"Shhh!"

"I don't think she can hear me."

"Someone else might."

"Pshaw! If I didn't know any better, I'd say she was making a play for Samuel."

"Making a play?"

"You know, trying to get his interest, his attention."

"Do you think so?"

"I do. You'd better get out there and interfere."

Lena shook herself out of her fog. "What are you talking about, girl? I don't need to be involved in their conversation."

"You can't lose your chance." Becky slapped her hand over her mouth.

"My chance for what?"

"To get to know Samuel again."

"We know each other as well as we need to. I already told you that Samuel and I are the past. If Sarah is his future, then so be it. It would be *gut* for him to have someone to share that house and his life."

"But he should be sharing it with you. I can see how much he cares about you and your *kinner*, even if you're too stubborn to admit it to yourself."

"I think Sarah might be just right for Samuel. They can fill that house with their own little ones." If she really believed that, though, why did her breath catch somewhere between that lump in her throat and her nose, making her want to cough or gag or cry?

"Sarah is too old for him." Becky stomped her foot like a defiant two-year-old.

Lena laughed. "What has age got to do with anything? People of all ages get together and are perfectly happy."

"Well, she should have looked for someone more her age a long time ago."

"She can't be more than a few years older than Samuel. That's not so bad."

"She should seek out Isaiah Kurtz. He's been looking for a *fraa* for some time now. And she could be *mudder* to his six *buwe*. They surely do need some help. Maybe I'll go right out there and steer Sarah in that direction."

"You will do nothing of the kind, Becky Stauffer. Samuel is a grown man and is free to make whatever choices he wants."

"He doesn't need to be distracted by Sarah while he's waiting around for you to *kumm* to your senses."

Lena elbowed the younger woman. "You're being silly. Sarah is probably only trying to be polite."

"Probably not. I know flirting when I see it. Trust me on that." She nudged Lena back. "Listen."

"It's rude to eavesdrop," Lena whispered.

"Sometimes it's necessary. Listen."

As she peeked around Becky, Lena glimpsed Sarah batting her eyes and twirling a *kapp* string around an index finger. Maybe Becky was right about the flirting after all.

"You have such a sweet, gentle way with the little ones." Sarah's slightly deep, husky voice blew in the window.

"I like *kinner*," Samuel replied, keeping his focus on the Frisbee-throwing.

"That's obvious. Maybe you'll have a whole passel of them one day."

Lena saw Samuel shrug but didn't hear any reply.

"Will you be attending the singing this evening?" Sarah stepped ever so slightly closer to the object of her pursuit.

"She doesn't still go to singings, does she?" Becky hissed.

"How should I know? I haven't attended one in a hundred years."

"Do you suppose Samuel has been going?"

"I haven't any idea whatsoever."

"Shhh!" Becky clutched Lena's hand, squishing the oatmeal cookie between them. "Let's see what he says."

"I probably won't." Samuel snatched Eliza before she wandered into the path of a flying disc and swung her high in the air. His smile, a genuine one unlike the polite smile he gave Sarah, lit his whole face. Lena could see that even from her distant hiding place.

Sarah persisted a moment longer. "Well, I'll be there. If you change your mind, it would be fun to chat." At that, she sauntered away, turning once to smile over her shoulder at the man who hadn't even watched her leave.

When he glanced toward the house, Lena drew away from the window, pulling Becky with her. "Do you think he saw us?"

"I doubt it." Becky struggled for balance. "You moved so fast you almost pulled me down."

"Oops! Sorry." Lena tried to wiggle her fingers, which seemed to be stuck together. She looked down at the smashed cookie adhering like glue to her hand. "Ew!"

Chapter Twenty-Three

Samuel pondered the day as dusk fell while he finished the necessary outdoor chores. He let loose the huge sigh that had been building for hours. Would it always be like this? He wasn't sure what he expected to happen when he returned to Maryland. He'd had his hopes, but so far Lena had kept quashing those. She mumbled a quick "*danki*" in his direction when she slipped away from the Swareys' before he could bat an eye.

That was depressing, to be sure, but he realized she would need time. What had taken him by surprise were the single, young women who tried to flirt with him, or whose *mudders* kept bringing him one so-called delectable treat after another, lauding the baking skills of their *dochders*. Most, he feared, needed a bit more practice in the kitchen.

It wasn't that Samuel was picky or hard to please. To tell the truth, he much preferred fruit or simple cookies and brownies to gooey shoofly pie, pecan pie, thick layer cakes, or heavier treats. He was polite, though. He always said "*danki*" and then sent his visitors on their way as soon as possible. How did he tell these ladies he was not looking for a *fraa*? Well, he was, but he had found her. He simply needed her to realize that.

Samuel didn't have a clue what he would have done earlier in the afternoon if he hadn't had the *kinner* to run interference. Sarah Swarey was the last person he expected to approach him. Why wasn't she married by now? She must be approaching thirty. He was twenty-eight, and he remembered she was a couple of grades ahead of him when they were scholars. Hadn't she courted any fellows in all this time? Were there any her age that still attended singings?

He had a sneaky feeling that Sarah's clutches would be harder to escape. The other girls were just that. Girls. Young. They had plenty of *buwe* to choose from and plenty of time to do it. He suspected their *mudders* would like to see them paired with a fellow like him, who was more settled and could provide for them. Probably most of the girls wouldn't really be interested in him, though. They would still want to go out and have fun, not be stuck with a homebody like him.

Sarah, though, would be different. She was probably getting desperate to get married and start a family. So why hadn't she? She was attractive enough—not beautiful, but far from ugly. She seemed nice. Why hadn't she hit it off with any of the fellows? Maybe she was too picky or too pushy. Or maybe things hadn't clicked with anyone. If there was *nee* spark, there would be *nee* fire. It was a wonder her *mudder* hadn't sent her off to visit relatives in another state, where her chances of finding a husband might be greater. *Jah*, he definitely had to watch out for Sarah Swarey, make sure he was never alone with her.

A second, smaller sigh slipped out. Belonging somewhere could be a huge problem. Where did he belong? He certainly didn't fit in with the young, unmarried fellows. They were nice enough for sure, but a little immature for him. He'd spent some time with Atlee, Atlee's older *bruder* Sam, and Timothy Brenneman and enjoyed their company. Even though they were all a bit younger, Atlee and Sam were already married and Timothy would most likely be marrying their *schweschder*, Malinda, in the fall.

Samuel felt at ease enough with the older men until they started talking about their families. Would he ever have a family to discuss? His *mamm* always told him the Lord Gott had a plan for everyone, but sometimes he wondered if the Lord had forgotten him. He prayed, but he never heard a voice or witnessed a flash like a lightning bolt to give him reassurance he was heading in the right direction. Rather, he simply stuck one foot out in front of the other and plodded on one day at a time, hoping he followed where the Lord wanted him to go.

One thought that never left him all the years he was away was the firm belief he should return to Maryland. He planned for the day he would return. When he wrote to Bishop Menno and the property transfer went through without a hitch, he knew the Lord Gott had a hand in the whole thing. He even got the impression he would have the bishop's approval if Lena ever gave him a chance.

But would that ever happen? Sure, he hadn't been back long, but he was basically the same person he was when he left, a bit older and, hopefully, a lot wiser. He'd been shocked a few years ago when he first got wind that Lena had married, but he couldn't fault her for that. When he discovered his letters had never reached her, he gained a better understanding of the betrayal and rejection she must have experienced. He'd never intended to cause her so much pain.

From time to time a flicker of anger tried to ignite when Samuel thought of all those letters. He always tried to douse it before it burst into a roaring fire again. He'd forgiven his *daed* for sabotaging his communication, for preventing any of them from communicating with folks from the past, and for trying to burn bridges behind them.

Poor Daed. He could pity the man now that he was gone. None of them knew at the time that he had been continually trying to flee his demons. The family, and probably everyone else who knew them, assumed he had an insatiable need for adventure, which prompted his need to keep uprooting his family to find something better or more interesting. But Samuel had discovered the truth, the real reason Daed had packed them up and moved great distances at the drop of a hat, and it wasn't pretty.

Lena decided to sit on the front step instead of collapsing in the rocking chair as she usually did after getting her three rambunctious little ones settled for the evening. She needed a bigger dose of fresh air than the living room window afforded.

With only a crescent moon suspended in the night sky, the stars twinkled like jewels. Lena searched for a constellation she could identify. Maybe she'd glimpse a shooting star. That was always a treat. But simply viewing the Lord's handiwork was an awe-inspiring experience. Lena could gaze at the amazing night sky for hours on end.

A slight rustle in the old oak trees hinted at a breeze. Lena tilted her head in the direction of the woods so whatever whisper of air made its way to her would cool her flushed cheeks. She'd grown quite warm cleaning up the kitchen and the *kinner*. And she'd grown rather weary as well, but an agitation deep inside would surely prevent sleep from claiming her.

She had to admit the irritation was directed at

herself, not any other person. *Really, Lena, would it have killed you to be a little more pleasant, a little more sociable, and a lot more grateful?* She clucked her tongue. *Shame on me. I would have reprimanded Mary if she had shown as little civility as I did.* Lena had scarcely thanked Samuel for taking an interest in her girls and for including them in the activities. She hadn't smiled, hadn't looked the man in the eye, and did little more than mumble in his direction.

She couldn't look him in those eyes that reminded her of ferns glistening in the forest after a spring shower. She couldn't give those eyes the opportunity to see into her heart and soul again. But she could have been more appreciative. Surely she could have shown better manners without giving Samuel false hope that she wanted to pursue a relationship. Lena studied the stars and followed one that shot across the sky. "I'll try to do better."

The cacophony of voices in Becky Stauffer's kitchen reminded Lena of swallows scolding one another in the top of the old oak tree, though the human voices were not actually upbraiding in any way. Many women of the community, young and not-so-young, had gathered to help the new *mudder* can the green beans overflowing from her abundant garden. Becky had tried to keep up with the produce, but the demands of nursing a newborn had made the task daunting. The hands of many helpers would make the job faster and more fun.

"You're looking chipper, Malinda." Lena had given care of her little ones over to the older girls who had accompanied their *mudders* expressly to perform childcare duties.

"I've been feeling great. I haven't had a flare-up of the Crohn's in ever so long."

"That's *wunderbaar* news. But I detect a definite sparkle in those big, brown eyes. Whatever could that be from?"

Malinda clapped her hands to her now rosy cheeks. "I-I guess . . ."

"I guess you're happy, ain't so?" Lena squeezed the younger woman's arm. "I didn't mean to embarrass you. I'm only teasing. I think it's great you've found someone, uh, I mean happiness." Lena winked. She knew she shouldn't mention anything about a fellow until the couple was published, but anyone could see that Malinda and Timothy Brenneman only had eyes for each other.

"*Danki*. It is pretty terrific."

"So, where are we with this mountain of beans?"

Malinda lowered her voice. "Knowing Mamm, she has a whole assembly line worked out. She'll give assignments directly."

"That's *gut*. Saloma will keep us all in line and on task."

"What's that, Lena? Did I hear my name?" Saloma pushed silver-rimmed glasses higher up on her nose with an index finger.

"I said you will keep us organized and moving."

"I'll do my best, but we'll have fun, too, ain't so? Work always goes better with a little fun thrown in."

"For sure." A little fun was exactly what Lena needed. Already she noticed some of the tension seeping from her stiff shoulder muscles.

Under Saloma's direction, the women got a system going. They washed beans, filled jars with beans and boiling water, dispelled air bubbles from jars with handles of wooden spoons, screwed on lids, and set jars in big canners. They chatted and laughed as they worked and switched jobs periodically to allow for breaks.

As they caught up on news from near and far and joked with one another, Lena felt more relaxed than she had in days. The agitation she'd fought since the last church day had been tamped down and covered over by the happy chatter. Of course they all took turns holding little Grace when she was awake.

"Hello, everyone. I'm sorry we're late. I'm sure there's still plenty to do, though, ain't so?"

Conversations halted abruptly as the workers all looked toward the door. Sarah Swarey flounced into the room as if dancing on a cloud, followed by her cousin, Emma Stauffer, who wore a pained expression on her usually serene face.

Saloma was the first to recover. "Of course there is always plenty to do. *Kumm* on in, girls."

Sarah dropped her purse on a chair and smiled at the room in general. "We had a little stop to make and lost all track of time. Isn't that right, Emma?" She hooked an arm through one of her cousin's.

"I guess so." Emma looked as if she wished a hole would open up in the linoleum floor, swallow her, and close in behind her.

Becky scooted over to the sink to stand next to Lena, who had taken over the bean-washing job. "Uh-oh," she uttered out of the side of her mouth.

"Where do you want me, Saloma?" Emma escaped from her cousin's clutches and hurried over to her husband's *mudder*.

"Why don't you spell Malinda on the bubble removing?"

"Sure." Emma acted like she wanted to disappear into the woodwork.

Sarah chattered on as if the whole world waited to hear the fine details of her day. She rubbed her hands together, warming up to being the center of attention. Her small, light brown eyes sparkled. "We stopped by Samuel Mast's place so I could drop off a shoofly pie. I made it extra-gooey; men just seem to love that. Samuel is an ever-so-nice fellow. He welcomed us warmly, and well, time got away from us."

Lena nearly swallowed her tongue. In the first place, unless Samuel's tastes had drastically changed over the years, he definitely did not enjoy rich desserts and would probably heave if he ate one bite of gooey pie. She was sure he would be gracious and accept the gift, but would probably try to pawn it off on someone else later. Or, if all else failed, he'd sling it far into the woods for the deer and raccoons to eat. Poor critters would probably go into a sugar coma if Sarah added extra brown sugar.

Becky's not-so-gentle nudge made Lena tune into Sarah's words again. She didn't know why a sudden annoyance with the woman overcame her, but she found she had clenched her teeth and curled her hands into fists when they should be washing beans.

"Isn't he dreamy to look at? I daresay, we are fortunate he returned to St. Mary's County. *Ach*, I mean, we can always use another farrier, ain't so?" Sarah's face blossomed into a bright, fuchsia color. She ducked her head slightly and picked at imaginary lint on her purple dress.

"Sure," Saloma agreed. "Levi is getting older and having a hard time getting around. I'm thinking that he will give up his business altogether pretty soon. Samuel will have plenty of work to keep him busy."

"She means she's glad Samuel is single and she might be able to get him to notice her," Becky whispered into Lena's ear.

Lena frowned and pursed her lips in a shushing position. If Sarah wanted to chase after Samuel, what business was it of theirs? And if Samuel was attracted to Sarah, well then, *gut* for them.

The women began chatting about other things, but Sarah couldn't leave the topic of Samuel Mast alone. "Samuel was ever so attentive, wasn't he, Emma?"

Emma's expression progressed from pained to sickly. Lena feared the girl was about to lose the last meal she'd eaten. Couldn't Sarah see her cousin's distress? Was she that blind or self-absorbed or desperate for attention that she was totally oblivious to everything else around her? Emma jabbed the wooden spoon handle into the jar so furiously, Lena expected the glass to shatter.

Sarah still babbled as if her tongue had worked itself loose at both ends, allowing it to flap uncontrollably. "I noticed how Samuel's eyes rarely left me to look at anything else. It was like I was the most important thing in the world to him. Isn't that sweet?"

"Sickening," Becky muttered. "I'm sure he was only being polite."

Lena jabbed her *freind* again.

Becky jumped and rubbed her arm. "Ouch!"

284

"Sorry."

"We've got to hush her up."

"She's happy."

"She'll be disappointed in the long run. Samuel only has eyes for you. A blind person could see that."

"Shhh!"

Saloma tried to break into Sarah's litany. "Let's see, Sarah, would you want to fill jars for a while?"

Sarah waved her hands about. "Sure. Sure. Whatever." She fastened her eyes on Lena as if suddenly noticing the petite woman at the sink. "You knew Samuel well, ain't so, Lena? Weren't you two sweet on each other before he left? I know that was all meaningless, youthful stuff, but what do you think? Do you think I'm Samuel's type? I'm sure I could be. Do you think you could talk to him and put in a *gut* word for me? Or maybe you could convince him to attend the next singing."

Lena's head spun with Sarah's prattle and a strange ache settled in her heart. She needed to reply to Sarah if she could squeeze a word in sideways, but what on earth should she say? And how would she get sound past that boulder filling her throat? She glanced at Sarah's hopeful face and blinked her eyes to dispel the moisture that filled them. "I-I'm sure I wouldn't have any influence over Samuel Mast whatsoever." Her voice came out in a silly, little squeak. "Excuse me." Lena dashed out the back door with her face on fire and her eyes dripping like a sudden rain shower.

Chapter Twenty-Four

Lena didn't stop her mad dash until she reached the heavily blossomed mimosa tree at the far edge of the yard. She leaned against the trunk beneath the fernlike leaves and inhaled the sweet fragrance of the feathery flowers. She panted to catch her breath and swiped a sleeve across her damp eyes and cheeks. *Get yourself together, Lena. You bolted like a skittish colt without any reason whatsoever.*

She should simply have answered Sarah's questions as succinctly as possible and turned back to her task. Now tongues would be wagging. Everyone would pity her. They would truly believe she cared about Samuel and was upset by Sarah's ridiculous requests. And that wasn't the case at all. *So why did you race out of the house like a lunatic?*

Lena had felt sorry for Sarah in the past, knowing how desperately the woman wanted a husband and family. Today, she acted like a scholar with her first crush instead of a grown woman, and her silly prattle was hard to stomach. But why should it bother Lena if Sarah wanted to pursue Samuel? He needed someone, too, someone who could devote herself to him and not have to share her time with another man's *kinner*.

If he truly did show an interest in Sarah today, Lena hoped things worked out for them. And she hoped the pain that wrenched her gut would ease.

"Lena?"

The whisper floated to her on a breeze. If she could shimmy up the tree, she surely would. She was pretty sure she could still physically manage that maneuver, but how would she explain why a grown woman sat in the tree to whoever pursued her?

"Lena?"

Becky. Now that the person had walked a bit closer and spoken a little louder, Lena recognized the voice. "*Jah*?"

"There you are. Don't these mimosa blossoms smell heavenly? I wish I could bottle the fragrance so I could get a whiff of it all year."

"It's one of my favorite scents." Lena forced sound past the lump nearly occluding her windpipe. Her throat ached from holding back a cascade of unshed tears.

"Are you all right?" Becky ducked under a low branch to stand beside her. Worry lines wrinkled Becky's brow. She reached out to pat Lena's arm.

Lena plucked the small hand from her arm and lightly squeezed it. "Erase that frown from your lovely face and stop fretting. I'm fine. I was overcome by an attack of the sillies."

Becky smiled. "Sarah did tend to go on and on, ain't so?"

"Just a bit."

"I'm sorry she upset you."

"I'm not upset. I-I think I got overheated." Becky's face told Lena that her *freind* didn't quite buy that excuse.

"You might have gotten hot, but I know you, Lena Troyer. I know when you're upset. I didn't live with you for months and not learn to gauge your emotions."

"I don't have any reason to be upset. Sarah is free to be giddy over any man she pleases. And if that fellow gives her some indication that a relationship might be possible, I wish her well. She's waited a long time." Lena's voice cracked a little at the end of her oration.

"You don't honestly believe Samuel led her on, do you? I'm sure Sarah is reading something into his politeness that wasn't really there."

"Who knows?"

"Emma does. Did you see her expression? She progressed from looking uncomfortable to absolutely miserable in a matter of minutes."

"She did appear as if she'd like nothing better than to fall into some deep, dark hole and stay there."

"Poor girl. I'll talk to her later to get the real story. I can trust Emma to be truthful and unbiased."

"Don't waste your time, Becky. It isn't impor-tant."

"That's what your mouth says, but I'm convinced your heart is saying something entirely different."

"I think your own wishful thinking is clouding your judgment. I'm sure Samuel could be very happy with Sarah, or anyone else he chooses."

"What if you are his choice?"

"I would have to be agreeable to that—and I'm not."

"Then why did you hightail it from the kitchen? And don't you dare say because it was hot or Sarah's incessant chattering gave you a headache, even though it was and she did!"

Lena shrugged. "It was a stupid thing to do. I made a fool of myself, and now I have to slink back in there and have everyone stare at me after I've been the topic of conversation and pity."

"I'm not sure how many people noticed. Emma spilled a jar of beans all over the place right after you left. That kind of took the focus off anything else, even Sarah. I'm wondering if Emma staged that little mishap on purpose to hush up her cousin." Becky slapped a hand across her mouth. "Oops! I shouldn't have said that. I have to remember I'm a *mudder* now and need to set a *gut* example for my little girl. I wouldn't want her to be unkind."

"I suppose I need to be brave and withstand a little mortification. It certainly isn't the first time I've done something to embarrass myself, and I doubt it will be the last time, either."

Becky smiled and squeezed Lena's hand. "You don't have any reason to be embarrassed. The room had grown very stuffy, and I daresay others had an urge to get some fresh air."

"Maybe, but they didn't tear off out the door like their hair was on fire."

"Please talk to me, Lena. I know you're troubled."

"I'm troubled because my *boppli* is cutting teeth and I can't get more than an hour or two of sleep at a stretch." She gave a nervous little laugh.

"I don't doubt that for an instant, but I know that's not really the issue."

"So you've perfected those mind-reading skills, huh?"

"I'm afraid not. But I do know you, and I'm almost one hundred percent sure your tangled feelings about Samuel Mast are at the root of your sleeplessness."

"Who said I had any feelings for Samuel Mast, tangled or otherwise?"

"This is me, your old pal, your former roommate you're talking to. You can't pull the wool over my eyes quite as easily as you think."

"I don't know what you're talking about."

"I believe you do."

"We need to get back inside." Lena took one step but halted at the pressure on her arm.

"Wait, Lena. I don't want to upset you. I care about you. I believe you still have feelings for Samuel, or maybe they resurfaced when he returned to Maryland. Just know that I'm here for you whenever you want to talk."

"I don't know, Becky. I'm so confused." Lena sniffed and blinked to prevent the hateful tears from trickling down her cheeks again.

"It's okay to be confused. You don't have to know all the answers. I'd just hate to see you close the door on any possible happiness you might have with Samuel and then regret that decision the rest of your life. I almost did that with Atlee, and I know my life would be miserable without him. You helped me realize that."

"Oh, Becky, Samuel and I were so young, but we were totally convinced we were meant for each other."

Becky nodded in encouragement. "Sometimes people know from an early age who their soul mate should be."

"When he left, I was devastated. When he didn't even correspond with me to let me know he was alive and well, I felt lower than the creepiest little earthworm slithering along on its belly. I figured he had been toying with my affection and didn't really care about me at all."

"You know now that he wrote letters you never received, ain't so?"

"I know that's what he says."

"Don't you believe him?"

"I'm not sure what I believe anymore. It took a long time to lick my wounds and get over Samuel. Then my parents died and I felt lost again. Joseph came along and was that bright spot at the end of a long, dark tunnel."

"I can understand that."

"Joseph and I had a *gut* life. It might not have been exciting and romantic, but we cared for and respected each other."

"There are different kinds of love, and that's okay. The romantic part is fun and exciting, but you need enduring, mature love to sustain a relationship."

"You sound like you've been married for ages rather than being a newlywed."

"I feel like Atlee and I have been together for ages. I don't know how it happened so quickly, but we share a bond I never dreamed possible."

"I'm happy for you."

"You deserve that happiness, too."

Lena sniffed harder. "I've had my chance. Now I have my *kinner*. That's all I need."

"I know they are the most important little people in your life. But you need an important big person, too, who can share life's joys and burdens with you. It doesn't have to be Samuel, of course, but someone who makes your heart sing."

"I'm fine exactly as I am."

"What are you afraid of? Don't you want that closeness again?"

"I'm not afraid. My heart doesn't need to sing. I'm, uh, I'm . . ."

"Afraid."

"Maybe."

"Of being hurt?"

"Of being left. Everyone I've ever loved, except for my *kinner*, has left me. I've experienced that pain far too much and don't care to do so again."

"Are you talking about Joseph?"

"Joseph, my parents, Samuel. I don't have a very *gut* record of keeping people around. Maybe it would be dangerous for anyone to be close to me. Maybe you should keep your distance. Run while you have the chance!"

Becky laughed. "I'm not at all concerned. Think of those people you listed, Lena. Did any of them choose to leave you?"

Lena thought for a second. "*Nee.*"

"See? Your parents and Joseph didn't choose to die. It was their time, and you couldn't do anything to change that. Samuel didn't choose to leave, either. He was young and had to do what his *daed* said. I don't know the details, of course, but I have the impression that he returned to St. Mary's County as soon as he was able."

"Ten years? It took ten years. Years of silence,

I might add, when we didn't have any news from him or his family."

"He said he tried to communicate. Again, I don't know, but I think there might have been some sort of bad situation with his *daed*. If you gave him a chance to explain, I'm sure he would tell you about it."

Lena shrugged.

"Don't give me that who-cares? attitude. I know better."

"You've already developed that *mudder*-knows-everything trait, and Grace is still a newborn."

"I think that and the *mudder*-bear attitude rush in as the infant emerges from the womb."

"It certainly did with you. We have got to get inside before they send out a search team."

"Okay, but promise me you'll think hard about dismantling that wall you've built and about the possibility of letting someone in."

"I don't make promises." Lena grabbed Becky's hand to tug her toward the house, but the girl wouldn't budge.

"Promise, Lena. At least think."

"I'll promise to think. Now help me get through the humiliation and questioning I'm bound to face as soon as I step foot inside that kitchen."

Before they reached the house, the back door swung open and Emma Stauffer fled as if a wild animal chased her. Lena and Becky exchanged a quick, questioning glance and hurried to meet the flustered young woman.

"*Was ist letz?*" Lena reached Emma first.

"Nothing is the matter. *Ach*, everything is the matter."

"Maybe you needed a breath of fresh air, too."

"I'm not sure what I need. I seem to have the dropsies today."

"I thought you might have dropped that jar of beans on purpose to, uh, to . . ." Becky bit her tongue, afraid to say the words clinging to its tip.

"I did mean to spill some beans, but not the whole jar. I thought that might hush Sarah because she wasn't taking any other hints."

"She was only excited." Lena tried to soothe the distraught girl.

"Excited bordering on annoying. Well, after I cleaned up the bean mess I made, I knocked over the salt. And you know how awful that is to try to clean up. It didn't help that Sarah called me 'butterfingers' and told everyone—even Samuel Mast—how she found me on the floor cleaning up spilled tea when she arrived at my house. She eagerly reminded everyone how clumsy I was as a little girl." Emma paused for a quick breath and plunged in again. "I was a clumsy girl, but I outgrew that. Really I did."

Lena patted Emma's arm. "We all have bad days, Emma dear, when nothing we do is right. Why, I remember one time I used salt instead of sugar in a recipe. Blah! It might not have been a total disaster the other way around. A real sweets lover might have enjoyed extra sugar, but I can't think of a soul who would like a ton of salt in their pie."

Emma smiled. "I can imagine how embarrassed you must have been."

"Totally mortified."

"I know I shouldn't be so sensitive. I don't know what's wrong with me lately."

Lena peeked around Emma to throw a knowing glance at Becky, who smiled and nodded. Lena remembered feeling extra-sensitive early on during all her pregnancies. Perhaps Emma would have an announcement to share soon. She looked back into the girl's sweet face. "You are just fine, Emma. Sometimes things from the past haunt us. We simply have to push them down and move forward. You are not the clumsy little girl any longer, if ever you were one. You are a lovely, capable woman, and a *gut fraa* to your Sam."

"I want to be. I try to be."

Becky stepped a bit closer. "You are, Emma. I can see the happiness on Sam's face every time we're in the same room."

Emma smiled. "Then I shouldn't let being called 'butterfingers' bother me."

"Absolutely not!" Lena again patted the arm she still held. "What's past is past and needs to stay there. Live today the best you can and hold high hopes for the future."

"*Gut* advice, my *freind*, for all of us—even you." Becky's voice was little more than a whisper.

Lena felt her lips form an O, but not a single sound passed between them as realization dawned. Did she really utter something so profound to Emma? Did those very same words apply to her as well? Could she let go of past hurts, disappointments, and heartaches? Could she embrace the present and anticipate the future with confidence that all would be well?

Chapter Twenty-Five

"Well, there you are."

Sarah's voice surely must be loud enough to wake the dead. Lena didn't remember the woman ever being so chatty or so loud before. She must have been emboldened by her earlier encounter with Samuel. What Lena wouldn't give to have been a fly buzzing around their faces during that meeting! Knowing Becky as she did, her *freind* would probably wheedle the details from Emma at some point in the not-too-distant future.

Lena stole a glance at the two women entering the kitchen with her. Emma rolled her eyes heavenward and appeared to be counting under her breath. Judging from Becky's tight jaw, her teeth must be clenched nearly to the breaking point. Lena forced her lips into some semblance of a smile and snatched a few deep breaths of air. "We're refreshed and ready to take over for someone."

Sarah focused her gaze on her cousin. "Have you recovered from your mishap? It must be at least your third or fourth today. Maybe you should do something like snap beans. You can't break anything there, except beans, of course." She giggled as if she'd uttered the funniest joke in the world.

From the corner of her eye, Lena saw Emma's

face flush a lovely scarlet color. "I think Emma will be just fine wherever she works. You know, we all have days when things seem to work against us. I suspect you've had those days yourself, ain't so, Sarah?"

"I reckon so. I can't remember the last time I had one, though."

Perfect, are you? Lena fought not to voice that thought. "I'm feeling much cooler now, so I can take over for someone at the stove."

The elderly woman who had been ladling boiling water over the filled jars of beans stepped back and sighed with relief. "*Danki*, Lena dear. I could use a breather."

"You go ahead and take a break." Lena took the ladle from the woman's wrinkled hand and prepared to assume her duties. To her dismay, Sarah sidled up to her. Lena was cornered. She'd be forced to listen to whatever the woman had to say.

"I'm sorry if I upset you talking about Samuel Mast. I remember you had a silly crush on him years and years ago when you were both mere *kinner*."

We weren't so young that we didn't know our feelings ran much deeper than a "silly crush." "I wasn't upset." *Forgive me, Lord Gott, if that's a teeny bit untrue.*

"You certainly ran from the room like you were angry or upset or both."

"I was neither, Sarah. Don't give it another thought." *And please hush up about it now.*

"Were you suddenly sick?"

Sometimes Lena had difficulty believing Sarah was actually older than she was. Yet she still had not learned to hold her tongue. "I wasn't suddenly sick. I needed a breath of air. I've been up with a teething *boppli* several nights in a row, and the heat got to me for a moment."

"You're such a bony little thing. I guess it's easy for you to be overcome by the heat. Look, I can get my fingers completely around your upper arm." Sarah grabbed Lena's arm to demonstrate.

Now Lena's face grew hot, and not from the steam of the boiling water on the stove. It took all her willpower to control her rising anger. Did Sarah think Lena didn't know she was skinny? She certainly didn't need Sarah to point out that fact to her and everyone else within earshot. Why would the woman deliberately embarrass her? Was she completely lacking any filter in her brain to stop her wild thoughts from traveling to her tongue? Lena mentally counted to one hundred by twos and yanked her arm from Sarah's grasp. "I'm well aware that I'm thin, Sarah."

"And we love her exactly the way she is." Becky threw an arm around Lena's waist and hugged her tight. "I wouldn't change a single thing about my dear *freind.*"

Sarah backed off a step or two. "Of course not.

I didn't mean there was anything wrong with Lena. I only meant she's tiny, so maybe she's more delicate."

Becky laughed. "If you'd ever seen this woman whip a house into shape while caring for three little ones, you'd rethink that idea."

"Oh, uh, I . . ."

"Sarah, could you help over here, please?" Saloma called out from the corner near the sink.

Bless Saloma. Even though Lena was embarrassed that Saloma overheard that conversation, she could have hugged her for calling Sarah off.

"Sorry," Becky whispered. "I don't know what's gotten into Sarah."

"It's okay," Lena whispered back. "Maybe Saloma can find her a job to do outside."

Becky covered her mouth and coughed to cover her laughter.

The women broke for lunch in shifts. Lena was grateful for a chance to sit in the living room to nurse Matthew. Becky joined her with Grace. The others who were eating at the time took sandwiches outside, where they could catch any hint of breeze that might blow. The teenage girls had taken the younger *kinner* out to picnic tables in the shade as well.

Becky eased into the rocking chair with a weary sigh with Grace in her arms. "Thank the Lord Sarah doesn't have a *boppli* to nurse. We'll get a little reprieve."

Lena kept her voice low. "If she has her way, she'll be married to Samuel in a flash and could be nursing her own little one within a year."

"Don't hold your breath on that."

"Hey, it could very well happen. Sarah seems awfully determined, and she's completely taken with Samuel."

"Too bad the feeling isn't reciprocated." Becky pushed with her toes to set the chair in motion.

"You don't know that." Lena raised Matthew to her shoulder and patted his back. She was immediately rewarded with a loud burp. She rubbed the little back a moment longer before repositioning him to continue nursing.

"I know what I see."

"Or what you want to see. Besides, Samuel could have been so captivated by Sarah and her shoofly pie that he has fallen madly in love."

"Not so. And he looked like he was going to throw up when he first glimpsed that pie."

Lena gasped. Her cheeks burned as if she had splashed boiling water on them. "Oh my!" Who had overheard their conversation?

"It's just me." Emma peeked into the room before stepping over the threshold.

"Who else is there?" Lena would have to apologize profusely if Sarah trailed her cousin into the room.

"I'm alone." Emma shuffled across the floor. "Don't worry. There wasn't anyone else nearby.

Everyone who isn't working in the kitchen hurried outdoors as soon as they grabbed their food. And it's so noisy in the kitchen, they wouldn't hear a freight train collide with a dump truck."

"That's a relief." Lena patted her chest above Matthew's head.

Becky sat up straighter in her chair and repositioned Grace. "Do tell us the details."

"I don't want to be a gossip, but I want you to know what really happened."

"The truth can't be gossip, ain't so?" Becky looked at Lena, who shrugged, and then looked back at her *schweschder*-in-law.

"That's what I think, too." Emma fanned herself with a flutter of her hand. "I don't know what possessed Sarah to bake a pie and deliver it to Samuel. I never even knew she'd spoken to him since he moved back to Maryland. Anyway, she was all excited about stopping at his place. I tried to dissuade her, to tell her she should let him make the first move—if he wanted to—but she wouldn't listen. I think she feels like time is slipping away from her and she'd better try to make a match before she gets too old."

"She certainly isn't old by any stretch of the imagination." Lena bent her head to kiss Matthew's fuzzy head.

"I tried to tell her that, in a roundabout way of

course. But once Sarah gets an idea in her head, wild horses can't drag it out."

"I'm sure Samuel was surprised by your sudden visit." Becky rocked a little faster.

" 'Shocked' might be a better way of putting it." Emma smiled, as if the very memory of the meeting was comical. "But being a polite man, he recovered quickly and was most gracious." She loosened a strand of pale hair that had glued itself to her neck and fanned herself again. "Whew! It's even warm in here, but I needed a break from Sarah's chatter so I didn't want to go outside." Suddenly she burst into a fit of giggles.

"What's so funny? Did one of us grow a second head?" Becky reached up and patted her head.

"I was remembering Samuel's expression." Emma hiccupped and gasped. "It was priceless." She slapped her knee and broke into another round of laughter.

Lena looked at Becky and the two began laughing simply because Emma's merriment was contagious. Neither spoke but instead waited for Emma to compose herself and continue.

"Oh dear. I'm sorry. I don't know what came over me." Emma swiped at her moist eyes. "When we first arrived, Samuel thought we'd been sent about a horse needing shoeing. When Sarah informed him the visit was purely social, Samuel's face paled and his mouth dropped open. I was glad pesky flies weren't buzzing around." Emma giggled again. "I have to hand it to him. Samuel recovered quickly and mumbled something like, 'What a surprise.'"

"Which probably meant he wished he was anyplace except where he was," Becky interjected.

"Probably. Anyway, when Sarah pulled out the shoofly pie and said she'd been thinking of him in that big house all alone and probably eating food out of tin cans so she just had to bake him a nice treat, he turned a little green."

Lena clapped a hand over her mouth to muffle her own chuckle. "I can imagine."

"Based on his reaction, I gathered he didn't like sweets too much. I don't think Sarah even noticed his brief look of disgust. I did hear him gulp and take a deep breath before saying he appreciated her thoughtfulness."

"Poor Samuel." Becky shook her head and then blew the swinging *kapp* string out of her face.

"It was nice of Sarah to think of him." Lena hoped a pleasant thought would calm the sudden churning in her stomach. Both Becky and Emma whipped their heads to stare at her. "What's wrong with you two?"

"I thought you might be interested in Samuel." Emma chewed her lip as if afraid she'd spoken out of turn.

"Why would you think that?"

"He's obviously interested in you, judging by

the way he looks at you. And I vaguely remember seeing the two of you together years ago."

"That was a lot of years ago."

Emma spoke softer. "But he still looks at you with big, caring eyes."

"See, I told you!" Becky stopped her furious rocking. "I wasn't making it up."

How many people had noticed the same thing and assumed she and Samuel would pick up where they'd left off? Now she would be even more self-conscious at community gatherings.

Emma reached over to pat Lena's leg. "Don't be embarrassed or upset, Lena. I'm a romantic at heart. I pick up on subtle cues. I'm sure other people haven't noticed a thing."

"You and Becky certainly noticed."

"I guess we're both romantics."

"And we both care about you and want to see you happy," Becky added.

"I don't understand why everyone thinks I'm so miserable. I'm not!" Instantly Lena regretted her outburst. She knew the other women had her best interests at heart. But what was best for her?

Becky tried to smooth things over. "I know you aren't miserable and that you adore your *kinner*, but . . ."

Lena held up a hand in a stop sign. "*Nee*. I'm sorry. I didn't mean to snap at you. You are both *wunderbaar freinden*, and I appreciate your concern. I'm not sure if I'm ready for another relationship, or if I'll ever be ready." *Especially with someone who broke my heart before.*

"We understand." Emma looked at Becky, who nodded and then turned back to Lena. "We certainly aren't trying to push you to do something you aren't ready to do. We merely want you to keep your options open." She paused for a fraction of a minute before hastily adding, "And if you are at all interested in Samuel Mast, don't let Sarah steal him away!"

Lena chewed her bottom lip until her tongue registered the metallic taste of blood. Could Samuel's encounter with Sarah today have sparked an interest despite what Emma said? The very thought turned her blood to ice and made her stomach tumble over itself.

Chapter Twenty-Six

When word spread that he was actually a farrier and had trained with a veterinarian in Wisconsin to care for horses' feet as well as shoe them, Samuel stayed busier than a cat in a mouse-infested hay barn. Today he'd had a little break to take care of things around the property and to work on his greenhouse. That was precisely where he'd been heading when his morning visitors appeared out of the blue.

What on earth had possessed Sarah Swarey to drop in on him with a pie? Sure, other women had brought him food from time to time. Older women who happened to bring their unmarried *dochders'* baked delights, along with the noodle or rice casseroles the *mudders* had concocted. Sometimes they even dragged the *dochders* with them. The mortified girls stared at the ground or at the fingernails they picked probably to the point of pain as their *mudders* extolled their virtues. Samuel always likened each experience to a horse auction and halfway expected the older women to coax him to examine their *dochders'* teeth and feet.

Samuel yanked off his straw hat, ran a hand through his hair, and plopped the hat back on his head. Today had been the first time a young lady had visited on her own. Well, Sarah had brought Emma along as a chaperone. Poor Emma looked as if she'd just as soon flap her arms and fly up to perch on the highest limb of one of the oak trees than witness the awkward exchange taking place in front of her. Awkward for him at least. Sarah chatted like they'd been *freinden* forever when, in truth, they were barely acquainted.

Sarah had been ahead of him in school and they hadn't shared the same activities or *freinden*. It wasn't really that age mattered so much, but interest was important. The only woman who interested Samuel now was the same one who'd interested him years ago. If Lena wouldn't or couldn't find it in her heart to even consider a relationship with him, he would stay single all his Gott-given days. Not his preference, but better than being yoked to someone he didn't love.

Now he had another pie to get rid of. A shoofly pie at that. The mere thought of biting into a piece of it set his teeth on edge. He barely suppressed a shudder. Samuel often wished he liked sweets more so he wouldn't offend anyone by not eating their homemade treats, but the more gooey and sugary the food, the more his stomach turned inside out. He *might* have been able to sample a teeny, tiny sliver if the pie had been plain old apple or peach, but even that would have been pushing it. Give him a small brownie or a cookie and he could be completely happy with that.

It looks like I've got another pie to deliver to Miriam and Melvin King. Melvin had a sweet tooth as big as the whole outdoors, so he would never refuse a pie or cake. Miriam seemed to enjoy the past treats he'd pawned off on them, too. Samuel didn't know if that was because she truly liked them or if it meant she didn't have to bake anything. The reason didn't matter as long as he didn't have to waste the food and didn't have to eat it himself.

Would Sarah be calling on him again? Not if Emma had any say in it for sure and for certain. Her misery had been obvious. And surely Sarah wouldn't be so brazen as to visit alone. Samuel hoped he hadn't given her any sign of encouragement. He replayed the conversation in his head and couldn't recall a single hint that he was interested in her. He'd been polite, nothing more and nothing less.

Sweat trickled down his neck and rolled down his back. He swiped a hand across his moist forehead. He hadn't known moving back to St. Mary's County would present such challenges as avoiding the desperate unmarried women or their more desperate *mudders*. What he needed right now was some tough, physical work to occupy his hands and to render his mind thoughtless.

Though the day was another scorcher, at least an occasional breeze whispered through the trees, and Lena had been enjoying it for as long as possible before entering the Kings' stuffy kitchen following the church services in their big barn. She hadn't heard anyone approach and gave a little yelp when a hand touched her arm. "*Ach*, Emma. You startled me."

"I'm sorry. I wanted to talk to you for a minute before we went inside."

Emma's voice had dropped so low that Lena had to strain to decipher her words. "Why so hush-hush?"

"I don't want to be overheard." Emma paused to nod and smile at a passerby.

Lena looked up into the face of the younger woman, who stood several inches taller. "Is something wrong?"

"*Jah. Nee.* Maybe. Oh, I'm not sure."

"That sounds pretty mysterious." Lena slowed her pace to a shuffle to give Emma time to gather her thoughts and speak her piece. She shifted Matthew to her other arm and watched her girls run off to play under the supervision of some teenage girls. Mary and Eliza were growing up so fast. Eliza did her best to keep up with her big *schweschder*. They certainly weren't *bopplin* any longer. She glanced again at the obviously agitated young woman beside her. If Emma didn't speak soon, they'd reach the house and she would miss her opportunity for a private conversation.

"It's Sarah!" Emma croaked at last.

"What about her?"

"She tried to get me to go with her to Samuel Mast's place again yesterday."

Why did Lena suddenly have trouble catching her breath? It must be the humidity. Where did that little breeze go? "R-really?"

"I didn't go of course. I told her I had too much to do. She was rather put out with me."

Lena couldn't contain her curiosity. "Why on earth did she need to go back to his house? Is something wrong with her horse?"

"That's just it. She didn't have a reason. She had baked some sort of rich cobbler or something. I couldn't quite identify the mess, but I saw lots of brown sugar and cinnamon. Oops. I guess that wasn't very nice." Emma paused to slap her own cheek. "Anyway, she wanted me to invent an excuse to visit Samuel."

"What excuse could you possibly have used?"

"None whatsoever, and I told her so. I might have spared Samuel a stomachache. *Ach!* What's wrong with me? I don't mean to be unkind."

Lena patted her *freind*'s arm. "It's okay. I'm sure her request took you by surprise."

"For sure. I guess she didn't notice, or didn't want to notice, how awkward the last visit was."

"D-do you think she went alone, then?"

Emma's hand flew to her chest and she let out a horrified gasp. "Surely she wouldn't have, would she?"

"You know her better than I do. Would she risk her reputation for an opportunity to, uh, to . . ."

"Flirt."

"*Jah*."

"I don't know. She really has been anxious to find a husband the last few years. I don't know why she's turned her nose up at every man around, but she certainly seems to have set her sights on Samuel now."

"M-maybe it will all work out for them."

"How can you say that, Lena? You've got to do something."

"It's not my place to get involved in their relationship."

"You have to prevent a relationship. You're the only one who can."

Lena forced a little laugh and patted Emma's arm. "They are two adults who can definitely make their own decisions." She quickened her pace for the last few steps to the house.

"Don't lose him, Lena!"

Emma's words had been whispered, but they echoed in Lena's mind like a shout in a canyon. A person couldn't lose something she didn't already have, could she? Something she didn't want? Lena didn't have Samuel. They were two completely different people than they were ten years ago. An entire lifetime had lapsed. And she didn't want him, either. *Then why do you get that pang from your belly to your heart when you think of him and Sarah together?*

Nonsense. That's what it was. Pure nonsense. And maybe a little nostalgia. A relationship couldn't be based on what could have been or what would have been if circumstances hadn't deemed otherwise. She and Samuel both needed to move forward, she with her *kinner* and Samuel with Sarah or whoever else he chose. There. That was settled.

Lena cleared the remnants of the common meal from the table with the help of some of the other married women. The young folks had already started a game of volleyball despite the heat and humidity. The younger *kinner* played in the shade of the trees in the side yard. The wee ones, including Matthew and Grace, napped in a spare bedroom.

Movement near the buggies drew her attention in that direction. She shaded her eyes with one hand to help her see without squinting into the sun. Her heart gave a tiny jump. Samuel. He'd pulled a clear plastic bag full of colorful Frisbees from his buggy. He must be planning to entertain the little ones again. They would be happy for sure. Warmth spread through her at Samuel's concern for the *kinner*.

Lena returned to her chore but stopped abruptly at the sound of a too-cheery voice. She knew she should go about her business and not pay them any mind, but her curiosity made her hone in on Sarah's syrupy words. Curiosity sounded ever-so-much nicer than nosiness or eavesdropping.

She really didn't need to worry about appearing to eavesdrop. Sarah obviously didn't care who heard her words because her voice was louder than normal. Did she want Lena to hear? Was that her intention? Was she trying to rub it in that she was interested in Samuel and determined to pursue him? Surely not. Lena had never known Sarah to be mean-spirited. They had never been great pals because they had different interests, but she'd never seen Sarah be anything other than polite. Then again, she'd never seen the woman use her wiles to ensnare a man. Even if Lena rustled the paper plates to make noise, Sarah's voice carried as clear as if she'd been speaking directly to her.

"*Ach*, Samuel. You've brought the toys again. You are so *wunderbaar* with the little ones."

"I enjoy them. I miss my little *bruders* and *schweschders*."

"You should have a whole house full of your own."

Now if that wasn't obvious, nothing was. Why didn't she just propose to him and get it over with? Lena tried to let out the breath she'd been holding slowly so it didn't expel in a giant whoosh that could be heard halfway around the world.

"Maybe someday." Samuel tossed a disc to a waiting little *bu*.

"You aren't getting any younger." Sarah's giggle seemed a mite forced.

What you mean is you *aren't getting any younger, and Samuel had better hurry up and notice you.* Ach*! Lena, you are being most unkind.* Why should she care if they married next week? She started to move away, but Samuel's words paralyzed her.

"I'm not so old that I can't wait for the right woman to marry. Everything happens in the Lord Gott's time, ain't so?"

Lena couldn't look in their direction, but Samuel's eyes burned a hole clear through to her heart. She'd experienced the power of his gaze on numerous occasions years ago. Its effect had not dulled. Did Sarah follow his gaze and look at her, too? She would never know. She pretended to be totally absorbed in her task.

"Catch!"

Lena heard Samuel call out to another child. She peeked in his direction in time to see him gently toss a red Frisbee to Eliza. The toddler giggled and hopped up and down when she caught the toy.

"Great catch, Eliza! Here, Mary, you catch the next one."

"Can I help you? I like *kinner*, too. It will be fun with the two of us playing with them."

317

You're trying too hard, Sarah. Ease up.

"Uh, well, sure, unless you'd rather play volleyball. They look like they're having fun, too."

Lena knew that tone of voice. Samuel was trying to discourage Sarah without being too obvious or mean. Sarah, however, didn't seem to pick up on the tone or the implied message behind his words.

"The volleyball players are a little young for me. I'd feel out of place with them."

Translation: The fellows are all younger and aren't interested in an older girl. Lena's cheeks burned. Where were all these sarcastic thoughts originating? Surely some little imp had entered into her brain and whispered such ideas to her. Well, she needed to cast him out right now before he loosened her tongue and she let words slip out that she would regret all the days of her life.

"They're all nice folks, so it seems. I'm sure they'd be glad to have you play, but you can certainly toss Frisbees if you want."

Samuel, the diplomat. Always truthful, yet always kind. Lena had dawdled long enough. She needed to move on or risk saying or doing something she shouldn't. A little shout from Samuel made her snap her head around. Did someone get hurt?

"Agh!"

"Samuel, I'm so sorry. I guess I don't aim these things properly. Are you all right?"

Samuel rubbed his cheek. Sarah must have hurled the hard, plastic missile right at his head. It was a *gut* thing one of the *kinner* wasn't on the receiving end of that toss.

"I'm fine. You sort of have to throw them with a twist of your wrist."

Sarah trotted close enough to touch Samuel. "Maybe you can help me position my hands correctly." She held up a disc so Samuel could place his hands over hers.

And maybe I'm going to throw up! Lena turned and marched to the big trash can near the house.

Chapter Twenty-Seven

You can't have it both ways, Lena, so get yourself together right now. What Samuel and Sarah do or say is not any of your concern. She shook her head and sniffed.

"*Was ist letz*, Lena?"

She jumped halfway to the sky. Had she spoken aloud? If so, she definitely was losing her grip on sanity. "Nothing is wrong, Becky."

"You could have fooled me. You looked upset."

"Not at all. I was lost in thought."

"They must have been some pretty disturbing thoughts."

Lena forced a smile. "Not really."

"Serious thoughts, then. And you were stomping like you were as mad as a wet hen."

"I'm not mad. Why were you giggling to yourself? Do I have my dress on backward?"

Becky nodded to the Frisbee throwers. "That situation out there was almost comical."

Lena failed to see anything amusing about the whole business but didn't say so. She raised a quizzical eyebrow at her *freind*.

"I guess you missed it. Sarah was trying desperately to get Samuel to help her throw the Frisbee." Becky paused for a breath.

I didn't miss that. And I didn't find it funny in

the least. Lena waited for Becky to continue.

"Well, Samuel called one of the bigger girls over and had her teach Sarah how to hold the Frisbee. The look on Sarah's face was priceless." Becky covered her giggle with her hand. "I do feel a little sorry for Sarah, though."

"How so?"

"Poor thing doesn't realize it's a no-win situation for her. She isn't going to be able to turn Samuel's heart and thoughts from you."

"Go on with you, Becky Stauffer. Samuel was simply displaying appropriate behavior. He couldn't very well stand so close to Sarah or touch her with half the community watching."

"I don't believe he even wanted to be close to her, gauging by the expression on his face."

"She had just clobbered him with a wild throw. His cheek was probably smarting."

"Think what you want, Lena, but one day you will need to face the truth."

"And you know what that is?"

"I do. It's written all over Samuel's face. He only cares for you."

Samuel's earlier words about waiting for the right woman echoed through Lena's brain. Did he still believe she was the right woman for him, as Becky declared? Give him time. He'll fall for one of the unattached young ladies for sure and for certain. Maybe even Sarah.

Lena resumed her march to the house. "I need

to check on Matthew and get everyone ready to go home."

"Why the rush? Matthew was barely beginning to stir when I peeked into the room before *kumming* outside. And the girls are having so much fun. Look at them."

Lena didn't want to look in that direction. She didn't want to see Samuel's smiling face or his big, green eyes. And she definitely didn't want to see him smiling at and focusing those beautiful eyes on Sarah. There. She admitted it. She was jealous. But she hadn't any right to be. If she wasn't interested in Samuel, she should be happy for him to find someone else. So why wasn't she?

"Look quick, Lena!" Becky pointed toward the *kinner*. "Eliza is getting ready to toss the Frisbee. You surely don't want to miss it."

Lena snapped her head around. Her little girl's smile practically split her face in two. Lena could see her dark eyes shining. She could tell Eliza struggled to control her movements. Knowing her *dochder*'s penchant for jumping up and down and squealing, standing still and focusing would be quite a huge accomplishment for her.

But there she stood, concentrating on her throw. She drew the disc toward her. With a flick of her wrist, she lobbed it right at Mary's hand. When Mary caught the Frisbee, Lena was the one who hopped up and down and squealed. "She did it!

Eliza threw it and Mary caught it!" She tugged on Becky's arm.

"I saw."

"Oops! Sorry." Lena dropped Becky's arm. "I got as carried away as the girls."

Becky laughed. "That's quite all right."

Almost shyly, Lena shifted her eyes in Samuel's direction. His grin rivaled Eliza's. Was that love for her girls she saw in his eyes? Lena blinked and refocused. Probably Samuel was simply excited the girls had learned so well under his tutelage. But she did detect a softening of his features when he gazed at Mary and Eliza that she did not notice when he looked at the other little ones. How odd!

Suddenly Samuel riveted and focused on Lena. He flashed her that brilliant smile that caused her heart to flop like a rockfish on the bottom of the little fishing boat Samuel had taken her out in years ago. *Stop it, Lena. You are not some silly scholar. You are a grown woman.*

Even the stern reprimands could not keep Lena's lips from pulling up into a smile. Her face flamed when Samuel winked at her. Involuntarily she raised a hand to one burning cheek. Becky nudged her and gave her a sly smile.

"Mamm! Mamm! Did you see? Eliza threw and I caught." Mary held up the Frisbee in triumph. Now that Eliza had completed her mission, she leaped up and down.

Lena's feet took off before her brain could issue the command. She snatched both little girls up in an embrace and twirled around with them. "I did see! I'm impressed with your skills." They twirled and giggled until they collapsed on the ground. Lena hadn't felt so lighthearted in, well, she couldn't remember when.

From the periphery, she caught Becky laughing and clapping. But right smack in front of her, she saw a large hand reaching out to her. Her eyes traveled up and up to connect with Samuel's.

"Need some help?"

Lena was sure she could hop to her feet just fine all by herself, even though the action might be terribly unladylike. But some strange urge compelled her to accept Samuel's offer. She tentatively stretched out a hand, which he clasped firmly in his own.

"One, two, three." Samuel tugged, pulling Lena to her feet with Mary and Eliza clinging to her skirt.

"*D-danki.*" Lena tried to free her hand, but Samuel held tight. He released her only a moment later, but the pressure and warmth sent a shock wave throughout her entire body. *Step back!* Her feet ignored the voice of reason as if they'd been cemented to the spot. Not only were her feet disobedient, but her eyes refused to disengage from Samuel's. A tug on her skirt sent reality crashing down.

"Play?"

Lena pulled her eyes from Samuel's face to look at her younger *dochder*, breaking the spell that had kept her focused on the tall man in front of her. "Y-you can play for two more minutes and then we need to go." She needed to go right now and get away from those mesmerizing eyes that could peer into her soul.

"L-Lena?"

Samuel's voice wobbled. Did he feel that same jolt that rocked her body?

"Samuel! Samuel! Look! I think I got it." Sarah trotted over with a red Frisbee in one hand. She wormed her way between Samuel and Lena, practically knocking Lena off-balance.

Samuel reached around her to place a steadying hand on Lena's arm. "Are you okay?"

"Oh, sorry, Lena."

Sarah didn't sound very contrite, but Lena tried not to dwell on that. "It's okay. I'm fine." She pulled her arm from Samuel's grasp. The interruption provided the douse of cold water Lena needed.

"I got so excited that I got carried away," Sarah gushed. "I was so eager to show my handsome instructor that I didn't even notice you standing there, Lena."

Lena sucked in the gasp that threatened to escape. Sarah really called Samuel handsome? To his face? In front of her? "Oh, don't mind me." She knew her comment sounded sarcastic, but she couldn't retract it. Maybe Sarah didn't notice. *Just like she didn't notice me standing right in front of her. I might be skinny, but I'm not invisible!*

Samuel covered up his snort with a cough, assuring Lena that he'd picked up on her sarcasm even if Sarah hadn't. Lena should be ashamed of herself. She wasn't.

"Watch me throw!" Sarah practically elbowed Lena out of the way.

Is she three or almost thirty? Lena resisted the urge to cluck her tongue. She had better skedaddle out of here before she said something totally inappropriate. She clapped her hands. "Let's go, girls. We need to get your *bruder* and go home. Tell Samuel *danki* for playing with you."

Two little mouths began to pout until Samuel spoke. "*Gut* job, girls. We'll play again soon, ain't so? Hey, maybe when I drop by to help with haying, we can play afterward. How does that sound?"

What? He planned to help the fellows renting her fields? Why? *Ach*, that's right. She did hear that one of the men broke his wrist, so they were probably a man short. But why did Samuel have to offer to help? Didn't he have enough to do?

Instantly Mary and Eliza brightened. "Okay. *Danki.*"

Okay for them, maybe, but not for me. "Let's go, my little champions." Lena grabbed their hands and herded them toward the house. She sensed several pairs of eyes following her movement but did not turn around.

"Watch, Samuel. I think I've got the hang of it now. Don't worry about her. She's too caught up in her own problems to even notice anything else."

Sarah's plaintive voice echoed through Lena's head. What problems kept her too preoccupied to notice her *freinden*? She wanted to tell Sarah to grow up and act her age, but compassion kicked in. Lena now clearly saw that Samuel was not romantically interested in Sarah. Though he strove to be polite, his disinterest was obvious. Only Sarah hadn't picked up on that.

At the sound of footsteps behind her, Lena glanced over her shoulder. She slowed to allow Becky to catch up.

"You're certainly in a hurry." She gasped for breath.

"I-I need to get home. Run ahead, girls. I'll be right there."

"Home or away from a certain person?"

"Both."

"I admire your honesty." Becky patted her chest, as if that would help her get more oxygen into her lungs. She lowered her voice. "That scene back there would have been funny if it wasn't so sad."

Lena nodded. "Maybe Samuel should give her a chance."

"What?" Becky grabbed Lena's arm and jerked her to a stop. "I don't think I heard you correctly."

"I think you did."

"Why should Samuel give Sarah a chance when he plainly, obviously, desperately cares about you?"

Lena chuckled. "Are there any other adjectives you'd like to throw in there?"

Becky tapped the side of her head, pretending to be in deep thought. "*Nee*. I think that about sums it up."

"You're *narrisch*."

"I am not one bit crazy. But you must be a few yards short of a full skein of yarn if you think Samuel Mast could possibly care for anyone other than you."

"Samuel cares for the girl I was when he left. He doesn't know the adult Lena."

"You could give him a chance to see that the grown-up woman is even more *wunderbaar* than the girl was."

"Ha! You are too funny."

"I'm sure you have the same endearing qualities Samuel loved ten years ago."

"Don't say that word. We were *kinner*."

"You were young adults. And I believe that

word applied back then the same as it does now."

Lena shook her head so hard her neck popped. "We need to face reality here. And Samuel needs to give someone else a chance."

"I don't believe that will happen. And I don't believe that is what you truly want. I saw the way you two looked at each other just a few minutes ago."

"Merely a throwback to the past." Lena resumed her march to the house.

"Be careful what you wish for, my *freind*." Becky trotted to catch up so she didn't have to yell. "Your wish might be granted, leaving you sad and sorry the rest of your life."

Chapter Twenty-Eight

Could anything have been more awkward? Maybe he would avoid all social functions from now on, even the common meal after church. *I'll simply live like a hermit until Lena* kumms *to her senses and realizes we're meant for each other. Nee.* He couldn't very well do that. He didn't want to disappoint the *kinner*. They always got so excited when he brought out the Frisbees.

He clucked to Stockings to coax him to trot faster. Only when he was halfway home did he allow himself to fully exhale and relax his tense shoulder muscles. He rotated his head to stretch his neck and passed a hand over his throbbing forehead. What a day!

How could Sarah have been that forward? He'd been so flabbergasted that he hadn't quite known what to say or do. And there stood Lena as a witness. Did she think he'd encouraged Sarah? Surely not. *Ach*! He'd never been in such a quandary—and he'd found himself in many a difficult situation in his life, not through any fault of his own. But he could honestly say that a woman he hadn't any interest in had never blatantly thrown herself at him while the woman he lived and breathed for looked on.

Samuel rubbed his stubbled chin. *Must not have*

shaved as closely as usual this morning. Funny how such inane thoughts could even poke through as his brain grappled with more serious issues. Whatever was he going to do to get himself out of this mess he'd landed smack-dab in the middle of? He sighed so loudly that the horse pricked up his ears and tried to whip his head around. "Easy, boy. It's just me. A befuddled, frustrated human. Be glad you're a horse."

Lena had played with her *kinner*, read to them, fed them a light supper, and tucked them into bed. Now she could finally settle into her rocking chair and try to make some sense of this strange, awkward day. She'd really rather pretend the day never happened, but that wasn't an option. She set the chair in motion and drummed her fingers on the wooden chair arms. If she didn't calm down, she would never get a minute's sleep tonight.

She dug her bare toes into the throw rug beneath the chair to momentarily stop the rocking. She stretched to reach the knitting bag and pulled it onto her lap. The weight of the half-finished afghan would probably make her hotter on this sticky evening, but knitting soothed her better than any other activity.

She loved the feel of the yarn between her fingers, be it wool from a neighbor's sheep or some of that soft, warm alpaca fleece Phoebe

Yoder had convinced her to try. The clickety-clack of the knitting needles provided a melody as sweet as any music she'd ever heard. Lena and Becky had spent many evenings knitting and talking about their lives.

Lena missed adult companionship in the evening. That was when the loneliness crept in to haunt her. Joseph hadn't been a great conversationalist, but his presence had been comfortable, reassuring. Becky had filled a huge void when she moved in during Lena's pregnancy with Matthew. They had quickly become as close as *schweschders*. Now Becky had her own husband and *boppli* to tend to, which was as it should be. Lena could only feel happiness for her dear *freind*.

The wooden needles continued to click and clack as they wove in and out of the yarn loops, filling the almost oppressive silence in the room. Lena's sigh seemed to echo around the house before returning to vibrate in her ears. Nothing, though, had been able to drown out Becky's parting words. Was Lena wishing for the wrong thing?

How would she truly feel if Samuel did take an interest in Sarah? If he courted her? If he married her? Lena tried to scrape away the memories of nearly overwhelming pain when Samuel left Maryland and completely dropped out of her life. The wound still festered after all these years.

She didn't understand it then and didn't really understand now why he hadn't found some way to communicate if he cared about her as much as he claimed.

If the shoe had been on the other foot, Lena would have done everything in her power to let someone know she cared. Did Samuel really try to write, or was that merely his excuse now to get back into her *gut* graces? How would she know for sure and for certain? How could she trust him not to rip out her heart and stomp on it again *if* she summoned the courage to offer it again?

Maybe she should adjust her thinking. Maybe she should envision Samuel and Sarah together, shepherding a passel of *kinner* with brown hair and magnificent green eyes. That made a nice picture, ain't so? She could live in a close-knit community where she'd bump into Samuel's *fraa* in the little Amish grocery store or the cheese shop. She could sit elbow to elbow with the woman at a quilting frame during a stitching frolic. She could . . . Right! She'd never be able to swallow that lump of misery that threatened to choke the life out of her.

Lena rocked harder and knit faster, needles flying in and out of stitches. She couldn't tell Samuel to leave her alone and find someone else with her mouth while her heart wept. The two body parts needed to be in sync. And then there was the part of her that felt as if she was betraying Joseph by even thinking about Samuel. She'd blocked thoughts of her first love out of her mind when she'd accepted Joseph's marriage proposal and concentrated on her husband.

She'd understood the two were completely different men, and she'd loved them in totally different ways. Samuel was a closed chapter in her life's book when she married Joseph. With his death, another chapter of her book ended. Did she really want to reopen the former one? Could a person go back and fan an old spark into flame?

If Becky and Emma were correct, Samuel had never extinguished the fire. If Lena was perfectly honest, she would have to admit she saw the flicker in his eyes every time she caught him gazing at her. But what did *she* feel? *Examine your heart, Lena.* She raised her eyes from her knitting and scanned the room. Had those words been spoken by some outside source or were they simply her own thoughts?

She was definitely alone in the room. The *kinner* slept in their beds. The front door never opened. The words were her own, unless the Lord Gott had whispered them into her brain. Lena wiggled in her chair. She'd been avoiding the examination of her heart. That activity could prove painful, and hadn't she had enough pain in her life? She looped the yarn around a needle and continued stitching.

Examine your heart, Lena.

"*Ach*! Go away. My heart is fine." She spoke to the empty room. *Now I'm talking to myself and hearing voices. Maybe I'm losing my mind.* She laid the knitting in her lap and leaned her head against the high back of the rocking chair. She squeezed her eyes shut so she didn't see the shadows dancing on the walls in the lamplight. She heard only the gentle squeak of the wooden chair and the chirps of crickets and other night bugs outside her window. Her sigh sounded like the thunder of a sudden summer storm. *Okay. Okay. I'll examine my heart.*

Lena's rocking all but stopped as she allowed the memories to wash over her. In her mind's eye, she was a girl again—well, not quite a girl, but not yet a woman. Fifteen. She'd certainly considered herself an adult even if she was the only one who thought so. Samuel, a whole two years older, treated her as a grown-up woman. Maybe that was because he felt older himself because he carried the weight of much of his family's needs.

"In three years you'll be eighteen, Lena. We'll get married then. I'm ready right now, but I'm sure your parents would never allow that."

He had taken her hand and gazed down at her so tenderly that the tears gathered in her eyes and threatened to cascade down her cheeks. Even the memory made her sniff. She was an only child and had been rather sheltered. Even if she had begged her parents to approve of her marriage, she knew they wouldn't relent. "Three years is such a long time." She remembered how hard she had struggled not to wail like a two-year-old.

"The time will go by fast. You'll be learning all sorts of things from your *mamm*. I'll be working and saving money and learning all I can to establish my own business, too."

She nodded, unconvinced those activities could make the years fly by.

"And we'll see each other often. We'll ride home from singings. I'll visit on Saturday evenings. We'll do things together." He squeezed her hand.

"Those things sound nice, but three years still sounds like an eternity to me."

"Me, too, my sweet Lena." He hugged her close.

She heard the steady thump of his heart beneath his blue shirt. She felt him press a kiss to her head, which barely reached his shoulder. She snuggled beneath his chin and knew without any doubt whatsoever she belonged with Samuel. "I suppose I'll have to resign myself to the idea that we have to wait. I'm sure all the older folks would say we're way too young to know what we want."

"We might be young, but I'm absolutely sure what I want. I want you to be my *fraa*."

Lena pulled away to look into those green eyes she likened to new spring ferns. "I know what I want, too." She dropped her head back against his broad chest. All his hard labor had turned his seventeen-year-old body into that of a man. "My *grossmammi* was only seventeen when she got married. And she and Grossdaddi were happy for all the years of their lives."

"Hey, there's a glimmer of hope. Maybe your parents will agree to our getting married when you're seventeen. Two years to wait doesn't sound quite as bad, ain't so?"

Ach! The dreams they'd shared that summer. They planned their house, though they didn't have a clue where they would build it. They decided what crops they would plant and toyed with the idea of raising sheep. They would learn how to care for them and shear them. Lena wanted to learn to spin and knit using her own homespun yarn. They imagined their *kinner* running in the yard, though that part had set Lena's cheeks on fire. They'd gone for rides and bought ice cream on sticks from the truck that clanged through the community. They'd laughed as the melting chocolate and vanilla concoction dribbled down their chins. Twice they drove in Samuel's courting buggy to the little carryout that sold frozen custard.

All their happiness ended abruptly one Saturday evening in mid-August. As the previous memories had brought a smile to Lena's face, this one caused the exact same searing pain that it had ten years ago, that gut-wrenching agony she had tried to forget all these years. She didn't want to relive that heartache now, but she had to if she ever wanted to push past it.

Like so many other Saturday evenings, Samuel showed up at Lena's house after her parents had gone to bed. Unlike other visits, though, this night they did not talk and laugh. Samuel spoke little. His eyes flicked from one object in the room to another as he avoided looking in Lena's direction altogether. He fidgeted, picked at a fingernail, and tapped a foot. Right as Lena opened her mouth to ask what was troubling him, Samuel spoke.

"I have some bad news."

The bottom dropped out of her stomach, and Lena feared she would be sick right there on the spot. "Wh-what kind of bad news?" She wanted to slap her hands over her ears to shut out whatever words Samuel might say. Was he tired of her? Had he found someone else?

"I'm moving."

"What?" He had spoken so quietly that Lena wasn't sure she'd heard correctly.

Samuel cleared his throat. "I'm moving. Well, not just me. My family is moving."

"Where?" Maybe they were moving to another district. That shouldn't be any problem.

"Pennsylvania, I think, or wherever my *daed*'s whim leads him."

Now that was a problem! "Why in the world is your family moving to Pennsylvania?" Lena struggled to regain some sort of composure and to make amends for her outburst. "I mean, you don't have relatives there, do you?"

"*Nee.* We don't know anyone there."

"Why so far away?" Her voice wobbled. She didn't know which would be worse, sobbing like a *boppli* or throwing up. She suddenly felt a chill even though they'd been in the throes of the dog days of August for several weeks.

Samuel took her hand and finally ventured to look into her eyes. "My *daed* says he wants to see someplace different." He shrugged and looked a little misty-eyed himself. "I don't want to go, Lena. I don't want to leave Maryland. This is my home. Most of all, I don't want to leave you."

"I can't believe your parents want to move."

"My *daed* does."

"Not your *mudder*?"

"I don't think so. I heard her crying, but she'll do whatever Daed says. We all have to, even me. If I was eighteen, I could say I'm staying here and live with a *freind* until I got on my feet a bit. As it stands now, I have to go with my family."

"This can't be happening." One tear after another slid silently down Lena's cheeks.

"Please don't cry, *lieb*."

Samuel tried to wipe away her tears with a large, callused finger. Lena wanted to throw herself into his arms, hang on for dear life, and never let him go. He couldn't go. He couldn't leave her. She couldn't stop the cascade of tears any more than she could keep the Potomac River from lapping at the sandy shore.

"Shh! It's okay." Samuel pulled her closer. She pressed her face to his chest and sobbed her heart out, soaking the green shirt that exactly matched his eyes. "We'll work something out."

Lena sniffed. "What? How?"

"Pennsylvania, if that's where we end up, is pretty far away, but it's not on a different planet. We can write letters, and I'll be back before you know it. I'm planning on returning as soon as I'm eighteen." He dropped a kiss on top of her head. "It won't be forever."

The pain that began that night intensified a few days later when the Mast family piled into the van that transported them away from Maryland. Their house and most of their belongings had been sold, so there wouldn't be any place for them to return to if they did decide to move back. It seemed like Samuel's *daed* wanted to burn all their bridges behind them. When months passed without any letters from Samuel and her own mail returned to her, any hope Lena had gave way to despair.

For months she went through the motions of

living. "Existing" might be a better word. She ate little, slept little, and socialized little. Only gradually did the fog lift, and that only after Samuel's eighteenth birthday passed without any sign of him returning to Maryland. At the pleading of *freinden*, she began to attend singings again, but she remained on the fringes of activities.

Joseph, who she discovered had been watching from afar, became a trusted *freind*. When Lena's parents were snatched from her in a buggy accident, she leaned on Joseph and soon accepted his marriage proposal. She did everything in her power to lay the past to rest and to move on with her life. The arrival of her *kinner* finally helped her to do that.

Now the past had galloped into the present. She reverted to the confused, scared girl who'd struggled to make the right decision. What should she do? Should her past become her future?

Chapter Twenty-Nine

"I'll be back before you know it. As soon as I'm eighteen. It won't be forever." He'd never forget the words he'd spoken before he left. They were permanently etched on his brain and haunted him on a daily basis.

Ten years. Ten long years. It might as well be forever. It must have seemed like an eternity to Lena, too. Had too much time elapsed for them to recapture the love they once shared? His love had never waned, but she had been through so much. He could understand why she didn't trust him. If only . . .

Nee. He was done blaming his *daed.* He'd spent too many years doing that. He wouldn't undo all the prayers he'd offered and all the effort it took to forgive the man and finally make peace with him before his passing. Samuel's eyes must be filled with every grain of pollen and speck of dirt blowing in the hot breeze. He rubbed them furiously as he grappled with a decision. The only remote chance he had of gaining Lena's trust would be if he told her the ugly truth he had learned after his family left Maryland.

Samuel dug at his itchy eyes. He'd kept that ugliness to himself for years, hoping if he buried it, it would disappear forever. He should have known that wouldn't work. He saw that the stick-your-head-in-the-sand attitude didn't help Mamm one bit. But talking about the whole mess wasn't something Samuel looked forward to doing. There was a chance that the truth could hurt his case instead of help it. What if Lena thought he would turn out to be like his *daed*? Could he take the risk? What choice did he have?

He snatched his straw hat from his head with one hand and raked his hair with the other. He squinted up at the bright, cloudless sky. If rain didn't put in an appearance soon, the remainder of the crops would burn up and he would surely melt. Maybe he'd become too accustomed to cooler Wisconsin summers. A cloud of dust alerted him to an approaching horse and buggy. Was it time for his customer already? Had he really frittered away half the morning?

Uh-oh. This buggy definitely did not belong to his customer, not unless he'd sent his *fraa*, which was highly unlikely. A churning in the pit of his belly shot a searing pain straight up to his throat. He coughed and swallowed hard. Why in the world was *she* here again? Wasn't his unspoken message on Sunday as crystal clear as spring water? *I guess I'll have to more explicitly verbalize that message.* He'd have to get rid of her fast because the customer he expected was none other than Bishop Menno Lapp, and the man did not need to arrive to find Samuel alone with another woman.

Alone? Surely Sarah Swarey hadn't driven here alone. She wouldn't, would she? He wanted to take another peek at the buggy to assure himself someone sat beside her, but he didn't want it to appear that he was eager to see her. If he could hide in the barn, he certainly would, but it was too late for that now. Sarah had already spied him.

"Hello, Samuel," she called out to him before she even got the horse stopped.

Should he wait for her to hop out and approach him or head over to the buggy? Maybe if he could catch her before she had a chance to disembark, he could quickly send her on her way. He forced his wooden legs to hurry down the driveway. "Hello, Sarah." He stooped to glance across the buggy, silently praying someone else would be sitting beside the person whose attention he wanted to deter. "Oh, hello, Emma." He almost didn't see the other woman slinking back into the shadowed corner as if she tried to blend in with the upholstery.

"Hello, Samuel." Emma's voice couldn't be any flatter. "Sorry to barge in on you. I told Sarah you would be busy." She rolled her eyes and shook her head.

Sarah, who stared intently at Samuel, missed both of those gestures. "I'm sure Samuel has a few minutes to spare for me, uh, us, Emma." Sarah threw the words at her cousin without turning to look at her. Her gaze stayed fixed on Samuel.

The fire in his stomach intensified. He might have to race to the house to search for an antacid or to chug down a little baking soda in a glass of water. "Actually, Sarah, I am expecting a customer any minute." *And I need you to leave immediately!*

"Oh. Well, I won't stay too long." She giggled like a much-younger girl and made motions to get out of the buggy.

Samuel wasn't sure how to be subtle, so he opted for a swift response instead. He placed a firm hand on the door, thinking she couldn't possibly misinterpret his meaning. "Is there something I can help you with? Is your horse having a problem?"

Sarah giggled again. "*Nee*, silly. I didn't bring my horse to see you. *I* came to see you."

A "hmpf" and a sigh from the corner told Samuel that Emma shared his own sentiments. He might even have rolled his eyes as she did earlier if Sarah hadn't been studying his every nuance. He waited for her to explain the reason for her visit, but when she kept quiet, he felt compelled to break the uncomfortable silence. "So, are you and Emma out for a ride?"

"Not exactly." Emma's muttering, though soft, reached Samuel's ears.

"I baked you another treat." Sarah finally tore

her eyes from his face and reached for whatever container she had stowed behind her.

In those brief seconds Samuel's eyes sought out Emma, who shrugged and mouthed, "I tried to discourage her." He nodded his understanding.

"Ta da!" Sarah produced a covered pie tin and held it out to Samuel.

"Another pie." He hoped his expression didn't give away his struggle with the nausea that now competed with the heartburn. "You didn't have to do that."

"I know I didn't have to. I wanted to try my hand at a pecan pie because I baked a shoofly pie last time."

Samuel's stomach roiled. A pecan pie would be at least as sweet and gooey as the shoofly pie he'd pawned off on the Kings. "That's, uh, nice of you." He couldn't quite move his hand to accept the proffered pie.

"Here!" Sarah wiggled the pan. "Take it."

"Oh. Right." He worked hard to keep his expression neutral, without any hint of the revulsion his stomach signaled. "You know, Sarah, you don't have to keep baking or cooking me things. I really do quite well fending for myself."

She clucked her tongue. "A bachelor cooking? Somehow I doubt it."

"Truly, I can cook and take care of myself."

"But can you bake delectable pies?"

I wouldn't even if I knew how. "That's not my area of expertise." From what the Kings—who were in no way picky—said: pies were not Sarah's area of expertise, either. Quickly he added, "But I could probably bake one if I set my mind to it. I'm not a very big sweets eater, though." There. He'd said it. He hoped he hadn't hurt her feelings, but he had to convince her to stop these ridiculous, awkward visits.

He needn't have worried. Sarah appeared unfazed by his words. In fact she acted as if she hadn't even heard them.

"Everyone likes sweets. Maybe I'll make you something chocolate next time."

Emma groaned. "Didn't you hear him, Sarah? He doesn't eat many sweets."

"Hush, Emma." Sarah threw a scowl at her cousin but turned a smile back on Samuel. "I'll think of something yummy. Don't worry."

"Please don't bother, Sarah. I appreciate the food, but I really am fine without it."

"Pshaw!"

"Please excuse me. I need to get ready for my customer." Samuel began backing away, the dreaded pie wiggling in his hands, which were clenched so tightly on the edges of the pan that they trembled and ached.

"Let's go now!" Emma obviously spoke through clenched teeth.

"Enjoy the pie, Samuel."

He didn't turn around, exhale, or relax his taut shoulders until he heard the buggy wheels crunch on gravel. Unfortunately he detected another set of hooves and wheels approaching. Those muscles immediately tensed again. This visitor could only be someone who would have to be blind not to recognize the occupants of the departing buggy. Samuel hoped the man noticed there were two people in that buggy. Could this day get any worse? And it was still only morning!

Bishop Menno leaped from his gray buggy as nimbly as a much younger man. Samuel braced himself for some sort of reprimand or inquisition at the very least. He was completely innocent of any wrongdoing again, but would the bishop believe that?

"*Gut mariye*, Samuel."

"Hello, Bishop Menno." Samuel held his breath, dreading the man's next comment but anxious to get it over with and move on to his work.

"You're a busy fellow."

Was that a smirk the bishop tried to erase from his face? The man appeared to be struggling to gain composure, but the edges of his lips kept curling upward. He cleared his throat and fidgeted with his wire-rimmed glasses. Whatever did he find so funny? Samuel identified nothing whatsoever about his current dilemma that warranted even a hint of amusement. "I expect I'm about as busy as most." Rivulets of sweat rolled down his back like loosened boulders tumbling down the side of a mountain.

"Maybe more." Bishop Menno coughed, but Samuel heard the snort that escaped first. "That was Sarah Swarey who just left, ain't so?"

"It was. And Emma Stauffer, too." Samuel knew the man had to have seen Emma. He was convinced the man's eagle eye could have picked out a gnat on the buggy wheel.

"Is she having a problem with her horse?"

"She has issues, but not with her horse." Instantly Samuel's cheeks burned red hot. Had he really spoken those thoughts aloud? He steeled himself for the upbraiding that was sure to follow. He stared at his foot swirling the dirt as if it had a mind of its own. He jerked his attention upward at the rumble of a deep belly laugh. The bishop laughed? Now Samuel didn't know how he should react.

Bishop Menno snatched off his glasses and rubbed them on the front of his blue shirt. He swiped at his eyes before resituating the spectacles. "That was a *gut* one." He slapped Samuel's shoulder and chuckled again.

Samuel, still confused, figured he'd better explain or apologize or something. "I didn't invite Sarah here. I, uh . . ."

"It's quite all right, Son. I understand. I was a young man once upon a time. You're a newcomer and all the *maedels* are vying for your attention. Some a bit more than others, perhaps."

"That's for sure and for certain. I haven't done anything to encourage any of them, and I haven't been here alone with anyone. Sometimes their *mudders* accompany them." Samuel rolled his eyes but then feared that was the wrong thing to do, too, but the older man chuckled again. Samuel had never seen him so jolly. He'd never have guessed the bishop had a sense of humor. *I guess I don't know folks here so well after all.*

"I can imagine. By the way, I didn't have any intention of accusing you of any wrongdoing. And I did see Emma hunkered down in Sarah's buggy."

Samuel exhaled louder than he'd intended. *"Gut."*

"Let me guess. She just happened to make pies and brought you one."

"Something like that." Samuel forgot he still held the offensive food in his hand; he hadn't made it to the house or even to his shop in time to squirrel the thing away. He looked from the pan to the bishop's face. Smile lines still crinkled around the man's eyes, and he looked for all the world as if he would burst out laughing again any second. "I don't even like pie!" Now the older man hooted. "Would you care to take it home with you?"

"*Nee.* My Martha makes about the best pie in

the community. That's what I've always told her. She'd be convinced I've been lying all these years if I go traipsing into the house with someone else's pie."

"The Kings have been reaping the benefit of my bountiful gifts, but I think they're about pied out. I'll have to think of something." Samuel hurried to his shop to set the pie on the edge of a workbench and raced back out to help the bishop unhitch his horse. "Let's check out this big fellow."

Bishop Menno sat in a green, metal lawn chair in the shade regaling Samuel with stories of the community while he worked. He paused in his narration to cough and clear his throat several times. "I feel like I swallowed a desert."

"*Ach!*" Samuel looked up and rubbed his dripping forehead on his shirtsleeve. "I'm sorry. I should have offered you a cup of water. I have a huge jug of ice water and cups in the shop. I can get you some."

"I can get it." The bishop hauled himself to his feet. "This heat tends to make a body lazy."

Unless that body is laboring or thinking hard to devise a way to discourage unwanted female attention. Dare he ask the bishop for advice? "I have some plastic utensils in there, too. And paper towels. Help yourself to some pie while you wait."

"You really want to get rid of that pie, don't

you?" The older man chuckled as he made his way to the shop. "I don't suppose it would hurt to look at it." After a moment he added, "Pecan pie—all nuts and sugar. You can hardly go wrong with that, ain't so?"

Samuel wasn't so sure. The Kings told him they could barely choke down the shoofly pie. Maybe if Bishop Menno really liked pie, he would enjoy this one. Samuel wouldn't hold his breath, though. He doubled up his efforts so he could hurry and finish with the bishop's horse.

A quick glance at the man's face as he emerged from the shop with a cup in one hand and a slice of pie wrapped in a paper towel in the other, told Samuel his hunch had been spot on. Bishop Menno frowned as he chewed. He swallowed with an audible gulp and followed that with a noisy slurp of water. Samuel had to look away quickly lest he be caught smiling. Now it was his turn to be amused.

"I think she needs to practice a little more."

Samuel struggled not to laugh. "You think so?"

Bishop Menno picked a pecan half off the pie and popped it into his mouth. He grunted and spat the nut onto the ground. "I think I might have broken a tooth. I wonder how old those pecans were."

Samuel couldn't hold back any longer. The bishop's wrinkled nose and disgusted expression were Samuel's undoing. He laughed loud and long. When he could catch his breath, he tried for a semiserious expression. "So, I guess the pie wouldn't win any blue ribbons at the county fair, huh?"

"Not even a yellow one, or a gray one, or any other color."

Samuel chuckled. "That bad?"

"Don't you dare tell anyone I said that!" The bishop strolled a short distance away from the shop and hurled the remainder of his pie as far as he could.

"Some critters will have a feast in a little while," Samuel said.

"Maybe not." The older man shook his head as he returned to his chair. He combed his long, salt-and-pepper beard with his fingers, as if removing any pie crumbs that might be lodged there. "I can't imagine what Sarah did wrong. She must not have sought her *mudder*'s advice. Maybe I should have Martha give her some pointers."

Samuel cocked an eyebrow as he ventured a peek at the bishop's face. "Maybe you could give me some pointers. I need advice."

Chapter Thirty

"I need advice."

"I'm not sure you came to the right person." Becky snapped off the tips of a green bean and tossed them into her scrap bucket. She added the long, tender bean to her enormous metal bowl. She and Lena sat in the shade of the old oak to work. Mary and Eliza played nearby while Grace and Matthew napped on thick blankets spread out on the grassiest spot they could find. With the recent dry spell, much of the grass had grown brittle. This mess of green beans would likely be the last of the season. "It certainly isn't like I've led an exemplary life that I can offer any pearls of wisdom."

"You overcame your past, Becky. You're exactly the right person to advise me. How did you do it?"

"Why, with your help of course. And with lots of prayers. Don't you remember your words to me?" Becky paused, holding a bean in midair to turn a startled gaze on her *freind*.

"Words. Pretty words. I was *gut* at offering those when I hadn't any firsthand knowledge of how you were supposed to *kumm* to terms with things. I hadn't even settled my own past in my mind. What a hypocrite I was!"

"You were not." Becky dropped the bean onto her lap and reached for the older woman's hand. "You were sincere. You told me I needed to forgive myself for my past mistakes and move on. I don't think you have such horrible deeds to forgive yourself for. You just need to lay your past hurts to rest."

Lena squeezed Becky's hand. "It isn't like you were some wicked Jezebel, you know."

"I hurt a lot of people when I ran off to New York, and I made a lot of mistakes while I was there."

"You were young and naïve. You came to your senses and returned home. We all forgave you and accepted you with open arms."

"Some people took a little longer than others to believe I'd changed. I can't blame them one bit. But I'm ever so grateful for you and Atlee, who saw me through the rough times."

Tears sprang into Lena's eyes. "Tell me how to put the past behind me. I-I b-believe I'm ready to move on now."

"I am so happy to hear that, dear Lena. I know you've made a *wunderbaar* life for your *kinner*, but it is time for you to find happiness and fulfillment for yourself."

Lena sniffed hard. She could only force out a whisper. "How do I let it go?"

Becky brushed the beans waiting to be snapped from her dress and back into the bucket. She scooted her chair closer to her troubled *freind* and took both Lena's hands into her own. "What is troubling you the most?"

Lena shrugged. "I don't know. Maybe it's nothing." She sniffed again. "Maybe it's everything."

"Do you want to start at the beginning? I know you cared very much for Samuel. Even though you were both young, you knew your hearts and minds. You must have been devastated when his family moved."

Lena nodded her head. "B-but I thought it was temporary. H-he said he'd be back."

"He had never lied to you before, ain't so?"

"*N-nee*. Not that I knew of."

"You must have been worried when you didn't hear from him."

"I worried that something happened to them along the way. Then I grew angry. I thought he forgot about me and never really cared for me at all. I felt kind of used."

"But you knew deep inside he cared for you. Right?"

"I suppose. But I was so hurt, Becky. I tried to push the memories and dreams of Samuel under all the other debris cluttering my mind. I tried to stow away the pain. I never wanted to experience anything like that again."

"I can understand that."

Remorse suddenly kicked in. Lena gasped.

"I'm so sorry, Becky. Am I making you dredge up unpleasant memories of your own?"

Becky smiled. "Well, I certainly have a lot of those, but I have made peace. I've forgiven myself and let it go. I can't change the past. I can only do my best in the present and hope for a *gut* future."

"I want to do that."

"Can you forgive Samuel for hurting you?"

"I think I did a long time ago, but I can't let go of the fear of being hurt again."

"But you married Joseph. You must have trusted him in order to take that huge step."

"I did. But Joseph was safe. He was dependable. He was there when I needed him after my parents' accident. I leaned on him. I did love him, Becky, but in a totally different way."

"There are all kinds of love. Your feelings for each other were mutual, ain't so?"

"I believe so. Joseph had been engaged once years before. He was ten years older than me, you know. Anyway, I wasn't his first love either, but we made our marriage work."

"Well, that's important. Your marriage to Joseph should help you see you are able to trust people."

Lena shrugged again. "Maybe. He was there to give me comfort and support at a terrible time in my life." She squeezed her eyes shut, but a tear escaped anyway. "He gave me my precious *kinner*."

"He did. But he's gone now, dear. Are you feeling guilty that you might be interested in another man, like you are betraying Joseph?"

Lena nodded but didn't open her eyes.

"I'm sure everyone who has lost a spouse must experience the same qualms about moving on." Becky squeezed Lena's hands a little harder. "Do you still have feelings for Samuel?"

"Is it terrible to admit that I do?" More tears coursed down Lena's cheeks. "I didn't pine for him when I was married to Joseph. Truly I didn't. But when he returned to Maryland, all those emotions threatened to smother me. I have moved forward by making my *kinner* my whole world. What if I trusted Samuel again—and worse, if my little ones got attached to him—and he disappeared again?"

"First and foremost, you are not a terrible person. We can love lots of people at the same time. You love all your *kinner*, don't you?"

"Of course, but that's different."

"You love your *freinden* and you loved your parents all at the same time, too."

"*Jah*, but . . ."

"Sometimes our first love is the true love, and that feeling never dies. I'm sure widows who have remarried still love their departed husbands but at the same time love the new one."

Lena remained silent. She felt the pucker in her brow that always arose when she thought deeply. "That makes sense." She wondered if there was a widow who would verify that for her.

"As for the trust issue, Samuel never lied to you when you were young."

"He could have."

"What does your heart tell you about that? Did you ever have reason to doubt him?"

"Not back then. But he could have told me rain was angel tears and I would have believed him."

Becky laughed. "Did anything he ever said ring untrue? Did anything make you pause and question his words or actions?" Before Lena could give a swift reply, Becky held up her hand in a stop sign. "Think before you answer."

Lena clamped her mouth closed and gnawed on her tongue. "I can't think of any time that I doubted him."

"There you go." Becky leaned back in her chair.

"That just makes it harder to understand why he lied to me about writing to me or returning when he turned eighteen."

"Didn't he tell you he tried writing letters to you?"

Lena nodded. "He said his *daed* wouldn't mail them or took them from the box or something. That doesn't make sense to me. Why would the man care if Samuel wrote letters?"

"Did you ask him to explain?"

"I tried. He sort of clammed up and got a sad, faraway expression on his face. It was like he wanted to say more, but he couldn't. That doesn't make sense, either."

"Maybe he and his *daed* had harsh words over the matter and he's had to work out the bitterness."

"I suppose that's possible." Lena sighed. "I just don't know. Maybe it's all too risky. Maybe I shouldn't upset the applecart. My *kinner* and I are happy, so I should leave well enough alone."

"Look me in the eye and tell me you would be completely happy if you turned Samuel away and told him to find someone else."

A vision of Samuel and Sarah together floated across Lena's mind, causing the bile to creep up her throat. She looked past Becky's head but couldn't bring herself to gaze into the green eyes. "I-I can't say that." The admission seemed to sap her strength. She slumped in the chair and closed her eyes until she felt a tap on her leg.

"When I returned to Maryland, you know I had to meet with Bishop Menno several times before I could join the church. Remember?"

Lena nodded, not trusting her ability to speak without sobbing.

"Well, he said a lot of things that made sense to me, but one Bible verse stuck in my mind all this time. It's in the book of Isaiah. It says something like 'Behold I will do a new thing; now it shall spring forth; shall ye not know it? I will even make a way in the wilderness, and rivers in the desert.' " Becky laughed. "Your expression tells me you're having the same reaction I did."

"Did Bishop Menno explain the verse?"

"He did, but he had me think about it for a few minutes first to kind of get my own interpretation."

"Okay. Let me think a second." Lena unconsciously raised a hand to her face and nibbled at a fingernail until Becky brushed away her hand. "Sorry. I've reverted to a bad habit from my youth. It sounds like the Lord Gott is going to do something new or different for someone, but I'm not sure I'm getting the gist of the verse."

"The Lord Gott can do new things in all our lives. We have to be watchful and take advantage of the new opportunities or gifts He offers to us. We can poke our heads in the sand and ignore his offering, or we can reject it altogether, or we can accept and embrace the gift with joy."

"So this newness for you was a life with Atlee?"

"*Jah*. You know how I resisted him because I didn't feel worthy of his love. You tried to talk sense into me for ages."

Lena chuckled. "Don't I know it."

"This Bible verse helped me realize what you kept trying to tell me. I finally understood that maybe it was the Lord offering me another chance by bringing Atlee into my life. If I let my fears and doubts hold me back, I wouldn't only be rejecting Atlee, I'd be rejecting Gott, too."

"You believe this something new for me is a relationship—correction, another relationship—with Samuel?"

"I don't presume to know the Lord Gott's plan, but you said you thought you were ready to move on, so perhaps He wants you to explore the feelings you've tucked away. Maybe He's calling you to trust yourself, Samuel, and Him."

"I-I don't know what to say." Lena swiped at a tear.

"At least you could talk to Samuel, find out exactly what happened while he was away, why he couldn't mail his letters to you. Then you can decide if you and he can build a new relationship. If you still don't trust him, you'll know to move on to whatever new adventure the Lord is calling you to."

"You make it sound simple."

"It isn't. I know how hard it is to let down your guard and trust, but I can't tell you how glad I am that I did."

Lena's throat clogged like the bathroom drain with a wad of hair stuck in the pipe. Her nose and eyes burned with the sob she only barely kept at bay. "I-I'm scared."

"I know." Becky reached out to hug her *freind*. "But you are one of the strongest people

I know—even if you aren't any bigger than a gnat's knee."

Lena giggled through her tears and swatted Becky's back. "A gnat's knee?"

"I don't know where that came from. It popped into my mind on a whim."

"You're *gut* for me, Becky Stauffer. And you give *gut* advice."

"Advice?"

"*Jah*." Samuel rubbed a hand over his smooth jaw. How should he word his request?

"You don't want my advice on baking a pie, do you? That would be a right sorry mess, I'm afraid." Bishop Menno laughed at his own joke.

Samuel smiled. The man's levity totally surprised him. The bishop apparently wasn't quite as formidable as he appeared. "*Nee*. It definitely isn't pie making that I need advice about. I wish it was something that simple, though maybe baking isn't so easy if that pecan pie is any indication."

The older man guffawed and clapped Samuel on the shoulder. "That's for sure and for certain. Okay, Son, I'll try to help you out as best I can. What's your problem?"

"Problems, actually. There are several."

"Name one."

"I'll start with the easiest, if either can be considered easy." Samuel picked up his tools to work. It would probably be easier to discuss his issues if he didn't have to look directly at the bishop or, more importantly, if the other man didn't have to see every expression on Samuel's face. "How do I get all these girls and their *mudders* to stop their visits? I'm up to my eyebrows in casseroles and pies." Samuel cut over his eyes in time to catch the bishop's lips twitching. He'd probably find the situation amusing himself if it didn't involve him.

"If you aren't interested in the young ladies, you need to let them know."

"I've tried to make sure I haven't encouraged any of them, but I'm not sure they all got the message." Samuel's eyes wandered to the spot where the bishop's uneaten piece of pie landed.

"I can have my Martha put a bug in a few ears to let the women know to ease up on their efforts. Don't worry. She'll be subtle. My *fraa* has a way with folks."

"*Danki.* I don't want to hurt anybody's feelings, but I sure would appreciate the help."

"Now, what's your bigger problem?"

If he experienced a little embarrassment discussing the first issue with the bishop, Samuel didn't know how he'd get through his next concern without succumbing to complete mortification. Maybe he shouldn't have even brought up the subject of another problem. Could he invent a substitute on the spur of the moment?

"Could your other issue have anything to do with a certain small, dark-haired widow?"

Chapter Thirty-One

Was he so transparent that Bishop Menno didn't even have to ponder what was on Samuel's mind? If so, everyone in the community must be aware of his dilemma. Heat crawled up the back of his neck and wandered around to sear his cheeks. Then one would think all the other girls wouldn't bother to pursue him, unless each hoped to be the one to change his mind. *Ach!* What an awkward mess. And the bishop's question still hung suspended in the air, waiting for an answer. "I-I guess you could say that." Of course Lena was his major concern. She lurked around the corner of his every waking thought and was the star of most of his dreams.

"Fine woman. Lena has been through a lot, but she has weathered the storms. She took in Rebecca Zook—well, Rebecca Stauffer now—and treated the girl like family. She's a splendid *mudder* and has done her best to keep her place up."

The man didn't have to sing Lena's praises to him. Samuel hadn't any doubts as to the kind of woman Lena became. He knew when they were young that she would be a *wunderbaar fraa* and *mudder*. "So I hear." Lame comment for sure, but he had to respond somehow.

"Lena is the reason you are not interested in any of the food-bearing *maedels* that have been vying for your attention, ain't so?"

The man didn't beat around the bush. That was for sure. "Lena has always been special to me."

"Even after all these years apart? You didn't court anyone in any of the other places you lived?"

"*Nee*. I guess I compared everyone to Lena, and they didn't quite measure up."

"And now you want to resume a relationship with her."

Samuel coughed. "I'd like to."

"Have you gotten to know her again? You were not much older than *kinner* when your family took off."

"Took off." That was definitely an appropriate term for their abrupt departure. They actually took off from a number of places over the years. "I've tried to get to know her again, and her little ones, too." Samuel finished his task, dropped his tools, and patted the horse's flank. He needed to face the bishop squarely so he didn't miss any subtle expressions.

"Hasn't that worked out for you?"

"One minute she almost seems like the old Lena, talking and laughing. But then she throws up that screen and goes into hiding. I've been here several months now, and I still don't know how to make her understand that I care."

"Do you think she's afraid you'll run off again?"

"I didn't run off before. I didn't have any say in the matter. I had to go with my family." Samuel struggled to keep his voice calm. Was he always going to have to defend himself? He didn't want to leave ten years ago. Should he have disobeyed and stayed here? Then he would have been throwing Mamm to the wolves, so to speak.

"I understand that, Son." Bishop Menno patted Samuel's arm. "I'm merely trying to look at this from Lena's point of view."

Samuel nodded.

"She might be afraid to trust again."

"She'll really be afraid to trust if she thinks I'm like my *daed*." Samuel bit his lower lip until he tasted blood. He hadn't meant that tidbit to slip out.

"How's that?"

"I didn't mean . . ." Samuel rubbed his forehead, trying to make the jackhammer stop pounding.

Bishop Menno led his horse to the pasture where Samuel's horses grazed. "Let's leave him there for a little while. *Kumm* sit in the shade and we'll talk."

Samuel shuffled behind the older man to the metal lawn chairs, feeling a bit like a sheep being led to the slaughter. He wished he had the guts to say he did not want to pursue the subject he'd accidentally alluded to. If he could stuff those words back inside his mouth and erase the bishop's memory, he surely would do just that. The throb inside his skull precluded any hope of inventing an alternative to the truth he had no desire to reveal.

Thirty minutes later the thumping in Samuel's head had eased off into a dull roar. Now he understood what people meant when they said they were "spent." He had spilled his guts, bared his soul, or whatever other terms could be used to describe his revelation, and now all shreds of energy had drained from his body.

Bishop Menno had stared at him with sympathetic eyes throughout his entire recitation. Samuel had caught that in his peripheral vision because he hadn't been able to bring himself to look directly at the man. He rubbed his suddenly moist eyes and waited an eternity for the bishop to speak. Surely it had been a mistake to confide in anyone. What advice did he expect the man to offer? Samuel should have carried his secret and his fears to his grave. He shifted in his chair, legs twitching with the urge to propel him far away. Bishop Menno's cough stopped his fidgeting.

"You are not your *daed*, Samuel, nor will you ever be him. I don't believe you are like him at all. I think you inherited your *mudder*'s kindness and strength. And I sense a deep faith all your own."

How on earth should he respond to that? "Mamm is a *wunderbaar* person. She worked very hard to teach us right from wrong."

"I believe she was successful. I also believe Lena will understand what you shared with me without being at all judgmental. You need to be completely honest with her, to give her that opportunity if you hope to establish any kind of relationship with her. In like manner, she needs to be honest about her own fears and doubts. A lot of give-and-take is always required for a happy union."

Samuel nodded. He hadn't witnessed a lot of that during his growing-up years, but he had caught glimpses of what a marriage should be when he visited the homes of *freinden*. He hoped with all his heart his *mudder* had found that happiness and peace now. And he prayed for it for his own life.

"I'm a pretty keen observer, Samuel. I've seen the signs with you and Lena. I believe you have a chance for a future together if you can both resolve your pasts and learn to trust one another again. Pray about it, Son. Pray without ceasing. And feel free to *kumm* to talk to me whenever the need arises."

"You know you can *kumm* talk to me whenever you want, don't you?" Becky had taken her bowl of green beans into the kitchen and moved

Grace to her playpen where she could gaze at her colorful toys. She bent to hug Mary and Eliza before enfolding Lena and Matthew in her arms.

"I know. *Danki* for listening and for helping."

"I'm not sure how much help I provided, but I'm pretty *gut* at listening."

"You're pretty *gut* at advising, too. I'll think about all you said. And pray about it."

"Great. But don't think so long that you miss your chance."

"Miss my chance?"

"You don't want someone else to step in before you get a chance to talk to Samuel."

"As in Sarah Swarey?"

"She's certainly persistent, I'll give her that. I really don't believe she'll worm her way into Samuel's heart, but don't give her any more incentive."

"I'll take that into consideration, too." Lena cast a wary eye at the sky. "It's clouded over."

"Maybe we'll get some much-needed rain— after you get home, that is."

"Rain I'm fine with." Lena lowered her voice so little ears didn't hear her confession. "But storms I could live without." She barely suppressed a little shiver. Even though the small tornado blew through several months ago and all debris had long since been cleared, the mere thought of that frightening evening sent chills racing up Lena's spine. She knew any storm, regardless of how minor it might be, made her girls fearful as well.

"I know what you mean." Becky's glance traveled to the playpen under the thick-trunked oak tree. "Look at her. I can hardly believe she's rolling over now and laughing and cooing. I think she might even be working on a tooth."

"They grow up so fast. This little monkey is crawling and getting into everything. I expect to find him standing up any day now." Lena hugged Matthew a little tighter. "Mary has become my little helper and Eliza, well, Eliza is my explorer. She wants to know the hows and whys of everything." Lena smiled at her girls.

"They'd probably like to have a *daed* around." Becky soundlessly mouthed the words.

Lena shook her head, sending her *kapp* strings fluttering around her face. "You're relentless. I think we'd better go before the sky opens up and drenches us with rain."

"Promise me you'll think about . . ."

"Everything. I'll think and pray."

Lena raced the raindrops from the barn to the house. She'd dropped off the *kinner* at the front porch and admonished them to stay put. She unhitched and cared for the horse as quickly as possible, not wanting to leave the little ones unattended for long. At least Matthew, like it or not, was still strapped in his infant carrier. Mary could be trusted to stay on the porch. Curious little Eliza was a completely different story. Lena hoped her wariness over storms would win out over her desire to play in the mud.

With the animals tended to and the barn door securely fastened, Lena was ready to race for the house. At least lightning didn't zigzag across the sky and thunder didn't boom like gunfire as it had in the previous storm. Huge splatters of rain drenched the earth. Lena flew from the barn, praying her black, athletic shoes wouldn't slip on the wet grass. When she reached the porch, she found Mary nibbling on a fingernail next to a squawking Matthew. "Where is Eliza?"

"She wouldn't stay with me. I'm scared." Mary lifted tear-filled eyes to the dark sky.

"It's okay, Mary. This isn't a thunderstorm. It's only rain. We haven't had any rain lately, so I suppose the Lord Gott decided the plants needed a *gut* soaking. Where is your *schweschder*?"

Mary pointed toward the side yard. "She went that way."

"Okay. Play with your *bruder*, please." Lena groaned and took off again. Most likely she would find Eliza happily digging in a flower bed, soaking wet and covered with mud. She panted as she rounded the corner of the house and then stopped breathing altogether. Eliza wasn't there. "Eliza!" She ran toward the woods. The little girl was only two and a half, with stubby legs. How could she possibly have moved so fast? "Eliza!"

Maybe Lena should have circled around the house before heading to the woods. Why didn't that little rascal answer her?

Lena leaned against a maple tree, panting for breath. The little girl surely hadn't plunged into the woods. Wouldn't she be afraid? Probably not, knowing Eliza. She would most likely only be afraid if thunder boomed. Where could she be? Lena looked from tree to tree, as if expecting one of them to give her an answer. Water trickled down her forehead and into her eyes blurring her vision. She blinked hard and swiped a wet hand across her face. "Eliza!" The only response was the sound of rain dropping on leaves.

Lena's heart pounded so hard it almost ached. A ball of fear shot from her gut and burned its way up to her throat, where it lodged. This was her fault. How could she have left three small *kinner* alone even for a few minutes? She thought she was doing the right thing by leaving them on the porch so they wouldn't get soaked. Wouldn't any *mudder* have done the same thing, or was there something faulty in her thought processes?

She should have taken the *kinner* with her. A drenching would have been preferable to this nightmare. She had zoomed through her chores in the barn at record speed, but evidently hadn't worked fast enough to keep one curious little girl out of trouble. How could Eliza have disappeared from the planet so fast?

Lena ran toward the house. Her soggy dress weighed her down. Her shoes squished and squashed with each stride. *Your fault. Your fault.* If anything had happened to her little girl, she would never forgive herself. Salty tears burned her eyes and mingled with the rain pouring down her cheeks. Maybe Becky was right. Her little ones needed a *daed.* If a man had been here to see to the animals, she and her *kinner* would be inside the house—safe, warm, and dry.

"Eliza!" She choked on the single word. She glanced toward the porch to assure herself that Mary and Matthew were still there and heaved a sigh of relief when she spotted them. She heard Mary yell for her but only waved in the direction of the house. Poor dear was nearly as frightened as she was.

Lena rounded the back edge of the house. She made another useless swipe at her eyes and squinted toward the garden. A speck of blue among the few remaining green tomato plants surrounded by metal cages caught her attention. She ignored the mud sucking at her feet as she plowed down the row. Anger, fear, relief, and gratitude all warred for prominence in her weary brain at the discovery of Eliza sitting smack in the middle of the row stirring mud with a stick.

"Eliza! Didn't you hear me calling you?" Lena snatched the little girl off the ground in a fierce hug, oblivious to the slime oozing from the tiny hands and smearing across her own back. "You frightened me to death. I told you to stay on the porch." Lena's voice shook. She should punish her *dochder* immediately, but relief won her emotional tug-of-war.

"I wanted to make you a mud pie, Mamm."

"So I see, but you disobeyed me." Lena hurried to the house as fast as she could while lugging a sodden little girl. Mary's song reached her before she made it to the front of the house. Mary always sang when she was frightened, right before she broke into sobs. Lena wanted to sob herself, but instead she joined in Mary's song.

"Mamm!" Mary jumped up from rocking Matthew's carrier. Her face crumpled.

Lena wanted to bawl right along with Mary. She'd have to beat herself up for her foolish mistake later. At the moment she had to appear calm and in control, although she felt anything but that. "Don't cry, dear one. We're all right. Let's get inside."

She managed to push open the heavy wooden door with one rain-slicked hand while gripping Eliza with the other hand. Grunting, she reached for Matthew's carrier and set it inside the house. Unless she wanted to scrub the floors again, she and Eliza would have to shed their filthy clothes on the porch. "Go ahead in, Mary. We'll be right there." The words of assurance she had offered her *dochder* bounced around in her head. Were they really all right? Would anything ever be all right again?

Chapter Thirty-Two

All the way to the Troyer place he rehearsed his words. Nothing sounded right. Even the horse snorted when he spoke them aloud. Of course that could have been Samuel's imagination. Stockings might not even have heard him.

Should he simply blurt out the truth? That seemed pretty harsh. How did one subtly lead into such a tainted topic? Maybe he'd been too impulsive. Maybe a little more thought and prayer were required. But once he'd mulled over the bishop's words, he knew the older man had been right. Samuel needed to give Lena all the details. The sooner he did that, the sooner he'd know if he stood any kind of chance with the woman he'd never gotten out of his mind or his heart. If she out-and-out rejected him, he didn't know how he would deal with the heartache, but at least he'd have his answer.

Samuel's plan had been to talk to Lena outside while the *kinner* played. He hadn't counted on the bottom falling out of the sky and the rain pounding the earth harder than a herd of wild horses stampeding across an open field. The *Englischer* he overheard at the grocery store yesterday must have been right. The remnants of that tropical storm must have blown up the coast at breakneck speed.

They needed the rain for sure if the fall crops were going to grow and if they hoped to get one more cutting of hay, but this driving rain might do more harm than *gut*. If they got strong winds as well, the crops might be doomed. He prayed the storm would blow out as quickly as it came and leave them with only a gentle rain.

He should have turned back toward home when the rain started. Samuel had been so intent on his impending conversation that he'd paid little attention to the darkening sky. The first huge drops of rain had startled him. Those drops had been followed by a downpour that caused the horse to quicken his pace without any urging from him. Now he'd get soaked even if he ran from the buggy to Lena's house, and he'd leave a trail of puddles on her clean floors. That certainly wouldn't put him in her favor. Oh well, he was out here now and would have to complete the mission he'd begun.

The rain rendered visibility almost nil, but Samuel could detect movement on Lena's front porch. Why would she be outside unless something was wrong? Had the roof sprung a leak, or was something wrong with one of the *kinner*? He didn't dare encourage the horse to move faster on the driveway, which had already turned into a slippery, muddy mess. He would reach the house in a minute or two anyway.

Lena had managed to untie her own soggy shoe-laces and kick off her waterlogged shoes. She peeled off her black stockings and stood barefoot on the cement porch floor. It took a few minutes to loosen the knots in Eliza's shoestrings. The double bows she'd tied earlier that morning had tightened into tiny, tight lumps. She had just yanked the muddy, sodden dress over the little girl's head when the approaching buggy caught her eye. The pouring rain and the muddy ground had drowned out the sound of horses' hooves and buggy wheels.

Who in their right mind would be out on a day like today, and why were they visiting her? Her dress adhered to her body like blue skin. Her *kapp* strings dripped water over her shoulders. Strands of hair had pasted themselves to her neck. And she stood barefoot and barelegged with a partially clad little girl. If the visitor was Bishop Menno, she'd be totally mortified. *Please let it be a woman.*

"Lena, is everything okay?"

Definitely not a woman. The smooth, deep voice calling from the buggy could only belong to Samuel Mast. Why did he always see her at her worst? *Why do you care what you look like if you don't care about the man?* That impish

380

little voice in her head could be so aggravating, especially when the words held some measure of logic and truth. She would mull that over later. "Everything is as okay as it can be for a couple of drowned rats," she hollered.

"Give me a minute and I'll help you."

"We're fine, Samuel. Don't get soaked on account of us."

"A little water never hurt anyone."

"A little? Look around you. We're in the middle of a flood at high tide."

The chuckle that floated over to her sent chills up and down her spine. She had always loved Samuel's laugh, but it must be the cold, soggy clothes giving her chills and goose bumps, nothing more. She rolled their stockings in Eliza's now mostly brown dress and kicked the shoes out of the doorway. "Step inside the house, Eliza, but stay right there where I can see you. Mary, please bring me some towels from the bathroom."

Lena looked down at her own mud-spattered dress. She had planned to pull it off before entering the house, but that was out of the question now. She wiped a hand down the side of her dress to wipe it clean. The dirt on her hand certainly couldn't soil the dress any more than it already was, and she needed a relatively clean hand to push her wayward hair back into its bun.

"What happened, Lena?" Samuel took the

porch steps two at a time. "Did you fall out of the buggy and into a mud hole?"

"Ha! Not exactly." She saw his lips twitching. She must look a sight. "Someone, some little someone, decided not to stay put on the porch where I put her to stay dry while I saw to the horse. I had to search high and low for her in this deluge."

"Uh-oh. Could that someone be the little girl I spy right inside the door?"

"She'd better be standing there."

"She is."

"Well, she definitely is the one who caused this ruckus and mess."

"I wanted to make you a mud pie." The wee voice trembled and ended with a little sob.

Lena glanced inside in time to see Eliza's lower lip quivering and tears shimmering in her big, brown eyes. The little girl was so sensitive. Lena needed to soften her approach. "That was very sweet of you, but I wanted you to stay where it was dry. You frightened me when I couldn't find you right away."

"Here are the towels, Mamm."

Lena could hardly see Mary over the pile of towels in her arms. She must have emptied the linen cabinet. Lena would have lots of extra laundry to do. She suppressed a sigh. "*Danki*, Mary." She pulled the top one off the pile and turned to Eliza.

"Why don't you let me tend to Eliza and you take care of yourself? You must be pretty miserable in those wet clothes." Samuel pulled the towel from Lena's hands and wrapped it around the little girl standing completely still for a change.

"Truly, Samuel, I can take care of things here. I'm sure you're eager to get home."

"I just left home." He gently wiped mud from beneath Eliza's eyes. "Were you trying to make raccoon eyes or do you cry chocolate tears?" He tickled her beneath the chin, eliciting a giggle.

"Chocolate tears!" Mary laughed and almost dropped her load of towels. "Nobody cries chocolate tears."

"Do you want to taste these to see?" He swiped a finger across the mud smear and held it out to Mary.

"Ew! I don't eat mud."

"Well, that's a mighty *gut* thing. I would hate for you to have a bellyful of worms and bugs."

"Ew! I don't like bugs."

Lena blotted her own face and peeked over the fluffy towel at the man who so easily made her girls happy. He looked completely at ease drying Eliza and teasing both *kinner*. "Samuel Mast, do you mean to tell me you deliberately set out in this horrible, nasty weather? What was so important that it couldn't wait a day?"

"You."

The word had been whispered, but it might as well have been shouted for the effect it had on Lena. Flabbergasted and confused, she pulled the towel higher and pretended to dry her face some more. She hadn't expected such an admission from his lips. Now that it hung out there in space, she didn't know what to do about it. Address it head-on? Pretend she hadn't heard it? Change the subject lickety split? She opted for the latter. "Mary, you can set down the towels on a living room chair so they stay clean. *Danki* for bringing them."

"Why don't you go ahead and change, Lena? I'll get Matthew out of his carrier."

"You might be sorry. He crawls now, you know."

"I can keep up with him, I think. And Mary will be my helper, ain't so?"

Mary smiled and nodded. "I like to help."

"*Gut* girl. So you see, Lena, we will be fine."

Her saturated clothes were beginning to leave a puddle around her feet. She hadn't wanted to drag her wet clothes upstairs, but she had no other choice now. Maybe if she moved fast, she could minimize the trail of water she'd leave behind. "*Kumm*, Eliza, let's get some clean clothes." She grabbed the little girl's hand and tugged her toward the stairs. "Let's hurry."

Lena paused at the top of the stairs and clapped her free hand across her mouth to stifle a giggle as Samuel's words rose to her. "How do you undo this contraption, Mary? Can you figure it out?" He might be comfortable with the *kinner*, but he apparently wasn't too familiar with their paraphernalia. She hoped Mary remembered how to work the clasp.

She got herself and Eliza changed and their hair smoothed into some semblance of order in record time. When she reached the living room doorway, she stopped so abruptly that Eliza bumped into her. "What on earth are you doing?"

Samuel was crawling on all fours behind Matthew, and Mary crawled behind Samuel. "You look like a herd of elephants following each other."

Samuel sat back on his haunches and winked at her, sending her heart into silly spasms. "How many of those have you seen?"

"None, actually. I can only imagine."

Eliza dropped to her knees to join in the adventure but started in the opposite direction. When she and Mary crashed into each other, both girls sat up and rubbed their foreheads. Lena hurried to kiss each little head before any tears or sniffles could form. "I don't think your *schweschder* realized it was a one-way street, Mary." That sent both girls into a fit of giggles. Lena snagged Matthew and quickly checked his diaper.

"I already did that."

Lena whipped around to stare at the big man sitting on the floor. "You did?"

"Of course. You know I don't mind doing such things, and I sure didn't want the little fellow to be miserable."

"Oh." Lena couldn't drag her eyes from his face. Something about those green eyes held her spellbound. Matthew's squirming in her arms forced her attention back to earth. She raised the *boppli* high and laughed at his squeal of delight. "Did you have some reason for stopping by?" Lena lowered Matthew and kissed his pudgy cheek. She didn't want to appear rude, but surely Samuel hadn't merely been out for a joy ride on such a miserable day.

He awkwardly got to his feet and wobbled, as if his long legs had grown numb. "I wanted to see if you and the *kinner* would like to go on a picnic on Sunday."

"A picnic?" He'd braved the elements to invite them on an outing?

"*Jah*. It's an off Sunday. We could take a lunch over to the beach and spend the afternoon, as long as the weather clears, that is."

Lena opened her mouth to refuse the invitation, but Becky's words came back to taunt her: "Don't think so long that you miss your chance." Should she give Samuel a chance? Should she give *them* a chance? "Okay. I'm sure the *kinner* would enjoy that."

"Would you enjoy it, too?"

Would she? A quick nod was her only response.

Samuel tried not to get his hopes up, but a surge of optimism shot through his body anyway. Even though she looked like a frightened rabbit caught in a trap, Lena had agreed to the outing. Now if she didn't back out before then, it would be nothing short of a miracle. It was too bad he hadn't extended the invitation loud enough for the girls to hear. Those two would probably badger her about it all week, thereby assuring Lena's cooperation if only to appease them.

He smiled and scarcely noticed the rain falling like a heavy curtain around his buggy. Did Lena have any idea how adorable she looked standing barefoot on the porch with a smear of mud across her cheek? It took every drop of his willpower to keep his arms pressed to his sides when they wanted to pull her into a hug. Samuel chuckled aloud. She probably would have slapped him or knocked him down the porch steps if he'd tried that. She was a feisty one, but he had always loved her spirit and her strength. For a little woman, she had a big personality.

Samuel had had every intention of baring his soul today, but he couldn't very well blurt out his family's shameful past with three little pairs of ears able to pick up and question his every word. Well, one of those sets of ears wouldn't be able to make any sense of the conversation, but the other two were most likely in the why, how, and what stage. He'd pray to have a quiet moment alone with Lena on Sunday while the *kinner* played.

He really wished the whole unpleasant business was behind him. Would Lena think he was like his *daed* and flee in the opposite direction? He should have pulled her aside today and made his confession and gotten it over with, but he couldn't bring himself to add one more problem to her day. Being soaked and covered with mud and dealing with a little one in the same condition seemed more than a person should have to bear for one day.

At least Lena had allowed him to help her today, albeit reluctantly. That fact alone gave his spirits a little boost. Her agreement to the picnic practically sent him soaring to the moon. *Please, Lord Gott, let her believe me when I finally tell her. Don't let her turn away from me. Let her see my feelings for her have only grown stronger. Help her see that I want to help her and her little ones. I want to be a part of their lives—a permanent part.*

What had she been thinking? Lena *hadn't* been thinking, not clearly, anyway. She shouldn't have accepted Samuel's invitation. She shouldn't encourage him, but she wanted to encourage him. Ach*! What's wrong with me?* She would simply have to find a polite way to get out of the commitment.

"Mamm! Mamm!" The tug on her skirt nearly yanked the thing off her body. She must have either lost more weight or not pinned her dress tightly enough. How long had Mary been pulling at her clothes. "What is it, dear?"

"Are we really going on a picnic?"

Ugh! Little ears heard more than they were meant to. Why did *kinner* always hear what parents didn't want them to? "Well . . ."

"You said '*jah.*' I heard you. A picnic will be fun." Mary hopped from one foot to the other. Eliza aped her and nearly knocked all three of them down.

The poor dears probably didn't even remember what a picnic was. How long had it been since they'd had one? "What do you know about picnics?"

"You take a basket of food, walk a ways, and eat outside."

"Eat outside!" Eliza echoed as she hopped again.

Lena dropped a hand to the little girl's shoulder to prevent the jumping. "Calm down."

"Are we really going?"

Mary could be relentless when something took hold in her mind. Now how was Lena going to get out of the promise?

Chapter Thirty-Three

Lena thought seriously about skipping the quilting frolic. The sun had finally returned, so she really needed to hang a ton of laundry on the line. All the diapers, *boppli* clothes, and little dresses she'd washed simply weren't drying well on her indoor clothesline. But after being cooped up inside with restless *kinner* for the past three days while rain steadily beat on the roof, Lena was more than ready to get out of the house and hold an adult conversation.

She truly did want to help with the quilts for several girls who would most likely marry in the fall. She remembered the fun and laughter at the frolic before her own wedding, and she'd appreciated the lovely stitching of all the ladies who attended. Besides, Becky had exacted a promise that she would show up bright and early with a plate piled high with her special, homemade fudge and would probably never speak to her again if she reneged. Lena had whipped up a double batch of her chocolate fudge as well as a single pan of a new peanut butter cloud fudge she'd made for the first time.

Lena wasn't a huge sweets eater herself, but Becky especially requested fudge. Hmm! There was another thing she had in common with Samuel. Would everything always make her think of him? With all the rainy, nasty weather they'd endured lately, she hadn't gotten word to him about canceling their Sunday outing. *Maybe you don't really want to miss the opportunity to see him again.* Nee, *I don't want to disappoint the girls. That's all they've chattered about.*

Lena dodged mud puddles and skipped over the mushiest areas of the driveway on her way to hitch up the horse. She carefully situated the containers in the back of the buggy, far out of the reach of little hands. She'd pull up to the door so the girls wouldn't have to maneuver through the swampy yard. Otherwise, knowing Eliza, the little girl would somehow find a mudhole to wallow in and Lena would have to get her dressed all over again.

She'd been leery of leaving the *kinner* in the house alone, but she couldn't drag them all outside with her every time she hung clothes on the line or cared for the animals. She prayed Eliza had learned her lesson and wouldn't venture off on her own again. What a little scamp! Lena couldn't suppress a smile. She had been a curious little girl herself and had probably caused more than a few of her *mamm*'s gray hairs.

Lena sighed with relief when she entered the house to find both girls entertaining Matthew by stacking blocks on the tray of his walker.

Would she always worry about her little ones? Probably. That seemed to be a *mudder*'s lot in life. But maybe she fretted a teensy bit more than most since she'd lost so many loved ones. "Is everybody ready for the frolic?"

"*Jah!*" the girls squealed in unison.

They most likely had a case of cabin fever to rival Lena's. It would be *gut* for them to have other little ones to play with under the watchful eyes of the older girls. It seemed they all needed a little break.

Only two gray buggies sat in the shade outside the Hertzlers' back door, so Lena had managed to arrive early. Nancy Hertzler was one of the older girls Lena expected would be published in a matter of weeks. The Hertzlers' house boasted a huge living room, and several quilting frames could be set up for the stitching. Several of the younger Hertzler girls would help care for the *kinner*. Lena smiled at Mary and Eliza as she helped them jump from the buggy. This should be a fun day for all of them.

Fourteen-year-old Ruth Hertzler whisked the little girls away to play a game while her fifteen-year-old *schweschder*, Hannah, relieved Lena of Matthew. Feeling strangely free, Lena trotted into the kitchen to pull the containers of fudge from the bag slung over her shoulder. This should be a fun day for the *kinner* and for her. Some adult time with her women *freinden* would be *wilkom* indeed.

As ladies, young and old, filtered into the Hertzlers' house, Lena figured she'd better claim a seat at a quilting frame. Two big wooden frames had been set up surrounded by assorted cane and oak kitchen chairs. The women could work on two quilts at the same time while sharing the latest news and telling stories from the past. The living room furniture had been pushed against the walls to allow freedom of movement between the frames. Lena wanted an end seat in case she needed to leave to nurse Matthew or tend to one of the girls.

Becky and Grace arrived with Malinda and Saloma Stauffer. Phoebe Yoder, now Phoebe Miller, arrived with her *mudder*, Lovina. Other women trickled in and took seats around the frames. Becky snagged the chair next to Lena and gave her *freind* a little jab in the ribs. "I already sampled your fudge."

"You didn't!"

"I couldn't help myself. Your chocolate fudge is the best. But that peanut butter fudge is a definite rival for first place. I've never had that before."

"It was a new concoction."

"It's definitely a keeper."

"I do hope you left a smattering of fudge for someone else."

Becky swatted Lena's arm. "I'm not quite that

big of a pig, but my sweet tooth is almost as big as Atlee's."

Lena assumed a horrified expression and gasped. "It can't be."

Becky giggled. "I know. I'll be as big as the side of a barn by the time I'm thirty."

"Somehow I doubt that. I think your metabolism is almost as fast as mine."

"Not quite."

Lena glanced down at her tiny wrist and slender fingers as she threaded her needle. Maybe Becky had a point. Oh well, it couldn't be helped. She'd always been the thinnest person around and very likely always would be.

Becky wiggled into the chair next to Lena and picked up her needle. "It's a *gut* thing I finally learned how to do needlework. I'm not the greatest or the fastest, but I'm certainly much better than I used to be."

"You don't have to be fast. And your stitching is just fine. Why, you took to knitting like a dog takes to a fat ham bone. I've never seen anyone gain proficiency so quickly."

"I do enjoy knitting. These tiny, even stitches for quilting can be a challenge, though."

Lena patted the younger woman's arm. She sucked in a breath and held it when a latecomer burst into the room.

"Hello, everybody. I'm sorry I'm late. I had a stop to make first." The woman's eyes traveled the room and lighted on Lena. Was that a smirk that toyed with her lips?

Sarah Swarey. Lena wondered if that stop was at Samuel's place. She tried hard to alter her thoughts and erase the scowl that most likely wrinkled her brow. She forced a smile. "Hello, Sarah."

"Sarah, it was *gut* of you to *kumm*. You're not really late. We're just getting started." Nancy saved Lena from trying to think up more pleasantries.

Lena focused on the fabric in front of her and blinked twice to clear her suddenly blurry vision. She certainly didn't want to jab the needle through her finger and bleed all over the lovely quilt. Surely she had been wrong. Sarah must have smiled, not smirked. Lena had never known the other woman to be mean or spiteful. True, she didn't know Sarah terribly well. They hadn't whispered to each other as scholars or played together on the playground except for when the whole school participated in some outing or game. Still, she'd always seemed a pleasant person. Lena had to have been mistaken a moment ago. That's all there was to it.

But you've never competed for the same man before. What? Is that what they were doing? Surely not. Where did that silly notion *kumm* from? Samuel could choose any woman he wanted, and if that woman happened to be Sarah Swarey, so be it.

He asked you to accompany him on Sunday. That must mean something. Or did he only feel sorry for her and her *kinner* and invite them on a picnic out of pity? *Nee.* Lena might not be the most experienced person in the world, but Samuel's green eyes did not shine with pity when he looked at her. When she allowed herself to be honest, she knew beyond the shadow of a doubt that those eyes held caring, compassion, and love. Love?

Lena's eyes jerked upward when the big, wooden quilting frame shook.

"Oops. Sorry. I guess my mind is elsewhere." Sarah plopped on the chair directly across from Lena. Now why in the world did she choose that spot? There were two other empty chairs at this frame and three empty ones at the other frame. Was she deliberately trying to taunt Lena? Surely not. *Stop being so sensitive, or suspicious, or whatever this disturbing sensation indicates.*

"How's the *boppli*, Becky?" Sarah wiggled in her chair like she had ants in her pants. Why couldn't the woman sit still? She seemed awfully excited.

Lena jumped when Becky kicked her under the table. She must have received the same vibes from Sarah that Lena did.

"She's growing like a weed. *Danki* for asking, Sarah."

"She's here, ain't so?"

"Of course."

"Great. I'll take a peek at her later." Sarah pulled a long strand of thread through her needle. "And at Matthew, too."

Lena simply nodded and studied her stitching. Sarah sounded sincere, but she'd never taken interest in a *boppli* before. At least not that Lena was aware of.

"Someday I hope to have a *boppli*, too."

"I'm sure you will," Becky assured her.

But not Samuel's. Lena bit her tongue. She didn't have any right to make such a presumption.

"You'll never guess why I was late getting here." Sarah's voice dropped, as if she was about to divulge some great secret.

Fear ran like an icy rivulet down Lena's spine. She braced herself for Sarah's next words. Had Sarah been with Samuel this morning?

"You haven't started stitching." Becky pointed to the idle needle that Sarah had only poked through the fabric once and then held aloft.

"I'll get to it. We've got plenty of time."

Everyone else stitched as they talked. Sarah couldn't seem to do more than one thing at a time. Unfortunately, as Lena saw it, anyway, the woman chose to talk. Lena tried to keep her breathing slow and even. She wouldn't give

Sarah the satisfaction of knowing her words had any kind of effect on her at all. She forced the needle in and out in small, perfectly formed stitches. Maybe if she and Becky focused on their quilting, Sarah would keep quiet.

"Not a single guess?" Sarah continued. "Well, I'll tell you. I got up really early to bake and frost a gorgeous coconut cake."

Lena unconsciously wrinkled her nose. She'd rather graze in the grass than eat coconut. She'd never cared for the taste, even as a little girl. She remembered almost getting sick at school when another scholar gave her a piece of chocolate candy with coconut inside. She shuddered at the very memory. Thankfully, Becky and Sarah didn't appear to notice her reaction.

"Did you bring it with you? I didn't see you carry anything inside." Becky raised her eyes and glanced toward the kitchen.

Leave it to Becky to probe in a roundabout but polite manner. Lena almost smiled at her *freind*'s ploy.

"*Nee*, silly. I didn't make it for here!"

"Oh. Some of us brought treats along with us today." Becky shrugged and turned back to her stitching.

"I didn't want to waste all that time and effort on women."

Lena sucked in a breath and held it. She didn't know a person could drag out one simple topic for so long. *Spill it, Sarah, if you're dying to tell us.*

"Well, I guess we don't count for anything, huh, Lena?"

Becky nudged her so hard that Lena almost fell off her chair. She dropped her needle to rub her arm for a moment.

"I'm sorry, Lena. I didn't mean to hurt your arm."

"I'm okay."

"Gracious, Becky. You know how puny those little stick arms are. Why, you could break one without even trying." Sarah giggled.

Lena silently counted to twenty and then added ten more. She would not defend herself or even acknowledge Sarah's insult. Maybe she hadn't intended her words as a slight, but Lena's feelings hurt anyway. It would be best for her to say nothing in her present state of mind. She hoped Becky wouldn't pursue the topic, either. She picked up her needle and stabbed the cloth. From the corner of her eye, she saw Becky do the same thing. Now, if Sarah would only take the hint.

Chapter Thirty-Four

"Anyway, back to my cake story."

Couldn't Sarah see they really were not interested? Why did she need to keep harping on the subject? What was her motive? Lena picked up her counting at number thirty-one.

"I worked hard to get my cake looking just right."

I wonder if it tasted just right. Bad, Lena. So bad.

"I carefully covered it and carried it to my buggy. It's so hot out today that I was afraid the frosting might melt."

"It's hot for sure." Becky paused a moment, gulped in a deep breath, and blurted out Lena's thoughts. "You really don't need to give us a minute-by-minute account, Sarah."

"Oh. Okay. I'll get down to the best part."

Becky kicked Lena under the table. Lena didn't dare reach down to rub her ankle, but she would need to move her leg farther away from Becky if she didn't want to be covered in bruises. She willed her heart to calm down. She shouldn't let Sarah rile her. Maybe the irritating woman sold her nasty coconut cake to an *Englischer* for some exorbitant amount of money. Then she could move to Florida or Mexico or some place far away.

Shame on you, Lena Troyer. What horrible thoughts. Forgive me, Lord Gott. Help me to be nice. She struggled to arrange her face in a pleasant expression, even if she couldn't manage a smile. She stared at the quilt she was supposed to be stitching.

"Like I said, I was worried about the icing melting, so I urged my poor old horse to trot as fast as he could."

Lena cut her eyes over to Becky for the briefest instant. She swallowed a giggle at Becky's exaggerated eye roll and quickly pulled her leg out of kicking range. She didn't dare look at Sarah's face. Neither she nor Becky commented, but that didn't deter Sarah in the least.

"Thankfully, my cake fared fine, and I got to Samuel's place before he got busy with any customers."

Lena jerked when her needle jabbed her finger at the mention of Samuel's name. She'd been expecting that so shouldn't have been surprised. She stared at the little bubble of blood on her left index finger. Becky passed her a tissue. At least Sarah didn't seem to notice the mishap. Lena wrapped the tissue around her finger and pressed hard to stop the bleeding.

"I think I surprised Samuel."

"Probably so." Becky drew her needle through the fabric.

"Disgusted" might be a more fitting word than

surprised. Unless Samuel's tastes had changed drastically, he hates coconut as much as I do. Lena wished she could have witnessed that encounter. She bit down hard on her tongue to keep a chuckle from escaping.

"Do you think you might be going a little overboard?" Becky held her needle still.

Lena stared at Becky. What was she up to?

"What do you mean?" Sarah's face scrunched into a frown.

"I mean, uh . . ." Becky faltered and glanced at Lena, who kept silent. "Well, I mean, you seem to be chasing after Samuel."

Lena's breath caught. How would Sarah take Becky's bluntness?

"I'm only taking him food and visiting, like a *gut* neighbor and *freind*."

"Are you two *freinden*? I didn't know you were that well acquainted. You're a bit older, ain't so?"

Motherhood must have made Becky more aggressive. Lena couldn't help but be surprised at the girl's bold speech.

"I am a little older, but that's not important." Sarah bristled like a defensive porcupine.

"Of course not." Becky's voice took on a more soothing tone. "We can have *freinden* of all ages."

"Exactly. Anyway, I figured Samuel probably ate cold cereal for breakfast every morning and some kind of horrible canned food for supper."

"Samuel can cook." Lena hadn't meant for the words to slip out.

"What? How would you know that?" Sarah shifted her attention to Lena.

"He told me."

"Oh. Well, I bet he can't bake cakes and pies." Becky rethreaded her needle and pulled it through the fabric. "I heard Samuel really doesn't care much for sweets."

"What man doesn't like sweets? They say food is the way to a man's heart or something like that."

"Maybe. If it's a food he likes." Becky chuckled. "I don't have to worry about Atlee. He'll eat anything."

Sarah stared hard at Lena. "Do you know if Samuel likes sweets?"

"Well, I'm sure people can change, but he didn't care for a lot of sweets when he was younger."

"Do you mean I've been making all these cakes and pies for nothing? What did he do with them if he doesn't eat such things?"

"I'm sure I wouldn't know what he's done with them." Lena knew for a fact that he had shared some of the treats with the Kings, but she didn't know about the others. "Maybe he developed more of a sweet tooth over the years." Lena almost felt sorry for the other woman. Deep down she knew if she didn't have feelings for

Samuel herself, she'd be totally sympathetic.

Sarah shrugged and gave a tight smile. "Well, it's the thought that counts, ain't so? I guess I can make something other than sweets. What do you think? I can always drop off a casserole."

I think Samuel might throw up if he receives one more casserole. Lena kept mum.

"Maybe you should wait and give Samuel an opportunity to approach you." Becky spoke softly enough for only the three of them to hear. "You know, sometimes a man wants to be the one to pursue."

"But if I don't try to win him over, he'll turn to someone else."

Lena didn't look up from her stitching but felt Sarah's gaze on her. The fire shot right across the quilting frame, threatening to consume her.

Becky patted Lena's leg out of Sarah's view before responding. "It's pretty much impossible to make a person feel one way or another. Samuel is a grown man. He knows his own heart and mind."

Sarah pushed back her chair. "I think I need a drink of water before I stitch."

Lena ventured a peek at Sarah's retreating back before turning toward Becky. "I hope we didn't hurt her feelings."

"You didn't do anything. I was the mouthy one. I wasn't trying to be mean. I only wanted to talk some sense into her before she makes an even bigger spectacle of herself. I'm not sure I succeeded, though."

Sarah had pasted a smile on her face by the time she returned. She picked up her needle and plunged it into the cloth. "I'll think of something else to do," she muttered as she attacked the quilt.

Lena wondered what the woman's next scheme would be in her desperate attempt to win Samuel's heart. Would he fall prey to the next one?

What in the world would he do with this lop-sided coconut cake? Ugh! He couldn't even make himself taste it so he could mumble some kind of compliment if asked about it. He couldn't imagine anything worse than having flakes of coconut stuck between his teeth. He fought a shudder. He'd rather eat hay with the horses than consume a sliver of this cake. Maybe he could offer it to his customers; Melvin King said he'd had quite enough of Sarah's baking.

Samuel had had quite enough of her flirtations. He thought she would have gotten the message by now. He wished he knew a fellow to introduce her to. She definitely needed to focus her attention elsewhere. Apparently Bishop Menno's *fraa* hadn't gotten around to putting a bug in anyone's ear, or else Sarah chose to ignore any advice offered to her. Samuel didn't want to hurt the woman, but he might have to resort to bluntness to drive his point home. If only Lena would agree to a courtship. That would put an end to Sarah's increasingly frequent visits, wouldn't it?

He'd never been pursued so relentlessly before. Sure a couple of times girls had flirted with him outright, but once they knew he wasn't interested, they backed off. Sarah, though, seemed to consider his disinterest a challenge. Should he talk to the bishop again, or maybe to Sarah's *mudder*? That would surely be as embarrassing for him as it would be for Sarah.

He couldn't stand here in the hot sun all day holding a foul cake with icing sliding off it. He'd better take it into the house. It wasn't much cooler in there, but at least the sun wouldn't turn the cake into a lumpy, gooey puddle.

Samuel spied a stack of paper plates on the kitchen counter and devised a plan. He would slice the cake, put the pieces on paper plates, cover them with plastic wrap, and set them in the cooler. He'd haul the whole thing out to the workshop along with a box of plastic forks and tell customers to help themselves. That should resolve the cake problem. Now how did he resolve the real problem?

Sunday couldn't arrive fast enough. Samuel prayed over and over that Lena would understand. He'd glimpsed a familiar little spark in her eyes on several occasions and observed that smile that made his heart want to burst with joy. Somehow he had to convince her to give them a chance.

Samuel slammed the lid of the cooler after tossing in the last slice of cake. He had several appointments scheduled. He would convince everyone to take a piece of cake and serve any leftovers to the forest animals. There were going to be a lot of fat deer and groundhogs around here if Sarah didn't stop her crazy visits.

The morning proceeded in awkward silence at Lena's end of the quilting frame. She tried to focus on the stories the old women told and politely laughed when everyone else did. Her mind journeyed elsewhere, though, and she'd been unsuccessful in calling it home. It was a blessing her fingers automatically knew what to do so her stitches remained small and even.

Grunts and groans from across the wooden frame told Lena that Sarah was not having as much success. Lena was vaguely aware that Sarah pulled out stitches several times. When Becky had been called away to tend to Grace, the uncomfortable silence became almost unbearable. A shroud of gloom threatened to smother her. So much for the fun day Lena had anticipated.

The lunch break took forever to arrive. Lena hadn't heard one whit of the stories or news shared by the others. She'd have to ask Becky what she missed when they had a chance to talk later. Her appetite had fled long ago and she wasn't sure she could even pretend to eat.

"Lena, are you eating?" Becky stretched as she stood.

"You really can't afford to skip any meals." Sarah clucked her tongue. "In fact, you need to add a few hefty snacks, I'm thinking." She smiled sweetly, but her lips didn't notify the rest of her face so it could join in the effort. "Men like women with a little meat on their bones, you know." With that announcement, Sarah flounced off toward the kitchen.

"I don't remember her being so catty before. Maybe I never really knew her." Lena scooted her chair back.

"I don't think we've ever experienced her desperate attempt to land a man before now. And you're her competition."

"Well, as she said, I'm too bony to be a real threat to a well-rounded person like her." Lena glanced down at her baggy dress. She would pin it tighter when she got the chance.

"You are fine exactly as you are. People *kumm* in all shapes and sizes. The Lord Gott made and loves us all."

Lena nodded, suddenly choked by a lump as big as her fist clogging her throat.

"Someone else loves you, too."

Lena squeezed Becky's arm and cleared her throat. "I appreciate your caring and concern."

"I do love you like a *schweschder*, but I was

thinking of someone of the male persuasion, and you know exactly who I mean." Becky leaned closer to whisper, "She doesn't stand a chance with Samuel. He only has eyes for you."

"You're *narrisch*."

"Not half as crazy as you think. Give him a chance. You'll see."

"Let's get you some food. I think your brain is starved."

Becky laughed and looped her arm through Lena's. "I am hungry, but my brain is functioning just fine."

The afternoon improved considerably when Sarah rushed off to another commitment. Lena's knotted stomach relaxed and her tense shoulders loosened.

"She probably went home to concoct a casserole." Becky shook her head. "Atlee said poor Samuel is seeing casseroles in his sleep."

Lena giggled. "Samuel did say he was tired of all the food brought by hopeful *maedels* and their *mudders*."

"How many casseroles and sweet treats did you take him?" Merriment sparkled in Becky's green eyes.

"Not a single one."

"Hmm. That could be a problem. That might throw you out of the running."

"I'm going to run get a leftover sandwich to stuff in your mouth, Becky Stauffer!"

Chapter Thirty-Five

Ready or not, Sunday dawned bright and beautiful. If she hadn't been so tired of rain, Lena might have wished for a drizzly day so the picnic would be canceled. But then the girls would have been disappointed. Why did a thousand butterflies flap their wings in her stomach? She'd known Samuel forever. Not this Samuel, though. This Samuel was a grown man. A competent, capable, kind man as far as Lena could tell. And a very handsome man, not that looks mattered.

Lena smoothed a few stray wisps of hair from her face and neck and poked them beneath her *kapp*. She ran her hand down her skirt to smooth out any wrinkles and frowned at the puckers made by the pins. Sarah's words came back to haunt her. What if men really did only want women who were healthier-looking? What if Samuel did?

She couldn't help it if she was thin. It apparently was part of her genetic makeup to be so scrawny. She couldn't even keep any weight on after giving birth. Once the infant exited the womb, her stomach collapsed against her spine again. Lena sighed. There was nothing she could do about it. She'd always been this way and probably always would be.

Samuel asked you to go on the picnic a few days ago. You looked exactly as you do now. He didn't have a problem with your looks then, or even ten years ago, so stop worrying. She was being ridiculous. They were two *freinden* taking cooped-up *kinner* on a picnic. End of story. Right?

"Mamm, is it time to go yet?"

Lena hadn't been aware Mary had entered the kitchen until she felt the tug on her skirt and heard the little voice. "Not yet, but soon."

"Soon?" Eliza echoed.

"Soon. Let's put some sandwiches in the cooler so we'll be ready. Should we add apples?"

"Okay." Mary trotted over to the fruit basket and plucked out two big, red apples.

"How about one more? You and Eliza can share the biggest one. Then there will be one for Samuel and one for me. We'll take applesauce for Matthew."

"Cookies?" Eliza tugged on her skirt now.

"I suppose we can toss in a few cookies, and maybe that jar of pickles."

"Pickles? Did I hear pickles?" The deep voice floated in through the open kitchen window.

"Samuel's here, Mamm. It's time to go!" Mary's eyes danced.

"Samuel!" Eliza jumped up and down.

Were her girls that excited to see Samuel? Were they missing a *daed* that much? They were probably only excited about going on a picnic. She should have taken them on one way before now.

"I like pickles." Samuel poked his head inside the back door. "May I *kumm* inside?"

"Of course." Lena's palms grew damp. Those butterflies took flight again, making her stomach queasy. She snatched up the dish towel and dried her hands. How would she get through this day if her nerves didn't settle down? She was a grown woman, not a teenager.

Samuel stepped into the kitchen. He reached down to tickle each girl under the chin, thereby setting off fits of giggles. Lena's heart melted at the obvious fondness he had for her *kinner*. When he raised his green eyes to meet her eyes, her knees wobbled.

"Hi, Lena." His voice was low and husky. He cleared his throat and spoke louder. "Hey, girls, did you know I love pickles, especially your *mamm*'s bread-and-butter pickles? Is that what's in the jar?" Before anyone could answer, he addressed the girls in a mock-serious tone. "Do you know why I like your *mamm*'s bread-and-butter pickles so much?" He paused to give the girls time to wag their heads. "Because she doesn't put onions in them! I don't care much for onions, and I especially don't want them in my pickles. Ew!" He crossed his eyes and scrunched up his face. The girls howled with laughter.

Even Lena chuckled. Her tension slowly drained. "Most people would call those plain, old sweet pickles, you know."

"*Nee*. They taste like bread-and-butter pickles, only without those nasty onions and peppers. What do you think, Mary?"

"I don't like onions and peppers, either."

"Either." Eliza didn't want to be excluded from the conversation.

"You do like your *mamm*'s pickles, though, ain't so?"

"She makes *gut* pickles." Mary carefully held up a pint jar and gave it a little shake. Uniform slices of cucumbers floated among the spices in the brine. "See?"

Samuel rescued the jar from shaky little hands and held it high. He pretended to study the contents. "I don't see a single onion or pepper. Hurray!" The girls giggled again. He winked as he handed the jar to Lena.

Her heart tripped over itself. She struggled to control her own trembling hands and quickly wrapped them around the jar. "I do have true bread-and-butter pickles, too. I could always throw a jar of them into the basket, too."

"These will do just fine."

Lena remembered Samuel's dislike of the traditional pickles. In fact memories of everything she ever knew about him rushed in to flood her thoughts. Her cheeks burned. They must have flushed a bright scarlet color. She turned away slightly to wrap a protective dish cloth around the jar and tuck it into the basket. "We have sandwiches, fruit, pickles, cookies, and pretzels."

"Those big, yummy, soft pretzels?"

"I'm afraid they're regular, old, store-bought pretzel twists."

"Perfect." Samuel patted his stomach.

"Cookies." Eliza hopped from one foot to the other.

"Let me guess. Chocolate chip?"

Eliza nodded.

"My favorite."

Lena remembered that, too. She knew better than to make some gooey dessert. She'd even made the cookies with a little less sugar, the way he'd always liked them.

"I'd say we're all set. Where is Matthew? I can get him for you."

Lena nodded toward the living room. "I had to confine him to the playpen to keep him out of trouble while I packed our food."

"I'll go spring him from *boppli* jail." Samuel strode off whistling. Mary and Eliza followed on his heels like little ducklings waddling after their *mudder*.

Lena smiled. She almost broke into song herself. Samuel always had a way of bringing a smile to her lips and joy to her heart. She'd better stay on guard, though. It would be too easy to get used to his presence.

"I think we need to make a slight change in our plans." Samuel flung the words over his shoulder on his way out of the kitchen.

Uh-oh. Lena's hope and happiness drained right out the soles of her feet. Instantly her mind flew back in time. Samuel had uttered the same words ten years ago. Was he planning to run out on her again? Then why bother to show up here today at all?

If he hadn't walked in the door, she could have told the girls something must have detained him. They could have gone on with a little picnic of their own, even if they had it in the backyard. Now Mary and Eliza would be so disappointed. They had looked forward to this outing and would be as heartbroken as she had been years ago.

The gash in her heart that had scabbed over opened afresh. For all her trepidation, she had looked forward to today's picnic, too, just as she had looked forward to being courted by Samuel when they were younger. She should have known better than to count on him again. Anger fused with hurt.

But wait. Why was Samuel retrieving Matthew if he was planning to back out on his promise? Why make a big deal about pickles and pretzels?

Wouldn't he have simply said he couldn't go when he first popped in the door? Or he could have sent word somehow. Lena forced herself to take a few deep, calming breaths so she could listen to his explanation without interrupting or flying off the handle.

Samuel swung Matthew high in the air and chuckled along with the high-pitched squeals. How could the man be so sweet the instant before he broke their hearts?

"Are you all right?" Samuel's laughter died and he looked at Lena with eyes full of concern.

"Sure. Why?"

"I don't know. You look pale. You aren't sick, are you?"

Lena shook her head and then reached to secure a few strands of hair that shook loose.

"I was about to say we might need to alter our plans just a tad."

"Oh?" One word was all she could manage.

"*Jah*. Yesterday an *Englisch* customer mentioned some kind of big to-do at the river today. The place is likely to be swarming with all sorts of people. If it's okay with you, we could hike back to the pond on Melvin King's property and have our picnic there. What do you think?"

Lena exhaled the breath she'd been holding. "I-I think that would be fine." She'd been a bit concerned the river would still be restless after

416

the recent heavy rains, so this change of plans might be for the best.

"Great. I'd rather have peace and quiet so we can talk and play. Miriam King even offered to let Matthew nap in the house, if you wanted to do that. I think she's itching to care for a *boppli*."

Lena smiled and relaxed once again. Samuel wasn't abandoning them. When was she going to stop jumping to conclusions—the wrong conclusions? When would she learn to trust again? "Miriam is such a nice woman. I might take her up on that offer, depending on how things go."

"Are we ready to load up?"

"*Jah*!" Two excited little voices cried out in unison before Lena could even form an answer.

"I think someone is excited." Samuel winked. "Make that two someones."

Make it three! Samuel's tenderness, concern, and that wink sent Lena's heart soaring once again. Dare she give it permission to fly or should she rein it in before it got too far away? Perhaps for one day she could throw caution to the wind and be carefree. That would be ever so nice. She would try really hard to enjoy this day. A quick glance at Samuel's smile and sparkling eyes told her that would probably not be difficult to do.

"Putting down the plastic under the blanket was a wise idea. Even though the last couple of days have been sunny, the ground is still a little damp." Lena patted the grass just beyond the blanket.

"Sitting on this little knoll helps, too. I'm sure the ground is soggier closer to the pond." Samuel reached over to wipe applesauce from Matthew's chin. "*Danki* for preparing the lunch. I would have done it. After all, I invited you on the picnic. I should have provided the food."

"Don't be silly. It wasn't any problem. Besides, I don't think we wanted peanut butter and jelly sandwiches." Lena laughed and poked his arm.

"Hey, I can make other things."

"I'm sure you can. You look like you've been eating well."

"Are you trying to tell me I look fat?"

Lena laughed harder. "You sound like a woman who's worried about her weight. I didn't mean that at all. You look *gut*." She felt the flush creep from her neck to the roots of her hair. He looked better than *gut*, to be truthful.

"Well, I have to say your ham sandwiches were much better than peanut butter, and your meat loaf sandwiches were the best. I had one of each, in case you didn't notice."

"Mine, too." Eliza looked up from the pickle juice she'd been dipping her pretzel in.

"Okay. Okay. I finished your sandwich, too, but you ate most of it. Anyway, I didn't eat breakfast, so I was extra-hungry." Samuel patted his belly.

"Are you girls finished eating?"

Mary swiped a napkin across her mouth. "*Jah. Can we play now?*"

Lena nodded her consent. "But you stay right around here where I can see you." She finished mopping Matthew's face and then wiped his hands on a damp wipe from the container she'd brought.

"He looks like he's ready to fall asleep any second."

"If I rock him in my arms for a few minutes, he will probably drift right off." Lena pulled the *boppli* into her arms and hummed softly as she swayed to and fro. From the corner of her eye, she could see Samuel picking at the edges of the blanket. Something must be bothering him. She remembered how he used to fidget when he had something on his mind. Carefully she lowered Matthew to the far corner of the blanket where he could doze undisturbed.

Samuel cleared his throat. "Lena, we need to talk."

Startled, her eyes flew to his face. The last time he needed to talk and looked so serious, she ended up with a shattered heart. Was he planning something equally bad? Maybe he really was like his *daed* and couldn't stay in one place for very long. She steeled herself to hear whatever troublesome news he prepared to impart.

"I need to tell you the real reason my family left Maryland—and every other place we lived."

Chapter Thirty-Six

Why did that stricken look cross her face? She hadn't even heard his story yet. Or had some rumor reached her from somewhere? He doubted that. He would have known if word had gotten around. Keeping secrets in such a small community was practically impossible. She must be reliving their conversation from ten years ago. He'd seen that exact expression on her face back then. She must think he was about to leave again. How could he reassure her that was not at all what he intended to do?

Samuel reached over to touch one of her hands. Ice cold. On a sunny, August day, a person's hands should not feel like she had just rolled snowballs in the middle of a January blizzard. If she was scared he was going to leave, that must mean she cared, ain't so? He would take some comfort in that thought, even if she told him to leave after hearing his confession.

"Y-you don't owe me any explanations, Samuel. That's in the past. What is done is done." Lena pulled her hand from beneath his big, rough, warm one.

"But I want to explain. I know I hurt you, though I certainly never intended to. I want you to understand. I want you to have all the facts, and then you can decide whether or not to hate me."

"I never hated you and I never could." Neither could she tell him her love for him had been buried but never completely snuffed out.

"Maybe 'hate' is too strong a word. I know you don't hate people. You're way too kind and caring. 'Dislike' might have been a better word."

"I don't dislike you, either." *I'm just not sure if I can trust you.*

"Will you hear me out?"

Lena's eyes darted from her sleeping *boppli* to her little girls picking wild daisies, violets, and buttercups in the sunny field. "Very well."

Samuel glanced toward the sky—asking for guidance perhaps—cleared his throat, and began his tale. "You know my family left here abruptly."

"For sure."

"I truly hadn't any idea my *daed* was about to uproot us and drag us off to Pennsylvania."

"People said he was an adventurer, that he couldn't settle in one place long."

"He couldn't stay anywhere long, but not because he sought adventure, unless that adventure lodged at the bottom of a whiskey bottle."

Lena gasped. "Wh-what are you saying?"

"My *daed* was fond of alcohol. Fonder of it than of his *fraa* and *kinner*."

"Oh, Samuel. I'm sorry. I didn't have any idea." She patted his arm as she spoke.

"I don't think anyone knew. I didn't know for sure until after we moved a couple of times. He was an expert at hiding his addiction. He could carry out his work most days, or had me do it. Eventually we figured out that he drank every evening."

"I-I hope he wasn't mean to you, that he didn't mistreat you."

"Not in a physical way, but emotionally his drinking took a toll on us, especially Mamm. Sometimes she seemed so small and frail, so beaten, but she always summoned up strength and carried on. Daed never hit anyone. He yelled sometimes, but we *kinner* learned to do our chores and stay out of the way. It probably didn't help matters that Mamm and I tried to cover for him once we knew what was going on. I think they call that 'enabling,' but we wanted life to be as normal as possible for the younger ones."

Lena swiped at the moisture in her eyes. "I never figured that out. Did anyone here know of his problem?"

"I don't believe so, but Daed feared the bishop was putting two and two together. That's when he invented the story about needing to see new places. The same thing happened everywhere we went. Right when we started settling in and getting used to new people and new routines, he snatched us away again. Indiana, Florida, Wisconsin. I've lost count of all the places."

"I wrote you tons of letters. I see now why you wouldn't have received them. But the letters you said you wrote . . ." Her voice fizzled out and she gulped to force back a sob.

Samuel grasped her hands and squeezed them. She allowed her gaze to travel to his face and couldn't tear her eyes from the sincerity and concern she saw in his eyes. "I did write to you, Lena. Please believe that. I wondered why you never wrote back. One day I found the answer." His voice broke.

Lena squeezed his hands in return. Maybe she could will him strength or encouragement, whichever he needed. She waited silently for him to continue.

"I had run from the field to the mailbox at the end of the long driveway. I was so sure a letter from you would be waiting for me. Instead I found Daed there, stuffing mail into his shirt. I thought he'd put it there for safekeeping, so I offered to carry it to the house for him. His words were slurred, so I knew he'd begun drinking earlier in the day than usual. He flailed his arms and told me to get back to work. That's when all the envelopes fell to the ground."

Samuel let go of Lena's hands and plucked a blade of grass from the ground. He studied it as if he'd never seen such a marvel before. Then he twirled it between his thumb and forefinger. Lena stayed perfectly still. She sensed he was struggling to control his emotions and wanted to give him all the time he needed.

"I was quicker than he was and scooped up the mail, but it seemed like a lot more than we usually received each day. I looked closer at the envelopes and realized it was all outgoing mail. Letters addressed to you, four or five of them. Letters Mamm had written to *freinden* in Maryland and a few other places we'd lived. Daed had collected them all. He must have watched every day and taken the mail before the mailman could get it. That's why you never heard from me. I'm not sure why he had them all with him at that time. Who knows why an alcoholic does what he does?"

"B-but why? Why wouldn't he want you to communicate with anyone?"

"From his twisted way of thinking, if we didn't keep in touch with anyone, his problem would remain a secret. I guess he thought Mamm or I might tell someone the real reason we moved so often. Daed had the presence of mind to be embarrassed, but apparently not embarrassed enough to quit drinking. Honest, Lena, I did try to contact you."

"I believe you, Samuel." She laid a hand on his arm. "You must have been so upset with your *daed*."

"I was furious. In my anger and frustration, I said things I shouldn't have. I accused him of

424

ruining our lives. I-I later regretted my words and asked his forgiveness."

"Your anger and hurt were completely understandable."

"Perhaps, but not right. And not like me. I am not an angry, mean person."

"Of course you aren't."

"It took a while for me to work through the pain of his deception and, worse, the pain of losing you."

Lena sniffed. "I was wrong, too. I assumed you didn't really care about me, that I was only a passing fancy. I let hurt and anger dictate my actions for a long while, too."

"I'm so sorry, Lena."

"H-how did you ever get to the point of forgiving your *daed*?"

"I did a little research at the public library. I learned alcoholism is a disease and people need help to overcome the addiction."

"Did your *daed* get help?"

"*Nee*. He died in a logging accident in Wisconsin. He had been drinking. His reflexes were too slow and he couldn't get out of the way of a falling tree."

"I'm so sorry. Your poor *mudder*, and all of you *kinner*, too."

"He shouldn't have been out cutting wood in his condition, but he always thought he was fine."

"Your *mudder* didn't want to return to Maryland with you?"

"*Nee*. Mamm said she would not uproot the family again. I worked every job I could to keep the family going, so I wasn't able to leave right away. When Mamm started seeing Gabe Schlabach, I started planning my own move."

"Did she remarry?" If Samuel's *mudder* found the faith and courage to trust again, couldn't Lena find those things as well?

"She did. Gabe is a very *gut* man and treats Mamm and the younger ones with love and kindness. He had two nearly grown sons and a younger *dochder*, so they have a very full house. Mamm is happier than I ever remember her being."

"I'm glad to hear that. I always liked her very much."

"She was fond of you, too. She was almost as upset as I was when we found out about Daed's scheme to keep us isolated. I know her heart ached for me when I was so distraught."

"*Mudders* always feel the pain of their *kinner*."

Samuel took Lena's hands again. "I see what a terrific *mamm* you are. I always knew you would be. Do you think you can find it in your heart to forgive all the pain I caused you?"

"I know now it really wasn't your fault, but I did forgive you long ago."

"My feelings for you have never changed.

Can you find it in your heart to trust me again?"

A shriek and a loud splash ripped the air.

"Mamm! Mamm!" Mary hollered and pointed at the pond.

"Eliza!" Lena screamed as she leaped to her feet. Her heart pounded so hard that it stole her breath. Her feet propelled her forward before her brain even issued the command. She threw a quick glance over her shoulder to make sure Matthew still napped. What was Eliza doing near the pond?

Samuel's long, powerful legs got him to the pond ahead of Lena. She squinted but couldn't see Eliza. Was her little girl on the bottom of the pond? Eliza didn't know how to swim. Lena didn't even know how to swim. "My *boppli*! My *boppli*!" Before she could plunge into the murky pond, a big hand jerked her backward.

"Stay here, Lena. I'll get her."

"I don't see her. Oh, dear Gott, where is she?"

"I'll find her." Samuel threw off his hat, kicked off his shoes, and waded into the pond. He shaded his eyes with one hand as his eyes roamed the pond's surface.

"There! Over there, Samuel. I see blue." A bump against Lena's leg nearly sent her tumbling into the water. She put out a hand to grab Mary, who slid down the hill. Crashing into Lena was the only thing that kept her from rolling into the pond. "Mary! You almost knocked us both in. Why was Eliza down here?"

Mary gasped and sniffed and tried to speak. "S-she did what I j-just did. S-she was ch-chasing a b-butterfly. She slid and couldn't stop." Sobs overtook her and she clung tighter to Lena's leg.

"Shh. Samuel will get her." Wouldn't he? He had disappeared beneath the water, too. Had she lost both of them? "Please run up and stay with Matthew." She gave Mary a little push in the opposite direction. "Stay there with him. Don't bring him down here. Okay?"

Mary nodded. Still crying, she picked her way through the tall grass and brambles. Lena had to trust her older *dochder* would do as she was told. Her attention needed to be focused here, and she needed Mary out of the way in case . . . *Dear Gott, please let them surface. Now!*

Samuel probably held his breath before diving under the water, but Eliza didn't know to do that. And even if some instinct might have told her to do it, she tumbled down the hill and into the pond so fast, she wouldn't have had time to draw in a deep breath.

Where were they? How long could they stay beneath the pond's surface? How long had they already been there? It seemed forever. All the recent heavy rain had swelled the pond nearly to overflowing and had made the water muddier. It was a wonder she'd even seen the blur of Eliza's dress. Why couldn't she see it now?

A splash to her left made Lena whirl around so fast that she almost lost her balance. Samuel coughed and gasped as he sloshed toward her with a limp little girl in his arms. Why didn't she cough or cry out? *Please, dear Gott. Please let her move or cough or something.*

"My *boppli*!" Lena rushed forward, her arms outstretched.

"Let me lay her down." Samuel moved quickly despite the mud sucking at his feet. He lowered Eliza to the ground and felt her neck. "I feel a pulse." He placed a hand on her chest.

"It's not moving. She's not breathing, is she?" Lena dropped to her knees and picked up one limp little hand. "Eliza!"

Samuel tilted back the little girl's head and began rescue breathing. Dread and fear filled Lena's heart as she helplessly watched Samuel breathe for her *dochder*. Suddenly Eliza's body jerked. She coughed and gagged as water spewed from her mouth. Samuel rolled her onto her side to allow the water to drain out.

Eliza's coughing turned into crying as she fought to sit up. "M-Mamm!"

"I'm here, sweetheart." Lena pulled the little girl into her arms and rocked back and forth with her. "*Danki*, Gott. *Danki*, Samuel."

Samuel wrapped his arms around two of the most precious people in his world. Tears mingled with the nasty pond water cascading down his face. Lena moved one hand from the little girl to clutch his soggy shirt. He held them tighter as she sobbed into his chest.

"Mamm! Mamm!" The cry floated to them on a wisp of breeze.

"*Ach*, Mary must be so scared."

Lena pulled from Samuel's arms, leaving him with an emptiness that was almost painful. How *gut* it felt to hold her. How right. "I'll run to reassure her. Just let me find my shoes." Before he could get to his feet, Lena grasped his dangling hand.

"How did you know what to do? I felt so helpless. I can't even swim."

"I can't say I would have known what to do if I hadn't lived in Florida for a little while. I learned to swim there. I took a first aid and CPR class there, too. I wanted to know what to do if one of my siblings got into trouble swimming or got hurt."

"That was smart thinking."

"I never in a million years expected to need that training."

"I was so scared, Samuel. I thought I'd lost my little girl." Lena coughed and choked back a sob. "When I couldn't see you under the water, either, I thought I'd lost you, too. I couldn't bear to lose either of you." She broke into fresh sobs.

"Everything is all right, Mary!" Samuel hollered over his shoulder before crushing Lena and Eliza in another embrace. "And I could never bear to lose you or Eliza or Mary or Matthew." He pulled back only far enough to stroke Lena's cheek. With a finger beneath her chin, he tilted her head so she had to look into his eyes. "I lost you once, Lena. I don't want to do that ever again." Her brown eyes stared into his. "Do you know what I'm saying?"

"I-I'm not sure."

"Not sure what I'm saying, or not sure of your own feelings, or not sure you can trust me?"

"I trust you, Samuel. You risked your life for my *dochder* without a moment's hesitation."

"I would gladly do it again for any of you."

Lena blinked, but a tear still escaped and trickled down her soft cheek. Samuel couldn't help himself. He leaned down to gently kiss away the drop. He heard her sharp intake of breath and felt the shiver that rippled through her body. Or maybe it rippled through his. He only knew for sure and for certain that he would give all he had for this woman and her *kinner*, and he would devote his entire life to keeping them happy and safe. "Do you know why I would do it again?" He couldn't force his voice much louder than a whisper.

She shook her head but kept her eyes locked on his. Big, dark, chocolate eyes that Samuel wanted to gaze into for the rest of his life.

"Because I love you, Lena Troyer. And I love Mary, Eliza, and Matthew. I love all of you with every fiber of my being."

Lena freed a hand to stroke his cheek, sending fire through his veins. "I love you, too, Samuel Mast. And I am sure of that."

Samuel tied his shoes, plopped his straw hat on his wet head, and lifted Eliza from Lena's arms. He shifted the little girl's weight so he could stretch out a hand to Lena. She clasped it hard, relishing the warmth and strength. She thought her wobbly knees would hold her now so she could trudge up the hill from the pond. Samuel dropped her hand and wrapped his arm around her waist to steady her.

Lena practically had to skip to match his long-legged stride until he noticed her effort and slowed his pace. She was grateful but actually wanted to run, twirl, leap, or turn cartwheels. Her little girl was safe. Samuel loved them. She loved Samuel. She didn't have a single qualm about that now. Any lingering doubt about his sincerity completely vanished when he plunged into the pond without any thought to his own safety. He hadn't hesitated for a second. He'd kept her from foolishly splashing into the murky water where she probably would have drowned. Samuel's quick actions and selflessness had saved them all.

Danki, *Lord Gott, for watching over us, for*

protecting Eliza, for sending Samuel back to Maryland and back to me. You've given me a second chance at love. Danki *ever so much.*

Mary's sobs pierced Lena's heart. Her *wunderbaar* older *dochder* obediently sat on the blanket beside Matthew despite her fears and anguish. Lena tore herself from Samuel's side and ran to them. Matthew, oblivious to the drama around him, continued to nap peacefully. Mary rubbed her eyes with her fists and gulped in shaky breaths. Lena scooped her up and held her tightly.

"Shh, Mary. Everything is all right now."

"I-I was s-so s-scared."

"I know, but you did exactly as I asked you to do. You were very brave and you were a big help. I always know I can trust you."

Mary hugged her so fiercely that Lena gasped for oxygen. She tugged at the little arms to loosen their grip a bit.

"Eliza?" Mary's voice still trembled.

"Eliza is fine. Samuel is bringing her."

"Did someone mention my name?" Samuel stopped beside the blanket. He knelt with Eliza still in his arms so Mary could see her little *schweschder*. Lena stooped beside him. Samuel shifted Eliza to one arm so he could include Mary and Lena in a hug. He chuckled. "We just need Matthew to complete this family gathering."

As if on cue, Matthew rolled over and crawled across the blanket. When he reached Lena, he pulled himself onto her leg, throwing her off-balance. When she and Mary toppled over, they pulled Samuel and Eliza with them. All five of them rolled in the grass, laughing.

"Are we a family?" Mary looked from Samuel to her *mamm*.

Samuel's beautiful green eyes searched Lena's face, his gaze reaching into her soul. She felt her own lips lift in a smile that matched his. She nodded at his unspoken question.

"We are, if your *mamm* agrees to become my *fraa*."

"I do agree. *Jah*, Mary, we will be a family."

Epilogue

Lena clicked the ink pen and laid it on the oak table beside the big, old, worn Bible that had belonged to her parents. She leaned back in the sturdy oak chair and allowed her eyes to roam the room that was so different yet so comfortable and homey. Her apple-shaped clock ticked on the far wall. Her brass teakettle perched atop the gas-powered stove. Her ceramic canisters lined the kitchen counter beneath the cupboard holding her *gut* white dishes. But all those familiar belongings occupied new spaces in a different house.

So many changes had occurred in the past few weeks. For a person so used to her set routines, change was not usually very easy. But this time she embraced the change. She often pinched herself to make sure she hadn't dreamed everything. Lena smiled. If she was dreaming, she didn't want to awaken. This *wilkom* change followed her escape from the wilderness of grief, fear, and mistrust where she had wandered for too long. Now she understood Becky's Bible verse. The Lord Gott had indeed done a new thing in her life. She was sure beyond any doubt that Samuel was her river in the desert.

"What has you smiling, Fraa?"

Strong yet gentle hands pressed her shoulders. Her smile broadened. She actually giggled when his scruffy beginnings of a beard brushed her cheek before he kissed it. "I'm smiling because I'm happy."

"I want you to always be happy. You aren't sorry you moved here instead of my moving into your place?"

"*Nee*. This house is perfect for us. The kitchen is big, with lots of work space. The windows look out over the fields. The *kinner* have a big yard to play in and their own rooms."

"And there's still plenty of space for more *kinner*."

Lena's face grew warm. She'd never thought she'd have more *kinner*, but now that was a distinct possibility.

"Did I ever tell you how beautiful you are, my *lieb*? Especially when you blush like you used to do when we were scholars."

"You're *narrisch*." She playfully swatted his arm.

"Crazy for you, that's all." He bent closer to brush his lips across hers. "I just checked on the little ones. Everyone is sleeping peacefully."

"You are so *gut* with them."

"I love them as if they were my own. And truly, I consider them my own now. I won't treat them any differently if the Lord decides to bless us with more."

Lena nodded, unable to speak. She blinked back the tears that sprang into her eyes. How had she been so blessed to win the love of this man? She knew. It could only have been the Lord Gott's doing. He'd helped her to trust again, to lay the past to rest, to banish the guilt of loving another man after losing Joseph. Only Gott could help Samuel forgive his *daed* and realize he was nothing like that troubled man. Only Gott could help Samuel find his way back to Maryland and give him the patience to wait for her to *kumm* to her senses.

Tears threatened once again. Danki, *Lord Gott, for this man who loves me and my little ones, who never gave up on me, who returned to me after so many years.*

"I am grateful every day for you, Lena. And for Mary, Eliza, and Matthew. The Lord Gott is so *gut*. He allowed me to find my way back to you."

"I was just saying *danki* to Him for you. I am so glad you didn't give up on me and that you chose to return to Maryland."

"I've always considered St. Mary's County my home. It's where I grew up. It's where you are. I never gave up the hope that I would return here and have a life with you." Samuel kissed her again. "What were you reading?"

Lena flipped open the Bible to the center pages. "I was writing." She turned to the page labeled

"Marriage Record." "See?" She pointed to the words she'd written.

Lena Troyer wed Samuel Mast

She had squeezed the date in the margin of the gold-edged page.

"Only three words could be sweeter than those you wrote."

She looked up into the green eyes she'd always treasured in her memories. "And those are?"

" 'I love you.' "

"I love you, too, Samuel. For always."

Center Point Large Print
600 Brooks Road / PO Box 1
Thorndike, ME 04986-0001 USA

(207) 568-3717

US & Canada:
1 800 929-9108
www.centerpointlargeprint.com